Murder in the Piazza

A Maggie White Mystery

MURDER IN THE PIAZZA

A Maggie White Mystery

by Jen Collins Moore

LEVEL
BEST BOOKS

First published by Level Best Books 22 September 2020

This novel is entirely a work of fiction. The names, characters and incidents portrayed in it are the work of the author's imagination. Any resemblance to actual persons, living or dead, events or localities is entirely coincidental.

Jen Collins Moore asserts the moral right to be identified as the author of this work.

First edition

ISBN: 978-1-947915-53-4

This book was professionally typeset on Reedsy.
Find out more at reedsy.com

To my family.

Praise for Murder in the Piazza

"Moore delivers, and with a kind of artistically unobtrusive skill… At the heart of it all is the charmingly innocuous protagonist…an achingly ordinary person who pines for excitement and, if given the opportunity, is so clearly capable of achieving more in life…. **An enjoyably dramatic tale**…[with a] mystery that delights"—*Kirkus Reviews*

"This book has everything: a rollicking plot, sparkling wit, thrilling twists, and a fascinating cast of characters, all set against the irresistible backdrop of Rome. Maggie White is a delightful, relatable, note-perfect detective, and *Murder in the Piazza* marks **the debut of a dynamite new voice in cozy mysteries**."—Abby Geni, award-winning author of *The Wildlands, The Lightkeepers,* and *The Last Animal*

"A fun-filled fusion of culture, history, and mystery! Jen Collins Moore's endearing and relentless sleuth tackles red herrings, plausible suspects, and well-timed twists in this **delightfully clever romp through Rome**, Italy. Find the nearest gelato stand and sit back for a terrific read!"—J. C. Eaton, award-winning author of The Sophie Kimball Mysteries, The Wine Trail Mysteries, The Marcie Rayner Mysteries

"Absolutely terrific debut! *Murder in the Piazza* grabbed me from the first page with the **perfect blend of funny and smart**! Jen Collins Moore, I want more!"—Molly MacRae, national best-selling author of the Highland Bookshop Mysteries and the Haunted Yarn Shop Mysteries

"Richly detailed and entertaining, Jen Collins Moore's debut *Murder on the Piazza* offers a well-drawn mystery set against the picturesque back-drop of modern Rome. Surrounded by an intriguing cast of characters, Maggie White—a sharp-eyed no-nonsense amateur sleuth—is determined to discover who among her tour group companions may have killed her new boss. **Fans of Agatha Christie will enjoy this cozy and intelligent read**."—Susanna Calkins, award-winning author of the Lucy Campion and Speakeasy Murder Mysteries

"The streets of Rome come to life (and death) in this fresh, fun mystery that journeys through the intersections of art, travel, secrets, and delicious Italian cuisine. **Jen Collins Moore is an outstanding tour guide**."—Kristen Lepionka, Shamus Award-winning author of the Roxane Weary mystery series

"*Murder in the Piazza* has **something for every reader**: a bustling, colorful Roman setting, a complex mystery, a city full of art, a wealth of details about Renaissance masters, a resourceful, intelligent, middle-aged sleuth, a villainous victim, an eccentric group of suspects, and some delectable descriptions of Italian food. But really, Jen Collins Moore, you had me at Rome."—Julia Buckley, best-selling author of the Writer's Apprentice series

"What could be better than a murder mystery plus an artist's tour of Rome?? **I was hooked from page one** of this wonderful debut and enjoyed every moment of Maggie White's search to find out who murdered her employer. Readers will fall in love not only with this tenacious and savvy heroine, but the entire delightful cast of characters on their luxury holiday in Italy. I can't wait for the next book in the series!"—Mindy Mejia, author of *Everything You Want Me To Be* and *Strike Me Down*

"Jen Collins Moore's captivating debut mystery, *Murder in the Piazza*, is **an absolute delight**. Maggie White is a refreshing protagonist and is every bit as unrelenting and persistent as her intrepid creator. I love the mix of mystery, art, and history and I can't wait to see where Moore's next book takes Maggie!"—Jessie Chandler, author of the Shay O'Hanlon Caper Series

Chapter One

T he city of Rome celebrates its defeat of the barbarians in 753 B.C. with reenactments of battle scenes and an impressive fireworks display. Guests of Masterpiece Tours will enjoy the view from Lord Philip's private terrace, staying, quite literally, above the chaos and crowds that spoil so many Roman holidays.

—Masterpiece Tours "Welcome to Rome" pamphlet

Maggie White started fantasizing about Lord Philip's death on her third day. Just a painless, but fatal, heart attack that would strike her boss down in the middle of the night. When that failed to materialize, she imagined him taking a wrong step in front of a speeding bus. Today she moved on to poison.

Maggie was the "new girl" at Masterpiece Tours, which offered exclusive painting holidays to well-heeled Americans. She was seated on the rooftop terrace of a minor 17th-century palace on the Piazza Navona with guests on the current tour. It was a lovely April evening, her chair was comfortable, and she was pleasantly full. But Maggie had had as much of Lord Philip Walpole as she could take.

Could she sneak arsenic into Lord Philip's whiskey? Maggie considered this as the tourists around her oohed over a particularly brilliant firework bursting over the Colosseum in honor of Rome's birthday celebration. Would he notice the taste? How much would it take?

Getting the deadly liquid would be a problem. She seemed to remember arsenic came from juniper berries, but perhaps that was cyanide. She took a sip of her drink. Espresso, smooth and strong. Maybe slipping the poison into Lord Philip's morning coffee would be safer.

It was only her sixth day on the job—four days with the tour group and two before the guests arrived—and the man had reduced her to tears five times. And Maggie wasn't a woman who cried easily. She'd been in Italy for five months, spent three of them trying to fit in as a woman of leisure, then two fruitlessly looking for a job, and it wasn't until she met Lord Philip that she'd lost control.

Maggie breathed in the scent of the flowers in the giant pots around Lord Philip's rooftop terrace and sighed. She wouldn't kill her employer, pleasant as it was to imagine. She'd managed to survive fifty-five years without killing anyone—including that awful Lana Harrison, who thought she knew more about managing an advertising campaign than Maggie—and she would survive without killing Lord Philip, too.

She could quit, just as her husband, Burt, said she should. But Maggie wasn't a quitter. Hadn't she been the youngest woman ever promoted to vice president at Bells & Wallace? Hadn't she single-handedly saved the PTA bake sale when 450 cupcakes, cookies, and Rice Krispies treats were savaged by Mrs. Simpson's basset hound, Napoleon? And hadn't she sent two high-spirited children off to excellent liberal arts colleges?

Quitting now would prove her husband was right about this job being a mistake, and Maggie wasn't about to admit that.

Footsteps echoed on the terrace. Maggie twisted in her seat. It was dark, but Maggie could just make out Vicky Barlow sliding into her chair a few feet away. She was the tour's youngest guest, only in her mid-twenties.

"Got it." Vicky's words carried across the terrace. She had complained of being cold soon after the fireworks began and now held a sweater in triumph.

Maggie hadn't even noticed the young woman leaving the terrace.

Vicky was English and carried herself like a dancer. She probably spent hours at those Pilates classes everyone seemed so keen on. The young woman rested her head on her husband's shoulder.

Daniel Barlow was older, late thirties. The only non-painting partner on the tour, he joined the group for meals but declined to take part in any sightseeing. He was American, a banker or something.

"I wanted to go to Spain," Daniel had told the group their first night. "I actually speak the language there. But since this trip was an apology for a little misunderstanding with my secretary, I didn't have much say in the matter."

His wife had blushed and quickly changed the subject. Rome's magic must be working on them now. The pair had been cooing all evening.

Maggie looked up at the colorful light show, thoughts shifting back to the problem of Lord Philip. Burt kept reminding Maggie she didn't need to work. They had come to Italy for his job. Her job was to relax after twenty-three years spent juggling a career and children. "You've earned a break, enjoy it," he'd said.

But they were five months into Burt's expat assignment, and Maggie still felt lost. She'd spent two decades climbing the corporate ladder at Bells & Wallace before the chairman told her they no longer needed her services. She'd known they were consolidating departments; it was only logical. But the decision to give her job to a woman ten years her junior—a woman who Maggie herself had mentored—was a blow. When Burt told her about the opportunity to move to Rome for two years, it was only natural she'd jumped at it. She just hadn't anticipated feeling so, well, inadequate without a job to go to each day. When she heard about the position with Lord Philip, she thought it would give her a sense of purpose. Instead, it made her feel bumbling and incompetent.

A chair scraped and an elderly voice quavered, "Oh dear, Charles, was that your foot? I'm so sorry, just off to the restroom." Eloise Potter, small and slightly hunched, moved off into the shadows to the stairs down to the apartment.

Eloise was on the tour with her sister, Helen, the most talented painter of the group. The women had taken Charles Rossi, a widower, under their wing, insisting he sit next to them at dinner, helping him set up his easel, and offering him a sun hat the moment they stepped outdoors. Maggie couldn't decide if he welcomed the attention or simply tolerated it out of politeness.

3

Maggie was startled by the loud crack of a firework exploding. There didn't seem to be a corresponding burst of color overhead. Funny how sound could play tricks, echoing off the old stucco buildings around the piazza. Maggie shivered and pulled her sweater tighter.

Lord Philip should be on the terrace by now. He had summoned the tour's young painting instructor, Thomas Evans, to his study for a conference after dinner. Lord Philip had been in a particularly foul mood and Maggie heard his angry voice when she guided the guests past the closed study door on their way up to the terrace.

Lord Philip ran Masterpiece Tours out of his penthouse, which occupied the entire fifth floor of a palazzo that had been divided into apartments a century ago. The tour brochure promised guests a home away from home with full access to the living room, dining room, painting studio, and rooftop terrace. Most of the guests were disappointed to learn they would be sleeping at a hotel two blocks away.

Maggie felt Thomas's presence before she saw him. "Everything all right?"

He slipped into the chair next to her. "Busywork assignment. All taken care of now."

Thomas was English, like Lord Philip, and had the lean, blond-hair-blue-eyed good looks Maggie associated with the English upper class. He was the best part of the job. Funny and eager to please, he didn't take anything too seriously. Maggie did wonder, sometimes, how he'd managed to graduate from Oxford three years earlier. He didn't seem to be the intellectual type.

Thomas wasn't bothered by Lord Philip's verbal attacks, the way Maggie was. What Maggie needed, she realized as Thomas stretched his long legs and leaned back, wasn't poison but thicker skin. If a twenty-five-year-old man could take whatever Lord Philip dished out, so could she.

Why had she given Lord Philip the power to intimidate her? She wouldn't have done that in a boardroom at home. But she'd been so attached to the idea of working she'd failed to keep perspective. What was she afraid of? That she'd be fired from a job she didn't even want anymore?

Maggie flushed. That was exactly what she'd been afraid of. Being fired after the Bells & Wallace debacle would be more of a blow to her ego than she could stomach.

There had to be another way. Maggie did a quick calculation. This was the fourth day of the ten-day tour. She would see it through, get the guests safely onto their flights home, then tender her resignation. She just needed to last six more days to escape from this job with a shred of dignity.

"Honey, can you get my camera? I want to get a good picture of all this," Vicky whispered, her voice carrying across the terrace.

Her husband's sigh was loud enough for everyone to hear, but he pushed his chair back and headed toward the stairs.

Another starburst filled the sky, then another. Maggie sipped her coffee and relaxed, enjoying the sound of the fireworks bouncing off the buildings. It was random, impossible to tell where each burst was coming from and disconnected from the colors exploding overhead.

Just having a deadline for her resignation made Maggie realize how ridiculous she'd been to let Lord Philip get the better of her. Imagining murder. She almost wished he'd appear now with some petty jab at her Norman Rockwell taste, giving her the chance to fire back with a cutting zinger.

"Is Lord Philip coming up?" Maggie whispered to Thomas.

"Who knows. He was on the phone when he sent me away."

Daniel returned with his wife's camera just in time for the grand finale. The group on the terrace applauded politely.

"Just lovely." Helen's sleeves fluttered as she lightly clapped her hands. Helen's taste ran to gauzy, brightly patterned fabrics so popular among women of a certain age. Tonight, in the darkness, it gave her a ghostly, almost ethereal effect, despite her six-foot frame. "Eloise and I are about ready to return to the hotel. Charles, will you join us?"

The widower pushed himself to his feet and wagged his cane toward the city below. "If you think the crowds have thinned enough."

The streets had been packed for the annual "*Natale di Roma*" celebration of the city's founding two thousand years ago. Maggie knew the bare bones of the story. Twin boys. Raised by a wolf. The city was named for one. She wasn't sure what had happened to the other, but she suspected nothing good.

Stories with twins never ended with both living happily ever after.

The brochure had been particularly flowery in its description: *A night worthy of the Caesars—five-course feast followed by unparalleled views of the city's breathtaking fireworks—inspiration for your personal masterpiece abounds on this night of history and romance.*

The meal and spectacular fireworks display had indeed been worthy of the Caesars. That was, if those long-dead dictators would have appreciated the charcuterie platter, crispy fried artichokes, lasagna with white sauce, monkfish with brown butter, chocolate semifreddo, and thoughtful wine pairings as much as Maggie had. They certainly would have cheered Maggie on if she *had* slipped a little poison into Lord Philip's meal. Rome's Caesars had been a bloodthirsty group.

Helen tucked her hand around Charles's left arm. "We can make it. We'll form a phalanx if necessary."

Eloise hooked her hand around Charles's free arm. She wore the same style of cashmere twinset and string of pearls Maggie remembered her mother wearing to her weekly bridge games.

"We're in Rome," Eloise said. "We should be a legion. Phalanx is a Greek military term."

"I was speaking in the general sense," Helen said.

"I'm sure Charles appreciates specificity." Eloise looked at Charles and winked.

He was a professor. Perhaps that made him a stickler for details.

"Shouldn't we wait for Lord Philip?" Len Cooper and his wife, Shelia, were from Texas.

Maggie guessed they were in their late-sixties, about fifteen years older than she was. Len wore a denim suit with a big turquoise belt buckle and cowboy boots. Maggie hadn't seen him in a cowboy hat, but he kept touching his faded hair combed over the crown of his head, as though missing something.

"Maggie can tell him we're leaving." Shelia's generous curves were zipped into a tight denim jumpsuit Maggie wouldn't have dreamed of wearing, but the woman pulled it off with pure self-confidence.

"I'll just let him know." The guests sat back down and Maggie almost trotted down the stone stairs, feeling more like her old self: confident, can-do Maggie, ready to face whatever petty criticisms Lord Philip had in store for her.

Maggie was conscious of her feet echoing when she reached the marble hall and how few lights illuminated the dark wood paneling. She slowed as she approached Lord Philip's heavy door, her confidence beginning to ebb. She listened for a moment. Silence. Maggie knocked, feeling uneasy. No answer.

She pushed the door open a crack and took a peek then jerked the door closed. Lord Philip was flopped over sideways, halfway out of his big green leather chair, blond head dangling unnaturally close to his feet.

Maggie took a deep breath. Lord Philip was probably just picking something up off the floor. She knocked more loudly then opened the door with a big, forced smile on her face. "Lord Philip? Is everything all right?"

But no. His face, so handsome in life, was swollen and pasty white, blue eyes staring. Blood soaked through his crisp white shirt. Maggie was no expert, but he was definitely dead.

She swallowed. She'd wished for Lord Philip's death, but not seriously. And not like this. Not a gunshot to the chest. For, surely, that was what must have happened. Blood had spread through his lovely grey pinstripe suit, dripping onto his expensive-looking oriental rug.

And the smell. The iron mixed with sweat. A lesser woman might have lost her head and run off screaming. But not Maggie. She averted her gaze and took a deep breath. Everything else looked just as usual. The picture of a child playing a piano on the wall behind the desk. The three framed sketches of a running horse off to one side, the big, brightly colored abstract painting on the other. The floor-to-ceiling bookcases, with their old-looking books and bits of antique-y odds and ends appeared just as they should. The tall windows were closed. Nothing out of place except Lord Philip himself. She quickly scanned the floor. Not even a weapon. Maggie stepped back into the hall, hand gripping the metal doorknob. He hadn't done this to himself.

She swallowed hard and focused on the sculpture at the end of the marble hall. A ballerina, frozen mid-twirl, standing in a niche. Maggie resisted the urge to smile. Magically—and, of course, tragically—her problem seemed to have been solved.

Chapter Two

Visitors are often impressed by the Alfa Romeo patrol cars driven by Italian law enforcement. Residents know the special models by their nicknames: Pantera *(Panther) for the police,* Gazzella *(Gazelle) for the* Carabinieri, *and* Civetta *(Owl) for undercover work.*
—Masterpiece Tours "Welcome to Rome" pamphlet

Maggie straightened her skirt, tighter at the waist than she liked, and pulled down the sleeves of her matching jacket. Someone had shot Lord Philip, and here she was standing around. His murderer could be getting away. Or worse, hiding inside the palazzo.

Maggie moved quickly down the dark hall to use the phone in her office and ran straight into Thomas. Maggie squeaked before she recognized the young painting instructor.

"Sorry Mrs. W. Didn't mean to scare you. Have you seen Ilaria?"

Ilaria DeMarco was the tour's young Sicilian cook.

Maggie shook her head. She hadn't realized she was afraid until she noticed her hands were shaking.

"Shelia asked for the recipe for the lasagna," Thomas said. "Wants to know if it was rosemary or thyme in the sauce. I told her it was probably both, but she sent me to get the specifics." Thomas squinted at her. "Something wrong, Mrs. W.?"

Maggie took a breath to try to steady her voice. "I need to call the police. Lord Philip is dead."

Thomas snorted. "Surely not. I was with him not half an hour ago. That man's as healthy as a horse. He must have just dropped off. One drink too many and all that."

Thomas brushed past her and opened the study door. She watched as he froze, taking in the scene, then stepped back into the hall. His face was white, the way a child's was right before he threw up all over the new carpeting.

"Well then." His voice was choked. "You didn't, ah, check his pulse, did you?"

"The man is dead, Thomas. I'm calling the police."

Maggie left him guarding the study door and ducked into the small room designated as Masterpiece Tours' head office. More of a closet, really. Her tiny desk was squeezed between filing cabinets and three towers of boxes containing unfiled paperwork. The emergency operator, who spoke lovely English and really sounded quite sympathetic, promised to send assistance.

Maggie joined Thomas outside the study. "I'll go up to the terrace and tell the guests. You can wait downstairs for the police."

She glanced around the dim hall as she spoke. Lord Philip's apartment occupied the entire floor. The rooms were arranged around a central marble hall, with the large dining room and tiny kitchen off to one side and Lord Philip's bedroom, Maggie's office, and the painting studio off to the other. So many places for someone to hide. But surely, whoever had done this had left. No one would stick around after doing that, would they? Still, Maggie would feel better when the police came and took charge.

Thomas seemed to read her mind. "Shouldn't we stay together?"

The guests might come down any minute, and someone needed to greet the police. Maggie shook her head and shooed Thomas down the hall.

He paused in the grand entry, with its mosaic floor and frescoed ceiling. "You and I will be the prime suspects, you know."

"What on earth do you mean?" The nice woman on the phone hadn't said anything about that.

"The police never trust the people who find the body."

Thomas sounded quite cheerful about the whole thing. But then, the idea of Thomas killing Lord Philip was laughable. If his meeting had turned murderous, Lord Philip would have come out victorious. He was that type of man.

Maggie paused at the top of the stairs. The group on the terrace was just as she'd left it. Seven tourists seated in a rooftop garden. No whiff of unease.

"We were about to send a search party." Helen stood. One of her scarves danced in the breeze. "First Lord Philip disappears after dinner, then you, then Thomas. Is something going on?"

Maggie heard the *nee-eu nee-eu* of a siren in the distance and swallowed in relief. "I have some news."

"Goodness. What's that noise?" Shelia walked to the wrought iron railing surrounding the terrace. The silver belt that cinched the waist of her pantsuit jangled musically as she moved. "It sounds like one of those funny European police cars. I hope the fireworks haven't caused a fire."

"Sounds like it's coming this way." Len joined Shelia at the railing and looked down.

Maggie joined them at the edge. Two police cars screamed up Via di Santa Maria dell'Anima, sirens blaring, lights flashing.

"If you'll all give me your attention for a moment—"

"There're two of them," Len said, excited. "They're slowing. They're parking. It must be close, whatever it is."

The artists crowded around, trying to get a glimpse of whatever it was the police were doing. Three uniformed officers and a large man in a suit emerged from the two small sedans below.

Maggie turned away from the railing to face the group. "The police are coming here. I have some sad news. Lord Philip is dead."

"Oh my." Eloise was still holding the puff of powder blue wool that was supposed to transform into a sweater for an infant. She carried it everywhere, but her progress was slow.

Maggie looked at the tourists, eyes wide, mouths gaping a bit in the moonlight, frozen in place while the lights of the city danced all around them.

"Well?" Shelia drew the word out into three long syllables. "What happened?"

Maggie gave the barest of information. Lord Philip was dead. Thomas was waiting for the police downstairs. They were sure to know more soon. She tried to ignore the knot forming in her stomach. She didn't mention she was going to be a prime suspect.

"I assume the tour's cancelled?" Daniel put his arm around his wife's shoulder. "You'll be issuing refunds?"

Vicky removed his hand. "Why would the tour be cancelled?" Her words were soft and soothing, like an old-fashioned nanny. She was English, like Thomas, but she had spent the last five years in New York. "Maggie's still here. Ilaria's still here. Thomas's still here. They can take care of us."

Vicky turned her gaze to Maggie and smiled. Maggie smiled back, even though Daniel was right. She couldn't imagine the tour continuing. Lord Philip *was* Masterpiece Tours. Sure, Maggie was learning the ropes in the office and Thomas gave painting instruction. But it was Lord Philip the guests signed up to see. An insider's tour of Rome led by the second son of a duke. That alone was enough to make most Americans go weak in the knees.

But Lord Philip was also charismatic and handsome. He was a few years younger than Maggie—in his early fifties, she guessed—and aging in the lean, attractive way some men did. And Lord Philip had been witty and charming with an uncanny memory. He could recall everything the guests said, and he'd used those little details to flatter them. And to mock them behind their backs.

No, Maggie would have to send everyone home and figure out a way to get them all refunds.

"It doesn't seem quite decent to be talking about this." Helen reached for Charles's hand and clutched it, as though for reassurance. "We've just learned the poor man is dead."

Len rubbed his head where his phantom cowboy hat should be. "How did he go? Heart attack?"

"How can she say, Len?" Shelia swatted his arm. "Does Maggie look like Quincy?"

It was surprising, really, how much Lord Philip had looked like the victims Maggie had seen on TV. Her stomach turned over at the memory, remembering the crimson stain spreading across Lord Philip's tailored suit, smelling the iron in the air.

"He was shot," Maggie said.

"Suicide?" Daniel asked.

She shook her head. "I didn't see a gun."

Eloise and Helen exchanged a glance. Daniel took Vicky's hand and gave it a squeeze.

"Let me get this straight." Shelia's southern accent was deeper than usual. Tougher. "We're talking about a murder. Here. Inside the apartment. Not thirty minutes ago. And we're just standing up here talking? This is insane." She made a move toward the stairs.

"The police are downstairs," Maggie said. "We're perfectly safe."

Len pulled a chair out for his wife. "Lord Philip was probably up to something he shouldn't have been. This isn't anything to do with us."

Would the police agree? Maggie's shoulders tightened when, at last, the large man she'd seen climbing out of the police car walked onto the terrace. He paused at the top of the stairs, as though assessing the guests.

"Good evening, I am Inspector Orsini." His words were accented, but his English was clear. "There is a body downstairs, as I am sure you are aware. The owner of this apartment, yes? I will strive to make this process as brief as possible for you."

Maggie relaxed. He seemed like a very reasonable man. A seasoned professional who would look past the ridiculous idea of suspecting people simply because they happened to find a body.

"Are you sure it's safe for us to be here?" Shelia asked.

Orsini nodded. He had a shock of white hair and a large belly straining the buttons of his rumpled suit. He looked a bit like Santa Claus after a long day at the office. "Whoever did this is long gone. My belief is the victim was killed during a robbery."

"Terrible security," Daniel whispered loudly to Vicky. "Something like this was bound to happen."

The door to the street was left open all the time, and Maggie had never seen the tenants of the other floors. Lord Philip had mentioned they were absentee owners, and Maggie imagined oil sheiks and South African mine owners. The door to Lord Philip's apartment was also kept unlocked during the day so the artists could come and go. It would have been simple for someone to stroll in.

"We're taking fingerprints." Orsini pulled a notebook from his pocket. "We will compare them to the records. I hope we will have a suspect very soon."

Burglary? Maggie's mind raced. Lord Philip was a well-known collector. Would a burglar have snuck in, expecting Lord Philip to be on the terrace enjoying the fireworks?

"What was taken?" Eloise asked.

The moon disappeared behind a cloud again and Maggie couldn't make out the guests' faces clearly any longer.

"That is not yet known. Now, we'll take your statements and get you to your beds, yes?" Orsini consulted his notebook. "We will begin, I think, with Signora Bianca. Who is this?"

Maggie's stomach dropped. Thomas had been right. She *was* a person of interest. Orsini's explanation of a burglar sneaking in for the art might have been a ruse to get her guard down. She stepped forward, half-raising her hand. "That's me. Or almost. I'm Maggie White, not Bianca. Though *bianca* means white in Italian, doesn't it?"

She was rambling. Burt's Aunt Gertrude said liars gave themselves away by talking too much. Would this inspector find it suspicious?

"Fine, fine." Orsini waved his hand. "We will talk first. Everyone else, please come to the living room. Yes, all of you." He shooed them to the stairs. Only the clicking of Charles's cane on the tile broke the uncharacteristic silence.

Orsini led the guests into the room Lord Philip had called the Grand Salon. It was enormous, decorated in a style that reminded Maggie of the movie about Mozart that had won all the Academy Awards years ago. Very European, very old. The ceiling was painted light blue with gold swirls and red geometric patterns. Maggie had tried to stencil a border around her kitchen with a too-short ladder once and knew how hard it was to work with your hands above your head.

Two sets of giant door-sized windows offered views south over the city. The furniture was that heavy old stuff that seemed just right here in a palazzo in Italy but would have looked ridiculous in her suburban house back home.

It was the artwork that made the room really special. Every wall was covered with pieces. Some old, fitting the period of the room. Others looked newer. Impressionist, perhaps? And whatever it was Picasso was. There were two sculptures in the corner, one of some ancient nymph, another of a child reading a book. Maggie didn't have the art bug, but even she could tell the collection was eclectic in a good way, pieces gathered for their beauty, not for some interior decorator's color scheme.

Maggie felt a mix of nervousness and, she had to admit, excitement as she left the others and followed the inspector into the dining room. She read a lot of mysteries, and here she was a key witness.

Orsini closed the room's double doors and gestured for Maggie to sit at the polished wood table large enough to seat twenty. The inspector's chair creaked as he settled his bulk across from her. He took out a pair of glasses and set them on the table. "Now, Signora Bianca. I understand you found the body. Is that correct?"

"Mrs. White. Yes, that's right." Polite, but accurate. She was off to a good start.

"And Mr. Walpole ran a tour company here, in his private residence, yes?"

Was running a business from a private home illegal in Italy? Surely some code violation wasn't at the heart of the matter. She hoped Inspector Orsini wasn't one of those bureaucrats so focused on minor regulations that they were unable to see the big picture.

Maggie looked at this inspector more closely. Judging by his age, he was a seasoned professional, not some eager rookie. No point in worrying yet.

"Yes, Masterpiece Tours. But his name isn't Mr. Walpole. Or wasn't. He's Lord Philip Walpole. His brother is some sort of duke in England, and we're supposed to call him Lord Philip or plain Walpole. But not ever Lord Walpole. It's over my head."

Be quiet, Maggie. He'd think she was up to something for sure the way she was going on. She attempted to get back on track. "Masterpiece offers painting vacations with some art instruction."

Thomas led a painting tutorial each morning in the palazzo's studio, then Lord Philip took the guests for some sightseeing and more painting, with Thomas offering one-on-one advice as they worked. This morning the guests had toured the Colosseum. The day before it had been the fountains of Rome. The guests came back for lunch and then had the afternoon for more painting or sightseeing on their own.

"The dead man was an artist?" Orsini was chewing on a breath mint. Wintergreen.

"No, he's an art collector and loves Italy. Or did." She swallowed, thinking of his body flopped over in his chair. She took a breath. "Lord Philip moved to Rome thirty years ago for the art and culture. He founded Masterpiece Tours to share his passion with artists of all ages and inspire them to create greater art of their own." Maggie had memorized the brochure on her first day.

Orsini grunted. "And how did you come to find the body?"

Maggie spoke slowly, choosing each word carefully. She still didn't know what to make of Orsini, and she didn't want to give him any ammunition. "Lord Philip was working in his study after dinner. I went to find him after the fireworks ended to tell him the guests were leaving."

Orsini put his glasses on and made a note then looked up, brown eyes intent on her for the first time during the interview. "And the gunshot? Did you hear it?"

"No, of course not." She'd hardly have strolled into the study if she had. She thought of the fireworks and loud cracks out of sync with the bursts of color in the sky. They sounded so much like gunshots. Had the killer planned it that way? To have fired a gun with the fireworks, masking the sound? She'd read a book where something like that happened. Or was it a gong being struck? She couldn't quite remember.

"Was anything out of place?"

Maggie thought about the scene again. The perfectly neat desk. The artwork on the wall. The bits and bobs on the bookshelf just as usual. "I can't think of a thing."

"Fine. Fine." He turned his notebook to a fresh page and pushed it toward her. "Now, please write your name, address, and title."

She took Orsini's pen and began to write then hesitated before listing her role. She and Lord Philip had never discussed an actual title. She settled on manager.

There. Facts out of the way, Maggie pushed the notebook back to him, ready for the intensive questioning to begin. Of course, she wouldn't tell this man she'd been wishing for Lord Philip's death. But should she admit how much she disliked working here? Did she need to tell this inspector Lord Philip had taken credit for her idea to include welcome bags in all the guest rooms? That he intentionally misunderstood Maggie's question about whether he'd met the Queen, teasing her mercilessly about whether she had dined with the president. Of course, she knew the average Englishmen didn't know the royal family. But he was nobility. Wasn't that different?

And then, the day before the guests arrived, Lord Philip had asked her to put a marketing plan together. Or so she thought. She'd stayed late, missing her anniversary dinner with Burt, outlining her ideas for increasing revenue. But Lord Philip had just tossed her detailed proposal aside, saying he'd have asked a person who actually knew something about business today if he'd wanted a plan, dismissing her twenty years marketing some of the world's most famous products with one casual comment. None of it was worth killing over, perhaps. But it might add to the inspector's suspicions of her if she told him.

Orsini took his glasses off. "Thank you. You can go."

"Don't you want to ask me anything else?" What happened to the questions? Digging into her possible motives? Even her opinion of the crime?

Maggie caught sight of herself in the giant gilt mirror at the end of the room. Her mousy hair, flat with streaks of grey, despite her daughter's frequent suggestions to dye it. Her face was flushed, giving her an eager appearance. Her jacket, which suited the meetings at the office back home so well, looked frumpy here. Had he written her off as not worth his time, no one of consequence?

"More questions? No. I think this is quite complete. Thank you for your assistance." He bobbed his head in a way that was part deference, part dismissal.

This wasn't how it was supposed to go. She gripped the arms of her chair. "Don't you want to know more? Whether I saw anything significant? If I heard anything in the hall? If I noticed Lord Philip acting out of the ordinary?"

"Did you?"

Maggie shifted in her seat. "No."

Laughter erupted in the salon. Shelia, probably. Maggie's face burned.

Orsini pushed his chair back. It was almost noiseless on the polished wood floor. "All of the signs indicate this was a burglary attempt. There is no need to delay you further."

She didn't stand. "What signs? I didn't see anything missing."

Orsini sighed. Maggie noticed the heavy bags under his eyes and the smell of stale coffee on his clothes. "Signora Bianca, I have extensive experience with foreigners. This is why I am assigned to this case, despite having been on duty for," he checked his watch, "twenty hours. There has been a lot of foolishness today, which required my attention. Other cases. Tonight, what do I see? A foreigner known to have a lot of valuables, shot in his own home. Burglary is the logical conclusion. And the sooner I can get these conversations with the witnesses completed, the sooner I can find the person who did this. Yes?"

Thomas was wrong. She wasn't the prime suspect. Not a suspect of any kind. That was good news. But why shouldn't she be treated to a proper interrogation? Asked some real questions? She'd found the body. She could easily have killed Lord Philip then pretended to discover him. How did Inspector Orsini know she hadn't?

If there was one thing Maggie couldn't stand, it was incompetence. From the bean counters in accounting to the salesmen who took her products to the stores, Maggie had spent her life making sure the powers that be did their jobs. And Maggie decided this Inspector Orsini was a type she'd encountered so often. A man tired of his job. A jaded paper-pusher who thought he had all the answers. She'd keep an eye on this Orsini. And if he didn't give the investigation the attention it deserved, his supervisor would hear about it.

Chapter Three

P iazza Navona is perhaps the loveliest of Rome's piazzas. Visitors are encouraged to linger as they take in the stately architecture, Bernini fountain, cafés, and attractive Romans strolling and being seen.
—Masterpiece Tours "Welcome to Rome" pamphlet

Maggie steamed as she walked back to her apartment in Trastevere, a modest neighborhood across the river from Lord Philip's. Orsini and his team had left the palazzo barely an hour after they had arrived. A uniformed policeman had led Maggie and Thomas through the apartment looking for anything a burglar might have taken. Not a single object looked out of place. By the time they returned to the salon, the inspector had completed his interviews of the guests. She doubted he spent longer with each of the others than the two minutes he spent with her. Barely time to get their names and addresses.

She'd been right. Orsini was lazy at best and incompetent at worst. He'd probably be back tomorrow for detailed interviews, but what if one of the guests had killed Lord Philip? They hadn't, of course. She was sure of that, but how did Orsini know that? He didn't even take away their passports. For all the inspector knew, one of the guests was racing off to catch a midnight train to Lisbon at this very moment.

Maggie cut through the Piazza Navona, passing the couples walking hand in hand and the dodgy-looking men hawking noisemakers and spinners. The square was bustling, despite the late hour. Two older men played accordions. Parents perched on Bernini's massive *Fountain of the Four Rivers* fountain watching their children chase each other around and around the enormous square.

The inspector wouldn't know a suspect if she walked up and handed him a smoking gun. Maggie dodged a soccer ball rolling across the piazza. The boy who chased it must have been five or six and was still awake.

Her husband, though, was asleep when Maggie got home. She stood in the doorway of their tiny bedroom. Burt was sprawled in the middle of their double bed. It was a change from their roomy king mattress at home, and he had complained about being squeezed in together like sardines when they first settled in. But Maggie thought it was cozy, even if she had to push him over a few times a night. Burt's tortoiseshell glasses were neatly folded on his bedside table. A stack of mysteries balanced precariously on Maggie's.

She sat on the bed next to him. "Burt." He didn't move. "Burt, wake up."

He rolled over.

Maggie sighed and started poking her husband in the shoulder, the way she did when he snored. "Burt, it's important."

He blinked at her sleepily. "Have a good night? We missed you at the party."

Burt had attended his own Natale Di Roma party hosted by expat friends. Normally Maggie would have asked him for all the details.

"Not now, Burt. Something's happened."

He sat up and reached for his glasses. His brown hair, thinning but not completely gone, was rumpled from sleep. "Is it the kids? I didn't hear the phone."

"No, no, not the kids. It's Lord Philip."

Burt frowned. "What's he done?"

Maggie told Burt about finding the body, working to keep her emotions in check. "The inspector barely interviewed me. Didn't ask me a thing about my motives or anyone else's. I think he was in a hurry to get home. Who knows what else he's missing?"

Burt blinked at her, as though still not fully awake. "Why would he suspect you?"

"I found the body. That's always suspicious."

He sighed. "You don't have a murderous bone in your body. The inspector is a professional. I'm sure he could tell that."

Maggie got changed then climbed into bed, thinking of the heart attack she'd wished on Lord Philip. The poison she'd imagined procuring. She didn't feel particularly innocent.

The light from the street below shone through the cotton curtains and made crisscross patterns across the ceiling. She stared at nothing for a moment then switched the light back on.

"I am suspicious, you know. I'm a brand new employee and my boss is dead." She propped herself on her shoulder and leaned over Burt, whose eyes were still closed. "I could have killed Lord Philip as well as anyone else, and that Inspector Orsini didn't ask me more than two questions. Probably didn't of any of the other guests either. Who knows what they're hiding?"

Burt opened his eyes. "This is isn't a game, Maggie. A man is dead. Let the police do their job."

Maggie didn't say anything.

He gave her a kiss on the cheek and lay back. "Just be careful. Please."

Maggie turned out the light and pulled the thin blanket that had come with the apartment up to her shoulders. She thought of Lord Philip inviting her into his office for a chat on her second day then asking why she'd lied about leaving Bells & Wallace to follow Burt's career.

Maggie's feet felt like ice as she remembered the smile on Lord Philip's face, more of a sneer really, as he'd caught her white lie. She'd told everyone she met in Rome that she'd left Bells & Wallace by choice. It didn't seem necessary to tell them she'd been downsized. The point was the same: she was a successful career woman. The details only complicated things.

But since that meeting, Lord Philip had made little digs at Maggie. Nothing big, nothing anyone else would notice. But enough to constantly remind her he knew her secret. And that he could do something about it at any moment, if he wanted to.

Maggie had worked for some terrible men in her time. But no one who had made her feel so powerless, so vulnerable. That was when she'd started thinking about ways Lord Philip might die.

Music drifted up from the apartment below. The kind of pop her children liked. She'd have to tell the kids about tonight. She began mentally composing the email, hoping the process would lull her to sleep, when Burt spoke. "I almost forgot. We got a postcard from Aunt Gertrude. She's arriving on Wednesday."

It was Sunday. "She didn't think to email? What if we were out of town?"

"Then she'd find somewhere else to stay," Burt said.

More likely she'd jimmy the locks and make herself at home. Burt's mother's older sister had married and been widowed sixty years ago, after which she'd lived an independent life, traveling with the Peace Corps, running a poetry magazine in Istanbul, and spending her time now visiting pals around the world. At least that was what she said. Maggie and Burt liked to joke that Gertrude was really a high-ranking spy or arms trafficker.

The woman made Maggie feel very conventional, juggling work and family like every other woman Maggie knew. Not that Maggie would have made a different choice. She couldn't imagine having spent the last twenty-three years of her life any other way. But with her children away and her career officially off track, Maggie worried about how she'd pass the next three decades of her life, assuming she was lucky enough to live as long as Gertrude, of course.

"Her train gets in at two twenty. You can meet her, can't you?" Burt asked.

Maggie nodded absently as she thought of the tour. The guests would probably all have gone home. And then what? Maggie would be back to taking history classes and cooking courses in one of the world's most beautiful cities. A life her friends at home were green with envy over. A life she'd craved when she was under Lord Philip's thumb. But it all left Maggie feeling incomplete, as though she didn't have an identity of her own.

Well, the least she could do was help the inspector hit the ground running tomorrow. What he needed was a timeline. Maybe background on the guests. The financials of the tour business. Maggie had told Burt she'd let Orsini do his job. And she meant it. But that didn't mean she couldn't give him a little help.

Chapter Four

*I*talian cafés are about conviviality as much as coffee. For an authentic experience, drink your espresso at the bar and join in the lively conversation about the day's news and events.
—Masterpiece Tours "Welcome to Rome" pamphlet

Maggie decided to make a list. She lay in bed the next morning thinking of all the things Inspector Orsini would need to know. Lord Philip's financial situation, probably. She had the bank statements and could pass those along. And certainly the name of his next of kin. Heirs were always suspects. She could check the files for a name.

It was too early to get up, but Maggie got out of bed anyway and padded into the tiny kitchen. Not at all like her spacious domain at home, occupied now by a very nice family, who was renting it while the Whites were away, this was a corner carved out of the living room. The expats all complained about how little space they had, but Maggie loved living with just enough and nothing else.

She filled the little stovetop espresso pot that had come with the apartment and found a pencil and pad of paper. The building was silent. The young people downstairs—French college students here for a year—would probably be asleep for hours.

Was Orsini's instinct correct? Had someone snuck into the palazzo intending to steal from Lord Philip's collection? Maggie leaned against the kitchen counter while she considered it.

Lord Philip said he had a keen eye, finding bargains, keeping some, selling others. He'd shown everyone his newest find on the first day of the tour. It was a small picture of a horse that certainly looked old. "Don't ask how I got it, but if my instincts are correct—and they most often are—this little gem is going to be worth a fortune."

But the picture had still been in the apartment after the murder. If it was the burglar's target, the intruder had failed.

The pot started to gurgle and she set it aside to percolate while she considered the timeline. Dinner was over by eight. Early, by European standards, but late for American tourists. Lord Philip and Thomas retired to the study to talk about the next day's schedule. At least, that was what Lord Philip had said. The raised voices Maggie had heard sounded like they were discussing something entirely different.

On the terrace with the guests, there was the usual discussion about who was going to sit where. Helen Potter seemed to have some idea one chair was the best and her sister, Eloise, made a show of claiming it first. After that, the group had settled back to watch the sunset over Janiculum Hill just west of the river. Those iconic Italian trees stood in silhouette against the setting sun. The expanse of terra cotta roof tiles glowed orange. And the dome of St. Peter's had been fiery red, looking both inspiring and ominous.

Maggie filled a tiny espresso cup. She sniffed. Better than Folgers. No question. She sat at the apartment's tiny table, right next to the window. Her neighbors were starting to wake up. An old woman with an ancient terrier was talking to the man rolling up the iron grates in front of his newsstand. A young couple across the street opened their shutters and the music playing on their radio drifted her way. She wondered if her son, Sam, knew the song. He was the music lover in the family. Maggie had two children, grown now, or nearly. Sam was twenty-three, just graduated from college and working in New York. Maggie didn't entirely understand what he did. Something with computers. Lucy was twenty and nearing the end of her sophomore year.

Maggie picked up her pencil and began jotting notes for Inspector Orsini:

8:00 Lord Philip & Thomas meet in LP's study
8:25 Fireworks begin

8:30 Vicky downstairs (sweater search)

8:40 Thomas on terrace (busywork complete)

8:45 Daniel downstairs (camera errand)

8:55 Fireworks end

She read it over again and made an addition:

9:00 Maggie finds body

The times were approximate, but should be enough to assist Orsini's search. Maggie set the list aside and stretched. The burglar, if that was who had done this, had been awfully lucky not to have bumped into anyone.

She glanced at her watch. Barely seven, but best to get to the palazzo early. After a shower—the hot water was working full blast, miracle of miracles—and only the briefest time spent trying to fluff her hair into something dignified, Maggie dressed in her most flattering pants and blouse. She was tying a silk scarf when Burt opened his eyes.

"I've left coffee." Maggie gave him a kiss. "And a casserole in the fridge. Don't wait up."

Maggie trotted down the three flights of stairs to the street and stood in her building's doorway a moment. The smell of baking bread mixed with the scent of detergent an old woman was using to scrub her stoop across the cobble street. She had on the type of zip-front work dress Maggie's mother had worn around the house, but in black instead of pink. Maggie said *buon giorno* to the widow every morning and was greeted in kind, but she still didn't know the woman's name or anything about her, other than she lived alone and was meticulous about her housekeeping.

The narrow road was still in deep shadow. The three- and four-story buildings blocked the light until late morning. Her lane opened onto the Piazza di Santa Maria and its 17th-century fountain. Neighbors would be gossiping and children playing here soon enough, but, at this hour, there were just a few businessmen staring at their phones as they walked purposefully toward the tram stop and two municipal workers in blue jumpsuits pushing trash bins.

Maggie turned the corner to another piazza. This one—she'd never learned its name—was just a small triangle with cafés on two sides and an upscale hotel on the other. Mario was arranging tables and chairs outside of Café Antica.

"*Buon giorno*, Maggie! You're early this morning." Mario, the café owner, was a few years younger than Maggie, early forties, and seemed to have boundless energy.

She waved. "I can't stop, Mario. I'll be in soon."

"Take a pastry at least. I want to ask your opinion about something." Mario pushed the last chair into place and guided Maggie to the café door with a gentle hand on her shoulder.

Maggie visited Café Antica nearly every day after Burt went to work. Mario and his wife, Giovanna, spoke excellent English, and Maggie had given up practicing her Italian with them. Instead, they had bonded over the challenges of raising teenagers.

A glass case dominated the café. It was filled with mini tarts stuffed with Chantilly cream and tiny strawberries, chocolate-dipped butter cookies, lumpy mounds of nuts in chewy meringue, perfect squares of layered chocolate, and ten different types of biscotti.

But, for Maggie, it had to be a cornetto. Smaller and less buttery than a French croissant, served up plain or stuffed with chocolate, jam, or anything else Giovanna dreamed up. And every day Maggie walked home, flaky pastry still fresh in her mouth, promising herself she'd eat something healthier the next day, yogurt and Muesli or maybe a piece of dry toast and cottage cheese.

Mario took his place behind the counter, tying a crisp white apron around his middle. His black hair was thick, and he had a muscular build. How did he stay so fit, surrounded by all of this pastry?

"What kind, Maggie? Strawberry? Honey? Or one of the *saccottino al cioccolato*?" Mario pointed to his "sacks of chocolate" pastries. They looked devilishly similar to chocolate croissants, which Maggie knew were strictly forbidden in her old Weight Watchers plan. She hadn't joined a group here, but memories of the weekly meetings stuck with her, even if the commitment to self-deprivation hadn't.

"Not today, Mario. I'll have a strawberry cornetto, *per favore*." At least she would be getting some fruit in.

Maggie took a bite and sighed as the buttery pastry began to dissolve in her mouth. The dieters didn't know what they were missing.

Maggie was the only customer, and she shook her head when Mario offered her a coffee. "What did you want to talk about?"

"It's Carletta. My middle child. You remember that boy I told you about? She wants to go camping with his family in August. She's sixteen. You know that age." He threw his arms in the air. "But what can I do? Giovanna says we'll make it worse if we tell her she can't go."

Maggie nodded sympathetically, brushing crumbs from her lips with a paper napkin. The bell on the door jingled and Faye Masters, a slim woman with stylish short black hair, walked in. She was Maggie's age but looked younger in her leggings and the tunic sliding off the shoulders. Faye was the self-appointed queen bee of the expat community.

"Maggie White, what a surprise!" Faye leaned in for the continental-style cheek kissing. "I had no idea you were an early bird like me." Without waiting for an answer, she began speaking to Mario in extravagant Italian, with lots of dramatic hand gestures and rolled Rs.

Maggie took another bite of pastry while the words flowed over her. She leaned against the bar and looked absently around the room. The tables for two were gleaming, ready for customers willing to pay the premium to sit while they took their morning coffee. A mural in the style of those uncovered in the ruins of Pompeii dominated one wall, a series of mirrors in all shapes and sizes covered another.

Faye and her husband, George, were in Rome on extended sabbatical from Stanford. He was an expert on historical astronomy, and Faye kept busy as the undisputed hostess of the expat set. She was always organizing dinners at charming undiscovered restaurants, hosting delightful cocktail parties, and arranging endless games of bridge.

Maggie entered Faye's orbit when she and Burt first arrived five months ago, gratefully accepting invitations to join pottery classes and lunch dates while Burt was settling into his job. But after a few months, Maggie was bored of the endless conversation about clothing and house decorating. She tried to get the wives interested in spending their time in more meaningful ways. She'd laid out plans for a charity drive and service day, but Maggie hadn't been able to enlist a single expat to help. She set off on her own, determined to make a difference in some small way but had been politely turned away at all the Italian charities she had approached.

Maggie couldn't imagine spending the next two years in Italy playing bridge with the girls—women she wasn't even sure she liked. Or perhaps, more to the point, with women who might not like her either.

The answer, she'd told Burt over dinner one night, was a job. A real job with a paycheck, coworkers to gossip with, and bosses to grumble about. But with limited language skills and no work permit, Maggie had gotten only three interviews in two months of looking.

Then she met Lord Philip at one of Faye's cocktail parties. Faye introduced them, saying Lord Philip needed help in his office and Maggie was a whiz, then she'd fluttered off. Lord Philip said he had a tour arriving in a few days and the office was a mess. A recommendation from Faye was good enough for him, and he hired Maggie on the spot.

Maggie took another bite of her pastry and wondered—not for the first time—if Faye had been the one to tell Lord Philip the truth about Maggie's departure from Bells & Wallace. She was the only expat Maggie had confided in, and she'd regretted it as soon as she'd made the confession. Just because Faye was the closest thing Maggie had to a friend in Rome didn't make the two best friends.

"We missed you at the party last night." Faye switched back to English as she took a white box tied with twine from Mario. She began rummaging in her purse, not looking at Maggie. "Burt said you were working. I know how much you wanted to find something *productive* to do."

Was Faye mocking her? The woman had a way of getting under Maggie's skin. Fluent Italian. Immaculate grooming. Charming hostess. She was a little too perfect. Maggie looked down and noticed the buttons on her blouse straining over her stomach and sat up straight. "Lord Philip was murdered in his home last night. I found his body."

Faye dropped her wallet. Coins rolled all over the tiled floor. Maggie felt somehow that she'd scored a point then immediately felt guilty. She dropped to her knees to help Faye collect the money.

"Giovanna!" Mario called from behind the counter. *"Venite fuori! Maggie ha trovato un corpo!"*

Giovanna walked out of the kitchen, wiping her hands on her apron. She was tiny, just five feet, and slim. She wore bright red lipstick and had a mole on her right cheek that gave her a 1940s movie-star look. "No! Maggie, I'm so sorry. Where did this happen? Not here in Trastevere? It was dangerous once upon a time, perhaps, but that was in my parents' time."

Faye was back on her feet and wrapped an arm around Maggie's shoulders. It was bony and not at all comforting. "Oh, darling, do tell. Was it simply awful?"

Mario passed Maggie a *saccottino al cioccolato.* "On the house."

She told them what had happened.

"Drugs, probably," Faye said. "It's only rumors, but people say Lord Philip was, well, entrepreneurial."

She drew out the word, making the most of each syllable, almost as if she were spelling a word in front of an illiterate child.

Maggie waited.

"Illegal entrepreneurial." Faye lowered her voice. "Some of the men joked once that Walpole must be selling drugs to pay for his apartment and asked would he bring some to the next party. They were just kidding, but Walpole said street-level dealers didn't make nearly enough to support his lifestyle, then he said he'd be happy to introduce them to a supplier. They laughed, but it was all a bit weird, if you know what I mean?"

It was. Burt earned a good salary and their relocation package was generous, but the White's apartment was still in the low-rent side of the city, and the whole thing was smaller than Lord Philip's Grand Salon. Then there was all that art. Maggie knew how much each guest paid for the tour. It wouldn't come close to covering those costs.

Still, Lord Philip was a member of England's nobility. Didn't they have estates and tenants and things that spun off gobs of money? Maggie had read most of Jane Austen's books and all of the Lord Peter Wimsey series.

Members of the upper class all seemed to manage quite well.

Giovanna disappeared into the kitchen and returned a moment later with a tray of tiramisu. She started filling the case. "I cannot imagine a successful drug dealer running a tour company. It doesn't feel, perhaps, very logical."

"Maybe the tour business was a cover." Faye tapped her finger on her pastry box. She hadn't even opened it to try a small bite.

"For what?" Maggie asked. "A drug empire?"

"To launder the money," Faye said. "Hiding ill-gotten gains. Isn't that supposed to be the hardest part of having a criminal enterprise?"

"That's out of my area of expertise," Mario said. "I studied literature at school, not accounting."

Maggie brushed crumbs off her front. She should be getting to the palazzo. "Mario, tell Carlotta you'll join her and the boy's family on the camping trip. That should take care of it."

He frowned. "She'll never go if it means the families will be spending time together." A moment later he grinned. "Ah, brilliant! She won't go. Why didn't we think of that?"

Chapter Five

*I*taly transformed itself from a poor, mainly rural nation into a global player through government policies and land reform. Its challenge today is how to stay competitive despite the country's deep risk avoidance mentality and employment laws that discourage hard work and innovation.
—Masterpiece Tours "Welcome to Rome" pamphlet

Faye's ideas about drugs and money laundering were probably nonsense. Maggie crossed the Tiber River and the busy three-lane road running alongside. And yet, it wasn't hard to imagine her boss as doing something, well, untoward. She would tell Orsini. It could be a good lead for him to follow.

It was still early for rush hour, but plenty of little cars and scooters raced past. Maggie walked into the heart of the old city and across the Campo Fiore. The rest of Rome was still waking up, but the city's most beautiful market was in full swing. Portable tables were crowded together, overflowing with colorful produce, fish nestled in crushed ice, and cuts of meat Maggie had never seen at home. And the flowers. Flower stalls everywhere gave their perfume to the air, all surrounded by lovely old buildings. Maggie couldn't imagine a nicer place to shop. Not today.

A man like Lord Philip would have made enemies. She cut through the market. These would be suspects for Orsini to interview. Maggie sped up, ignoring the honk of a car as she crossed the street and made her way to the palazzo.

She pushed open the door from the street and paused at the foot of the grand staircase winding all the way up. There were only four apartments in the building, one per floor, and an ancient elevator ran up alongside the stairs to each landing. It was only big enough for three or four small people and had no solid door. Stepping inside made Maggie feel a bit like she was walking into a cage, so she opted for the stairs. It would be good for her to work off that *saccottino,* anyway.

Maggie puffed up to the fifth floor and found a tall, well-dressed businessman waiting outside Lord Philip's door. His dark suit, crisp blue shirt, striped tie, and polished wire-rim glasses were too conservative for an Italian. And his blond hair, clearly styled with care, failed to disguise a distinctly Anglo-Saxon hairline. The man looked to be in his thirties or forties, but Maggie saw he was younger when she got closer.

"John Aldrich, representing the estate." British accent. Just as she thought. He held out his hand. "I came as soon as we were informed of Lord Philip's death. And you are?"

Maggie introduced herself. One thing off her to-do list. The executor would know who the heirs were. She was impressed the firm had sent someone so quickly. This man was rather young for what must be an important assignment. Still, everyone seemed young to Maggie these days.

She unlocked the door and they stepped into the foyer, with its marble floor and ceiling covered with cavorting cupids, pink and plush against a painted blue sky.

Aldrich whistled. "Looks as though Walpole's done all right for himself." He moved into the Grand Salon just beyond. "I'll need to get an appraiser in to take a look at all this. See what the family wishes to keep and sell the rest. Will be worth a mint."

There was no sign of Thomas or Ilaria yet. Maggie hoped the tour's painting instructor and cook would come soon. She remembered her promise to Burt to be careful. Surely this man was who he said he was.

"There's a tour on now." Maggie forced herself to sound light and unconcerned. She hoped Aldrich couldn't hear her heart pounding. "Seven guests. They'll be here soon. The police too."

"Right, that travel business," Aldrich said. "Hate to issue any refunds. You'll have to keep it going, I suppose, until we begin liquidation. The guests are all paid up in advance, I presume?"

She relaxed. A murderer wouldn't be interested in the logistics of keeping the tour open.

"I'm not sure they'll want to continue…" Maggie began, but Aldrich waved her off.

"Now, what else is tucked away here?"

Maggie trotted after Aldrich as he barreled through the apartment, glancing here and there at the art and furniture, making notes on a legal pad. Maggie's mind raced. Could she persuade the guests to stay on? They might think it macabre to continue painting and sightseeing, but the guests hardly knew Lord Philip. And, as Vicky said the night before, they had Ilaria, Thomas, and Maggie. Besides, if Inspector Orsini had any sense, he wouldn't allow the guests to leave the country anyway, so they might as well stay occupied.

Aldrich's tour ended at the studio at the end of the hall. The room was a pleasant jumble of brushes, paint, and canvasses. Aldrich took a handkerchief from his pocket and fastidiously wiped the surface of the cleanest of the paint-splattered tables then placed his briefcase on top. He snapped open the clasp, carefully folded the handkerchief, and tucked it into one of the case's interior pockets before handing Maggie three sheets of paper covered with handwritten questions. "We'll bring in a forensic accountant, but this will get us started."

Maggie glanced through the notes. Mr. Aldrich wanted to know the guest counts over the last two years, numbers of prepaid reservations, other sources of income, payments to personnel, contractors, and outside agencies, cost of accommodations and meals, payments on the apartment, and assets including office supplies. Was she really meant to count paper clips?

"Just some notes I sketched out on the flight to give me the lay of the land, as it were," he said while she flipped the pages.

"Johnnie Boy!" Thomas appeared in the doorway looking like the member of a rock and roll band in tight jeans, a striped red and white T-shirt, and a thin leather tie. "I'd know that voice anywhere." Thomas clapped Aldrich on the shoulder. "Don't tell me you're wrapped up in this business?"

Aldrich returned Thomas's hug. "I'm Lord Philip's executor. I heard you were in Rome, Mittens. But I didn't expect to find you here."

Thomas beamed at Maggie. "Johnnie and I were rugby mates back at university."

Maggie couldn't picture the two at school together. Aldrich acted prematurely middle-aged while Thomas was holding onto his youth with both hands.

"So, you're in charge of the estate." Thomas sat on the stool next to Aldrich. "How did you manage that?"

"My godfather is the solicitor of record, but I've been handling this work since I joined up." Aldrich leaned forward, his voice confidential. "If you want to know the truth, Mittens, most people in the office didn't want to have too much to do with Walpole after the flap over that mineral rights scheme. Still, it's a chance to show the higher ups what I can do and all that."

This, Maggie realized, explained the young man's ridiculous list of questions. He was trying to impress his boss.

"What flap?" Thomas asked.

"You must have heard about it," Aldrich said. "The diamond mine in India."

"I didn't know there were diamonds in India," Thomas said.

Aldrich sighed. "There aren't, old man. That's the point."

"Wait a jiff." Thomas sat opposite Maggie and Aldrich. "He wasn't the one who cleaned the pockets of the bright young things back in the nineties, was he?"

Thomas might be living a bohemian life in Rome, but his background was solidly English upper class. He'd told Maggie his family had butlers, at least when he was young.

"The very one."

Thomas whistled. "He made off with a fortune, from what I heard."

"Took money from nearly thirty idiots. A veritable Who's Who, including my half-brother and sister, I'm sorry to say."

Maggie was glad Burt wasn't here right now. First the rumors Lord Philip was dealing drugs, now the news he had swindled a good portion of the

English aristocracy. Her husband had been right when he said there was something wrong about her employer.

"Was he prosecuted?" she asked.

Aldrich snorted. "And have the stupidity of the young leaders of tomorrow brought to light? No. Walpole was allowed to walk with the understanding he stay away. Far away. That's how he ended up in Rome. Not a bad place to be exiled, I must say."

A very different story than the romantic tale Lord Philip told about leaving England to escape the memories of a youthful love affair.

Aldrich tapped his pen on his yellow legal pad. "I don't see the old scam stretching to all this, though. This tour operation must be really humming."

"I'm not a whiz at maths," Thomas said, "but I don't see it even covering the rent."

"Didn't he inherit from his family?" The metal stool was digging into Maggie's bottom. How on earth did the artists manage them? She shifted, trying to find a more comfortable position.

Aldrich snorted. "He was the second son of a nearly penniless duke. The family sold off most of their land to pay death duties in the forties, and his older brother rents the family home for weddings to scrape together enough cash to keep the roof watertight."

Faye's suggestion that Lord Philip was up to something illegal was seeming more and more likely.

"Did he ever say anything about where the money came from?" Maggie asked.

Thomas shook his head. His hair was spiked today. The day before it had been combed down, very professional. Maggie liked that he was a bit of a chameleon. Still trying on different personalities.

"I did sometimes wonder, though…" Thomas trailed off.

Maggie leaned forward. "You wondered what?"

"I'm not sure exactly. He just seemed to be awfully lucky when it came to his art purchases. Buying low and selling high."

Aldrich took another handkerchief from his briefcase and dabbed at his forehead. The room was warm, despite the early hour. It must be all the windows.

Thomas pointed to a brown-paper package in the corner. It was small, about the size of Aldrich's legal pad, and thin. Thomas had opened it last night for the police to confirm it still contained Lord Philip's newest picture, the *White Horse*. "Appraiser's coming for this today. Old Walpole was very proud of the fact he'd acquired it for a song."

Maggie remembered Lord Philip showing the picture to the guests the first night, saying he had a hunch it was a lost masterpiece from Italy's Macchiaioli movement. Helen had been particularly taken with that painting, asking if she could look at it in the brighter lights of the studio.

The pair had chatted about Italy's early Impressionists, a group Maggie gathered had predated the French superstars and were more focused on the depiction of light and darkness than whatever it was the French were known for. Maggie's understanding of the Impressionism movement extended only as far as the water lilies and haystacks she'd seen at the big Monet exhibit at the Met, which she'd dutifully taken her children to.

Aldrich laughed. "What's the problem, Mittens? Buying low and selling high is the name of the game, isn't it?"

Thomas wrinkled his nose, as if smelling a dog that had been skunked. "Forced someone to sell, so I gather. Walpole said something like, 'he won't be happy when the appraisal comes in, and there's not a thing he can do about it.'"

Thomas was an excellent mimic, and Maggie could imagine Lord Philip's sneer as he'd said those words. If Lord Philip had acquired the *White Horse* in a less-than-legitimate way, that could be one motive for his murder. Orsini would need to track down the original owner.

Aldrich held up his hand. "I shouldn't have asked. The less I know, the more room for plausible deniability."

Would Lord Philip's heirs get to keep the picture if Thomas was right and Lord Philip had acquired it under false pretenses? "Who inherits the estate?"

Aldrich relaxed, as if relieved at the change in subject. "Lord Philip's nephew, Edward Innes-Fox."

"Old Neddy?" Thomas looked genuinely pleased. "Good job, him. He's the one who found me this spot."

Aldrich pursed his lips. "How'd he put you two together?"

"Neddy heard about my need for a new situation and put me in touch with his uncle. Walpole took me to coffee, liked that I rowed crew and played rugby, as well as my degree in art from Oxford."

"Thank God we didn't go to Cambridge," Aldrich snapped his briefcase closed. "Ghastly chaps there. Wasn't your focus aboriginal and Pacific art?"

Thomas winked. "Walpole never asked about my concentration. Besides, art is art."

That explained Thomas's frequent encouragements for the guests to throw off the shackles of civilization. Maggie had overheard him lecturing Shelia the previous day saying, "You can learn as much about art by turning your back on the classics as by studying them. Just think what it did for Gauguin." A message perhaps more appropriate for a painting tour of the Pacific than a visit to the center of civilization for more than three millennia. Still, the guests' work was improving. Maybe Thomas was on to something after all.

"Can't see Neddy running this place," Thomas said. "Have you met that fiancée of his?"

"Pretty thing, but not quite our sort," Aldrich said. "You missed a rather good engagement party, Mittens."

"Couldn't get away. All the old boys there?"

"Nearly. Tancred was in usual form, going on about his uncle to anyone who would listen."

"Still? That was years ago." Thomas turned to Maggie. "You'd like Tancred. Can do fifteen different bird calls—more when he's had a few drinks. But his uncle had an accident and he's convinced the widow had something to do with it. He tends to drone on, if you know what I mean."

"Ridiculous," Aldrich said. "Terrible Tory didn't get a shilling. Had to start all over again hunting for some other rich husband."

"Tancred's uncle Albert died on his honeymoon," Thomas said. "He was eighty if he was a day, but Tancred can't believe any twenty-year-old girl would have married the man for his personality. It was a sightseeing excursion, I think. Fell off something."

38

"Madrid. Retiro Park," Aldrich said. "Beautiful place. Went there with the pater and mater one summer."

Maggie was relieved when Ilaria's voice interrupted the reminiscing.

"We're in the studio," Maggie called.

Ilaria walked in, unwrapping a pink silk scarf from her head, tossing her long brown hair like a woman in a shampoo ad. She had moved to Rome from Sicily four years earlier with her brother, who came to expand the family laundry business into the capital, and she worked part-time for Lord Philip when he had a tour on. Ilaria was in her mid twenties, tall, and slim, with the dark good looks that seemed a part of every Italian woman's DNA.

The young woman had left right after dinner, and it wasn't until Ilaria asked where Lord Philip was that Maggie realized she didn't know about last night. Maggie broke the news about finding Lord Philip's body and told her about the police investigation. Maggie wasn't sure what reaction she was expecting. Italian women in the movies all made extravagant shows of emotion, but Ilaria simply frowned.

"It was only a matter of time, I suppose. Silly man."

"What's that?" Aldrich unbuttoned his suit jacket, flashing a red and blue suspender when he put a hand on his hip. Maggie thought of a male peacock, fanning his tail feathers to impress a hen.

"The idea a robber broke in. It's absurd," Ilaria said. "Why choose last night, when the house is occupied, and not any other day, when the house is empty for hours at a time?"

Her accent was musical, and she had an attractive habit of frowning slightly whenever she paused for a word. Maggie felt like a dowdy old Yankee with her flat vowels and frumpy dress next to these three.

"What do you think happened?" Maggie asked.

Ilaria had worked for Lord Philip for two years. She would know more about him than anyone.

Ilaria crossed one pink-high-heeled foot casually over the other. She was sitting on the stool next to Maggie and leaned forward. "I have no idea. I can think of at least seven people who wanted him dead. No, eight. I should have included whoever inherits this place."

"Classic motive." Thomas drummed his fingers on the table in front of him. "Except that it's a chum of Aldrich's and mine. Next?"

"There's his family," Ilaria said. "His brother and his sister disliked him very much, from what I understand."

Aldrich yawned. "All a long time ago. Not relevant at all."

"That's three," Thomas said. "Who else?" He was moving to the imaginary music now, shoulders shifting to a beat that matched his fingers.

"There's the French man. Pierre." Ilaria said. "He swore revenge on Lord Philip. This would certainly qualify, yes?"

It certainly would. There weren't any French expats in the group Faye choreographed. Those were mostly Americans and Brits, probably because of their shared native tongue.

Thomas stopped drumming. "Art-thief Pierre? Master-criminal Pierre? It's a bit far-fetched. Simply stories art dealers tell when they have too much to drink."

Maggie leaned forward. Thomas had worked at one of the city's prestigious auction houses before coming to Masterpiece Tours. His parents gave him a generous allowance, enough to live a few blocks from Lord Philip, but with the stipulation he have a job, any job. If he was out of work for more than a few weeks, he would need to go home to London and join his father's firm, end of discussion.

Aldrich frowned. "You've heard of this man?"

"People say Pierre is hired to acquire pictures for special collections." Thomas coughed. "Private collections for wealthy collectors. Pictures that wouldn't come on the market on their own. You know, some family's had it for generations and can't bear the idea of parting with it or they don't need the money, so why sell?"

Thomas tapped his fingers faster now, seeming to enjoy the story. "Pierre's men sneak into private homes like cat burglars and swap out the original works with brilliant fakes. The owners never realize their art has been stolen, or at least not until too late." Thomas paused. "But I'm not sure the man's real. All seems a bit far-fetched."

"What's his connection to Lord Philip?" Maggie asked. "Does this Pierre fellow live in Rome?"

"No one knows," Thomas said. "He's the original man behind the curtain. Everything done through his agents. Or that's how the story goes. Art dealers are romantics at heart. They can't resist a great story, no matter how ridiculous."

"Are you saying Walpole was in business with this crook?" Aldrich asked. "If so—"

Ilaria cut him off. "It was about six months ago. Lord Philip came out of his study so excited. He said he'd gotten the best of someone named Pierre. I didn't follow all of it, but I think they had some sort of agreement and Lord Philip double-crossed Pierre."

"This is irrelevant." Aldrich stood. "Unrelated, clear as day. I should be off."

Thomas ignored his friend. "You don't know any details?"

Ilaria shook her head.

The studio windows were open the hum of street sounds floated in. A horn honked. Someone shouted in Italian. Then the buzz of scooters zipping along. Burt had suggested buying one of those terrifying bikes when they arrived, but Maggie refused on principle. She was too old to be climbing onto something so small.

"All I know is Lord Philip made sure he came out on top of any—" Ilaria paused and frowned for a moment, as though searching for the right word. "Negotiation."

"You think Pierre killed Lord Philip?" Maggie asked.

Ilaria pushed her long hair over her shoulder. "I don't think anything. I am just saying he's a man with a motive."

"One of the fellows at the auction house said he knew a chap who referred a client to Pierre," Thomas said, suddenly serious. "Said the referral commission was out of this world. But it came with strings. The old iron fist, velvet glove type of thing. When the dealer got cold feet and tried to get out of the arrangement, Pierre taught him a lesson."

Aldrich laughed. Maggie noticed a brittle edge to it. "This is a bit much, Mittens. I hardly think there's some master criminal out there taking out anyone who pulls a fast one on him. The art world would be decimated. From what I understand, unsavory dealings are the bread and butter of the industry."

Thomas shook his head. "Pierre destroyed this man's reputation, or at least the story goes. Wife left him for a neighbor. Took the dog. My friend said working with Pierre was like taking a deal from the devil."

"Well, if you're not talking about murder, I hardly think the story is relevant," Aldrich said.

Maggie hated to agree with him, but it was sounding a bit fantastic. Which detective said the simplest explanations were the right ones? Adam Dalgliesh? Hercule Poirot? She wasn't sure. The problem, of course, was you had no way of knowing what was simple until the case was solved.

"Whoever Walpole snagged the *White Horse* from would have wanted it back," Thomas said. "That's another suspect for your list."

Aldrich held up his hand. "I really shouldn't be party to any of this speculation. I'm a member of the bar. That comes with certain responsibilities." He glanced around as though a spy from the ethics department might be hiding behind the easels.

"Wouldn't he have taken the picture with him?" Maggie asked. "If he was angry enough to shoot Lord Philip?"

Aldrich took off his glasses and began polishing. There was something unsettling about the way he snapped the handkerchief open and kept his eyes on Thomas while he worked. "There's nothing to be gained from all this talk."

Thomas seemed immune to Aldrich's stare. "Okay, you've given us five people with motives. Who are the others?"

Ilaria smiled. "There's Maggie."

Maggie's heart skipped a beat as Aldrich turned his gaze on her with new interest. "Mrs. White? Now this *is* interesting."

"Me?" Did anyone else hear her voice squeak? "You mean because I found him? That's hardly evidence. The body was cold then. Right, Thomas?"

"Lord Philip wasn't a pleasant employer," Ilaria said. "And I got the sense it bothered you more than it should. As though there was something else going on. That Lord Philip knew something you didn't want anyone to know. Maybe you had enough, yes?"

Was this woman some kind of Sicilian fortune-teller who could see inside your heart? Maggie opened her mouth, but Ilaria continued, "I said people with motive. I include myself on the list. And you, Thomas. Lord Philip threatened to fire you just last night, didn't he?"

"That was nothing." Thomas's voice rose an octave. "Didn't like me criticizing his new picture."

Maggie willed her face to look natural. The others weren't paying attention to Ilaria's idea about Lord Philip's power over Maggie.

"What's your motive, Ilaria?" Aldrich asked.

The young woman smiled. "I don't mind telling you Lord Philip was pressuring me for an introduction to my father. He said he could make things difficult for me with my family." She uncrossed and re-crossed her legs. "No, he wasn't a nice man, and any of us could have easily taken it into our own hands to put an end to it all."

"The man enjoyed power," Thomas said. "I'm sure there are loads of people who could have had enough of him."

Maggie thought what it would take to have "had enough." She hadn't really been at the breaking point. But for her to have even contemplated it? Well, maybe it didn't take so much.

"The guests didn't see anything, I suppose?" Aldrich's his tone was casual.

"I'm sure it would have been quite simple for one of them to come down and—" Ilaria made a firing gesture with her hand.

"What possible motive could they have?" Thomas said.

Ilaria shrugged, unconcerned. "It would be a secret, would it not? Something no one knows?"

"They were on the terrace the entire time." Then she thought of the timeline she'd written out. Daniel and Vicky had each gone downstairs. Still, Thomas was right. They could hardly have a motive.

"You didn't see anything, Ilaria?" Maggie asked.

"Ah, so you do suspect me." Ilaria smiled. "Very wise. I cleaned the kitchen and watched the fireworks from the piazza with Gregorio."

43

"How romantic," Thomas's tone made it clear he thought it was anything but. He rolled his eyes whenever Ilaria mentioned her boyfriend. It reminded Maggie of her daughter when Sam had his first serious high school girlfriend. She felt so threatened by the girlfriend stealing her brother's affection that she teased her brother constantly.

"It was, actually." Ilaria's tone was light. "He proposed."

Thomas turned white. "You didn't accept?"

Ilaria frowned. "Of course not. Gregorio knows I don't want to get married yet, but he let my father pressure him. He's not normally a weak man, but when it comes to my father…"

Gregorio was best friends with Ilaria's brother and a key member of the family business. Maggie could understand Ilaria's father wanting to cement the relationship, but she was glad Ilaria had stood her ground. Maggie married Burt when she was only 25, but times were different now. There was no rush.

"If you were outside, Ilaria, anyone could have snuck in," Maggie said.

The three sat in silence a moment.

"What's your alibi, Mittens?" Aldrich asked.

"Don't have one," Thomas said. "I wrapped up the *White Horse* in the dining room. Had the door to the hall shut. The whole of the Tottenham Footballers could have come through the front door and I wouldn't have seen them."

Maggie thought again how lucky whoever had done this had been. Ilaria, Thomas, Vicky, and Daniel had all been downstairs at one point or another. Had the killer hidden in the study, waiting for his moment to slip away? She shivered, thinking of being locked in with Lord Philip's body until the coast was clear. It would have taken nerves of steel.

Inspector Orsini would be busy with this case. She'd make sure he had all the information he needed to do a thorough investigation.

"Bad luck, old man," Aldrich said. "The last thing anyone needs is the Italian police force bumbling through his private life. My advice is don't get involved. Let them look for their burglar. Best for everyone."

"A man is dead, Mr. Aldrich," Maggie said. "Our convenience shouldn't be our first consideration."

"People die." Aldrich picked up his briefcase. "Finding the killer won't change that."

Chapter Six

Gian Lorenzo Bernini's grand fountains, beautiful squares, and over-the-top churches define much of the city we see today. Think of him as the head architect of the church's marketing machine, creating a spectacle to attract pilgrims to the center of Catholicism. His most famous work—the massive Fountain of the Four Rivers—*can be found in the Piazza Navona, just steps from Lord Philip's palazzo, your home away from home for the duration of the tour.*

—Masterpiece Tours "Welcome to Rome" pamphlet

There was the hum of voices in the hall. Maggie followed Aldrich to the salon, where the guests were assembling. Shelia was talking with Eloise about something, and Maggie recalled an inspirational poster about a peacock and a sparrow. A falcon, maybe. She couldn't remember the message now. Something relentlessly cheerful and hopelessly naïve, probably. Vicky and Daniel trailed behind, holding hands. Daniel didn't typically come to the palazzo until lunch since the morning was dedicated to painting, but Lord Philip's death seemed to have been enough to persuade him to take a break from his work, something his wife had failed to do for the past four days of the tour. For a man who was on the trip to make amends for an indiscretion with his secretary, Daniel didn't seem to be working very hard.

Maggie heard the rattle of the old elevator settling at the landing and the metallic clank of the gate opening. Len entered the apartment first, followed by Charles and Helen. The tall woman had her hand on Charles' elbow, guiding him to a chair far from her sister's perch. Eloise popped up to join them.

Ilaria excused herself to prepare coffee and Aldrich introduced himself as the man in charge. He shook hands all around and was almost out the door when Daniel took him aside, speaking loudly enough for everyone to hear.

"Look, I'm really sorry about Lord Philip and everything, but we paid for a tour, and if he's not available, I expect you'll be issuing some form of compensation."

Daniel reminded Maggie of an older version of Lucy's high-school class president. Perfectly cut short brown hair, tight-fitting button-down shirt and crisp slacks. More than anything, though, it was that they both had a way of talking with a smirk, especially when saying something rude.

"Oh, Daniel." Vicky joined them and swatted her husband playfully on the arm. She'd dressed for the day in capri pants and a sweater that was so simple it probably cost more than Maggie's wedding dress. "It's not as if the money makes a difference."

"You're in excellent hands with Mrs. White and Thomas. The tour will continue as planned." Aldrich nodded at Vicky. "I know you from somewhere. You weren't at Oxford, were you?" They were about the same age. They could have overlapped in college.

But Vicky shrugged. "Not me. Straight into secretarial school."

"You remind me of someone." Aldrich frowned. "Doesn't she remind you of someone, Thomas?"

Daniel put his arm around his wife, as though claiming her as his own. "It's the principle of the thing. This tour isn't what was advertised."

Aldrich pursed his lips. "If you desire, applications can be made to the estate. Carry on, Mrs. White. I'll be in touch with further instructions."

He turned on his heel and the elevator clanked as he descended. The guests turned to Maggie expectantly. Shelia and Len sat together on an antique cream couch, their bulk out of place on that delicate piece of furniture. Shelia's tote bag, decorated with Van Gogh's *The Starry Night*, rested near her feet. It was probably weighed down with the guidebooks and painting manuals she carried everywhere.

Shelia pursued her painting and sightseeing with a dogged commitment that seemed born more from determination than passion. Len, on the other hand, had taken to the activity with a natural flair. His painting from the Forum the other day had been a simple tree with the vaguest hints of broken columns and fallen stones behind it, yet the picture managed to give the impression of the ruined grandeur of the place. It was the type of art Maggie would like to hang in her own home.

Eloise and Helen stood near one of the door-sized windows. Eloise wore sturdy walking shoes and had her umbrella and knitting bag beside her. Helen wore a purple straw hat and layers of gauzy scarves. Maggie wondered idly if they'd always been this different, or if they'd grown apart as they'd aged. Charles sat between them tapping his cane expectantly.

Then, finally, there were Vicky and Daniel. There must have been a ten- or fifteen-year gap between them. That wasn't necessarily a problem, but the guests all knew Daniel had had an affair with his secretary.

"Well, what's the plan?" Shelia asked. The teal sequins on her top sparkled, as if to reinforce her point.

Maggie took a deep breath and turned on her "Corporate Maggie" personality. She needed to convince these guests to stay on with the tour. "Lord Philip's death is a shock and a loss, and we're all very upset." She looked around at the guests, making eye contact with each one in turn. All except Daniel nodded dutifully. "But you've invested a great deal in this tour—not just your money but your time—and I would hate to see it go to waste. As Mr. Aldrich said, Thomas, Ilaria, and I are standing by, delighted to continue with the tour if you are."

She gave Thomas an encouraging mile. Surely he'd want the tour to continue while he searched for another job to appease his parents.

"Maggie's absolutely right," Thomas picked up her cue. "You've made so much progress, and we've just gotten into the meaty part of the instruction. Today we're covering sketching—thinking and planning before you even pick up a brush. What do you say?"

The guests glanced at each other.

Helen licked her lips, as if about to speak, but Vicky got in first. "That sounds wonderful. Daniel and I will stay. Won't the rest of you?"

Helen hesitated then nodded her assent. "Eloise *does* need every moment of instruction she can get." She turned to her sister. "That picture you did yesterday. Was it supposed to be a rooster?"

"It was a gladiator, Helen, as you well know." Even standing, Eloise's posture was slightly bent. Hours spent peering at her knitting probably didn't help. "We didn't all study painting in college, dear. Some of us chose more practical topics of study."

Helen snorted. "I hardly call library science a practical subject, dear. What, exactly, is scientific about a library?"

Ilaria entered the salon, bearing a large tray of coffee, interrupting their squabble.

"And after the lesson?" Charles asked once the guests helped themselves to coffee.

Maggie frowned. They were scheduled to tour the gardens at Tivoli, a good hour and a half in traffic. She couldn't very well send the guests out of the city when the inspector might arrive at any moment to continue his questioning.

"The Piazzas of Rome." They could set their easels up at the Piazza Navona a block away. There was plenty to paint there, and it would be easy enough to fetch everyone back when the inspector arrived.

Shelia spoke from the couch. "I can't stop thinking about Lord Philip's death. Shouldn't we have heard something last night?"

Maggie thought of the fireworks and the sound bouncing randomly off the buildings.

"No chance," Charles said. "With these old walls, the sound would have been muffled."

Len leaned forward. "Was Lord Philip shot from outside the building, do you think?"

"Afraid not." Charles set his cup on the coffee table inlaid with some sort of oriental pattern.

An antique, like all of the furniture in the apartment. Maggie worried they should be using coasters.

"Lord Philip's body was slumped toward the window. If he'd been shot from outside, he would be lying the other way."

"You know so many interesting things, Charles." Helen squeezed his shoulder.

"How do you know the position of the body?" Daniel's eyes narrowed.

"Thomas told me last night," Charles said. He played with the handle of his cane. "But the body's position is only part of it. It would be an impossible shot from the building across the way. Same for the buildings on the side. There's no place for a sniper to be positioned with a clear shot to his lordship."

"What did you say you did, Charles honey?" Shelia's drawl was casual, but her smile looked forced.

"Military intelligence, then academia." So much for the professor buried in books about the ancient world that Maggie had imagined.

"I'm largely retired," he went on, "but I still edit the occasional article and consult from time to time. Just to keep my hand in."

"I assume he was killed with his own gun." Len was dressed in denim from head to toe again today. He seemed like a man who would know about guns. "I told the police about it last night, and they checked his desk. It was gone."

Lord Philip had told the guests about his gun on the second night of the tour when Shelia asked if he was afraid of intruders.

Maggie shivered. It was time to distract the guests. "Let's get started in the studio, shall we?"

"I'm going back to the hotel," Daniel said.

It was early in New York. Still the middle of the night. "I'm not sure that's a good idea," Maggie said. "The inspector might be here any minute. You're more than welcome to use the dining room to work."

"I need my computer." He gave Vicky a kiss then stood. "The police know where to find me."

"You'll be back for lunch?" Vicky still held onto Daniel's hand. There was a pleading note in her voice.

He shrugged. "Can't say."

Maggie herded the guests into the studio, and Thomas began arranging the easels in a semicircle. The artists took their positions, Vicky at one end, Shelia in the center, Len next to her. Eloise and Helen jockeyed to have

Charles between them.

The room was long, stretching across the entire width of the palazzo like the top bar of a T at the end of the hall. The floor was tile, and three walls were made almost entirely of glass. Lord Philip said the room had been designed as a greenhouse when the palazzo was carved into apartments. Maggie liked to imagine some eccentric prior resident owner puttering about in this room tending his orchids.

Thomas dragged a ficus plant into the center of the circle. "Good watercolors begin with good sketches. You can work out key issues before you pick up a paintbrush. Now look at this plant. If I were to start painting, I might get the proportion wrong, or the angle, and then have to start over. But with just a few strokes," he sketched with his pencil on an easel facing the group, "I can see where I'm wrong."

Maggie left him to his work and retreated to the office. She checked her watch. Nine fifteen and still no sign of Orsini. It was looking like her instincts were correct—the man was lazy. She'd give him fifteen more minutes then call the station and ask when, exactly, he was planning to return to the apartment. She had important information for him.

Maggie settled down with Aldrich's list. The sooner she started the exercise, the sooner it would be complete. She opened a drawer and began looking for information about trip deposits. She found the file then looked back at the clock. Nine eighteen.

Maggie drummed her fingers on the desk. Close enough. She'd call the station. After a few confusing exchanges, she understood from a secretary that Inspector Orsini was not in and they didn't know of his plans. She left a message for him to call her and settled back down to work, stopping only to say goodbye when Thomas left with the guests to paint in the piazza. She gave him strict instructions to keep an eye on his phone so he could bring the group back as soon as Orsini arrived.

The paper files were well organized and easy to navigate. Maggie had spent her first few days on the job bringing order to the chaos the "old girl" had left behind. It had taken Maggie almost an entire day to find out who was even coming on the tour. The computer records were a mess, and paper printouts had been stuffed into three different drawers, each of which seemed to be organized in some kind of chronological system: Len and Shelia had booked in June, Charles in December, and Vicky and Daniel in February.

There hadn't even been a record of Helen and Eloise's booking. The first Maggie knew of their arrival was when the Hotel Fortuna called saying they had two unexpected guests in Lord Philip's party. Maggie had sorted out the hotel side of things and was relieved when Helen offered a check the first night.

"Our bank account wasn't debited," she explained. "And I do worry. I told Eloise I'd bring my checkbook, just in case."

Could Maggie get Aldrich to consider keeping the agency running beyond this current tour? She could show him the business plan Lord Philip had tossed away. The costs were low, and the guests paid a fortune to attend. The problem was Lord Philip didn't run enough sessions. Just six a year. Maggie made a mental note to talk with Aldrich about her ideas. Surely an eager beaver like him would welcome the opportunity to impress his bosses.

Chapter Seven

Collectors of modern art have long ignored the works of the Italian impressionist movement—the Macchiaioli. At last, the market is placing a premium on this art which pre-dates the French masters by nearly a decade and has a freshness and authenticity all its own.
—Masterpiece Tours "Welcome to Rome" pamphlet

Maggie was sitting awkwardly on the floor, surrounded by papers, when a man's voice called out from the entry.

"Walpole? You here?" The voice was American. From Chicago, maybe?

Maggie pushed herself to her feet and found a big man about her age standing in the hall. He wore a turquoise jacket, sleeves rolled to his elbows, and a pink T-shirt. He carried a leather folio under his arm.

"Walpole still out? He warned me he had a tour on. Why he does them, I'll never understand. Did he leave it for me?" He brushed past Maggie into the salon, walking with a clumsy gait. Not quite a limp but more than a shuffle. He looked around, as if expecting Lord Philip to appear.

"I told him I've been working nonstop, nose to the grindstone on other jobs, but he said it was urgent. I said I'd make time to pick the picture up today. Don't tell me he hasn't left it?"

Was this the man Lord Philip had hired to appraise the *White Horse*? Maggie looked at him more closely. He had beady eyes and licked his lips expectantly. She should tell this man Lord Philip was dead. Of course she should. But for some reason, she didn't.

She held out her hand, instead. "Maggie White, Lord Philip's manager."

She'd hesitated writing a title last night, but not today. John Aldrich had said she was in charge, hadn't he?

The visitor handed her a crisp business card. "Walter Jones. Fine arts." He squinted at her. "We've met before. Give me a moment..."

Maggie pulled her shoulders back, uncomfortable under Walter's gaze. Finally, he snapped his fingers. "I've got it. We went out to dinner in Testaccio with some of the gang in December. I talked with your husband at Faye's party last night. He's a funny man. Told me he misses your gnocchi."

Maggie remembered the dinner now. They'd all squeezed into two taxis to go to a hole-in-the-wall restaurant in a gritty working-class part of the city. The food had been wonderful, but Maggie had struggled to follow the conversation, which consisted mostly of inside jokes about past dinners. She'd been relieved when she and Burt finally returned to their apartment.

Maggie relaxed in Walter's company now. This man was wasn't a stranger. He was part of *the group*, as Faye called it. A collection of forty or so Americans and Brits working in Rome. It wasn't all of the expats in the city, of course. Not the diplomats or permanent residents married to Italians. Not the young people taking time off to find themselves or the jet setters with homes around the world. It was people working in Rome, mostly on expat packages, but some, like Walter and Lord Philip, who ran businesses here. Socializing with the group didn't feel all that different from what Maggie was used to back home, except for the small apartments and the presence of the Brits, of course. Maggie had somehow expected life here would be more, well, different.

She sat and gestured for him to do the same. "I understand there's a lot of interest in the *White Horse*." She chose her words carefully. All accurate, if perhaps misleading. Walter might be part of the group, but she wasn't going to give anything away that she didn't have to. Not yet.

He leaned back and drummed his fingers on his knee. They were stained with nicotine. "Abbatis don't come up every day. Not really appreciated outside of Italy, but he was one of the greats. I've been doing my research. If this is genuine—and Lord Philip has an excellent eye—it'll be worth a good deal."

The aroma of roasting vegetables wafted in from the kitchen. Maggie's stomach rumbled at the thought of Ilaria's caramelized eggplant and butter-soft zucchini. The Sicilian cook said the trick was to use very high heat and lots and lots of olive oil.

Maggie refocused on the stocky man in front of her. "You haven't seen it yet?"

He gave a cough. "Lord Philip only recently picked it up, and this is, quite literally, the first chance I've had to come over." The sun reflected off Walter's carefully styled hair. How did he get so much volume? Maggie unconsciously put her hand up to her own limp hair.

She remembered Thomas's suggestion that Lord Philip had strong-armed the previous owner into selling. "How did Lord Philip find it? Did he tell you?"

Walter shook his head. "No idea. Probably spotted it in some estate sale. Pictures get put away in attics all the time. From what I understand, this one may have gone missing during an exhibition in the eighteen sixties, but, of course, there are no photographs from back then. There was a lot of turmoil in Italy at the time. Abbati himself fought in the Independence War and was sent off to Croatia. Didn't die there, though. He got out, eventually, and died of rabies. Bitten by his own dog."

He put his hands to his knees and pushed himself into a standing position. "But I shouldn't be going on like this. Where's the picture?"

She sighed. She couldn't put it off any longer. "I'm afraid Lord Philip is dead. He was killed in his study last night."

Walter sagged. "My goodness." He took a step back, like he'd been punched. His face drooped as he seemed to process the news, then he brightened. "Last night? Word hasn't gotten out then. Wait until Faye hears this."

The expat world operated on the same commodity as Maggie's group back home. Having the best gossip, and having it early, was a sign of your standing in the community. Maggie didn't have the heart to tell Walter that Faye had already heard the news.

"I suppose you can't provide any inside details?" Walter stepped close to Maggie, his tone confidential.

His breath, all stale smoke and breath mints, made Maggie take a step back.

"Do the police have any leads?"

She shook her head.

"Well, the appraisal will come in useful for the estate, I'm sure."

Maggie thought back to her conversation with Thomas and Aldrich that morning. Thomas had said the painting was ready for the appraiser and Aldrich hadn't said anything about not moving forward with it. Maggie took Walter to the studio and pointed to the wrapped package Thomas had shown them earlier.

Walter placed it on one of the tables and carefully unwrapped it. He did it slowly, as if relishing the moment of unveiling. She could almost imagine him rubbing his hands together with anticipation. Inside was a small framed oil painting, barely larger than a sheet of legal paper. It was picture of a white horse standing in the sun. The animal was luminous, the light reflecting off its side. Head up, wind blowing its mane. A handful of chickens scampered in the dust nearby. They were in a courtyard next to a rustic stone barn that cast deep shadows over everything, except the horse and chickens.

Maggie could understand why Thomas had turned his nose up at it, with its dark colors and extreme detail. She'd overheard him telling Charles, "Classic art can be so dreary. The colors of the primitive schools are more joyful, more alive."

"Well, well, well. It will give me a great deal of pleasure to examine this. Unfortunate for Walpole not to get to hear the results of my analysis himself, but he was confident in its value. We can take comfort in that." Walter paused, as if holding a moment of silence in Lord Philip's memory, then slid the picture into his folio and zipped it up tight.

"How long will it take?" Maggie asked.

Walter tapped a stained brown finger on the folio. "Barring any surprises, my report will be delivered next week."

He was at the front door before Maggie thought to ask about the man Ilaria said had threatened Lord Philip. "Have you heard of someone named Pierre?"

An expression of surprise passed over his face, which he quickly replaced with a professional smile. "I didn't realize you were a collector, Maggie. I could make some introductions if you're looking for something special." He put an extra emphasis in the word special.

"What is it he can do?"

Walter coughed. "He's a man who can acquire pictures no one else can."

"A thief?" Maggie asked.

Walter colored. "I believe he calls himself a specialized dealer. What is it you collect?"

"Nothing. Just heard his name somewhere."

Walter gripped the folio. "Give my best to Burt. Will we see you at Faye's on Thursday?"

Maggie remembered Faye mentioning she was holding a bridge party on Thursday. Most of the men had the day off for the annual celebration of Italy's liberation from Nazi occupation.

Maggie was a decent player, but Burt had never learned, so they'd not been included in the dinner bridge parties Faye always seemed to be organizing. Maggie hadn't minded. And besides, she would be working this Thursday.

Maggie watched Walter walk to the elevator cage, an awkward step-shuffle as he favored his right leg. How important was that picture? If Orsini's theory was correct that a burglar had killed Lord Philip, had he come for the *White Horse*? If so, how had he neglected to look for the picture in the studio? Perhaps he expected it to be on display in Lord Philip's study and panicked?

Maggie wandered back into the studio, looking at the easels the guests had left set up with their sketches of the ficus plant. One was excellent, capturing the plant with near three-dimensional precision. The artist had added a bit of whimsy, a cat peering around from behind the pot. Helen's, no doubt. Two more were clearly plants, with lots of erasing and shorter, more cautious lines. The other three were more haphazard. Thomas had his work cut out for him.

Maggie returned to the office and dialed the police station again. Still no information on Orsini's whereabouts. She hung up and sat back, thinking about what to do next. Her mobile phone rang before she could decide, and Maggie grabbed at it, hoping for Orsini on the other end. But it was Burt calling to check in. Maggie swiveled in her chair to look out the window. The terra cotta roofs spread out in front of her, broken up by lines of laundry flapping in the breeze. A young woman stood on a roof terrace a few buildings away, tending her plants. Two children were playing next to her.

Maggie told Burt about John Aldrich's arrival and the police's nonappearance at the apartment.

"I'm sure the police are working on it," Burt said.

"Maybe." She heard Helen's voice in the hall. "I need to go. I love you."

Chapter Eight

V iolent crime is unusual in Rome. The city is, however, plagued by gypsies who prey on unsuspecting tourists. Protect your valuables and send the undesirables away with a firm "Via!"
—Masterpiece Tours "Welcome to Rome" pamphlet

Maggie met the guests in the hall and took the portable easels from Helen and Eloise, who were arguing over the history of water coloring.

"Preservation is the challenge," Eloise was saying. "It always was a big line item in the museum's annual budget."

Maggie had forgotten Eloise worked at a museum in Massachusetts. Maggie could imagine her as the secretary to the president. The small woman would have been no-nonsense and highly organized, a lot like Burt's old assistant back home, who was more on top of the deadlines than her boss and knew the office politics better than anyone else. She also kept a list of family birthdays and made sure Burt brought flowers home on his anniversary. Not like the young Italian outside his office now, who barely remembered Maggie's name.

Charles stacked the easels in the studio and Maggie collected brushes to clean in the sink. She ran them under warm water then carefully washed each with a bit of soap. Thomas said taking care of watercolor brushes was a snap, unlike brushes for oil painting, which had to be cleaned immediately with paint thinner.

"Any news from the police?" Charles asked. He had excellent posture, despite his cane.

Eloise clicked her tongue when Maggie said there was none. She reminded Maggie of Mrs. Dillard, her third-grade teacher, who had sat at her big desk clucking each time she circled a spelling error in Maggie's compositions. Eloise even wore her white hair in the same short style, cut close to her head, reinforcing the birdlike impression Maggie had had earlier.Not a benign bird, Maggie decided. Something more aggressive. A hawk, maybe.

"You can't rush the authorities." Vicky clipped her picture to the clothesline. She'd attempted to capture the *Fountain of the Four Rivers*. The perspective was right, but the background felt empty, as though she'd put her entire focus on one section of the picture and forgotten the rest.

"Expecting the police to return and complete their investigation is hardly rushing." Maggie would call the station again after lunch and talk to someone who could give her a real update.

"But they searched last night," Vicky said. "What more could they need?"

"They wouldn't have had time to go through every piece of paper. Who knows what's hidden in that office?" Perhaps the name of the previous owner of the *White Horse,* Maggie hoped.

Ilaria appeared and said lunch was on the terrace. Vicky stayed behind to "powder her nose" and Eloise said she wanted to take one more look at her sketch to see where she'd gone wrong. The others climbed the stairs to the rooftop, where Ilaria had set a long iron table and chairs in the shade of a striped canvas awning. The seating area was ringed by small potted trees and flowers. Maggie drew in a deep breath. Out here it was easy to forget she was in the middle of a big gritty city.

Roasted vegetables, olives, slices of meat and cheeses, and big loaves of crusty bread sat on another table, ready for the guests to help themselves.

"Len, for goodness sake," Shelia said as her husband loaded his plate. "The food's not going anywhere. You can always come back for seconds."

"I'm planning on it." He took the chair closest to the buffet, round stomach extending over his silver belt buckle. "Have you had this stuff yet? I'd never have guessed it was provolone." He was right. The provolone in Italy was rich and flavorful, with a delicious sharpness. Nothing like the rubbery blandness sold at Maggie's Food Lion.

Maggie made a trip downstairs to retrieve ice for Charles's soda and found Vicky on her knees in front of Lord Philip's study. The sleeves of her sweater were pushed up and the young woman flushed as she sat up and brushed off her knees. "Goodness, you gave me a start. Have you seen my hair clip? I thought maybe it had fallen out here."

Her blond hair was pulled back on one side, and Maggie had assumed it was a style statement. Her daughter, Lucy, often wore hers in a similar way. Maggie got down on her hands and knees and joined the search, but they had no luck.

"I'll tell Ilaria to keep an eye out. I'm sure it will turn up." Maggie sent Vicky up to lunch and went into the kitchen.

"Vicky isn't fortunate with her belongings," Ilaria observed when Maggie asked her if she'd seen the hair clip.

It was true. Vicky's bracelet had been stolen two days earlier when she was out sightseeing alone. She'd returned to the palazzo in tears, saying she'd given money to children begging in front of the Pantheon, only realizing later that one of them had stolen her bracelet. It had been a gift from her first husband, who'd died shortly after their marriage. Maggie had thought the gold piece with large blue stones a little old-fashioned, but surely valuable.

Maggie carried the ice upstairs and paused a moment before rejoining the group. The traffic sounds were reduced to an almost pleasant white noise up here, leaving the sound of forks clanking on plates and occasional sighs of pleasure as the guests focused on eating. A visitor walking in would see a group of happy, relaxed travelers. No one would think the owner of this home had died the night before.

"What kind of painting do you do, Thomas?" Charles neatly cut his grilled asparagus into equal, one-inch lengths. He ate deliberately, one piece at a time.

"You know what they say about teachers. Those who can't and all that." Thomas tore off a piece of bread and dragged it across the balsamic vinegar and bits of tomato left on his plate.

"Oh, Thomas, I'm sure your work is wonderful," Eloise said.

"Well, some of my pieces did sell for a few thousand at auction last year."

"What? That's brilliant," Vicky said. When she smiled she reminded Maggie of one of a American magazine cover model, all shiny straight white teeth and perfectly smooth blond hair. Only her accent signaled her English roots.

He grinned. "Bit of a gas, actually. Some friends dared me to slip a few pieces of my own into a batch of minor sketches we were selling at the auction house. I was as stunned as anyone no one noticed." He could have been a pop star answering questions from an adoring TV interviewer, proud and a little cheeky at the same time.

"You forged them?" Helen leaned forward, interested.

"As a joke." Thomas popped an olive into his mouth. "Back at university I forged a Renoir for a seminar on imitation and forgery. Did pretty well on it, too. The sketches were easy compared to that. But my boss didn't think it was very funny when he had to call the customer and explain."

Ilaria appeared with dessert: tiramisu and fresh fruit. Vicky shook her head no and Eloise took her knitting out of her bag and began clicking away. The others dug in. Maggie took a bite. The mascarpone and custard filling were creamy but not too sweet, just the way Maggie liked it. She promised herself she'd eat just two bites.

Maggie thought about Orsini. It would be easy for him to avoid her over the phone.

Shelia leaned back in her chair, the sequins on her top rippling as she moved. "Are you expecting us to stay here all afternoon, Maggie? I know we want to help the police, but I was hoping to see the Capitoline Museum this afternoon."

"And I would very much like to go back to the hotel to rest," Eloise said. "Surely, if we tell the police where we are, that wouldn't be a problem. Charles, what do you think?"

"Perhaps Charles would like a walk." Helen re-wrapped her colorful scarves around her neck. "We could stroll along the river to St. Peters. It might be fun to mail a card, just to get the Vatican postmark."

"It *is* a shame you missed the Sistine Chapel," Shelia said for the fifth time since the tour began.

Helen had been unable to participate in the first two days of activities, laid low with a migraine. She'd been fine the night of the welcome party then woke up in agony. Eloise waved off the concerns about poor Helen missing the Forum and the Vatican, saying her sister had seen them all before on previous visits.

"I think I'll work here," Charles said. "I want to take another go at that picture."

"Good show," Thomas said. "I think it's the dome that's tripping you up. Let's break it down into its geometry and see where that takes you."

Maggie looked at her plate and realized she'd eaten her entire dessert. Well, it was worth it. She had a walk ahead of her. She had information the police needed, and if they weren't going to come to her, she would go to them.

"I'm going to the police station." She pushed her chair back. She'd have to check the map and see where this station was, exactly. "I'll get some answers about where things stand." And give them some of her ideas.

"Are you sure that's best?" Thomas had lost his care-free-rock-star look. He looked worried. "Johnnie Boy was pretty clear..."

"If everyone had that attitude, nothing would get done. The world was built by meddlers."

He looked at her blankly. His family came from money, of course, so perhaps they didn't share the can-do, up-by-the-bootstraps spirit.

"Thomas, we have no idea what the police are doing, but what we *do* know is they aren't here. They aren't searching Lord Philip's office. They aren't looking at drugs. At blackmail. At Pierre. At the *White Horse*. They don't even have the timeline down."

"Oh dear." Eloise fumbled with her knitting. "I seem to have dropped a stitch."

"Drugs? Pierre? What are you talking about?" Vicky asked.

Maggie paused. She hadn't meant to talk about this in front of the guests. Still, she couldn't put the cat back in the bag. "There are questions about the legitimacy of Lord Philip's income. Rumors that might be relevant to the investigation."

"Thank goodness we didn't go any further with that investment," Shelia said to Len. "I knew it was too good to be true."

He shushed her, but it was too late. Everyone was staring now.

"Just something Lord Philip mentioned yesterday," Len said. "Some kind of land for sale. Nothing we were thinking seriously about."

Another thing Orsini might have learned if he'd done a proper interview with the guests.

"What were you saying about a timeline, Maggie?" Shelia reached over for the last of the tiramisu on Len's plate.

"I made a list of who was downstairs during the fireworks so the police can see when Lord Philip might have been killed."

"Are you saying they're suspects?" Shelia asked.

"Of course not." Though, last night Maggie had told Burt the police should at least consider the guests. Vicky and Daniel had both gone downstairs, though, looking at Vicky, it was hard to imagine her killing anyone.

"Did you hear anything when you went down?" Charles asked Eloise.

"Eloise? You went downstairs?" Then Maggie remembered Eloise stepping on Charles's foot, murmuring something about too much coffee. It was so easy to forget the elderly, wasn't it? Eloise had gone down just after Vicky came back with her sweater. Then Vicky sent Daniel for her camera, and Thomas had come up after that.

They all pivoted to look at Eloise, who was looking at her knitting "What's that? Oh yes, and Lord Philip was still alive."

Maggie's skin tingled, the way it always had when her daughter was about to score in one of her soccer games. It was like time slowing and a feeling the outcome was inevitable. "Did you see him?"

Eloise shook her head. "I heard him talking, presumably on the phone." She pursed her lips. "You don't think he was talking to the person who killed him, do you?"

Maggie shuddered. No one else had been downstairs. Who else could it have been?

"Do you think I ought to have told the police this last night?" Eloise asked. "That policeman just asked if I'd seen anything, and so I said no. If he'd been interested in things I heard, he would have asked, wouldn't he?"

"You did the right thing." Helen leaned over to squeeze her sister's hand. "The policeman should have been more specific." The group was silent a moment. Eloise looked frail and old. Helen, seemed to sit even taller, as if on guard.

Vicky finally broke the silence. "This does help narrow the time of death down, though, doesn't it?"

It most certainly did. Finally they had something concrete for that inspector. Lord Philip had been killed between 8:40 and 9:00, when Maggie came downstairs. This was progress, real progress. Maggie pushed her chair back. Enough of this sitting and waiting. It was time to force the police to act.

Chapter Nine

T he streets of Rome are neither symmetrical nor laid out on a grid. They are labyrinths, with curves and roundabouts and stairs that suddenly, and most unexpectedly, open onto majestic piazzas.
—Masterpiece Tours "Welcome to Rome" pamphlet

The streets were jammed with lunchtime traffic when Maggie set out for the police station with Vicky at her side. The young woman had been reluctant to give up painting time to file a police report for her missing jewelry, but Maggie insisted they tackle the Italian bureaucracy together.

She plugged the address into her phone and checked the route. The police station was a mile away, and it would be more pleasant to walk than sit in traffic. Rome's four commutes had been a shock when Maggie first arrived. Morning and evening she expected, but the crush of workers going home to eat lunch and then back on the roads to return to their offices was so inefficient. Burt went to work and stayed there.

The women crossed the Piazza Navona and walked along a winding medieval street. The road was narrow, just wide enough for the cafés to have a single line of outdoor tables hugging the wall. Window boxes overflowed with all shades of flowers and open-arched doorways provided glimpses into private courtyards. This was the Rome Maggie had imagined. Sun shining, streets charming, and being free from the cares of managing a big house and two busy children.

The smell of blooming wisteria was intoxicating. Maggie was tempted, just for a moment, to suggest they stop for a coffee. To join the men and women lazing their afternoons away with a cup of espresso and a biscuit.

But no. If good people stood by, chaos reigned. Nearly fifteen hours had passed since Lord Philip's death. And weren't the first twenty-four hours supposed to be the most critical? The sooner she got to the station, the sooner she could get the police on track.

Maggie picked up her pace. The street led downhill to the Pantheon, a giant round building with a Greek-style portico on the front. It was Rome's best-preserved ancient building. It had been converted from a heathen temple into a Christian church in the Middle Ages and was supposed to be the inspiration for all sorts of Renaissance folks who wanted to learn how to build big domes. Tourists crowded around the tall obelisk in front, and a guide with a microphone led a group of teenagers and two harried-looking chaperones into the church.

"When did you start painting?" Maggie asked, turning a corner. She couldn't find a street sign, but they should be heading west.

"I took it up when Daniel and I got married. I left my job after the wedding, and it's been nice to have time for some new hobbies."

"Do you miss working?" Maggie knew plenty of women who didn't work, of course. Raising children was a full-time job. Just one without sick leave, promotions, or a paycheck. But not working without children was unusual.

"I hated going to an office every day. Formatting presentations. Sitting in meetings. I met Daniel there. That was the only good thing." Vicky would have fit into an office. She was good looking, dressed nicely. She could have been promoted at least a few times based on those qualities alone. But Maggie knew the corporate ladder it wasn't for everyone.

They passed a small crowd watching an artist spray painting a picture of the Colosseum onto a canvas laid out on the sidewalk. He was adding Technicolor yellows and pinks to the night sky he'd created over the old monument. He had similar pictures with garish blues and purples, neon orange, and metallic silver and gold all arranged for sale next to him.

Maggie paused for a moment to consult her phone. They didn't seem to be exactly on course, but they must be close. "Daniel worked in London?"

"Oh no, I have dual citizenship. My father was American." She was wearing ballet flats that couldn't have offered any protection from the rough streets, but she matched Maggie stride for stride. Vicky kept pace with Maggie. "I came to New York for a fresh start after my first husband died." Vicky had offered the minimum of details about her young husband's death, and no one had liked to ask anything more.

They were back in the older streets of Rome now. A group of children ran hooting past, their voices bouncing off the tightly packed buildings, followed more slowly by three women pushing baby carriages.

"Daniel and I met on the lift," Vicky said. "I tipped a box of donuts on him. He was livid. He had an important meeting and I got jelly on his jacket and powdered sugar everywhere. I'd seen him a few times before, and I told him this was the only way I could think of to get him to talk to me. He asked for my number, and the rest is history."

Maggie and Burt had met in college over glasses of terrible wine in someone's apartment. They'd been married so long it was hard to remember actually being in love with him. She loved him, of course she did. And he loved her. Anyone who'd been married as long as she had, with two children, no less, knew that love changed.

"You did it on purpose?"

"No, I've always been a bit clumsy. But Daniel believed me. And it gave him a good story to open his meeting."

The temperature was probably in the 70s, but it felt warmer here in the direct sun. Maggie's shirt clung to her back, sticky with sweat. And walking on cobblestones was tiring, even in her solid shoes. Vicky's pushed-up sweater sleeves were the only sign she felt the heat as well.

They crossed another busy street.

A car honked when Maggie hesitated in the crosswalk, looking for a street sign. "What does Daniel do again?"

"Finance. South American markets." Vicky shrugged, sidestepping a pair of Japanese tourists taking selfies in front of a shop selling old-fashioned nuns' habits and priestly garb. "What did you mean about Lord Philip's income not being legitimate?"

"Just some rumors, at this point," Maggie said. "But it looks like the tour company wasn't his only source of income."

They passed a young man locking a heavy chain around the wheel of his scooter.

"He wasn't living on family money?"

"Apparently not," Maggie said. "None of it's very clear. Only that he was a man a lot of people had reason to dislike."

Vicky reminded Maggie of herself. Not on the outside, perhaps. Vicky had a better fashion sense and more self-discipline when it came to dessert. But they had the same natural curiosity. The same interest in learning new things. And both had forgiven men who made mistakes.

Months could go by without Maggie thinking of Burt's affair. It was so long ago now—nearly fifteen years. Burt had been foolish to think she wouldn't notice the increase of cash withdrawals on nights he'd said he was working late. But Maggie hadn't left him. Not with two small children.

Self-help experts all made it sound like a breeze. Get a divorce and live an independent life. But she'd seen what happened to divorced mothers. Burt had said it would never happen again, and Maggie believed him. She hoped Vicky would regain the same trust in Daniel.

They turned the corner and a giant stone obelisk rose up in front of them. Maggie groaned. They were back at the Pantheon. She must have led them in a circle. So much for all those years as a Boy Scout den mother.

Maggie pulled out her phone and tried to figure out what she'd done wrong. She traced a route with her finger then led the way back across the busy street. She veered left into the medieval maze again. They should be at the station in ten minutes. Fifteen at the most.

They'd been walking a few minutes when she noticed the growing rumble of voices, a characteristic sound at sights like the Vatican, the Colosseum, and the Forum. But here it was different, heightened, almost echoing. Maggie knew even before they rounded the corner into the little piazza with two gelato shops and one very large fountain that she'd led them off course again.

The Trevi Fountain was hidden away in a nest of narrow streets, hard to find even on the best of days. But now, when they were supposed to be half a mile south, Maggie had stumbled onto the darn thing.

She stepped around the throngs of tourists snapping photos, reading from guidebooks, and admiring the Baroque masterpiece. She squeezed onto one of the crowded stone benches that ringed the fountain.

The guests had come to paint here already. Maggie remembered Vicky's picture with Oceanus, that stern, bearded Greek god holding court above the mythical folks rising out of the water. It was competent, but the style mechanical.

Vicky squeezed in next to her. "Are we supposed to be here?"

Maggie sighed. "No." A trickle of perspiration ran down along her hairline. She felt like she was in one of those nightmares where she was running late and couldn't find her shoes, her car keys, or her bag. A thousand little things stopping her from her goal, and that frantic feeling that she'd miss something if she didn't get her act together. Maggie closed her eyes and tried to focus on the sound of water splashing, to tease it out from the sounds of voices all around her.

"Are you sure this is a good idea?" Vicky asked after a moment. "What if the police don't want our help?"

Maggie opened her eyes. "Of course they do. They just don't know it yet."

They arrived at the station fifteen minutes later. Vicky hesitated in front of the imposing doors guarded by two policemen in bulletproof vests, but Maggie pulled her inside.

The central hall looked like a waiting room anywhere in the world. Beige walls. Bulletin boards full of official-looking notices. And plastic chairs occupied by people filling out forms, playing with phones, reading books, and, mostly, staring off into space.

A single policeman sat behind the central window. Maggie took in the long line in front of him. Tourists, by the look of them. Probably reporting stolen wallets. Maggie stopped one of the policemen walking down a hallway to a swinging door marked *Privato* but he shook his head and pointed to the central window.

Maggie stepped to the front of the line, saying, "I just need a quick word," to the couple waiting at the window then turned her attention on the officer.

Gatekeepers—the secretaries, receptionists and the *agenti* of the world—were the ones who held the key to power. Maggie smiled apologetically. *"Buon giorno.* I'm sorry to interrupt you, but I'm here to see Inspector Orsini's supervisor, *per favore."*

The young policeman wore a starched blue shirt with some kind of metal insignia clipped to the corners of his open collar. He had badges on the shoulder and a white leather strap extended diagonally across his chest, giving him a faintly military look.

He frowned. "There is a queue, madam."

"You don't understand. I'm not here to file a report. I'm part of an active case." She lowered her voice. "The murder in the palazzo on the Piazza Navona." Maggie understood Rome's murder rate was exceedingly low compared to American cities. Surely this man, Brunello, according to his name tag, would have heard of it.

"There is a line, madam." He turned back to the Americans she had cut in front of. "Please fill out this form."

The line would take thirty minutes to get through. Maggie folded her hands on the counter. "I want you to call the supervisor on the case. I don't need to fill out any paperwork." She was aware of Vicky inching slowly away, as if not wanting to be associated with her.

"Get to the back of the line, lady," said the female half of the American couple. She had a strong Bronx accent. "We've all been waiting. You're nothing special."

The woman was thin, with a face like a rat. They didn't tolerate line cutting in New York.

Maggie dropped her smile. "Fine. We'll get in line. But they won't be happy about this upstairs." She didn't know where the supervisor's office was located, but it seemed like the right thing to say.

Maggie and Vicky joined the end of the line. Maggie fanned her shirt away from her body as she waited. It was stifling in the station. She looked around at the tourists forced to take time out of their vacations to sit here filing paperwork.

Three college-age kids with grubby backpacks and a guitar resting against a chair were laughing. The two girls wore braids and the boy had his dirty hair in a ponytail. She could practically smell the marijuana on them. Sam had wanted to spend the summer before his senior year youth hosteling across Europe. She and Burt insisted he find an internship instead.

There was also a young Japanese couple, three European women in their 50s, impossible to say which country they were from, and an American couple wearing shiny wedding rings, probably on their honeymoon. Maggie guessed not one of these visitors wore a money belt. The line inched forward.

Vicky fidgeted with her watch. "I knew I should have gotten an international calling plan. I hope Daniel doesn't worry."

Maggie understood. Cautious Americans turned their cell phone service off in Rome to avoid the exorbitant international fees. She'd felt like a local when she had popped a European SIM card into her phone and could text her husband without thinking of the expense.

Maggie offered Vicky her phone, but Daniel didn't answer. "Probably has it turned off too," Maggie said. But he didn't answer the phone in his hotel room, either.

Finally, they reached the front of the line.

Agente Brunello said *"Si?"* without even looking up at them.

"Hello again," Maggie said. "We're the ones here to see Inspector Orsini's supervisor."

"Do you have an appointment?"

Maggie stifled the urge to shout that she would have missed any appointment if she had been fortunate enough to have one. She forced a neutral tone instead. "We thought it best to come here in person. I'm afraid my Italian isn't what it should be, and I didn't think to use the phone." No need to mention her calls. "Please, *Agente* Brunello. He'll want to see me."

He looked at her, appraising. She was probably his mother's age.

Finally, he shrugged. "One moment."

Brunello typed something into his computer, glared at the screen, and then typed again. Finally, he dialed the phone and spoke in rapid Italian. Maggie only understood "yes," "because," and "when."

Agente Brunello said thank you several times and hung up. "Please have a seat."

"We also want to file a police report about some missing jewelry." Maggie gave Vicky a gentle push toward the counter.

The large Frenchman behind Maggie groaned.

Agente Brunello handed Maggie a clipboard. "This form, please."

The women settled in the chairs nearest the hallway. Vicky sat, fiddling with her pen, while Maggie mentally practiced what she would say to the supervisor. *I have concerns about the investigation... Someone able to focus his attention... Information that could shed a new light...*

But it was Orsini himself who came through the *Privato* door ten minutes later. Brunello must have gotten the message wrong.

Orsini looked harried. His green shirt appeared to be stained with coffee, and his hair was wilder than the night before. Had he slept? He had, at least, changed his shirt. "I understand you wanted to speak with my supervisor, signora?"

The young man had not gotten the message wrong—Orsini had outplayed her. She would have to change tactics.

Maggie held out her hand and gave him a firm handshake, a partner's handshake. "We're here to help, Inspector Orsini. I'm sure you were busy this morning, investigating the burglary theory and your other cases, whatever those are. I've learned some things that have direct bearing on this case. Where can we speak privately?"

He winced. "You are kind, Signora White. But you should not have bothered. I am at a—what is it?—a critical point in another case. You can give the information to my *agente*—"

Maggie was supposed to be going up the food chain, not down. She wished Vicky would help and join Maggie in the fight. But Vicky stayed in her seat, looking at the two.

"It's important. Now, I've put together a list of everyone's movements last night. To save you time." Maggie extracted the page out of her purse and handed it to him. He glanced at it then folded it and put it in his pocket. His gaze moved back to the hallway with its door marked *Private*.

"Please listen to Maggie, Inspector," Vicky stood up now as if she had finally read Maggie's mind. She ran a hand through her hair in a way that body-language experts might categorize as flirtatious. "Eloise Potter heard Lord Philip alive at eight forty. And Maggie found him at nine. That gives you a very definite time to investigate."

Orsini sighed and took the piece of paper out of his pocket again. He read a moment then looked at them, mouth tight. "And what would you like me to do with this? You're suggesting that this Eloise Potter was the last person to see Lord Philip alive? She is, what, eighty? You suspect her? Or is it your husband, Daniel, you want me to investigate, Mrs. Barlow? He appears to have been downstairs during the critical time. Or is it the painting instructor, Thomas Evans, you suspect?"

Maggie winced at his tone. "Of course not. Any more than I'm saying you should investigate me. Though I *did* find the body, and you have only my word that I didn't kill him."

Orsini sighed again. Maggie smelled coffee on his breath. Mixed with something. Salami. He hadn't been home to lunch. He'd been at the station, working at a time most Italians relaxed. Maggie warmed to him a hair. Perhaps he could handle this job after all. With the assistance of her information, of course.

"But have you checked Lord Philip's phone for calls? Whoever he was speaking to is important. And I've heard several rumors about his source of income, none of them legitimate. Not to mention the long line of people with a grudge against him." Maggie paused for a breath. She couldn't read Orsini's expression.

"Lord Philip acquired a very valuable picture under questionable circumstances, and, I'm sorry to say, has a history of seeking investors for fraudulent projects." Maggie thought of Len's discomfort when Shelia mentioned the investment Lord Philip had proposed. It didn't sound like they'd signed onto Lord Philip's scheme, whatever it was. "I don't have all the details, of course, but—"

Inspector Orsini cut her off. "You seem like a well-intentioned woman, Signora White. A bit too overly interested, perhaps, but you are an American. That is your way. You must understand, however, this is not information I can act on. My hands are tied."

The backpackers walked past, the boy bumping his guitar into Maggie's shoulder, and moved off without apologizing.

"What do you mean, tied?" The heat in this waiting room was making it hard for Maggie to think clearly. "Is it a case of manpower? Who allocates the resources here? I'll have a word with him."

"You misunderstand me." Orsini's eyes were bloodshot and ringed with dark circles. His posture stooped, as though he carried a heavy weight on his shoulders. "My superior called me this afternoon. He has closed the case. That happens only when someone very important gives us instructions. Someone from above. You understand?"

Vicky sucked in her breath, but Maggie stared at him, not answering. Orsini had been told to lay off? Was that what Inspector Orsini said? Maggie took a step backward as though she'd been pushed off balance.

The air was pungent with the odor of so many people in this closed space. All of them diligently filing out their paperwork, totally unaware that the police wouldn't do a thing unless it suited them.

Maggie felt Vicky's gaze on her. Vicky shook her head, as though warning her not to speak.

But Maggie felt her feet under her, sensible shoes keeping her grounded. She straightened to her full five feet five. She looked Orsini right in the eye. "No, Inspector, I'm afraid I don't understand. What, exactly, are you saying?" A trickle of sweat ran down her back.

Orsini looked pained. "I'm sorry, Signora White. I've told you more than I should. Good day to you both." He turned and walked away.

It took a moment for Maggie to realize what had just happened. The man had admitted to corruption and was scurrying off. Her nostrils flared, and she chased after him. "You're going to bow down to some order from above? Is this country a democracy or is it not?"

Maggie felt the gazes of the clipboard crowd on her.

Vicky caught up with her and put a hand on Maggie's arm. "Maybe we should go."

Orsini turned. "Life here is not easy, Signora White." Then he looked at Vicky's hand still holding the clipboard. "You're filing a theft complaint as well? That I can help with. I'll file the papers."

He took the clipboard and nodded at them both. "Good day."

Chapter Ten

*V*isitors will delight in Rome's innumerable cats living amongst the ancient ruins. Sitting on a stump of an old Roman column or napping on a stone step of the Colosseum, these cats are fat and healthy, taken care of by the doting Gattare, or Cat Women, of the city.
—Masterpiece Tours "Welcome to Rome" pamphlet

Maggie and Vicky stood outside the police station, blinking in the bright sun.

"Corruption." Maggie whispered. It was everything she had expected when she moved to this country, bribery and power sold to the highest bidder.

"Who would have the power to shut down an investigation?" Vicky asked. "It's just, I don't know, unreal."

Taxis were lined up outside the station. Maggie signaled to the first one, and the two women climbed in. Rush hour was over, at least for the moment. Maggie sank back into the upholstery, suddenly very tired.

"What are we going to do now?" Vicky asked.

"Go back to the apartment." And after that? She had no idea.

Everyone knew about the Mafia's power in Italy. Were they the ones who shut down the investigation? From TV and movies, she understood drug trafficking was their bread and butter. Her mind raced. Was it possible the expat gossips were right? Had Lord Philip been involved in the drug trade and now the Mafia was covering it up?

At home, Maggie would meet with the police chief. Call the newspapers.

Organize a letter-writing campaign insisting on a full investigation. But what could she, a foreigner, do? Not a thing. The taxi pulled up in front of the palazzo.

Maggie buried herself in the Masterpiece office for the remainder of the afternoon, while Vicky went back to the hotel, where she hoped to find Daniel. The lawyer's list of questions didn't take her mind off Orsini's announcement, but it did keep her busy until the guests returned for cocktails.

Maggie walked up the stairs to the terrace behind the Potter sisters, listening with only half an ear as Helen described their visit to the Torre Argentina, an excavation boasting four ancient temples and an old Roman theater. Her hat was in her lap and her grey hair was tied back in a loose bun. With her tall, slim frame and tendency to lecture, she reminded Maggie of some benevolent old witch from her children's books of myths.

Ilaria had arranged the chairs in a circle around a low table loaded with bruschetta and olives. Thomas acted as bartender while Ilaria passed glasses of prosecco. The two were laughing about something. Maggie liked watching them together. Thomas brought out Ilaria's lighter side.

Thomas would make someone a good boyfriend, but his taste so far seemed to run to party girls more interested in his family's wealth than in Thomas himself. He said his last relationship ended when his girlfriend tried to push him to take a cushy job in London and live off the family fortune.

"And the cats..." Helen took a sip of her wine. "One reminded me of my darling Nibbins. I may just have to work him into a picture. Maybe stretched out in front of that temple."

Helen's pictures all included a cat or two roaming the scene, sometimes peeking around a plant, other times front and center. They were whimsical and charming. Or would be, if Helen weren't such an earnest cat lover. Maggie couldn't imagine anything tongue-in-cheek about her art.

"What's the word from the police?" Len sat with his jean-clad legs crossed in a figure-four, right leg crossed over his left. Such an American posture, compared to all the Italian men Maggie saw seated at cafés and restaurants with their legs neatly crossed at the knee, or else both feet simply planted squarely on the ground.

Vicky coughed on her cocktail.

Maggie met her gaze then looked away. "They have it in hand. And I don't think they'll need our assistance any further."

Len whistled. "Damned efficient. The folks at home could learn something from the way they're handling this."

"They caught someone? It really was a burglar?" Thomas was sitting across the circle, next to Charles, who wore a skeptical expression.

Maggie was at a momentary loss for words. She would be letting everyone down if she told them the police had shut the investigation without a solution, so she simply shook her head. "They didn't say anything more. Just that we won't have to stay here waiting for them. Which is good news, since we're all set for the Borghese tomorrow."

She gave Thomas a meaningful nod, and he picked up her cue.

"Be prepared to have your socks knocked off. Everyone goes on and on about the art at the Vatican, but I'll take the Borghese any day of the week."

"Michelangelo would roll over in his grave," Shelia said. "Poor man already had an inferiority complex to Titian."

From what Maggie remembered, Michelangelo hardly needed an ego boost. The man considered himself the best sculptor in the world, and Pope Someone—they were impossible to keep track of—treated him like a prize stallion when he hired Michelangelo to paint the entire Sistine Chapel.

Lord Philip had told a story about a spat Michelangelo had with someone over the price of a commissioned painting, and Michelangelo had refused to hand it over until the patron paid double the original price. Lord Philip had made it clear his sympathies lay with the artist, not the patron who Michelangelo was strong-arming.

"I'm looking forward to seeing the gallery." Vicky spoke with more enthusiasm than was strictly necessary. "Is the rest of the itinerary staying the same? We're still visiting Bonaventura on Wednesday, I hope."

"I called to confirm this afternoon," Maggie said. "We'll be there with about a hundred German visitors, apparently." Bonaventura, a palace with a magnificent garden at the edge of the city on the Aventine Hill, was open only through pre-purchased tickets and sold out months in advance.

"I think you're wonderful," Vicky said. "Keeping it all organized."

"She's just doing her job. That's part of the fee." Daniel spat an olive pit into a napkin and reached for the bottle of white wine he'd put on the side table next to him. He topped off his glass.

"Did you enjoy your afternoon, Daniel?" Ilaria asked.

Maggie was pleased Ilaria had joined the group for cocktails. With Lord Philip's death, it felt like they were all in this together. Talking with the young woman this morning, passing ideas back and forth, had been the most fun Maggie had had in a long time. Then Maggie instantly felt guilty. Having fun discussing the death of another human being—what a terrible thing to do. But she'd felt different than she had in the last few months. More competent. More interesting. Like she had something to contribute again.

"I took in the sights, as a matter of fact." Daniel smoothed a crease in his khakis. "Thought I might find Vicky around but no luck."

"And I went back to the hotel looking for him." Vicky gave a little laugh. "We must have just missed each other."

"How nice, Daniel." Helen's tone was distracted, her words almost perfunctory. "What did you see?"

"Museum of Modern Art," he said. "Thought it might be nice to see some new things. I get tired of all the old stuff."

Church bells rang out the hour nearby. Shelia's eyes narrowed, like a cat who'd caught the scent of a mouse. "How lucky for you. I understood the museum is closed on Mondays."

Daniel looked away.

There were two types of liars. The ones who denied it to the hilt when they were caught, and the ones who acted as if they couldn't care less. The latter type was the worse of the two. Maggie's daughter had had a friend who'd just shrugged when Maggie caught her taking bills from her wallet. Maggie had always known that girl was trouble, and she'd been relieved when the family moved across the country.

"These Italian museums." Eloise shook her head and tugged on her knitting.

"You never know when they're open and when they're not."

Eloise's blanket didn't appear to have grown. She seemed to work the same rows over and over again. Maggie's grandmother had been a wonderful knitter, making beautiful cabled Aran sweaters and intricate lace shawls.

"We'll have to remind Francis of that," Helen said absently. She appeared completely relaxed with a glass in one hand, long legs crossed in front of her. "My goddaughter's son. He's coming to Rome with some friends on a whirlwind trip. Are they visiting three countries, Eloise?"

"Four." Eloise set her knitting in her lap. "We're taking him to dinner on Friday. Ilaria, you don't need to plan a meal for us that day."

Maggie noticed the music coming up from an open window nearby. It was Tina Turner's voice asking *What's love got to do with it?* Tina was one of the few musicians her whole family loved. Maggie remembered singing along to the *Private Dancer* album with Lucy and Burt on the long drive to deliver Lucy to college. Maggie and Burt couldn't listen to it for a month afterward without feeling the ache of their children flying from the nest.

Burt would be heating the lasagna she'd left for him right now. He'd talked of watching a movie. She'd been too busy—and too tired—to watch movies when she was still working for Bells & Wallace. But since moving from Connecticut, she and Burt seemed to watch them all the time, or else binge watch some television series.

Maggie sighed, remembering how cheerful she'd felt this morning. She'd been energized by having a project, something that would keep her busy again. Soon enough, she'd be back to cooking hot dinners for Burt and spending the evening in front of the television.

It was dark when Maggie finally left the palazzo. She'd told Ilaria and Thomas the details of her conversation with Orsini after the guests returned to the hotel. Ilaria had said something in Italian that sounded like a curse, but both agreed there wasn't anything to be done. Thomas offered to drop Maggie home on his scooter, but she wanted to be alone. After keeping up the conversation over dinner, she needed some silence.

The temperature had dropped fifteen degrees, and Maggie wished she'd brought a warmer sweater as she hurried through the Piazza Navona, sticking close to the restaurants with their outdoor tables. The small groups of people, sitting on benches or leaning against the giant fountain, seemed almost sinister tonight, their faces hidden in shadows. The narrow lane leading off the square was almost deserted. Lights were on at the small hotels she passed, but the tables outside the restaurants had been put away. Too cold, here on a side street.

Footsteps echoed behind her, but it was just a young couple holding hands. Still, Maggie couldn't shake the feeling of unease. *Not surprising, with a killer on the loose.*

But what, exactly, could she do? If there was corruption in the Italian police, she couldn't change that. And if the murder was some kind of Mafia-related hit, it didn't have anything to do with her or the guests. They were all safe.

Maggie crossed the busy Corso leading up to Victor Emanuel. Two lanes of traffic in each direction and good streetlights. She followed the crowd into the Campo Fiori and out toward the river and then home. A car raced past her. She wished she'd stayed on the main street—a longer walk, but more public.

Maggie gave a sigh of relief when her front door locked behind her. The vestibule light flickered, and a pile of mail lay on the floor. The neighbor who shared their landing was still out of town. Maggie's shoulders relaxed as pop music came from the apartment with the terrier on the second floor. She didn't recognize the song, but it had that bubblegum, synthetic sound of all music today. She'd never realized how optimistic it was.

Maggie climbed the stairs faster, eager to see Burt and tell him everything. But the apartment was dark when she opened the door. It was 10:30 and her husband wasn't there. No jacket on the coat rack. No shoes by the door. The single serving of lasagna she had left for him was still in the refrigerator, covered, and waiting to be reheated at 375 for twenty minutes.

Maggie wandered the apartment, tidying the pile of newspapers and emptying the dish drainer. She sat at her laptop to write an email to Sam. He'd been excited about a project at work she really should ask about. But she was at a loss when she tried to describe what had happened here in the last twenty-four hours. Maggie pushed the machine away.

She looked at the overflowing laundry basket and sighed. She missed her washing machine in her nice clean basement at home. She'd never let the laundry pile up there. Here she had to walk to the Laundromat, and she didn't like folding her clothes in front of all those strangers. But she was so worn out from the trip back last time, she'd left it all in a jumble.

Burt came home as she folded the last pair of slacks. "What a day I've had." He kicked off his shoes in their tiny bedroom. "You haven't been waiting up, have you? I tried calling, but there wasn't an answer."

Maggie remembered she'd set her phone to silent before dinner. Silly of her not to check it when she was looking for Burt.

Maggie kissed her husband and listened as he talked about his company's Swiss owners moving his project audit up by a month.

"I was on a conference call with New York all night. It's still the afternoon there. I'm trying to remember why basing me here was supposed to be helpful."

"You promised us an adventure. Gelato and romantic walks up the Spanish Steps."

Burt had said it would be a second honeymoon, of sorts. He would work a lazy job, enjoying the more relaxed European work schedule, then they would wander arm in arm around the magical city. But he was working more than ever, and no one told her how cold it would be here. She was just starting to warm up after the wet, damp winter.

"Tell that to the Swiss." He pushed himself to his feet. "Sorry, honey. Going on like that. Did the police get things sorted out?"

"They have, in a way."

"What's that mean?" He pulled his flannel pajamas out of a drawer.

"They're not investigating."

"What?" He stopped mid-button. The red pajama top was open across his chest. Burt's stomach was flatter than it had been when they left Connecticut. Rome agreed with him. He'd bought some new clothes with a slimmer, European cut. He'd made a real effort here and seemed truly happy.

Maggie felt the waistband of her pants biting into her as if in response.

"The inspector says he's been told not to investigate. End of story."

"That can't be right, honey. What did he say, exactly?" His tone irritated her, as if she'd misunderstood Orsini.

"He said he was told not to investigate, Burt." She unzipped her slacks. Relief at last.

Burt's phone rang. Unheard of at this hour. Burt lunged for it. "Probably more questions from the team."

He took it into the kitchen and she heard bits and pieces. "I'll be there" and "Yes, just like we agreed."

"Everything all right?" Maggie asked when Burt came back.

His face reddened. "Everything's fine. Now, tell me what happened."

Maggie told him everything Orsini said as she tidied the bedroom. "I guess our hands are tied."

"Rome is rubbing off you on, hon."

She picked up the pants he'd dropped on the floor, his tartan scarf left hanging on the one small chair that they could squeeze between the bed and little dresser. Was it a compliment? Sometimes she had trouble reading her husband, even after all these years. "What do you mean?"

"Letting go. You wouldn't have done that if we were still at home."

Maggie went into the bathroom to begin her nightly battle against aging. Cold cream. Eye lotion. She looked into the mirror. Had she changed? The same brown eyes stared back. Those eyes that had stood up to any executive. Anyone from market research who thought they knew her products better than she did. Burt was right. Since when did she just roll over?

Maggie wiped off the cold cream. Why should she leave this alone on the inspector's say so? She wiped faster. Someone out there was a murderer. Killed someone she knew, for goodness sake. There had to be someone she could appeal to. Someone in the government who wouldn't take kindly to an outside influence—the Mafia?—corrupting an investigation.

Burt was right. Maggie White didn't stand by and let things happen. This case would be solved. She would see to that.

Maggie climbed into bed, feeling better than she had in months.

Chapter Eleven

Though Italy may conjure up images of Don Corleone and his Hollywood progeny, you won't come into contact with the Mafia during your time in Italy, other than in the newspapers. The "Cosa Nostra," as the Italians sometimes refer to it, is focused on its own business and poses no risk to tourists.
—*Masterpiece Tours "Welcome to Rome" pamphlet*

Café Antica was Maggie's first stop the next morning. The café was quiet, just a few other customers at this hour. Two elderly men played backgammon at a table near the front and while two young women dressed for the office sat at one of the tables outside.

Mario passed Maggie a cappuccino and leaned his elbows on the marble bar. His sleeves were rolled up, revealing muscular forearms. "What has happened with the death of your employer? Was he dealing drugs for the Mafia, do you think?"

"Last night I was sure of it. Now I have no idea." Maggie told him about Orsini's announcement that the investigation was shut down.

"I know only what I read in the paper. They use legitimate businesses as a cover. Ones that make a lot of deliveries, have a lot of cash. Waste removal. Things of that kind. But, Maggie, these businesses are about family. Why work with a British lord?"

Maggie took a sip of her coffee. Mario had made it extra milky, just the way she liked it. She'd gone to bed full of fire to find some sort of anti-corruption bureau, but this morning she had the same concerns as Mario.

He moved off to steam milk for another customer, an older man with a striped maroon tie who nodded to Maggie. They were both regulars, though he always took his drink to the far edge of the bar and drank it while standing, reading the newspaper. Maggie looked idly out the window while the men chatted in Italian. Two scooters zoomed past. Then a white van rolled by. It had DeMarco printed on the side. Ilaria's family must be successful.

Who else would have the police under their thumbs? Could the thief, this Pierre character, be involved? If he was infamous enough for Thomas to have heard of him but still be at large, he might have the right sort of pull.

Giovanna came from the kitchen carrying a tray of cornetti that nearly dwarfed her slim frame. The smell was heavenly. Buttery, flaky, and a little bit fruity sweet. This batch must be filled with jam. Mario said something to his wife in Italian. Giovanna pursed her crimson lips as she arranged the pastries inside the glass case. "There is a lot of corruption here. Powerful businesses. Individuals. Not just the Mafia."

Two Italian mothers parked their strollers at a table outside. They each wore perfect makeup, tight jeans, and high heels. Back home, new mothers all wore leggings and commiserated about not having time to shower.

Giovanna left to take the women's orders and Maggie looked at her cup. Almost empty. Only few drops left at the bottom. It had been so easy to tell herself last night she'd do what it took to see the case solved. To take on the Mafia, if she had to. But knowing there were other possibilities, other, less dangerous options to consider, well, that was a little less daunting.

The bell on the door jingled as Giovanna returned. "How's the tour going?"

"We're going to the Borghese today. The van is set, and I have Thomas studying the guide books."

"Guide books? You can't run a tour from a guide book." Giovanna looked as shocked as if Maggie had told her she was going to give up sweets and train for a marathon. "It would be my pleasure to be your guide."

"Oh no, Giovanna. I couldn't impose like that. You have a business to run."

"As do you, Maggie. We have to help each other."

Maggie had moped to Burt only last week about having no friends in this city, and here was Giovanna offering to give up her morning for a woman she hardly knew.

"Giovanna wrote her thesis on pagan myths and the counter-reformation." Mario gave his wife an affectionate squeeze. "She should be lecturing at the university, but instead, she's stuck in a bakery. Please let her tell you all she knows."

Giovanna flicked her towel at him. "I'm not stuck."

Mario said something in Italian and Giovanna blushed.

"You're really sure?" Maggie asked one final time, but Giovanna insisted.

They made plans to meet in front of the museum in a few hours.

Mario handed Maggie a white paper bag on her way out.

"What's this?"

"To help you think. You're still looking for a way around the police, aren't you?"

She looked inside. A cornetto. Chocolate. Damn the diet.

The pastry was delicious, and halfway through, Maggie had her inspiration: John Aldrich. Maggie might not have the pull with the local police, but they could use Lord Philip's executor to get the case reopened. It was the kind of thing she'd done when the library needed a new roof. Find a high-profile sponsor and enlist his support. She should have thought of it sooner.

Thomas had already begun the morning's instruction when Maggie arrived at the palazzo. He looked like a 1950s letterman today, dressed in crisp pants, a sweater, and a tie. He had sketched a landscape using only rectangles, triangles, and circles. On another easel was a castle, again drawn using simple shapes.

Vicky and Shelia were eagerly taking notes while Len, seated at the worktable with them, was doodling three-dimensional cubes. Charles was seated between Helen and Eloise. Helen was looking out the open window. She was such an accomplished artist, perhaps this was all review for her. As usual, Daniel was absent.

"I want everyone to be looking for these geometric shapes when we're in the Borghese." Thomas tapped the easel with his pencil. "Every object can be broken down to its basic form. This is easy enough to see at a place like the forum, where it's all bits of columns and arches and crumbling old stone blocks. But even the most elaborate forms are basic shapes."

Maggie called Aldrich's hotel while Thomas continued the lesson, but the phone in his room was engaged. She left a message at the front desk for him to call. She felt better. He'd get the police organized.

An hour later they met Giovanna in front of the Borghese Gallery. She'd changed from her café clothing into trim trousers and very high heels. Maggie looked at her comfortable sneakers and wished they weren't quite so white. Giovanna greeted the guests like cherished relatives with exuberant hand shaking and cheek kissing.

Maggie had visited the Borghese with Burt in their first month in the city. The architecture was over the top with inlaid marble floors, vaulted ceilings painted with gallons of gold, and the walls—oh, the walls. Pink and white marble was laid out in geometric patterns and miles of sculptures were set into niches. And this was all background for the main event, a collection of all that was beautiful from every age and culture, at least in the opinion of a wealthy 17th Century Italian.

Giovanna led the group into the main entry hall, a big room filled with ancient mosaics and sculptures beneath a vaulted ceiling covered with some mythological scene. Maggie joined Shelia next to a mosaic featuring gladiators using all kinds of vicious weapons to fight wild animals and battle each other. It had been relocated from an ancient villa.

"What does it say about the Romans that they decorated their homes with scenes of death, do you think?" Shelia was wearing an embroidered white shirt tucked into jeans, with more embroidery around the ankles today. She'd told Maggie she liked to add her own personal touches to her clothes. Just a little something to make them more fun.

Maggie shivered. Certainly nothing good. Then again, the churches in Rome were covered with similar scenes, though with a biblical bent. All in the eye of the beholder, she supposed.

Her thoughts moved to John Aldrich. She hoped he wouldn't resist the idea of going to the police. She'd have to convince him. Maggie thought about the angles of investigation they already knew about. Lord Philip had been threatened by a criminal named Pierre. The previous owner of the

White Horse might have killed Lord Philip to get his painting back. And the guests needed to be checked into, for formality's sake if nothing else.

She still didn't know much about the proposal Lord Philip had made to Len and Shelia. She'd need to get more information on that. It might mean nothing, but, with Lord Philip's history selling shares in a diamond mine, it felt important.

They followed Giovanna into a room dominated by a naked woman reclining on a bed. She was life-sized and carved from white marble. Her hairstyle was classical and her pose was the same adopted by so many of the women in ancient Greek and Roman sculptures. But Maggie knew this one was modern. The model was Napoleon's sister.

"Notice the sheets. It's hard to resist touching them to check if they're as soft as cotton, is it not?" Giovanna talked about the technique required to achieve this type of effect from stone, then moved on to the next room.

Maggie hung back in the doorway and gestured for Len to stay behind. "Tell me more about the investment Lord Philip was proposing."

He snorted and hooked his fingers through his belt loops . "A load of baloney. Lord Philip invited Shelia and me into his study for a little chat. Those were his words, 'little chat.' Said he could get us in on the ground floor of some land coming up for sale in one of the hill towns outside the city. Said he had inside information that some kind of development was planned and we could make a fortune."

"You didn't invest?"

Len's face seemed to harden. "I've met con men before, and this had that smell, if you know what I mean. If you're thinking that Shelia or I had some kind of motive to kill Lord Philip, you'll need to find something else."

It was cold inside the Borghese. Maggie wouldn't have enjoyed living in this palace in the winter two hundred years ago. "Of course not, Len. But if Lord Philip was a con man, you probably weren't the first people he tried it on. Maybe there was someone out there who wasn't as cautious as you and didn't like being swindled."

"Could be." Len gave Maggie the particulars of the proposal and the location of the town Lord Philip had said was slated for development. She'd never heard of it, but they could find out if a development was even possible there.

"Could he have approached anyone else on this tour?" Maggie asked.

Len touched a hand to his forehead where his hat would have been if Shelia hadn't told him to leave back home, a story his wife had told everyone the first night. "I don't know. Daniel and Vicky seem to have plenty of money. A lot more than Shelia and I had when we were that age."

Maggie remembered the small apartment she and Burt had shared when they were first married. They certainly weren't taking luxury tours to Europe.

Maggie and Len joined the group gathered around Bernini's *David*. The young shepherd stood twisted with his slingshot pulled back, ready to take on Goliath. She felt a bit like that now. Ready to fire a rock off at the establishment. Had David felt as excited as she did?

Maggie noticed the oil paintings above the twin doorways, flanking the statue. They must be twenty feet off the ground. Did anyone else even look at them? An immoral museum curator could have swapped them out for fakes years ago and no one would ever know the difference. She imagined a young man balanced on a wobbly ladder, carefully replacing priceless originals with slapdash fakes. Was that how Pierre worked?

Maggie seemed to remember that the Italian police had an arm specializing in art thefts. She'd have to talk with Aldrich about getting that team involved. They'd know how to handle the Pierre-side of the investigation.

Maggie followed the group to the next room, where a naked woman running from a handsome man was captured in marble. The poor girl was transforming into a tree, leaves sprouting from her fingers as she pulled away.

"Notice how Apollo's back leg is raised in the middle of the air?" Giovanna circled the statue. It was on some kind of marble platform, putting Apollo and Daphne's knees at eye level. "This, in marble, is extraordinarily difficult. Bernini removed more than half the block of stone. It is these open spaces, it's what has been removed, that is so marvelous."

"It's a pretty good sculpture, too," Len said.

"Yes, yes. Bernini is a master. He makes us believe this story, this myth, was real. That a girl would suddenly turn into a tree. That is Baroque art at its best."

Thomas whispered to Maggie, "Giovanna's a godsend. The guests are eating it up."

Giovanna was in her element. With her quick smile and air of old Hollywood about her, she would have been a popular teacher if she'd continued in academia.

"Wasn't it the Renaissance artists who did all the old myths?" Shelia'd left her bag of guidebooks in the van today and appeared almost weightless without them.

Giovanna pressed her hands together, almost in a clap. "Yes, yes, that's it. The Baroque artists were *building* on what the Renaissance did. The Renaissance brought humanism to art for the first time since the classical age. The Baroque artists, though. They cared about irregularity. Not the perfection of humanity, but its drama, its emotional moments."

She led them through to the next room. It had the same vaulted ceiling, every inch painted a decorative pattern. And the marble. Deep reds and blues and greys were everywhere. Maggie had never known it could be so colorful.

How on earth did the cardinal who built this place justify the sheer opulence of it all? The palace wasn't open to the public back then, like those churches built to impress the impoverished peasants of the day. This was a private home. Maggie was far from a socialist, but perhaps displays like this gave detractors some of their ammunition against the West.

Maggie looked at the guests, listening attentively to Giovanna. Charles leaning on his cane, so much sharper than she'd given him credit for. He seemed so harmless when he was talking about his paintings and his dead wife. But once he started in about sniper angles and gunshots, she realized there was more to him.

Maggie could imagine a story in which Charles was the killer, seeking revenge for some old affair between his dead wife and Lord Philip. Except that Lord Philip must have been about thirty years younger than Charles's wife, and Charles had been on the terrace for the entire evening. Maggie found it was too easy to let her imagination run away with her.

But three guests *had* been downstairs—Vicky, Daniel, and Eloise. The police would need to give them some kind of vetting. Or perhaps just Daniel, since Eloise heard Lord Philip alive after Vicky went back upstairs.

She focused on Giovanna, who was talking in front of one of the gleaming white statues. "You do know these sculptures wouldn't have looked anything like this in their prime? Roman taste was more—what is it?—more colorful."

"What do you mean colorful?" Shelia seemed to perk up at the idea.

"Roman statues were painted. The hair, the eyes, the clothing. As were all of the buildings. Bronze roofs. Painted pillars. It was all very bright."

"What happened?" Vicky had been staying close to Giovanna, asking lots of questions. She was making the most of her time in Rome, even if her husband insisted on working.

"They faded after two thousand years. A few retained hints of their color, and early archaeologists actually cleaned the paint away so they'd look like everyone's image of the ancient art."

"Well I'll be," Len said.

Giovanna led them to the next room, but Charles held Maggie back. "May I have a moment of your time," he said in a low voice.

Charles had missed a button on his cardigan this morning. Maggie braced herself for some complaint about noise at the hotel keeping him awake all night.

"Are you entirely satisfied with the status of the police investigation?" he murmured.

Not the hotel, then.

Charles tapped his cane on the marble floor thoughtfully. The sound blended into the white noise of the other visitors to the gallery. Lots of small groups wandering, guidebooks in hand. No one was paying attention to them. Charles leaned on his cane and looked at her intently. He could be useful. An ally in this investigation. With his military history, he was an expert, in a way. And he was interested.

"No. Not at all."

The hard stone echoed with what sounded like a herd of elephants approaching. A guide led a group to *Apollo and Daphne*, speaking loudly in a language that was similar to Italian, but not quite the same. About twenty Spaniards, or perhaps South Americans, leaned in, straining for a view.

Maggie and Charles walked slowly to the next room, where Giovanna was talking animatedly in front of another sculpture of a woman fleeing from a man. This time the pursuer looked more brutish, the woman's sprint more earnest. But she held one arm in the air in the same useless gesture as Daphne. How different would the old myths have been if the young women of Greece had taken proper self-defense classes?

"Inspector Orsini has been warned off the investigation," Maggie said.

Charles stopped and turned to her, eyes serious. "Corruption."

Eloise approached them, her movements slow and deliberate, like a woman too cautious to risk falling and breaking a hip. "There you are. Giovanna's telling us about the economics of marble. So much of it was stripped down in the Middle Ages and burned for cement. Fascinating, isn't it? Full cycle of life. Skeletons of sea creatures turned into limestone, turned into marble, then burned back into limestone and used for roads for us human creatures. Though, Charles, you must know more about these things than I do."

Charles sighed and waved Maggie forward with his cane. "After you, Mrs. White."

Chapter Twelve

*A*rt is subjective. One man's Caravaggio is another man's hack. But the value of art is indisputable: whatever the market will pay.
—*Masterpiece Tours "Welcome to Rome" pamphlet*

Ilaria was standing at the palazzo's street door when Maggie arrived. "I've been watching for you." Ilaria's voice was breathless, as though she'd raced down the four flights when she saw Maggie's taxi pull up. "There's someone here looking for the man in charge. He wouldn't give his name, but he seems angry."

Maggie had left the guests painting in the Villa Borghese gardens, with Thomas urging them to take what they'd learned that morning and choose one subject they found beautiful to focus their energies on. A flower. A sculpture. The view. A picnic basket. Anything they could pour their passion into.

"Should we be worried about this man?" Maggie squeezed into the small elevator with Ilaria. There was, after all, a killer on the loose. Until the police caught him, she'd wonder if every unexpected visitor was a potential danger.

Ilaria shook her head. "I don't think so. I offered him a cup of coffee, and he asked for a scotch instead. That seemed to help."

"Mr. Aldrich hasn't called?"

"Not a word."

Maddening man.

The elevator shimmied and creaked ominously as it passed each landing.

Ilaria held the heavy metal accordion door open and Maggie hesitated before walking into the apartment. What was it Aunt Gertrude said? "Anger is your opponent's greatest weakness. Use it to your advantage." Or had that been her daughter's karate teacher? Either way, it seemed like good advice.

Maggie straightened her shoulders and walked into the salon, where a middle-aged man sat on a couch with his arm draped across its back and feet planted firmly on the ornate rug in front. He held his heavy glass in a tight grip, knuckles white. It was Faye Masters' husband, George.

He squinted at her, then realization dawned for him, too. "Good grief. Burt's wife. What are you doing here?"

"I work here." Maggie took a seat across from him in a heavy wooden chair.

Ilaria sat in the one next to her. Her dark hair caught the light, and Maggie wondered idly if the shine was all genetics, or if Italians had particularly good shampoo.

George took a swallow of his drink. "Bad business."

It was quiet, except for the sound of ice shifting in his glass. Maggie looked at him, appraising. George's face was puffy, the red veins on his nose contrasting with his faded yellow hair. He didn't look angry, exactly. More worried, with a veneer of anger. What would Aunt Gertrude say? Something about cornered dogs being the most vicious.

Maggie shook off the image of her aged relative and focused instead on the man in front of her. "What can we do for you, George?"

"Right." He finished his drink. "I'm here for my picture. Walpole borrowed it, and I want it back."

"What picture is that, Mr. Masters?" Ilaria asked.

"George, please." He put the glass on the table in front of him. "A painting of a horse. Fit right above my desk. When I heard Walpole died, I wanted to pick it up so it doesn't get included with his estate accidentally."

Maggie and Ilaria exchanged a glance. This was the former owner of the *White Horse*. The man Lord Philip had swindled, if Thomas had the story right.

"He borrowed it?" Ilaria put a particular emphasis on the word borrowed, as if unsure of its meaning.

George bristled. "I was being polite. The man stole it." He leaned forward, looking Ilaria right in the eyes. "I picked it out for Faye's last birthday, but she said it was too drab, in that charming way of hers. She wanted nothing more than for me to get rid of it, but I hung it in my study to make a point."

He shifted his gaze to Maggie, and she looked away. Faye and George squabbled constantly, but Maggie had assumed the couple thrived on tension. George's tone made her wonder, though. Faye was a woman used to getting her way, and perhaps hanging a picture his wife hated had been George's act of rebellion, albeit a small one.

"Walpole liked it and asked all kinds of questions about where I found it. How the previous owner got it, that kind of thing. He offered to buy it, but I didn't want to give Faye the satisfaction of getting rid of the damn thing."

"How did Lord Philip change your mind?" Ilaria's voice was soft, all accusation gone.

George leaned back and crossed his right foot over his left knee. He began playing with his loafer's leather tassel. "He said he'd hate for Faye to find out about certain—things." George's tone was bitter. "He said he'd have no choice but to tell her if I didn't sell him the picture."

Maggie winced. Blackmail. Would Lord Philip have tried the same thing on her if she'd had something he wanted? Her secret was embarrassing, but nothing she'd have let Lord Philip hold over her, at least not for very long.

Maggie assessed George. How serious was the secret he was keeping? "Why tell us all this?"

"What choice do I have?" There was a sheen of sweat on his upper lip. "I thought the painting was a pleasant picture that had the side benefit of irritating my wife. Then I hear Walpole has been crowing all over town that he's acquired a masterpiece worth a fortune. If I'd known what it was worth, I'd never have given in to him. I'd rather Faye found out about the—" he paused, as if searching for the right word. "The *thing* than miss out on a fortune. What he did was illegal. And now that he's dead, we can just turn back the clock, as if it never even happened."

George drummed his fingers on his leg. "Now, if you can just get it back for me, there's no problem. I'll even have it appraised. That would be a real coup to tell Faye she turned her nose up at a genuine Abernathy or whatever it is."

Ilaria clucked her tongue. She disapproved, but Maggie felt sorry for George. Living with Faye couldn't be easy. The woman was more concerned about planning the perfect party than having a conversation about a topic of substance. And, perhaps, a genuine Abbati would be enough to give George the financial freedom to leave his wife. She'd heard Faye had family money tied up in an iron-clad prenup.

George looked so eager, so confident he was going to get out of this mess. What was it Aunt Gertrude had told the children about people with something to hide being the most gullible?

"People will believe anything, no matter how improbable, if they think there's a chance they can get out of trouble." Of course, Gertrude had been telling Sam not to buy the magic glue his sister, Lucy, had offered to sell him when he'd broken Maggie's crystal pitcher into forty-seven pieces, but surely the idea was the same.

"I'm afraid it's too late," she said. "The picture's already at the appraiser's. Walter Jones picked it up yesterday."

George turned white. "But I saw Walter last week. He said he was swamped. He even left our fireworks party early to get back to work. Said he wasn't going to be able to get started on Walpole's project until next week. It's only Tuesday..."

A fly buzzed around the room. Maggie heard it before she saw it land on the gilt mantle. Lord Philip owned so much. Perhaps the heir *would* give the picture back to George rather than face a scandal. A scandal which could, perhaps, raise questions about how Lord Philip had acquired his other works.

Maggie made her voice as gentle as possible. "I guess his timeline moved up."

George looked grey. "I'll have to tell Faye before she hears from someone else."

They sat in silence for a moment.

Maggie's chair was too large for her to be really comfortable. Her toes barely touched the ground. "Did Lord Philip blackmail anyone else, do you think?"

George flinched. "Blackmail's a big word."

Maggie and Ilaria kept their gazes on him.

"I don't know," he said finally. "After he pulled this trick on me, I did get to wondering about his other windfalls. But the expat set is small. He'd run through us pretty quick."

"I'll talk with the lawyer handling his will." Maggie tried to sound encouraging. "Maybe he'll decide the picture doesn't belong in the estate, given the circumstances."

"You think he might?"

"You never know."

At the door, George hugged Maggie and Ilaria. "I can't thank you enough. And give Burt my best. Will we be seeing you for on Thursday?"

"Thursday?" Maggie drew a blank. All she could think was that it was the day after Gertrude arrived.

"The bridge game."

"Oh, no. We don't play."

"No? My mistake." He looked more like his usual self, scattered and vague. "I've been a bit distracted lately. I just finished a project at the Basilica of St. Mary of the Angels and Martyrs. Some very interesting findings. The meridian measurement. But you don't want to hear all that."

Maggie held the apartment door open, mind racing. The tour was scheduled to visit the Basilica on Thursday. She knew Michelangelo had constructed the church out of the ruins of a vast ancient Roman bathhouse. It was as economical as it was symbolic, turning one of the great heathen gathering places into a testament to Christianity. It also had served as the city's official sundial and calendar for years, which explained George's connection. Maggie thought about the morning and what a success Giovanna had made of it with her specialized knowledge.

"It's fascinating." She looked at George with her best rally-the-troops smile. "Is there any chance I could persuade you to give our guests a private tour? Tell us all about your findings? They would learn so much from a behind-the-scenes view."

He flushed with obvious pleasure. "Well, that subject does happen to be right in my wheelhouse. When?"

"Thursday? Could we steal you away from the bridge party?"

"Faye will be livid." He grinned. "Nothing would give me greater pleasure. I'll meet you here, shall I?" He pumped the women's hands and wandered off down the stairs.

"What did you think?" Maggie asked as she helped arrange lunch.

Ilaria had already prepared a green salad, with fresh fruit, and cookies for dessert, and now she stood at the stove stirring risotto.

"Of Mr. Masters? Not much." Ilaria handed Maggie a stack of plates. "I hope he's very wealthy, otherwise I cannot imagine what his wife sees in him."

Maggie thought of the prenup. "No, it's Faye who has the money."

Ilaria sniffed and turned back to the stove.

"How are things with you and Gregorio?"

Ilaria turned to face Maggie. "If I am honest, not good." Ilaria was a private woman, and this was the most personal information she had shared with Maggie.

Maggie made the encouraging "mmm" noise she'd used when trying to tease information out of her children when they were teens, trying to stay as invisible as possible.

"We grew up together, practically since babies. He is like a member of the family, and when we began dating, it was understood we would marry someday. Now my father is getting impatient."

Maggie made another "mmm" noise. Ilaria's father seemed to keep a tight grip on the family. The plan had been for Ilaria's brother, Petro, to run the family's business in Rome. But when the operations took off, Ilaria's father had come to take charge.

Ilaria had been working side-by-side with Petro, but her father put an end to that. He didn't think women should be involved in business, so Ilaria had to disappear behind the scenes. Maggie still wasn't sure how involved the

Ilaria combed her fingers through her hair, pushing it off her face. "This

---

sound like the man we just met. Besides, would this George have the power to close a police investigation?"

Maggie shook her head. Even if George had it in him to shoot Lord Philip, he wasn't the type to have Italian policemen in his pocket.

"I cannot imagine many tears were shed for our Lord Philip." Ilaria grated Parmesan onto the risotto. She tasted then added pepper and more cheese.

The aroma of simmering mushrooms and rice made Maggie's stomach growl. "How would you have done it?"

Ilaria didn't even hesitate. "Not this way, this shooting. Too clearly a murder. I would have used poison, slow and steady until he died of it. Make it look like an accident."

Maggie blanched and filled a glass of water. "Do you think the person who did this was acting on the spur of the moment?"

"Who can say? Not everyone is as clever as I am." Ilaria transferred the risotto into a serving bowl as they heard the door open and guests returning. Her timing was, as always, impeccable.

Chapter Thirteen

Two thousand men and nine thousand animals were killed during the
Colosseum's first 100 days. This can be a shocking fact to learn. Before
dismissing these acts as the bloodlust of an ancient people, however,
consider the popularity of the action films which Hollywood produces year after
year.
—Masterpiece Tours "Welcome to Rome" pamphlet

The guests went their own ways after lunch. Eloise and Helen left the palazzo
carrying easels, while Charles pulled a copy of Lee Iacocca's biography from
his bag and announced his plans to relax on the terrace. Len and Shelia
invited Vicky to join them at the Colosseum.

"It's not on the itinerary and you'll kick yourself if you leave without seeing
it." Shelia sat with four guidebooks open in front of her.

Vicky hesitated. "What if Daniel comes and finds I've gone?"

Len gathered up Shelia's guides. "Then he shouldn't have left in the first
place. It's not the worst thing in the world for a man to know you're not at
his beck and call."

Vicky flashed a grateful look. "All right then. Thank you. This will be fun."

Maggie and Thomas walked the guests to the door then retreated to the
office. They needed to discuss the next day's tour to Bonaventura, but first,
she wanted to tell him about her idea to have Aldrich intervene with the
police.

She had just begun when there was a clicking in the hall.

Charles stuck his head in a moment later. "Is this a good time?" He stood leaning on his cane. Helpful, interested, and eyes sharp. "I wanted to continue our conversation from this morning. See how I can assist."

"I have a plan." Maggie waved him in and he settled into a chair next to Thomas. "The attorney for the estate can force the police to act. I've left him a message, and he should be here any time."

A horn honked outside, and Maggie heard the whine of a Vespa on the street. She had spent so much time waiting these last two days. First for Orsini, now for Aldrich.

"I don't know if justice is really Johnnie Boy's thing." Thomas leaned back. His chair bumped the wall behind him. "He's more of an ends-justify-the-means kind of fellow."

"We'll convince him," she said. "I'm good at that."

"Don't be so sure," came Aldrich's dry voice.

Maggie's stomach dropped as he appeared in the doorway. She hadn't even heard the front door open. The light from the office illuminated him against the darkness of the hall. Without his suit jacket, the muscles of the rugby player Thomas had known in college stood out through his dress shirt.

"You're right, Mrs. White. As the agent for the estate, I do have the necessary influence to sway the police." He leaned against the door jam and spoke lazily, drawing out each word. "In fact, I had a quiet chat with the embassy on the family's behalf when I arrived. I was assured they would see to it the investigation was shut down, and they have done their job jolly well."

Charles thumped his cane on the desk. "This is highly unethical."

Aldrich stepped farther into the tiny room, right next to the desk. Maggie had to look up at him when he spoke. "Walpole was a bit of a black sheep. His family doesn't know what he was doing here in Rome, and they prefer to remain in the dark."

"You asked the embassy to do something, and they did it?" Thomas tugged at his tie. "You have that kind of influence?"

"Things have changed since school, Mittens." Aldrich pulled his lips tight. Maggie hadn't noticed how hard his eyes were behind his glasses. For a moment, she considered what else this young man was capable of. "My clients rely on me to make things right."

"That doesn't give them the right to interfere with a police investigation," Charles said. "Just because his brother has a title."

"No police investigation will bring Lord Philip back," Aldrich said. "And thank goodness. He was a bad seed from the start. He blackmailed his nanny when he was eight. Can you believe that? Saw her with the married gardener and demanded sweets for his silence. He didn't even like them, apparently, just wanted to see her squirm. That's the man we're talking about here."

"That's a boy." Maggie's throat was dry.

"Who grew up to be an equally unpleasant man." Aldrich's tone was patronizing. "The decision has been made. It's time to move on. This is how the world works."

Maggie was suddenly claustrophobic, squeezed into this room with these men. The dark green walls felt like they were pressing in on her. She pushed her chair back, bumping it against the file cabinets behind her. "Not my world, young man."

He shrugged. "I've made my position clear. Who do you think the police will listen to? You, Mrs. White? I don't think so."

It was as if he'd given her a shot of adrenaline. Her heart pounded and her senses were heightened. Maggie noticed Aldrich's musky cologne, the sound of Charles's watch ticking, even the way the light from the window reflected off her desk.

Aldrich's voice sounded like it was coming from a long way away when he spoke. "Now, I will see you tomorrow for the tour. Nine, yes? I need to see what this Masterpiece business is all about if I'm going to complete my report for young Innes-Fox. Good day."

Maggie sat back and began tapping her fingers on the desk.

"He always was a bit of a thug on the ruby pitch," Thomas said. "Relentless. But I never figured him for anything so, I don't know, illegal."

Thomas played with Maggie's mug of pens on the corner of the desk. "And he's got some cheek calling Neddy 'young Innes-Fox.' Neddy was our year. Still, I guess that's that."

But Maggie was already pulling out a notepad. "Let John Aldrich decide who gets punished and who doesn't? No, I don't think so, gentlemen."

She clicked the end of her ballpoint pen. "The police won't help? Fine. The family won't help? Fine. We're going to get to the bottom of this ourselves."

Aldrich's visit left her with a taste of bile rising in her throat. Making a list was the only thing she could think to do.

Chapter Fourteen

O utdoor markets are a charming slice of everyday Roman life. Locals exchange gossip, choose from an array of fresh meats and produce, and banter with the decedents of the very vendors their grandparents patronized.

—Masterpiece Tours "Welcome to Rome" pamphlet

Maggie spoke while she jotted down notes. "Blackmail victims…they should be prime suspects… George Masters should go back on the list. Pierre, too… We need to find out where the relatives were when Lord Philip died. It's possible Aldrich is covering up for them…" She looked at Thomas and Charles, who had been watching wordlessly. "What?"

"You'll have the whole city on the list soon," Charles said.

"I'm being thorough. We'll get enough evidence the police can't brush this under the rug, no matter what the embassy says. Now, the guests should be on the list, too."

Charles nodded approvingly, but Thomas said, "What motive could anyone here have?"

"I have no idea." Maggie made a note on her pad. "But it's worth checking into, don't you think?"

Vicky had returned to the terrace before Eloise heard Lord Philip on the phone. That left Daniel among the guests who had access to Lord Philip before he died. He was an unpleasant young man, certainly. And he'd proven to be an unreliable husband. She needed to find out more about him.

Of course, there was also Eloise. It was only her word that she'd heard

Lord Philip alive. Maggie struggled to imagine that old lady killing Lord Philip then coolly returning to the terrace as if nothing had happened.

"What's going on?" Ilaria stuck her head into the office. She listened with her hands on her hips as Thomas told the story of Aldrich's visit. "Politics. This country is corrupt. They talk about a war on the Mafia, on students who protest. But what do they do? Nothing. Just follow the path that will line their pockets."

"Oh, come on," Thomas said. "It's just a few bad apples. My experience has been a delight here, start to finish."

"An English citizen was able to subvert justice," Charles said. "Hardly a delight."

Ilaria towered over them in her heels. "You're visitors to this country. You have no idea what it's like to live here, good and bad. Soon enough, you'll go home and back to your real lives."

Thomas sat up. "That's not fair. Italy's my home. I may not know where I'll be in twenty years, but does anyone?"

"Not everyone's born with the money to float from place to place whenever he chooses." Ilaria's tone was bitter.

Maggie felt sorry for Thomas. Ilaria was taking her stress about Gregorio out on Thomas, but he had no way of knowing that.

"But your family's doing all right, Ilaria," Thomas said. "More than all right. You have built something really big here."

"Not according to my father. He thinks it's all Petro and Gregorio." Ilaria shook herself, as if trying to get back on track. "I'm not saying corruption is a bad thing. It creates certain—" she paused, "—opportunities."

There was the sound of the front door opening, then a voice called, "Charles, you in here?" Helen peeked into the office a moment later. The old woman was wearing a black hat printed with black cats playing with bright balls of yarn today. "Goodness, is there a game of sardines on? I'll play."

"For heaven's sake, Helen." Eloise came into view next to her sister. Her bent posture emphasized the difference between the pair. Helen, tall and bohemian, and Eloise small and all business, as though weighed down by the realities of the world. "It's clearly a business meeting. Oh, Charles, what

107

are you doing in there?"

"Picking Thomas's brain. I'm having trouble getting that fountain right."

"Water's jolly tricky." Thomas scooted his chair back, bumping it back against the wall. He made a show of stepping around Ilaria, as if not wanting to set her off again. "Let's see what you've got."

He and Charles disappeared into the studio, Potter sisters trailing behind.

"I'm off to the market." Ilaria had lost her edge, as if she'd let off whatever steam she needed to release. "I need to see how much longer my man will have artichokes."

"I'll come with you." Making a list was one thing. But what, exactly, was Maggie going to do next? Her best ideas came when she was thinking of something else. Then, like magic, the solution would come to her.

Wasn't that how she'd handled the Great Caramel Crisis when a competitor started to claim the Bells & Wallace candies were made from inferior sugar? There'd been a board meeting, where all the executives were competing to out-do each other with ideas to stop the negative advertising. But Maggie had put it out of her mind, focusing instead on writing out a shopping list for her son's birthday party. And then, when she had written down the color scheme to match her son's favorite flavor of ice cream, she'd had the idea of a caramel cooking contest. They'd created an entire advertising campaign around grandmothers cooking caramel with their grandchildren and sales of Bells & Wallace candies had soared.

Now Maggie strolled along the winding cobblestone streets with Ilaria to the Campo Fiori. Flanked by crumbling brick walls and balconies dripping with flowers, the walk was a pleasant contrast to Maggie's drive to the mega market back home. Even the graffiti—a colorful blur of letters Maggie couldn't translate—added to the atmosphere.

They paused at an intersection and another DeMarco van drove past. "I see your vans everywhere," Maggie said.

"It hasn't been easy expanding into this city, but we've made some important connections. Navigated the political waters, as you say." The pride in Ilaria's voice was unmistakable.

"It must be hard to be on the sidelines."

"I kept hoping my father would come around. I didn't think he'd use Gregorio as a bargaining chip."

"You've chosen hard men to work for, your father and then Lord Philip." Maggie had been thinking of killing the man after just six days. How had Ilaria worked for him for so long? Then her face burned. She'd been too forward. "I'm sorry. I didn't mean…"

"I can handle anything anyone throws my way." Ilaria was like Gertrude. A woman who wasn't going to be pushed around.

Ilaria waved away two children, begging. *"Andare! Zingari.* Vicky should never have let them get close enough to steal her bracelet."

"What was it Lord Philip wanted from your father?"

"You're investigating me? Good. Don't trust anyone. Lord Philip wanted an introduction. He said he could make them both a lot of money. I refused. For Lord Philip's protection, as much as my family's. It wouldn't have ended well for either party."

They arrived at the Campo, a big Medieval square lined with restaurants and cafés and filled with vendors selling produce, cheese, meat, and flowers.

A young man walked past, holding a radio. The stark, synthetic sound of the music was at odds with this timeless scene. *People are people, so why should it be…* The singer's voice sounded almost robotic. It was the sort of retro music her son, Sam, liked. Lucy preferred more cheerful pop.

Ilaria made a beeline for an elderly man standing at a stall filled with produce. She had a serious conversation with him, nodded, then walked to a table loaded with enormous wheels of cheese and plastic tubs filled with fresh mozzarella soaking in water. Maggie trailed behind as Ilaria began another conversation in Italian. "What do you think?" Ilaria asked in English, breaking off a bit of the sample she had just been handed.

Maggie put the soft cheese into her mouth. It was moist and sweet, sharing its texture only with the bland balls of mozzarella at home. Cheese in Italy was truly a revelation. "Delicious."

Maggie looked around the market as Ilaria handed over some colorful bills and moved to the next table. Romans of all ages were shopping, chic mothers in tight jeans pushing strollers, middle-aged men in business attire, and the usual assortment of elderly women with headscarves and dark coats.

Maggie tried to plan her next move. Dig into birth records so see if Daniel was some kind of illegitimate heir to Lord Philip's family fortune? Or check to see if one of the Potter sisters was a former domestic for Lord Philip's family? Maybe bring all the expats together in a living room and say she knew their secrets and hope they confessed all. That was what the detectives in her novels did. But she wasn't a retired Belgian policeman or a shrewd spinster. She was a well-educated, well-intentioned woman of a certain age. Who, Maggie was starting to worry, also happened to be in over her head.

A woman's giggle rang out, and Maggie saw Faye Masters with one of her bridge "girls." She caught sight of Maggie and waved her over. "The very woman we were chatting about," Faye gave Maggie continental air kisses. Her perfume—Obsession?—was overwhelming.

Faye introduced her friend. "I can't believe the police aren't looking into Lord Philip's death. It's shocking. Really shocking."

How had Faye heard that? With her ear for gossip, she was wasting her talents. She should be an investigative reporter.

"Well at least you'll have more free time now," the friend said. "Because I just found a fabulous new painting instructor—" she winked at the word instructor. "Faye's taking the class, too. You should join us. We'll all have some fun."

"Now you know Maggie wants to do something *important* with her time." Faye's tone was teasing, but Maggie thought she could detect an edge in it. Faye had no idea her husband had given away a fortune, Maggie thought with satisfaction. Or a possible fortune. Walter Jones would tell them for sure when he made his report next week.

"I'll still be working. The tour company is staying open." *For the time being*. Maggie had done an excellent job of burning her bridges with John Aldrich this afternoon. He was unlikely to make a positive recommendation to Neddy about keeping the agency up and running now.

"Well, let me know if anything changes." Faye walked off, laughing about something with her friend.

Maggie thought about Faye's husband. She would put him on her list of suspects, no matter how unlikely. She needed to at least confirm he didn't slip out of the Natale di Roma party.

Maggie sighed and focused her attention on the stall in front of her. There were more than a dozen different shallow tubs of olives and pickled vegetables. Everything from tiny capers no larger than a pencil eraser to giant ones the size of a marble. There were dark green *"niçoise"* olives, shiny black olives with dried herbs, and pickled cauliflower. Burt loved them, and Maggie decided to surprise him with some when she got home.

"Buon giorno," she said to the elderly man behind the table and pointed at the giant green olives speckled with hot peppers. *"Per favore, signore."* She held her fingers about three inches apart.

He scooped a cup of olives into a plastic tub and looked at her.

"Va bene."

He weighed the cup and showed her the total on his calculator.

Ilaria joined her at the table. "You're like a child."

"I failed out of language school." Maggie had joined a weekly conversation group when she first moved to Rome but was told politely—and in English—that a private tutor might serve her needs better. Maggie had found a woman claiming to specialize in challenging students, but, after a month, the teacher said she was moving to Parma. Maggie couldn't be sure, but she thought she'd seen Flavia on a bus two weeks ago.

"I thought you were making a joke," Ilaria said.

"What do *you* think happened to Lord Philip?"

"I have no idea."

They began the walk home.

"Perhaps it's best to leave things as they are, Maggie."

"Leave it alone?" Maggie thought she'd misheard the woman. "Why would we leave it alone? There's a killer out there."

Ilaria paused, dark eyes serious as she looked at Maggie. "The murder has nothing to do with us. Lord Philip was up to something. He was killed for it. The only danger is if we insist on getting involved."

Chapter Fifteen

H otel rooms in Rome can be small compared to American standards and street noise can be a problem. Be assured guests of Masterpiece Tours enjoy luxury accommodations.
—Masterpiece Tours "Welcome to Rome" pamphlet

When they returned from the market, Ilaria waved away Maggie's offer to help with dinner. The apartment was quiet. Perhaps the guests had gone back to the hotel to rest. Maggie tried to shake her feeling of failure. She hadn't come up with a credible action plan, despite the excursion.

Maggie noticed the hall was dark. The formerly grand rooms of the palazzo had been divided when it was turned into apartments, and the long ago architect had neglected to ensure natural light filtered into the hall. The studio usually provided enough light during the day, but the door must be closed this afternoon. Unusual. She walked down the hall, her footsteps ringing out in the darkness like a hammer striking.

Hearing a voice coming from the studio, Maggie hesitated, hand on the doorknob. It sounded like Daniel. She couldn't make out the words and leaned closer, head against the door. She strained to hear. Did he just say, "We'll settle it tomorrow"?

Maggie pulled her hand away, heart pounding. She pressed her body against the door and could make out the words "agreement" and "necessary changes."

A jolt of electricity surged through her body. Daniel. She'd known there was something not right about him. He was the guest who didn't fit in on this tour of painters. The one who'd been downstairs after Eloise heard Lord Philip. Now, here he was, having a covert conversation in the one room he had no business in. Maggie knelt down to try to see through the keyhole.

Light flooded the hall. "Lost something, hon?"

Maggie bumped her forehead at the sound of Shelia's drawl. She stumbled to her feet and saw Shelia at the light switch. Maggie's thoughts raced as the Texan walked toward her. She needed to explain herself, and the memory of Vicky kneeling outside Lord Philip's study the day before passed through her mind. Maggie mimed bending down and picking up something tiny. She tucked her hand into her skirt pocket. "Got it!"

Maggie's back was to the studio door and she smelled simmering tomato sauce wafting from the kitchen. "Ilaria's getting dinner on. Why don't you ask that question about the lasagna the other night?" *Please go away.* She put her hand on the doorknob. *Please, please.*

Shelia squinted at Maggie. "What were you doing here in the dark?" Then she put her tote down. "I could have spent all day walking around the Colosseum. Those old stones. So much history."

Maggie couldn't make out what Daniel was saying over Shelia's voice.

"Did you know admission was free in Roman times? It's really something to think of all those seats filled with people. I wonder what they did for restrooms?"

If I can just find out who's inside with Daniel. Maggie put her hands behind her back and twisted the knob gently, but it didn't turn. She tried again, harder. Nothing happened. The door must be locked.

"Fascinating," Maggie said. "I'll join you and Ilaria in a minute, and you can tell me all about it."

"Well, as a matter of fact, I was coming to find you. Can we talk in the dining room?" Shelia tucked her arm into Maggie's and pulled her down the hall before Maggie thought to protest. Shelia closed the double doors and put her hands on her hips. "You know I don't like to make a fuss, Maggie, but something's got to be done."

Maggie kept her gaze on the dining room's doors, as though she could see through them and into the studio if only she tried hard enough. Finally, she gave up and turned her attention to Shelia. Her face was flushed from the sun this afternoon, her embroidered blouse rumpled.

"Len and I were woken at five this morning," Shelia said. "Just like yesterday and the day before. I don't like to complain, you know that, Maggie. But I told Lord Philip, and he said he'd do something about it. Enough is enough."

Len and Shelia's room was at the back of the hotel, Shelia explained, and deliveries started early. Maggie quickly promised to arrange for a room change. She might still be able to get back to Daniel in the studio.

Shelia stayed where she was. "It's not just us. Vicky and Daniel are right next door, and the sound has to be just as bad there. I know Daniel talked to Lord Philip about it, too. I heard them in the study."

Maggie took a half-step toward the door. Shelia took a half-step back. *It would look ridiculous to anyone walking in on us.* Two small women at one end of this massive room intended for parties of twenty. Had Lord Philip ever eaten in here alone?

"I thought being right next to the fire escape would be a good thing in that type of old hotel," Shelia continued. "Because, you never know. But not if loud men are going to be unloading things at all hours, shouting at each other in Italian."

Maggie promised again to talk to the manager and then raced out of the room. Maggie's her heart sank when she saw the door to the studio was open. She knew Daniel would be gone even before she walked in.

The room had an empty, abandoned feel. Easels were put away, brushes back in the cabinets. Had Daniel been in here with someone, or had he come in to make a private call?

A few windows were open, and Charles's painting of a rowboat on the lake at the Villa Borghese waved gently in the breeze. It was bright and confident, almost exuberant in feeling. It was a big improvement from the stilted Forum he'd painted when he first arrived. Thomas's influence, no doubt.

Next to it was a picture of a bench with a fountain in the background. A cat peeking around one of the legs marked it as Helen's. She'd captured the color of the city in a way that Eloise, whose skyline picture hung next to it, hadn't managed.

There was a clatter from the corner and Maggie nearly jumped out of her skin. "Daniel?" But then she noticed Eloise standing at the sink.

"Just me." Eloise held up her knitting bag, bright red and patterned with hordes of cats. Cats sleeping. Cats rolling on their backs. Cats reading books. A gift from Helen, she'd said over cocktails one night. "I'm tackling some paint I got on this the other day. Clumsy of me."

"Was Daniel in here?"

Eloise raised her eyebrows. "In the studio? That man hasn't set foot near here as far as I've seen."

Maggie should have put Shelia off. She just hadn't had time to think.

"I don't think that man has any interests outside of work." Eloise unscrewed the lid of a small metal can. The familiar odor of paint thinner filled the room. Eloise tipped the can over a rag and blotted the top edge of the bag, where a streak of thick blue paint covered the heads of two playful kittens.

"Was anyone else here when you came in?" Maggie asked.

"Just me and these cats." Eloise continued patting at the spot, and the paint was coming off. "At least these don't shed. Not like Helen's. How those four creatures manage to cover every surface of her house, I'll never know."

Maggie's children helped with a neighbor's cats one summer when they went out of town. She'd remembered thinking Helen had the same number. "I thought it was three." Maggie knew it was irrelevant, even as the words left her mouth.

"Three? Four? Who can keep track of them? Anything more than two is too many." Eloise held the bag to the light. "There. All better."

Maggie stayed behind when Eloise left to show her bag to Helen. Maggie needed to organize her thoughts. Daniel could have been chatting on the phone about anything. Talking about a deal or making dinner reservations. But what was he doing in the studio? And with the door locked? And hadn't he said he visited the Museum of Modern Art on a day it was closed? The man was up to something. There was no doubt about it.

Eloise had her knitting out when Maggie stepped onto the terrace. The clicking sound of the metal needles was strangely domestic in this urban setting. Maggie remembered the time she decided to knit a hat for Burt one Christmas. She'd still been working after he went to bed on Christmas Eve, frantically knitting and hoping her husband wouldn't notice the crooked cables.

The other women were grouped around Eloise, Shelia showing Helen and Vicky something in her guidebook. Thomas stood with Charles and Len near the railing, pointing out this and that in the skyline. Only Daniel was alone, drinking a glass of white wine, gaze focused on his phone.

Maggie stood at the buffet, trying to organize her thoughts. Daniel was dressed in a light blue blazer and chinos rolled up, exposing bare ankles above lizard-skin loafers. What if Faye was right and Lord Philip *was* involved in the drug trade? On TV, drug dealers were all from South American cartels. Could Lord Philip have been helping them make inroads into the European market? Daniel said he spoke Spanish. Was Daniel some kind of liaison between the Colombians and Lord Philip?

Maggie watched the news. The drug war was continuing. Why wouldn't the Colombians want a piece of the Italian market? And why wouldn't they use an American financier to facilitate it?

The connection fit. It really fit. She needed to call Inspector Orsini.

A hand touched Maggie's elbow. Vicky was next to her, saying something. "I'm sorry?" Maggie tried to focus.

"Are the plans for Bonaventura still set for tomorrow?" Vicky looked like she'd just stepped out of the house for the day, hair and clothes perfectly in place. The poor woman was completely in the dark about her husband.

"Yes, yes, all set."

Maggie checked her watch. With any luck, the inspector would still be at the office. She excused herself and dialed his number. She leaned back, heart thumping, while she waited to be put through. This was evidence the inspector couldn't ignore, whatever his supervisor said.

Someone finally came on the line to report Inspector Orsini had left for the day. Maggie left a message and headed back to the terrace. She was halfway up the stairs when the doorbell rang. Maggie hurried back down and found a disheveled Inspector Orsini standing at the door.

Maggie beamed at him. It was synchronicity, the universe coming through for her at last. "Inspector! I was just trying to call your office, and here you are."

Orsini frowned. "Yes, as you say, here I am." He looked tired. And a little annoyed. He gestured toward the dining room. "We need to talk, Signora White."

Maggie led him through the salon into the elegant dining room. She was careful to close the double doors. She didn't want to risk Daniel interrupting them.

Maggie chose a seat at the head of the massive table and gestured for him to sit at her left. This meeting would be nothing like their last conversation in this room. "I have some information for you. It's about one of the guests. I heard a conversation I think you would be very interested in, and—"

Orsini cut her off. "Another time, Signora White." The inspector wasn't wearing a jacket, and his shirt cuffs were rolled up to his elbows, as though he'd been in the office working on paperwork. "No, it's you I'm interested in. Your work history prior to coming to Italy, specifically." Orsini took out a notebook and looked at her expectantly.

Maggie didn't understand at first. "I was an executive at a candy company, Bells & Wallace."

He cocked his head at her, bushy eyebrows raised, and then it clicked. Somehow this inspector had learned she fudged the details of her departure from Bells & Wallace. She swallowed. Fessing up was the best policy. Of course it was, but somehow she couldn't bring herself to do it. "I thought your investigation was shut down."

The room was warm. The windows were closed. The guests would find it stifling after the terrace. Ilaria was usually much more attentive to these details.

"And it was, Signora White. And yet, I couldn't stop wondering about you. An American woman so intent on our investigation that she comes to my office with her own notes of the crime. It's very unusual, no?"

Maggie said nothing. She wished she had a glass of water. Why on earth were the windows closed?

Orsini leaned forward, elbows on the tables, chin on top of his interlaced fingers. "We looked into you, Signora White. Retired executive, left her job to follow her husband to Italy. That's what we were told. And yet, when my officer called your company for confirmation, that isn't what I learned."

Maggie couldn't read his expression. His eyes crinkled at the corners, as though genuinely concerned about this disparity.

She looked away and fanned herself. "It's warm in here, isn't it?"

Orsini ignored her. Instead, he put on his reading glasses and made a show of flipping through his notebook, as though refreshing his memory on the details. "You were let go six months before you and your husband moved. And I asked myself, what if Lord Philip knew this too? And then, perhaps, did he attempt to do something with this information?"

Orsini removed his glasses and leaned back, hands in his pockets, like an actor playing a cop on TV who knew he had his case sewn up. If he was bothered by the heat, he didn't show it. "Lord Philip doesn't seem to have been universally liked. No one says what, exactly, but there seems to be something that was unlikeable about the man."

The police were investigating at last, just as she'd asked—no, just as she'd demanded. And they seemed to have moved past the ridiculous burglary idea. But this inspector had somehow gotten it all wrong after that.

Maggie wished she had a pad and pencil. Something to hold onto while gathering her thoughts. She drummed her fingers on the table, instead. The solid table felt reassuring, just like the conference tables back home. It was a trick she'd learned early in her career when she'd had to explain disappointing sales performance. It made her look calm and in control while her mind raced to come up with a solution.

"You had the opportunity," Orsini continued. "You made a point of telling me that. And now I find a motive. Is there something you'd like to tell me?"

This inspector reminded Maggie of Tim Beloit, the sales manager for their biggest customer. He flew under the radar in their planning meetings, then dropped a bombshell when everyone was ready to wrap up for the day.

Maggie had never liked Tim Beloit. But she'd climbed the ladder at Bells & Wallace faster than he had, making it to Vice President, while he'd been sidelined and moved to a small regional customer.

This inspector wanted to rattle her, and she wasn't going to give him the satisfaction of knowing he'd succeeded. Maggie looked Orsini straight in the eyes. "As I told you, Inspector, I called you with important information about the case. I overheard Daniel Barlow, one of the guests, making suspicious plans for tomorrow. He has lied about his whereabouts on this tour and I suggest that you—"

But Orsini cut her off again. "You have no comment about Lord Philip's death?" Maggie noticed Orsini's reflection in the room's big mirrors. It was as though an army of inspectors were judging her from all sides. She shook her head.

Orsini grunted as he pushed himself to his feet. "All right then, Signora White. If you change your mind, you know where to reach me."

Maggie stayed where she was until she heard the front door close, then she opened each of the room's big windows as wide as they would go. She leaned against the last one, letting the cool air wash over her.

She, Maggie White, was a suspect. An honest to goodness suspect. Maggie didn't know whether to be terrified or delighted.

The rest of the night passed in a daze. Maggie barely followed the conversation as she thought about her interview—for that was what it was, an actual interview—with the inspector.

Here she was, sitting across from the likely killer, and the police thought she was the guilty one. Maggie watched as Daniel tore a piece of bread. His hands were smooth, with buffed nails. He wasn't the type to strangle someone or use a knife. A handgun would have suited him perfectly.

Finally, Maggie couldn't sit still any longer. She asked Thomas and Charles for help in the kitchen while Ilaria served dessert. The room was compact; the swinging door bumped up against a refrigerator three-quarters the size of Maggie's back home. Even the stove was miniature. Maggie kept her voice low as she told them about her theory, leaving out Orsini's visit. There didn't seem to be a point in explaining why Orsini thought she was a person of interest.

Thomas boosted himself onto the counter and listened with elbows on knees as she spoke. Charles leaned against the stove, nodding along.

"I suspect Daniel is the money man," she concluded.

"Why would he kill Lord Philip?" Thomas asked.

"I have no idea. Drug types are always getting into trouble, aren't they? It's one of the hazards of the profession. The important thing is he doesn't have an alibi for Lord Philip's death, and now we know he was involved in a cartel with Lord Philip." Maggie knew she was stretching the truth. She didn't have proof of anything, but her gut said she was right.

"When he lied about being at the museum, maybe he was giving an update to his employers." Thomas picked up the ice cream scoop Ilaria had left on the counter and licked it.

Maggie nodded. "I think you're right."

"Did you tell Ilaria?" Thomas's voice was casual, but his expression was serious.

Maggie shook her head. "She thinks we should stay out of it."

Thomas gave a bitter laugh. "She made her opinion about visitors not understanding life here pretty clear this afternoon."

"Any chance Vicky knows?" Charles asked.

"Absolutely not," Maggie said. "She's as innocent as they come. She thinks she's on this trip because her husband cheated on her. It'll break her heart when the truth comes out."

"Poor lady," Thomas said. "She's had a hard time of it, after losing her first husband."

The baked cheese scent of Ilaria's tomato and artichoke casserole still hung in the air. Maggie turned on the water and began washing the dinner plates while she considered what to do next.

"We need to call the police," Charles said.

"I tried that." Maggie gave a laugh that sounded false, even to her own ears. There was nothing to do but fess up, at least partially. "Something about me being the one to find the body, just like you said, Thomas."

Thomas hopped off the counter and began drying dishes. "That's mad.

The three of us will go to them in the morning and explain it all."

Maggie shook her head. "I don't trust this inspector. We need to catch Daniel in the act."

"What act?" Charles asked. "Lord Philip is already dead."

"Daniel said he would settle 'it' tomorrow, didn't he?" Maggie said. "Maybe he's doing a hand off or something. We'll follow him and get proof the police can't ignore."

Thomas blinked. "We? I've got to stay with the tour, Mrs. W."

"I would help, but I'm afraid I would slow you down." Charles gestured at his bad leg.

Fine. She'd do it herself. Burt would hate it, but, with any luck, he'd be asleep when she got home and she wouldn't have to tell him.

"Keep a safe distance," Thomas said. "Daniel won't suspect a thing. And before he knows it, bang! You'll get a picture of him meeting some criminal type, and Daniel will be in prison where he belongs. I don't envy him. My uncle said they're awful here. He warned me to run for the border if I was ever caught up in anything. Said to make the judicial system claw me back."

Maggie wished Thomas would stop talking. And the aroma of dinner combined with the hot, soapy water was starting to turn her stomach. Maggie told herself she had nothing to worry about.

The kitchen door swung forward a bit, just half an inch, then swung closed again. The hair on the back of Maggie's neck stood up. She pointed to the door.

"Probably the Potter sisters." Charles's voice was low. "We should get back."

There was a knock at the door and the three exchanged glances. Maggie opened the door and found Daniel in the hall. His expression was cold, like her children when they were teens and mad about having an earlier curfew than their friends.

Daniel's voice was flat. "Vicky's not feeling well. We're leaving." Then he turned on his heel and walked stiffly away before anyone could answer.

Maggie felt Thomas and Charles's gazes on her as she let the door swing closed again. "You don't suppose..." She faltered.

The three looked at each other. Only the dripping tap broke the silence.

Finally, Thomas spoke. "He looked angry. You don't think he'll, well, come after us?" Thomas's voice lacked its usual bounce.

"Impossible." Maggie was firm. "Not with all three of us. Besides, whatever beef he had with Lord Philip was just that—a beef with Lord Philip. We'll go ahead with the plan. Stick with the Potters tonight, Charles, just to be safe. Let them walk you to your room. We'll follow the Girl Scout motto: be prepared."

"You were a scout?" Thomas asked.

"I set new cookie sales records three years in a row." She'd enjoyed the camping and badge skills as a girl, but her children hadn't shown any interest in following in her footsteps. "Trust me, gentleman, it'll be fine."

Chapter Sixteen

Rome is a unique city, with modern residents living next door to ancient ruins. Romans pay dearly for modern conveniences, and apartments tend to be small and cramped, with uneven services.
—Masterpiece Tours "Welcome to Rome" pamphlet

Burt was stretched out on the Whites' couch when Maggie opened the door a little after ten. He took off his reading glasses and carefully marked his page. He was reading a thick biography of some past president. Maggie preferred lighthearted stories about sedate English villages.

Thinking about her plans to follow Daniel the next day, Maggie thought she might have been better off reading spy thrillers.

"Let's have some cocoa and you can tell me about your day." Burt stood. "I think we have some packets left from Lucy's care package."

Their daughter had taken to sending them shipments of peanut butter and instant hot chocolate, both hard to find in Rome. Usually Maggie loved digging into these deliveries, but tonight she wished Burt had been asleep at his usual time. She wasn't ready to tell him about Orsini's visit or her plans with Daniel, but she couldn't say nothing.

Maggie sank onto the couch. A wave of guilt for resenting her husband's thoughtful gesture washed over her. He was still in his work clothes, she realized. His dress shirt fit him well. His pants were cut slim. Even his reading glasses were fashionable. She couldn't put her finger on it, but he looked stylish, something she'd never have said about her old Burt. It suited him.

She took a sip of her cocoa. Lucy had bought the kind with mini marshmallows, and the gooey sweetness melted against her lips. Burt began rubbing Maggie's feet. She felt so relaxed sitting here with her husband, the man she trusted most in the world. She was being foolish, keeping things back from him. She'd start at the beginning and tell him everything. Including her plans for tomorrow. Burt would tell her to be careful, but he'd support her.

She started with George Master's revelation about the *White Horse*.

Burt whistled. "To have let a fortune slip through his fingers."

"He couldn't have snuck out of the party, could he?" Maggie took another sip. George's alibi for Lord Philip's murder hardly mattered now, but it would be information to show the police she'd been thorough.

"George was too busy refilling drinks to sneak out anywhere," Burt said. "Walter was the only one who left before the fireworks ended. Do you think Faye knows about the picture?"

"Of course not. I'd love to see her face, though, if she were to find out the picture she'd turned her nose up at was a masterpiece." Maggie enjoyed the pressure on her Achilles; her tension drained way.

"You and Faye were good friends." Burt rubbed her feet harder, moving up to her ankles.

Maggie hadn't told her husband that Lord Philip knew about her white lie to the expats. It was just too embarrassing to admit she'd been caught. She'd have to tell him about Orsini's accusation—if that was what it had been—but she didn't want to dwell on it by going into her suspicions about Faye being Lord Philip's source.

"Faye was helpful when we were getting settled, but she's vapid. Just concerned about parties and card games."

"That's a little harsh. I've been thinking we might have more fun here if we did more things with them. Got into the regular mix. Speaking of which—"

"Wait, I'm just getting to the important part," Maggie said. "When I got back from the market, I heard Daniel making plans to meet someone tomorrow."

"Daniel?" Burt seemed to be searching his mental rolodex.

"The young one married to the English girl. The man who's on the tour making up for an affair with his secretary."

She told him about Daniel slipping downstairs during the fireworks, his lying about visiting a museum, and his refusal to take part in any of the tour activities. "He speaks Spanish and travels to South America. Added to the rumors about Lord Philip's involvement in the drug trade, I think it's pretty suspicious." Maggie drank the last of her cocoa and set the mug on the scratched coffee table like someone who had just downed a beer in a drinking contest.

Burt stopped rubbing. "A South American cartel setting up business with an English lord then killing him using an agent disguised as a tourist?" He didn't bother to hide his disbelief. This from a man who'd seen *TheBourne Identity* three times, a movie she understood was about an amnesiac assassin on the run from a secret government program. Burt's tone was cool. "Are you sure you're not blaming Daniel because he had an affair."

Burt sometimes accused Maggie of being judgmental, unable to move past petty grievances. His tone made it clear he thought she was doing that now. Burt should know better. Maggie had forgiven him, but she wasn't going to have that conversation again.

"No." Her icy tone matched his. "It's because he lied about going to the museum." She certainly wasn't going tell him about Orsini's visit and the plan to follow Daniel now. Nothing good would come of it.

Burt shrugged and took their mugs to the kitchen. Maggie heard him head to the bedroom, but she didn't move. The students downstairs were out on their balcony, their laughter filtering in through the open window.

Maggie sighed and went into the kitchen. She washed out the mugs Burt had left sitting on the counter. The hot water was out. Again. She'd chosen this apartment for its charm. Burt's company had first set the couple up in an antiseptic unit in a modern block of flats on the outskirts of the city, but Maggie had immediately set out to find something with character. She wanted to live like an Italian, hanging her washing out over the street, having some old grandma on the first floor who kept tabs on them.

Of course, most of their neighbors in the sterile apartment were Romans, and Maggie would die before hanging her underwear for everyone to see, but that wasn't the point. She'd gotten herself an English newspaper and circled apartments that might suit them. Faye made the phone calls and even came with Maggie on the visits.

Maggie had fallen in love with this one, a fourth-floor walkup just off the Piazza di Santa Maria in Trastevere. The neighborhood was a fifteen-minute walk from all the sites and filled with locals. It had a little more garbage on the streets and graffiti on the walls than the high rent area near Lord Philip's palazzo, but these walls were ancient walls. And the old women on her street really did spend their mornings gossiping out front. Most days Maggie loved it. But the hot water was a problem.

Maggie went into the bathroom to complete her nightly ritual, still thinking about those first weeks in the city. She'd forgotten how helpful Faye had been then.

Burt finally broke the silence. "Did you see the email from Lucy?"

"Yes. I'm glad she and her roommate are getting along better." This was how they ended fights. One of them changed the subject, and they both moved on. Maggie wiped off the cold cream. Was that an age spot near her cheekbone? Were those supposed to start already?

"What about the other suspects?" Burt said from the bedroom. "You had some good leads, didn't you? Guests who left the terrace during the fireworks?"

Maggie took a final look in the mirror. Maybe she should consider a new hairstyle.

"Eloise went downstairs. She's the one who heard Lord Philip, so that helped narrow the window. Daniel's wife was downstairs, but she came back before Eloise, so she's in the clear." Maggie rubbed a final batch of lotion onto her hands. "Really, Burt, I'm sure it's Daniel."

Burt's clothes were in a heap on the bedroom floor. She hung up his suit and put his shirt in the hamper.

"Could Vicky and Daniel be in it together?" Burt asked. "Like Bonnie and Clyde?"

Maggie thought of Vicky's story of spilling donuts on her husband, losing her bracelet and then her barrette. "No, she's just a sweet girl who married the wrong man.

"Thomas and Ilaria don't have alibis, do they?"

"Ilaria was with her boyfriend." Maggie climbed into bed next to him. "She was busy refusing a marriage proposal."

Burt put his book down. "Poor man."

Maggie nodded absently. "I just hope Ilaria can hold off. She's dated this man since she was a girl. She needs to have some time on her own, try other people."

It took a minute before Maggie realized what she'd just said. Was she suggesting loyalty wasn't important? That having a history with someone was irrelevant?

Then she shook herself. The romantic life of a young, single woman wasn't the same as that of a married couple with two children.

"Ilaria probably has it in her to kill Lord Philip," Maggie said, "But she would have done it differently. Smarter. And Thomas was packing up a picture for Lord Philip, then he came right up. None of the others were involved. I'm sure of it."

Burt went back to his book and Maggie mentally ran through her plans for the morning as she lay in silence next to her husband. Their good camera was in the closet. She'd need that, plus a guidebook in case she needed to look inconspicuous. She'd bring her backpack with a water bottle and some chocolate. A raincoat, too.

It was unfortunate Daniel had overheard them in the kitchen. She hoped he wouldn't alter his plans for whatever meeting he had worked up. On the other hand, maybe a little pressure wasn't such a bad thing. It might make him careless. People got caught when they panicked, didn't they? This could work to her advantage.

She was drifting off when Burt spoke. "You'll get Gertrude tomorrow, won't you?"

Maggie had forgotten. "Can't you?"

"I'm in meetings all day. Just meet her at the station, give her a key, and send her on her way."

Maggie wasn't going to tell him she'd be busy following Daniel. She'd figure something out. She always did.

Chapter Seventeen

M ost have heard Rome was founded upon seven hills, but centuries of development have rendered them nearly invisible. Peaks have been shaved off, valleys have been filled in, and the city today simply rolls up and down for no apparent reason.
—Masterpiece Tours "Welcome to Rome" pamphlet

Maggie arrived at the hotel early the next morning, parking herself in the lobby with the vague plan of sneaking behind Daniel whenever he set out for the day. But he emerged from the elevator with Len and Shelia promptly at eight, and the three walked toward the breakfast room. She listened from behind her copy of the *Financial Times* as they passed.

"Vicky was sick as a dog all night. Still can't be more than a few feet from the bathroom. She was really looking forward to today's tour, and she insisted I go in her place." Daniel was the image of a wealthy young American on vacation. Bright yellow sweater, powder blue polo, madras shorts, and polished loafers. If he'd lost any sleep caring for his wife, it didn't show.

Maggie considered the implications for Daniel's meeting. Admission to Bonaventura was limited to guests of Masterpiece and the German tour, so his contact wouldn't be able to meet him there. Whatever he had planned was likely set for later in the day, during the free time.

Maggie folded her newspaper and pulled her backpack on as she slipped out of the hotel and down the narrow street to the palazzo. She would stay close to Daniel on the tour, just in case.

There was just enough room for a single car to travel down the street, and drivers bolder than Maggie had parked on the sidewalk. She skirted the parked cars, enjoying the feeling of her bag on her back. She had a thermos, camera, and floppy sun hat. She was ready for whatever came her way today.

Maggie opted for the stairs when she arrived at the palazzo, too impatient to wait for the elevator. She pushed away the niggle of concern about Orsini's interview the day before and was barely out of breath when she reached the apartment. The elevator whirled into action and Maggie peered over the railing. She spotted John Aldrich stepping into the elevator in his usual uniform of a suit and tie.

She forced a smile and waited for him at the door. "Good morning, Mr. Aldrich. What can we do for you today?" Maggie breathed in the scent of brewing coffee as she walked into the apartment.

"Joining the tour for the morning. Need to see how it works firsthand for my report and all that."

Maggie remembered her promise to George. "There's a matter we should catch up on. The owner of the *White Horse* wants his picture back."

"What do you mean?" Aldrich asked. "Neddy owns that picture, or will after probate."

She told him about George's visit and the pressure Lord Philip had put on him to sell.

"Well, tough luck on him." Aldrich stood with his hands in his pockets, double-breasted jacket stretched across his chest, as if the commander of some navy ship.

Maggie thought Aldrich had probably perfected this pose in a front of a mirror.

"I may not approve of Walpole's approach, but it sounds like he got it fair and square. And I hardly think your Mr. Masters is going to raise a fuss and risk his wife finding out whatever dirty secret he's hiding."

"And you're just going to keep it?"

"I'm keeping it for Lord Philip's heir. He can make amends if he chooses. Though Neddy's hardly in a position to do that with his marriage around the corner. A man needs capital if he's making that type of match. Now, where's Thomas?"

Aldrich walked off to the studio and Maggie went into the kitchen, where Ilaria was preparing a tray of coffee. Maggie remembered the morning after Lord Philip's death when the young woman suggested their employer was holding something over Maggie.

"Thomas told me everything," Ilaria said. "Ignore the police. They are idiots."

Maggie was glad that whatever tension had been between Ilaria and Thomas the day before had blown over. She began to relax under Ilaria's confident smile.

"Now," Ilaria counted out cups and saucers, "you still are planning to follow Daniel?"

"I'll be careful."

"I wasn't going to tell you to be careful, I was going to tell you to bring something to eat." She reached a white paper bag on the counter and handed it to Maggie.

It was warm and Maggie smelled pastries inside. She unrolled it and saw three cornetti.

"Stakeouts can be tedious." Ilaria tapped the bag with a long, manicured finger. "It's best to be prepared."

Maggie decided not to ask how Ilaria knew this. She had just tucked the bag of treats into her backpack when the guests arrived. Daniel settled in the salon with a newspaper, while the others filed into the studio. If he was bothered by what he'd overheard the night before, he didn't show it.

Maggie poured herself a cup of coffee and settled into a chair across from him. "What are your plans after the tour today, Daniel?"

He lowered his paper an inch. "Can't say. Depends on how long the pictures take." He'd brought a camera bag with him, saying Vicky asked him to take photos of everything this morning.

"You're welcome to download them to the computer here..." Maggie began, but Daniel had already gone back to his paper. She sat looking at him a moment. His plaid shorts looked ridiculous in this fashionable country. She wasn't proud of the twinge of pride she felt knowing her own husband would never make the same choice.

Aldrich joined them a moment later, helping himself to coffee and settling onto one of the couches. "Seems like Thomas has the lecture side in hand. Talking to them all about some rule of thirds. They seemed to be lapping it up." He took a sip then turned to Daniel. "I'm sorry about your wife, by the way. I understand she's under the weather."

Daniel put the paper down. "Probably something she ate. Bit ironic, since she refused to go to South America saying she had no intention of getting hit with Montezuma's Revenge." He was sitting in one of the wooden chairs whose arms had been carved to look like roaring lions. He moved his right hand back and forth across the end, as if petting the wooden creature.

Maggie looked at the men. Two young go-getters. Both of whom played fast and loose with the law.

"Such a pretty girl." Aldrich removed his glasses and began polishing them on a handkerchief. "Can't think where I've seen her before. Not in our set. I somehow think she was with someone older when I met her. Her father perhaps?"

"No," Daniel said. "Her father died when she was a baby."

"Not that then. A husband? Thomas said she was married before, I think?"

Daniel frowned. "Widowed. First husband died young."

Aldrich shook his head. "That's bad luck. Though it worked out in the end, didn't it? Marrying you, I mean."

Daniel returned to his paper, and soon enough the artists emerged from the studio and crowded into the van downstairs. Daniel and Aldrich took seats in the very back row, leaving the others to fill in the three rows behind the driver.

Maggie gave the address and settled back as the driver navigated the busy road that wound around the Colosseum and past the Porta San Paolo with its odd Egyptian-style stone pyramid next door. The old Aurelian Wall that surrounded the ancient city had skewered the pyramid. It looked like a trapped beast, strangely out of place in this realm of European culture. The Romans had always gathered up specimens from other cultures, importing elephants and parading prisoners of war through their streets.

"What's the story with that thing?" Len asked.

Maggie knew the answer. She'd visited the tiny museum next door only a month ago. "Egyptian things were all the rage in ancient Rome. There were lots of pyramids like these, apparently, but they were all torn down for one reason or another. This one survived because they built the city walls right around it. It was built by one of the early emperors. I can't remember which one."

"Not an emperor," Shelia held up her guidebook. "It was built for a magistrate in eighteen B.C."

Damn her.

"I'm sure he was less impressive than his tomb," Helen said. "Those men always were."

"Aren't we supposed to be inside the Aurelian walls, dear?" Eloise asked.

Maggie checker her phone. Eloise was correct, as usual. Maggie must have given the wrong address. Thank goodness Lord Philip wasn't there to see it. Then Maggie felt a pang of guilt. His death was a terrible thing. In a moment, the driver had the directions sorted and drove through the gates to Bonaventura.

"Oh my," Helen climbed out of the van. "This *is* something."

An oasis of green stretched out beyond. Lord Philip had told Maggie it was quite a coup that Masterpiece had these tickets. The grounds were open on a restricted ticket basis to keep the space quiet for contemplation.

And it was strangely calm. Birds were singing. A lawn mower buzzed in the distance. But nothing else. No scooters whizzing around. No traffic. And no conversation. It was as if the place had cast a spell over the artists. They all got out without saying a word, even Shelia. A miracle.

They were still in the city, but it was a quiet, more elegant neighborhood than the one they'd left. The Aventine neighborhood was on top of one of Rome's fabled seven hills, and the city center stretched north in front of Maggie. It was easy enough to pick out the giant Colosseum, the ruins of the Forum, and the Vatican with its shiny dome on the left side of the river.

"Well, let's get on with it," Aldrich said. "Where is this famous pile?"

Thomas checked the group in with the elderly guard and they passed through into the garden. There was a rolling expanse of lawn studded with large trees in full leaf and modern sculptures sprinkled everywhere. The garden felt enormous, but Shelia helpfully informed them it was just two acres. The clever designer, whoever he was, had played with perspective and plantings to create a haven in the middle of the city. Perhaps most amazing of all, there were no other visitors.

A man walked out of the main office. "Don't miss the tower," he said with an Italian accent. "Everyone comes for the famous altarpiece, but there are some nice views from the top. Just don't get too close to the edge. The wall is low."

The man, clearly a manager, stood with his hands tucked into his pockets. "I told the board of directors we need to install a railing, but no. They won't hear of it. Said it would spoil the appearance. There was even an article written in an American magazine a few months ago about the correct balance of restoration and public safety."

"We'll be careful," Thomas said. He was dressed like an affluent boater that day in a form-fitting t-shirt, blazer and silk scarf tied around his neck. The manager looked at him a moment, then drifted away.

The group crunched along a gravel path toward the chapel, passing modern sculptures of steel and copper. It was a welcome change from the marble all over the rest of the city.

Len and Thomas were at the front of the group. Daniel was right behind, with Shelia talking about something at his side. Aldrich was flanked by the Potter sisters and Charles trailed at the rear. He caught Maggie's eye and she slowed her pace to match his.

"Thomas," Charles called. "Do you have a sketchpad? I seem to have forgotten mine."

Thomas hurried the few yards back to join them. "I don't like this," Charles said in a low tone. "We could be adding pressure into a situation we don't understand. We should call the police."

Maggie thought about her interview with Orsini the day before. He'd made it clear he didn't want to hear from her. "We can't just sit on the sidelines. Bad things happen when good people do nothing." She didn't need to prove Daniel's guilt to show the police she was innocent, but it certainly wouldn't hurt.

Up ahead, Daniel stopped to take a photo.

"Well, he's not likely to do anything here," Thomas said. "The tickets for the day are sold out."

"We should stay with him anyway," Maggie said. "Daniel shot Lord Philip in cold blood over some illegal business arrangement. He could be up to anything."

"What are you looking for, exactly?" Thomas asked.

"I don't know," she said. "Anything unusual. We'll know it when we see it." *Hopefully.*

They caught up with the group outside the chapel. It was small and nondescript, flanked by a boxy tower. The effect was strangely un-Roman. It was the green space around the church. Most of the city's churches were squeezed between ancient buildings or surrounded by paved plazas.

The interior was small and dark, with just ten rows of pews facing an altar. The walls glowed with gleaming golden halos, writhing sinners, and smirking Madonnas. There was gilt leaf on the ceiling, and colorful stained glass sparkled in every window.

"The gardens have been open to the public for centuries, but the chapel just reopened." Thomas led the group through the dim room. "Every piece has been restored over the last ten years. And the one we want to see is right here." Thomas stopped in front of a three-paneled painting behind the altar. It showed elegantly dressed women tending a bare-chested man with cloth draped around his shoulders.

The chapel smelled crisp and new. Not a hint of the musty, smoky scent that seemed to define the other churches in the city. Those cleaners had done a good job.

"The Samaritans aiding the traveler on the road to Jericho," Thomas said. "Does this painting look familiar to anyone?"

"It looks like most of the paintings we've seen." Len was right. Strapping young man being tended to by comely women.

"Very good," Thomas said. "In particular, it looks like paintings by

Caravaggio."

"Which one was he?" Len hooked his fingers around his belt loops.

"You saw his *Deposition from the Cross* at the Vatican," Thomas said.

"The one with Jesus being crucified?" Len asked.

Daniel snorted. "I think that describes most of them." He was pacing around the small space, taking photo after photo, as though trying to complete his wife's errand as quickly as possible.

"Art often appears that way when you don't take the time to appreciate it, Daniel." Helen's voice was crisp, in the tone she usually reserved for sparring with her sister. Maggie could imagine her as a teacher, usually easy going, but could rule with an iron fist when necessary. "We've learned many interesting things on this tour that show the differences. Go on, Thomas."

Thomas coughed. "What's important here is that Caravaggio was one of the most widely imitated artists in history. This painting looks a lot like his style, but it doesn't have his psychological intensity."

The writhing man looked awfully intense to Maggie, but she tended to go through museums mentally choosing the pictures she'd want in her own home, mostly sunny landscapes from the 19th and 20th Centuries. Caravaggio never made the cut.

"You're saying it's a fake?" Aldrich had been looking at his phone during most of the tour, and Maggie hadn't been sure he'd been paying attention. But he seemed focused on the conversation now.

"No one knows," Thomas said. "It's not one of his best works, certainly. But it also looks very much like his style. It was hidden under another picture for over a century, and they only found it when they began cleaning. The experts can't agree whether the triptych we're looking at is a bad Caravaggio or something that resembles his stuff."

"Why would the church have a forgery?" Len asked.

"It wouldn't have been considered one." Thomas leaned back on the wooden pew in the first row. "Lots of people painted in Caravaggio's style. He didn't have a studio that churned out students the way other artists did. There were just people who imitated his dramatic lighting and his shadows. They weren't trying to pass themselves off as him. They were just doing their own work."

"Who gets to decide if it's the real thing?" Daniel snapped a photo of a window then turned his attention back to Thomas.

"The decision comes down to the poses, the energy, and the details." Thomas said. "If it were ever sold, they would call its origins contested. The auctioneers would play up the mystery. Gives it a bit of magic and make people feel they have the chance to buy a Caravaggio at a bargain."

Maggie thought of the *White Horse*. George had picked it up for a song, and Faye didn't even want it in her living room. But that was true of everything, wasn't it? We didn't consider something precious until we were told others valued it.

"The provenance over the last few hundred years is rock solid, at least," Thomas said. "It's the pictures that come out of private homes that raise more doubts."

Their voices echoed in the church. Maggie wondered what the early priests who'd overseen the construction of this church would think of it now, a tourist site with visitors talking clinically about the value of the artwork, leaving the religion out entirely.

"Provenance?" Len rubbed his head as though pushing a hat back.

"It's the paper trail associated with a picture to show it's the real thing," Helen said. "There's no question this picture is old, because it has to be older than the picture painted on top of it. Modern forgers have to create the impression of age, making new work look old with scavenged pieces of wood and canvas, artificial aging, things like that."

Eloise laughed. "My sister, the know-it-all. This is Thomas's tour, dear."

Daniel had moved away, toward the baptismal font. He took a picture, the flash temporarily bathing everything in light. "Right, what's next?"

Chapter Eighteen

P rominent bell towers, campanile, *so common in the north, are associated with Rome's smaller churches, often following a Romanesque pattern dictated by the popes of the 12th and 13th centuries.*
—*Masterpiece Tours "Welcome to Rome" pamphlet*

The door to the chapel swung open and five Germans talking loudly walked in.

"Who's going to climb the tower with me?" Shelia asked.

"I'm towered out, hon," Len said.

Shelia had insisted he climb to the top of the dome of St. Peter's and Len said his thighs were still sore.

Eloise and Helen shook their heads, murmuring about sore hips. Charles waved his cane apologetically, and Thomas muttered something about not having a head for heights.

"I'm going to get Vicky's pictures outside." Daniel moved his big black camera from one hand to the other. "I'll just catch a taxi back to the hotel."

"Let me know before you go," Maggie said quickly. "I need to get back early, too. Perhaps we could share."

He shrugged and moved toward the door, with Aldrich close behind.

"Oh goodness, you all are no fun," Shelia said. "Maggie, you'll come with me?"

Charles nodded toward Daniel, and Thomas gave a thumbs-up. They'd keep watch.

It might be good for her to get her bearings from the tower. She and

Shelia found a wooden door labeled *Torre* and pulled it open. A narrow stone staircase curved upward. Shelia puffed gamely on up, but Maggie stopped midway to catch her breath. She didn't have a sense for how far she had left to go. In the dim light, all she could see were stairs winding above her.

Maggie grabbed the iron handrail and climbed the rest of the way. The space at the top was larger than she expected. It could easily hold ten or more tourists, but she and Shelia had it all to themselves, for the time being at least. There were two buses in the parking lot, and tourists clutching cameras and backpacks seemed to be everywhere on the grounds. They would be the German tour group sharing the gardens that day.

"Germany's second invasion of Italy." Shelia was slightly out of breath. "Let's hope this batch is more civilized."

The view of the city really was marvelous. Green patches, where the ancient ruins stood, appeared like islands in the modern city's sea of orange and red roofs. Maggie picked out the big leafy park full of orange trees around the corner from Bonaventura and, further on, the 28-acre ruins of the Baths of Caracalla, a testament to the opulence of ancient Rome. It all looked so peaceful from here, the cars and scooters and throngs of visitors hidden from sight.

Shelia waved energetically to their group below, who all looked quite small from up here. Eloise and Helen were walking slowly across the gardens with their painting gear. Thomas was arranging easels for Len and Charles, and Daniel was snapping pictures nearby. And Aldrich, where was he? Maggie finally spotted him near the entrance, talking with the manager who'd greeted them when they arrived. Probably asking if he was looking for a new lawyer.

"They don't see me." Shelia moved closer to the edge. The wall was, indeed, very low. Shelia reached over the wall, rhinestones on her jeans pockets sparkling as she stretched forward, and waved again.

"Don't get too close," Maggie's heart caught.

"I'm as solid as they come. Not about to lose my head up here."

"Photo?" Maggie was startled by a voice from behind. She hadn't heard anyone come up, but there were two Germans almost on top of them, one holding a phone. Maggie obediently took their picture.

She looked down into the garden again. Daniel was moving faster now, extending the distance between the group and himself. Maggie gave a silent prayer of thanks for the man's colorful wardrobe, which made him easy to spot. "Let's get back down. I need to catch up with Daniel."

Shelia gave her a questioning look but said nothing as they made their way downstairs. It took Maggie a moment to find Daniel again when they emerged from the church, blinking after the dim interior. He was wandering toward a sculpture of a horse balancing on a circus ball. He crouched and snapped some pictures, bumping into a German couple as he got back to his feet.

Maggie caught up, following him toward the back wall, using the garden's sculptures as an excuse to stop and stand when she got too close to her quarry.

A small group stopped Maggie. "Photo?"

She took a nice one of the smiling foursome with the tower in the background and handed the phone back. She turned to where Daniel had been, near a granite sphere. He was gone.

Another couple approached, smiling and holding out another phone. "Photo?" There was a delay while they took off their hats—so many of the Germans wore sun hats—before she could take their picture.

Then a group of five young women asked her and Maggie cut them off impatiently as they tried to tell her how much background to include in broken English and simply snapped their picture. She'd always cursed selfie sticks, but now she wished this group were a little more like the young tourists she saw occasionally whacking other sightseers in the face. Another couple approached, holding a camera, and Maggie hurried off before they could make a request.

When she felt she was a safe distance away, Maggie stopped and scanned the grounds. No yellow sweater. No Daniel. No Charles. She looked over and saw Thomas having an animated conversation with Shelia. Then she caught sight of Daniel walking toward the church. Charles wasn't anywhere to be seen. A group of Germans passed in front of her, blocking her view.

Len approached Maggie. "Thank you for fixing our room situation. Shelia got the best night's sleep of the trip yesterday."

"My pleasure, any time." Maggie was distracted.

Now four Germans passed behind Len, posing for a photo with the horse. Still no Charles. Maybe he had caught up with Daniel inside the church.

He didn't move. "I also wanted to talk with you about the arrangements for Sunday."

Maggie looked down at Len's cowboy boots and took a deep breath before answering. "Sunday?"

"I wanted to visit Duty Free before our flight. Can we get to the airport early?"

Shelia giggled. "Thomas, you're too much. I'm a grandmother, you know!"

"We'll get you there in plenty of time." Maggie strained to keep the tension from her voice. "Why don't you find a nice spot to paint. How about here by the wall?" She rushed off without waiting for an answer. Where was Daniel? Maggie scanned the grounds. No Charles. No Eloise. No Helen. No Aldrich. No Daniel.

It was fine. Of course it was. Daniel hadn't been walking toward the exit. He couldn't slip away from Bonaventura yet. She hurried over to Thomas, who was explaining the difference between Polynesian and aboriginal art.

"Let's give Shelia time to paint, shall we?" Her voice sounded artificially cheery to her ears, like a parent trying to convince a toddler to eat pureed peas.

"What do you think of giving the number seventeen brush a go?" Thomas said. "It paints like a dream—"

"Thomas," Maggie interrupted. "I've lost Daniel."

Realization slowly dawned on Thomas's face. "I'll leave you to it, Shelia, shall I?"

Maggie took his arm and hurried him toward the chapel. "Daniel was heading this way when I lost him. You go into the chapel and see if he's there. If not, climb the tower. You'll have a good view of the grounds. I'll look down here."

Thomas tugged at the scarf around his neck. "I can't do heights."

"You'll be fine." Maggie gave him a push, harder than she'd intended. "Go!"

Thomas strode toward the church, and Maggie moved at a trot, dodging Germans chatting in small groups, while scanning the grounds for Daniel. The ingenious garden design made it impossible to get a good view of the entire place. She looked left and right as she followed the winding paths. Where was he?

She'd search the church. If Thomas was going straight to the tower, she should check the interior. Maggie stepped inside and scanned the room. No sign of Daniel. Maybe he'd gone to the basement to view the crypt. Maggie made her way down the stairs, but it was empty. Maggie hoped Thomas was doing better. Then sharp, high-pitched cries pierced the air.

Maggie hurried up the stairs and outside, The screaming had stopped, but a crowd was gathering nearby. And there, next to a bronze sculpture of a girl turning a cartwheel, was a man in a bright yellow sweater lying spread eagle on the ground.

Daniel was limp, almost deflated. His arms and legs were at an impossible angle, and his head was slightly misshapen. A thin trickle of blood ran out one ear, and his eyes were open, unseeing. Daniel was dead.

Chapter Nineteen

D ial 112 to reach emergency services from anywhere in Europe. Calls are free and can be dialed from any landline, pay phone, or mobile phone.

—*Masterpiece Tours "Welcome to Rome" pamphlet*

Maggie was aware of the hum of excited voices as a crowd gathered around her, but she couldn't make out any words. Her stomach turned over, and she stepped back to catch her breath, bumping into the soft belly of a man behind her.

Thomas stood a few feet away, breathing hard. A middle-aged woman in a pink knitted cardigan patted his back and murmured what must have been the German equivalent of "there there."

Maggie stepped around the crowd to join him. "What happened?" Her heart pounded so loud she didn't think she'd be able to hear his reply. "You checked the tower, didn't you?"

"I couldn't do it, Mrs. W." Thomas's voice was shaky. "I told you, I can't do heights. I got inside the stairway but couldn't climb up. I checked the chapel instead then came out to try to see from here."

They must have just missed each other inside.

"The man fell," a middle-aged woman said in a German accent. "He's dead."

"He was taking a lot of pictures," another woman said. "He wasn't making room. He stepped on my foot." She made it sound like a crime that couldn't be forgiven, even in death.

Maggie thought of the low railing and how uncomfortable she'd been

143

when Shelia stretched out. "Were you with him when he fell?"

The woman shook her head. "Not me. I already came down."

Shelia spoke from the back of the crowd. "What is it, Len? Can you tell?"

Maggie's knees buckled. One minute Daniel was there. The next minute he was, well, not. Thomas put his arm around her. Maggie stood in a daze until uniformed police arrived, shooing everyone toward the parking lot.

Maggie stopped one of them. "The dead man, Daniel Barlow, he was involved in a murder." Maggie's voice caught. "We need Inspector Orsini. He's in charge of the case."

The officer waved Maggie away, but she noticed him picking up his radio. She was suddenly too tired to check whether he'd actually made the call. She allowed Len to guide her to the parking lot, where Charles was standing with John Aldrich and the Potter sisters.

"Is it true?" The hem of Helen's crepe pants floated in the breeze. "Daniel is dead?"

A lump caught in Maggie's throat. She nodded.

"My God." Charles thumped his cane. "I lost sight of him and thought maybe he'd gone to the gift shop, so I doubled back."

The sisters clutched portable stools and easels. They said they'd been painting in the back corner of the estate when a guard informed them the garden was closing. Aldrich said he'd been in the loo when he heard the commotion.

Maggie's head spun. Could this have been a terrible accident? Daniel leaning out too far, trying to get a perfect picture for his sick wife?

"The edge was low," Shelia was saying. "Just like the manager warned us."

Maggie tried to imagine Daniel leaning out over the edge to get a picture for his wife, camera to his eye, then suddenly losing his balance. No, it would be too much of a coincidence.

Could he have been meeting a contact here, after all? Maggie considered it, looking at the Germans gathered in small groups around them. Could Daniel have known one of them? Was someone posing as a tourist? It would be an elaborate cover, traipsing along on a week-long bus tour. Surely drug cartels didn't work that way.

Helen set up her stool and offered it to Charles. He shook his head.

"We left the rest at the entrance," Thomas said. "Should have thought of it sooner. Give me a hand, Johnnie Boy."

The two men managed them all in one trip and arranged the portable stools in a little circle in the dusty parking lot. Maggie was grateful for the shade of a big pine.

"I can't stop thinking about Tancred's uncle." Thomas sat with his elbows on his knees, chin resting in his hands. He looked like a boy.

Maggie was again struck by the difference between him and Aldrich, who looked older after the day's events. She noticed wrinkles around the corners of his eyes.

"Who?" Eloise asked.

"Friend from school," Thomas said. "His uncle fell from a tower in Spain on his honeymoon. I wonder if he looked like that."

"Don't be gruesome," Aldrich said.

"Ignore me," Thomas said. "Just talking for something to say."

They were silent again. Helen's skirt fluttered in the breeze. Eloise appeared strangely at rest without her bag of knitting.

"Looks like we're going to be here a while," Aldrich said finally. "May as well look around."

"And I should let Ilaria know we'll be late for lunch." Thomas reached for his phone and began typing a message.

"You're so considerate, Thomas," Shelia said.

Aldrich read over Thomas's shoulder as he typed. "You're a regular Romeo. I thought she was taken."

Thomas tipped his phone away from Aldrich's view. "We're just friends."

Aldrich shrugged. "If you say so." He strolled off, hands in his pockets. He returned a few minutes later with packets of chips from the gift shop, which was doing a brisk business selling to the stranded tourists.

"Got the last ones." He passed them out.

Maggie opened a bag. The greasy saltiness of her first chip was like an antidote, waking her up from this nightmare. The other guests were coming back to life too.

"Almost had to fight a granny for them," Aldrich was saying. "Though, I suppose, we could have gone to the café."

Several Germans were sitting at tables outside a café across the street. For all its tranquility inside the gates, Bonaventura was in still in the city, with several cafés, a *Pharmacia,* and a *Tobaccheria* across the street. The more enterprising Germans could easily catch taxis back to their hotel rather than wait for the police to officially release their buses.

Maggie remembered Ilaria's cornetti. She silently handed the bag around.

"Poor Vicky." Shelia tore off a piece. "Knowing Daniel died because she asked him to get some photos. Not that it was her fault."

Something was bothering Maggie. Something more than his death—or perhaps less. A detail. Something out of place. She blinked away the image of Daniel lying spread eagle. Then she knew what it was. "Did anyone notice Daniel's camera?"

"What about it?" Charles asked.

"It wasn't there, with his body. It would have fallen, too, wouldn't it? If he'd been leaning out for a shot."

"You can't trust people around crime scenes." Shelia's drawl made it sound like she was settling in for a bit of gossip with e neighbor. "Remember that time in Abilene, Len?"

"Three-car fender bender," Len said. "Someone lifted all the ladies' purses out of the cars while we were exchanging insurance information."

"What are you saying, Maggie?" Eloise's eyes were sharp, like a hawk, circling its prey.

Maggie thought of that camera. Daniel knew she suspected him. He'd heard them talking about prison. Had he put that camera down then climbed up to the edge of the tower on purpose? Had he decided to end everything, rather than face the consequences? Daniel wouldn't be the first person to think he could solve his problems with a fall.

"I don't see how it could have been an accident."

Had Daniel come on the tour today with suicide in mind? Capture pictures for his wife as an apology and then, mission complete, take his own life?

Charles cleared his throat but didn't say anything. Thomas dug the toe of his shoe into the ground. Were they thinking the same thing? If they hadn't been plotting in the kitchen, if Daniel hadn't heard them, he wouldn't have felt cornered, forced to choose between a lifetime in prison and death.

It wasn't Charles and Thomas's burden to carry. Maggie was the one who was snooping around. If she'd left all this alone, Daniel might still be alive. Because he had killed himself because of what he overheard, hadn't he?

Len and Shelia excused themselves to find something to drink, and the Potters joined them, saying they were getting stiff with the sitting. Aldrich turned to Thomas. "What are you going on about?"

"Daniel was the prime suspect," Thomas said. "He heard us talking. And maybe…"

Aldrich crumpled his chip bag. "Lord Philip's case is closed."

Maggie opened her mouth to say the police were ignoring his order and investigating anyway but stopped herself just in time.

Charles explained the theory anyway.

"And you think he killed himself here, rather than face prison?" Aldrich asked.

Maggie felt sick. She hadn't meant for any of this to happen. What was it Aunt Gertrude said? Intentions were irrelevant? It was actions that mattered.

Gertrude. Maggie had forgotten all about arranging for someone to meet her train. She checked her watch. She had an hour. "I'm supposed to meet my husband's aunt at the station."

"Have someone else pick her up." Aldrich began polishing his glasses. "Are you going to finish those crisps?"

Maggie handed him her bag. She'd lost her appetite. But he was right. She stepped away from the men and dialed Burt's phone. There was no answer. He was probably in a meeting. She texted him and stood, staring at the phone, waiting for his reply. No answer.

Why hadn't she gotten Gertrude's phone number from Burt? She'd never have missed that at home. She would have sent Gertrude a message telling her to wait at Café Antica. Now she was stuck, responsible for her husband's aunt on this awful day.

She sighed and called Burt's office. *"Buon giorno,* Lucia. It's Maggie White. Is Burt there, please?"

"Buon giorno, Signora White," said his pert Italian assistant. "No, he's not in today."

"Not in? Of course he's in. He has meetings all day." What was wrong with this woman?

"He's not here, Signora White. Can I give him a message if he calls in?"

"No. Yes. Tell him to call me. It's important." Burt's old assistant in New York, grandmotherly Pauline, would have heard Maggie's voice and known something was wrong. *And* known where Maggie's husband was.

Maggie tried Ilaria next. No answer. How could Maggie have forgotten to arrange for Gertrude's pickup? Was she completely incompetent?

Maggie knew she was getting carried away. A therapist had once told her she had a tendency toward catastrophic thinking. Maggie had always assumed everyone imagined the worst. She tried his tricks for breaking the cycle now. Keep everything in perspective. Don't let ideas snowball.

I'm a highly organized, capable woman. I am a fixer. This is no different.

Maggie took a deep breath and scrolled through her contacts, trying to think of anyone who could pick Gertrude up in her place. Mario and Giovanna would be rushed off their feet at the café. Her landlord certainly wouldn't help. Maggie's eyes fell on Faye's name. She'd be a hypocrite to ask Faye for help after calling the woman vapid. But Burt had been right. Faye had been nothing but friendly to the Whites. Maggie dialed the number, promising herself she'd be more open-minded in the future. Maybe she'd even pass along some of Lucy's peanut butter.

The phone rang for a long time. Just when Maggie expected it to go to voice mail, Faye answered. *"Pronto."*

"Faye, thank goodness. It's Maggie White. I'm in a jam and hope you can do me a favor. Are you busy?" Maggie was clenching the phone and made a conscious effort to relax her hand.

"Why? What do you need?"

"I can't explain now, but I'm trying to find someone to pick up Burt's aunt at the train station. I've tried everyone else I can think of. She's arriving on the two twenty from Paris."

"I don't know, Maggie. I'd love to help, but Termini is all the way across the city."

"Please." Maggie's cheek was hot from the phone pressed so close. "Something really awful has happened, and I can't get away." Maggie heard the television on in the background, Italian voices talking back and forth.

"I'm sorry, Maggie. Another time, maybe."

Maggie threw the phone onto the ground in frustration, sucking in her cheeks to hold back the tears she'd been fighting since seeing Daniel's body. Maggie might as well have pushed the man from the tower herself. So what if he'd killed Lord Philip? So what if he was involved in some drug cartel? She hadn't meant for him to die. Not like this.

Typical of her, rushing in without thinking things through. What, exactly, had she thought would happen? That she'd catch him doing something illegal, turn the information over to the police, and wash her hands of it all?

A tiny yellow sedan turned into the Bonaventura parking lot, and Orsini climbed out. Maggie swallowed. She had to face this head-on. Maggie picked up her phone, undamaged from the fall, thank goodness, and ran to catch the inspector.

Orsini's expression was grim. "Not now, Signora White. The officers called me about an accident. A foreign man involved in the death of another."

"Daniel Barlow. And not an accident." She paused to catch her breath. "I think Daniel killed Lord Philip. He knew I was going to turn him in to you, and he killed himself, instead."

The police radio crackled, filling the long silence before Orsini answered. "Come with me, Signora White."

Orsini sat Maggie in the manager's office while he went out to talk to the officers at the scene. Maggie looked out the window. Two young men in uniforms were talking to her group. They had their notebooks out, probably asking where everyone had been.

Maggie glanced around the room. There was a photo of the manager on the desk, arms wrapped around a family. He was slim and his hair was still dark in the picture. His children would be grown now. Otherwise, the room was impersonal. Just a bare desk and beige walls. Potted plant in the corner. And a picture of some politician on the wall.

Finally, Orsini returned, expression stony. He was going to say she should have stayed out of it. Well, she'd tried to tell him. This wasn't her fault. Maggie straightened her back, wishing she believed that were true.

"Why were you following Daniel Barlow?" Orsini asked.

Maggie blinked. How did this man know that? Then she remembered telling Shelia she needed to catch up with Daniel. And then later being panicked because she couldn't find him. Shelia must have told the officers.

Maggie forced a tight smile. "As I told you yesterday, Inspector, I had reason to believe Daniel Barlow killed Lord Philip. He was setting up some sort of meeting today, and since you weren't prepared to follow up on it, I did. I wanted to find out who he was meeting."

"And you followed him to the tower. And then he, what? Fell over the side by accident?"

"It couldn't have been an accident. His camera wasn't with the body."

Orsini rubbed his hand through his white hair, frowning. Maggie noticed what looked like an egg stain on the cuff. He took a breath mint from his pocket and chewed it loudly. Maggie was aware of the sound of her own breathing while she watched him.

Finally, Orsini spoke. "For once I agree with you, Signora White. I don't believe Daniel fell. I think, perhaps, it is more likely you were in the tower with him. You were, as you say, following him. It would have been easy enough to push him over the edge, would it not?"

Maggie felt like she'd been punched in the stomach. *Stay calm.* She gripped the arms of her chair. She hoped the inspector wouldn't notice how hard she was holding on. She managed to keep her voice steady. "I was in the basement, Inspector. Nowhere near the tower."

"With which witnesses?" Orsini asked.

"Some of the Germans must have seen me…" Maggie heard the sound of a bus engine outside. The Germans would be loading up and on their way to their next sight.

Sitting here meekly answering the inspector's questions wasn't going to change his mind. Maggie needed to go on the offensive and set this man straight. "Inspector Orsini, you seem to have some ridiculous idea I'm responsible for Daniel's death. I'm not. I was following Daniel to do the job you refused to do. And I lost him. I admit that. But Daniel knew we were on to him, and I'm very sorry, but the man killed himself. End of story."

Orsini narrowed his eyes. "Explain yourself."

And she tried to. Orsini listened as Maggie described Daniel's lie about visiting a museum and the phone call she'd overheard. He made a note and muttered about checking the phone records.

"This doesn't look good for you, Signora White. You have no alibi for either death. Tell me one other person here who could have done these crimes."

Thomas had no alibi for Daniel's death, or for Lord Philip's. Maggie opened her mouth to say so then closed it. If Orsini looked into Thomas's background, he'd learn that Thomas had been fired from his job at the auction house for forgery. And if Orsini thought Maggie had a motive, he'd be all over Thomas, probably saying Lord Philip was blackmailing Thomas, too. Ridiculous, of course, but Maggie didn't trust this inspector.

She looked away. If she gave the inspector Thomas as a suspect, he'd get off the crazy idea Maggie was involved. But she couldn't throw Thomas under the bus just to save herself.

Maggie shook her head. She wouldn't sacrifice a friend. And she wouldn't sit around, waiting for the police to clear her name on their own, either. The only option now was to get to the bottom of things herself.

Chapter Twenty

*If Americans can count on death and taxes, Italians can count on dust and
delays when taking the country's rail service.*
—Masterpiece Tours "Welcome to Rome" pamphlet

The guests were gone when Orsini concluded the interview. Thomas had
sent her a text saying they were on their way back to the palazzo. She
checked the time. She could still catch Gertrude's train.

Maggie's taxi pulled up to Termini station five minutes after Gertrude's
train was due. Maggie pushed her Euro at the driver and sprinted up the
concrete stairs. Well, perhaps not sprinted, but she moved as fast as her legs
would carry her. She dodged a group of black-habited nuns and a young
mother walking with a toddler.

She arrived at Aunt Gertrude's track only to find the platform deserted.
For the first time in Italian rail history, the train had been on time. Maggie
bent over, hands on her knees, to catch her breath and decide what to do
next.

"Don't tell me you've taken up yoga."

Maggie straightened.

Aunt Gertrude was bearing down on her, carrying a big floral duffel,
nylon carryall, and a worn shopping bag from Harrods. "Help me with
these." Gertrude's hair was in a flawless grey bob, and she wore a trim
pantsuit. Perfectly put together, despite the long train trip.

Maggie hoisted the carryall to her shoulder. It was heavy enough to have
bars of gold sewn into the seams.

"How are you faring in the City of Light?" Gertrude lead the way across the platform. "Burt's letter said you have another job. How is it back in the lion's den?"

Maggie staggered under the weight for a moment then found her balance. "Not very well, I'm afraid."

"Well, your old job was pretty cushy. All those people reporting to you, you never really had to get your hands dirty, did you?" Gertrude took a deep breath and let it out slowly. "I remember the last time I was in this station. Must have been thirty years ago. My pals and I had to get out of town fast. We caught the first train that pulled in and didn't even bother to see where it was going. We ended up in Romania. Now that was an adventure."

The women emerged onto Via Giolitti, the busy street facing the huge Pizza die Cinquecento in front of the city's main train station. Not the most attractive view in Rome, with cars whizzing, bland concrete, and a few scraggly trees. With the Fascist era railroad station on one side and ruins of the Baths of Diocletian and Servian Wall on the other, it was the real Rome, though. Old and new, housed ear to ear.

"This isn't the City of Light," Maggie said as they passed travelers dragging heavy suitcases. Four teens wearing heavy backpacks were consulting maps.

"What's that, dear?"

"Paris is the City of Light. Rome's the Eternal City." Maggie dropped Gertrude's bags into the trunk of the first available taxi and climbed in. "*Trastevere, per favore.*"

The driver raced into traffic then jammed on the brakes, throwing Maggie and Aunt Gertrude forward. He shouted something at a pedestrian then zoomed forward again.

"Well," Gertrude said. "What's wrong?"

"I killed a man." Maggie braced herself with both hands as the taxi rounded a corner. "Or at least, a man's dead because of me." Despite her pep talk before the interview with Orsini, that was how it felt. If Maggie hadn't come up with the plan to follow Daniel, he wouldn't have felt cornered, wouldn't have committed suicide.

"Not exactly the same thing." Gertrude turned her gaze on Maggie. Her makeup was nearly invisible, brows just so. She looked like a woman in her early 60s, but Maggie knew she was well more than a decade older.

"Near enough."

"Depends on your religion, I suppose," Gertrude held herself in place with the handle above the window as the driver braked hard. "I've been an atheist for a long time now. We're more flexible."

Maggie looked out the window as they circled the immense monument to Victor Emmanuel, the first king of the modern, unified Italy. It had gleaming white columns, larger-than-life chariots on the roof and a general we-love-imperialism feel. Maggie imagined the civic buildings in ancient times looking the same way. Grand. Intimidating. And a little showy.

Now the only visible remains of those days were columns and stubs of building walls. She had a hard time connecting the ancient power with this modern city. She imagined Julius Caesar time-travelling forward. Would he feel as out of step as she did?

Gertrude didn't say anything more until they rumbled across the Tiber. "Well, you must have told me this for a reason instead of asking me about my journey, about the health of Burt's sister, who I saw last month. Her back is much recovered, by the way. Or about my blog, which is going very nicely. What happened?"

Maggie told Gertrude everything. About Lord Philip and his untraceable income. About his swindling George Masters out of the *White Horse* and the threat Ilaria said Pierre made. About John Aldrich shutting down the investigation and, finally, overhearing Daniel making his plans in the studio.

"But before I could tell the police, they came up with a crazy idea that *I* was the one behind it all."

Gertrude laughed. "You? My dear, you must be joking."

Maggie wished Gertrude didn't think the idea was quite so ridiculous. "They think he was blackmailing me. Or was about to."

"Stop speaking in such a roundabout way, Maggie. It's not flattering. Say what you mean."

Maggie took a deep breath. The taxi smelled of old shoes. "I didn't tell people I was let go from Bells & Wallace."

"Oh, my dear…" Apparently Burt hadn't told his aunt that Maggie was let go either. He was such a stickler for the truth, Maggie was touched. "What happened?"

Maggie explained about the department consolidation and losing out to her protégé. "I didn't want to meet everyone here as a housewife. I wanted them to know I was someone real back home. Does that make any sense?"

Gertrude sniffed. "Everyone's real, Maggie. Your job doesn't define you."

The driver turned onto Maggie's street, bumping along the cobblestones. He paused when a cat ran across in front then pulled up at her front door. With many *grazies*, they were left standing on the sidewalk surrounded by Gertrude's luggage.

Gertrude picked up her floral duffel. "What made you suspect this Daniel fellow?"

"The man was the only one of our group downstairs after Eloise heard Lord Philip on the phone. He even lied about where he was one afternoon. His being on this tour only made sense when I realized he was up to something with Lord Philip. And then he heard us saying he was going to prison." Maggie's mouth was dry. "What choice did the poor man have? He killed himself, and it's all my fault."

"I've found it's best not to consider ourselves the center of the universe, Maggie. You may have asked some questions. You may even have said some things you regret. But you didn't push the man off a tower. Don't put that on your conscience."

Maggie picked up the heavy carryall. "You're saying Daniel had freewill. But if I hadn't interfered, he wouldn't be dead."

Gertrude strode up the stairs. "For heaven's sake." Gertrude's voice was impatient. "Don't give yourself so much credit. The man was clearly pushed. Now which door is you?"

Maggie unlocked her door. "Pushed? It was just our group and the Germans."

Maggie dropped the bags onto the floor and rubbed her shoulders while Gertrude made a brief tour of the apartment.

"Well, this is lovely. How about tea?"

Maggie filled a pot of water.

"From everything you've said, that man wasn't the type to off himself at the first sign of trouble." Gertrude opened the door to the balcony and stepped out. "Someone must have shoved him off, Maggie, then disappeared into the crowd when the body was found."

Maggie followed Gertrude. "I considered that. Someone from the cartel going undercover on the German tour group."

Maggie's neighborhood smelled different in the afternoon. Gone were the yeasty baking smells from Café Antica, replaced with the tomato and onion scent drifting out from someone's kitchen. She heard children laughing and the thump of a ball being kicked in the distance. Probably the piazza, the neighborhood's shared living room.

"This city hasn't changed." Gertrude leaned against the railing. "I remember Tillie's gentleman friend lived just off the Spanish Steps. Those were good times."

"Maybe you should go see the building," Maggie said. "Enjoy some of the memories. Who knows, maybe he still lives here."

Gertrude hooted. "No, I'm afraid we may have burned a bridge when we absconded with some of his business papers. Best not to open that can of worms." Aunt Gertrude had so many stories it was hard to keep track of them.

"This was the casino owner?"

"Good heavens, no. That was Nice. This was the gentleman with all the horses. I'll tell you another time."

Maggie thought of the guests back at the palazzo. She stepped into the bathroom to splash water on her face and reapply her lipstick. Maggie tried to tell herself Gertrude was right. Maggie might have made some bad decisions, but this wasn't her fault. She'd try to remember that.

Maggie gave herself one last look in the mirror. She tugged on her skirt, wishing it weren't quite so wrinkled.

Gertrude was sitting on the couch with her feet up when Maggie came back into the living room. She had her tablet out and was busy typing.

"Will you be here long?" Maggie asked.

"I leave Friday night." Gertrude took a sip of her tea. "You know the saying, fish and guests start to smell after three days. Have you considered that Daniel didn't kill your Lord Philip?"

"You think the cartel killed both of them?"

"The cartel theory feels a bit artificial. I wonder if the Germans weren't involved at all."

Typical Gertrude. Put an idea out there then shut it down, as if she hadn't suggested it in the first place. "What are you saying?"

"Someone killed these unpleasant men. Odds are it was one of your guests."

Maggie caught a taxi to the palazzo. As the car waited at a long light, she thought of her suspicions about Daniel. The lying about his whereabouts, the furtive phone call, and the cartel. She'd been so sure she was right, but Gertrude had shaken her confidence.

Should she tell the police what else she'd learned about Lord Philip? About the *White Horse*, Pierre, and the history of blackmail and swindling? Maggie wasn't sure it was still relevant. Or if Orsini would be interested in hearing any of it from his prime suspect.

She thoughtlessly took a sip of coffee from her thermos then grimaced. She must have burned the beans in her hurry to find Daniel this morning.

Gertrude's suggestion that it was someone in their group didn't leave many possibilities. Len and Shelia were in sight when Daniel died, and neither had left the terrace during the fireworks. Charles had been out of sight when Daniel died, and he *had* helpfully asked about the investigation, always suspicious in books. But he never left the terrace the night of Lord Philip's death, ruling him out unless he was working with an accomplice.

Maggie hated sitting here, thinking of these lovely people as potential murderers. Who next? The Potter sisters? Gertrude would jump on the fact they had no alibi for Daniel's death. Maggie smiled, imagining the women working as hit men in some kind of criminal enterprise. Maybe all that cat talk was an act too.

The driver honked his horn then changed lanes and raced forward. Maggie played with the strap of her backpack, rolling the strap between her thumb and forefinger.

That left just Thomas and John Aldrich at Bonaventura that day. Thomas was Thomas, of course. She knew men like him. They didn't bother worrying about problems. They simply floated from one thing to the next, confident that everything would sort itself out.

But John Aldrich...Maggie reflexively took a sip from her thermos again before remembering how awful it was. John Aldrich had chosen the very day Daniel died to join in the sightseeing. He'd actually been out of sight when Daniel fell. And he had gotten to Rome awfully fast after his client's death.

It was, perhaps, possible he'd flown in on the earliest flight, assuming his office had been notified of Lord Philip's death in the middle of the night. But wasn't it also possible, more likely even, that he'd already been in Rome when Lord Philip died?

Maggie felt a flicker of excitement. Aldrich could have been on the scene on *Natale di Roma* and arranged a meeting with Lord Philip that ended in her boss's death. No one had seen Aldrich, so he could pretend to arrive the following morning. His mistake was coming too soon.

Maggie paid the driver and stood outside the palazzo a moment, organizing her thoughts. She remembered Aldrich's endless lists and questions. Maybe that insistence on counting paper clips was just a cover, to keep her away from the real issues of the business. Aunt Gertrude said details were the best disguise there was. "Flood 'em with paperwork, if you're ever in a jam. Ten to one they'll never find the missing invoice." She'd been talking about embezzling funds, but the logic still held.

Should Maggie tell Orsini? She had no evidence, not even a theory. Just an inkling, a feeling she might be on to something. Unless she had something concrete, he'd think she was coming up with suspects to distract attention from herself. No, what Maggie needed was proof.

Chapter Twenty-One

Rome's narrow cobblestone streets make owning a car impractical. Many citizens opt for the "motorino," a motor scooter. Be advised, drivers of these vehicles consider themselves outside the rules governing motorcars. One-way streets are a suggestion. Sidewalks are fair game. And any space between two cars is a designated scooter lane.

—Masterpiece Tours "Welcome to Rome" pamphlet

Aldrich wasn't inside the palazzo.

Thomas said he left Bonaventura as soon as the police released them. "Apparently Johnnie Boy wanted to get to work on the liability side of things. Sounds like he may try to make a case for Vicky to sue Bonaventura. Or perhaps to defend Masterpiece, if she decides to go after us."

Thomas was on the terrace with the guests. It was nearly four, but the remnants of their late lunch were still sitting on the buffet. A slice of meat here, a stray piece of bread there. Not enough left to know what the meal had been. Maggie was ravenous. She hadn't eaten anything since breakfast, except a few potato chips and a bite of cornetto. She took a plate and scavenged a few grapes and a slice of pear from the fruit tray.

The group was somber. Len reported that Vicky was holed up at the hotel and didn't want any visitors. "Broken up on top of being knocked down with her stomach."

Len's voice had lost its usual enthusiasm. He was frowning, hands fidgeting. The guests were all gloomy. Shelia's tote bag lay untouched at her feet. Thomas played with a spoon. Helen and Eloise weren't even bickering. And Charles was staring off into the distance. Was he thinking about his wife's death?

Maggie pushed her plate away. She remembered the awful time when a coworker had died in a car accident. Everyone had walked on eggshells for a week, and Maggie had felt guilty rifling through his files to get the status on an important project.

Maggie shook herself back to the present. The guests couldn't spend the rest of the trip mourning these two men they had barely known. "We've been through the ringer the last few days, but I know I speak for Vicky and Lord Philip's family when I say we owe it to their memories to enjoy ourselves. What do you say?"

"I do need fresh air," Eloise said cautiously. "Perhaps a walk?"

Her sister nodded. "I could use a change of scene."

"I was hoping to see the Museum of Modern Art," Shelia said. "Perhaps it would be good to have a little distraction. What do you say, Len?"

Maggie swallowed, thinking of Daniel's claim to have visited the museum on Monday and how it had led her to her conclusions. Could he have been meeting John Aldrich instead? If the lawyer was behind all this, there must be some connection between the two men. Had they been in league together?

Charles and Thomas stayed with Maggie on the terrace.

"I'm sorry I lost him," Charles said when the others had departed. "This leg." He tapped his cane against his knee.

"It's not your fault," Maggie said.

Charles shook his head. "I might have stopped him."

Charles thought Daniel had killed himself. She was about to tell him Gertrude's theory when she stopped. She trusted Charles, of course she did. But he'd been out of sight when Daniel died.

Maggie held her tongue. She wouldn't help anything by sharing her ideas again.

Maggie walked to the hotel after making herself a sandwich in the palazzo kitchen. She needed to pay her respects to Vicky, even if the poor woman had told Len she didn't want visitors.

Maggie rode the elevator to the top floor and followed a frayed red carpet to the end of the hall, which terminated at a battered door opening onto a fire escape. Maggie peered out a window. Several employees smoking cigarettes lounged next to three large dumpsters. Maybe Daniel's complaints about the noise hadn't been so unreasonable.

Vicky's room was the last door on the left. Maggie fluffed her hair and knocked loudly. The widow opened it a moment later, blond hair mussed and eyes rimmed red. The room was very dark, shades drawn and just one dim light. Clothes covered the floor, and Maggie could make out the bed behind Vicky, a mess of sheets, tissues, and magazines.

The young woman sniffed. "Come in." Her accent was less refined than usual. Less BBC, more, well, whatever the less refined British accents were. She'd said she was from East London. Daniel's death had shaken off some of her veneer.

"I'm so sorry." Maggie gave her a hug.

Vicky squeezed her back.

"Is there anything at all I can do?"

"I don't suppose you can keep that beastly policeman away from me?" Vicky gave a hollow laugh as she pulled away. "I know it's silly, but that inspector was asking all kinds of questions. Whether Daniel was in any kind of money trouble. Whether he'd been depressed. The inspector doesn't seem to think what happened to Daniel was an accident."

"You think it was?"

"What else could it be?" She dabbed a crumpled tissue at her eyes. "He knew how disappointed I was to miss Bonaventura, and he offered to take photos for me of everything. I'll never get over it."

"It was his idea to go?"

"He was such a thoughtful man. Oh, I know he wasn't particularly charming on this tour. But you didn't know him. He was considerate. Loving. Everything a woman could want." She choked back tears. "And now he's gone."

Maggie put her arm around the young woman's shoulders. "I know you can't imagine life without him, but you're strong. You'll get through this."

Vicky looked at her, blue eyes pleading. "You really think so?"

"I do."

They sat on the bed, Vicky's hands gripping the coverlet. Her fingers were ghostly white against the red fabric. "It was almost as if the police thought Daniel killed himself, but he would never have done that. His life insurance policy wouldn't pay out if…if he did that. It was brand new. And he wouldn't let a big insurance company get the best of him."

Maggie hesitated. "I do wonder…"

Vicky looked at her with her bloodshot eyes. "Yes?"

"Two deaths in three days. That seems a coincidence." Maggie stood to open the drapes. The sky was overcast. Rain was forecast for tomorrow. She hoped it would hold off. "Could there be a connection?"

"Between Daniel and Lord Philip? How could there be?" Vicky blew her nose again.

"Could Daniel and Lord Philip have known each other? Before the tour, I mean?"

"The inspector asked me the same thing. No. The tour was my idea."

"Did Daniel know anyone else before? Maybe John Aldrich?"

Vicky looked confused. "The lawyer? Just because he got me confused with someone else?"

Maggie had forgotten Aldrich had said Vicky looked familiar when they met the morning after Lord Philip's death. She'd written it down to Vicky's generic beauty. Long blond hair. Wide blue eyes. Almost a carbon copy of the celebrities grinning on the covers of magazines today.

"I'm just trying to understand it all." Maggie paused, trying to make her next question sound natural. "Do you know what Daniel was doing on Monday? He said he went sightseeing, but the museum he said he visited is closed on Mondays."

"He lied so he could call the office, of all things." Vicky dabbed her eyes. "I told him to relax and spend less time working. He pretended to go to a museum, but I came home and found him on one of his conference calls." Her voice rose an octave, and she blew her nose again.

Maggie stepped away from the window and stumbled over an open suitcase. A jewelry bag the size of an envelope slid across its bottom. It was unzipped and a gold bracelet slipped out. The same bracelet Vicky had said pickpockets had stolen. Maggie looked up and saw Vicky blush.

"Don't hate me." Vicky put her hand out for the bag. "I told Daniel I lost it to get him to buy me something special. He wasn't paying a lot of attention to me, and this was the only thing I could think of." Her eyes welled up again. "But now it just feels petty."

Maggie had underestimated this girl. Vicky had more spunk, albeit misguided, than she had given her credit for. "Do you really think Daniel's death was an accident, Vicky?"

Vicky looked at the jewelry bag and started fiddling with the zipper. Maggie resisted the urge to fill the silence. It was a trick she'd used in her last go-round with the candy buyer at their biggest account. Maggie had let the silence drag on until Cindy Ballaroo agreed to give Bells & Wallace more promotional space and a secondary location in the toy aisle, an unheard of consideration for a brand like the one Maggie managed.

"I didn't want to say anything before but, well, there was one thing." Vicky appeared to be thinking something through.

Maggie's heart thumped. She gave an encouraging nod.

"I'm afraid Daniel might have been doing something, well, something he shouldn't have." Vicky played with her hair, winding and unwinding it around her finger.

Finally, she pushed it behind her ears, as though she'd made a decision. "I saw part of a text on Monday night. It was something like, 'You'll meet me if you know what's good for you.' I didn't tell the police because, I don't know, it makes Daniel sound bad, doesn't it?"

Maggie's mind raced. It sounded like George Master's version of events when Lord Philip got the *White Horse* away from him. A threat. Blackmail. *Slow down.* The police would be looking at Daniel's call history. If there was something to find, they'd find it. Unless Daniel deleted his messages.

Daniel had a big ego and a greedy personality. Was she right that Aldrich killed Lord Philip? And then Daniel had simply stumbled onto an opportunity and taken it.

Maggie thought of John Aldrich, who Thomas had said was ruthless on the rugby pitch. He wouldn't have put up with a blackmail attempt. He'd have eliminated the threat. Maggie remembered Aldrich and Thomas reminiscing about their friend whose uncle fell to his death. Could that have given him the very idea of pushing Daniel, hoping it would look like an accident?

"Is it possible Daniel saw something the night Lord Philip died?" Maggie asked. "Something he was hoping use to his advantage?"

Vicky nodded miserably. "I don't see another way around it."

"You've got to tell the police." Maggie's heart pinged with excitement.

If Daniel had been blackmailing the killer, that would put her in the clear. Daniel was already back upstairs when she found Lord Philip's body.

Vicky drew in a breath. "And tell them my husband was a blackmailer? That he knew who killed Lord Philip and tried to profit from it?"

"It's the only way they'll get to the bottom of this, Vicky. I'll stay while you make the call."

After dinner, Maggie accepted Thomas's offer of a ride home. The air was cooler tonight, and Maggie pulled her sweater tighter around her as they walked to his scooter. She'd told him and Ilaria about Vicky's call to the police, but she waited to share her suspicions about Aldrich until she and Thomas were alone. The two men were friends, and she put it off as long as she could, but when they found the scooter, she had to speak. "How well do you know John Aldrich?"

"Johnnie Boy?" Thomas bent down to unlock the heavy chain around the yellow bike's front tire. "Our families go way back. Grandmothers were debs together back when things were pretty flush. Still, my family hasn't had it as bad as Johnnie Boy's."

"Don't you find his arrival a little suspicious?"

Thomas looked at her blankly. "Suspicious? He's a go-getter. Always has been."

Maggie explained her theory, but Thomas shook his head.

"Trust me. Johnnie Boy isn't the one we're looking for. Now, let's get home. It's been a bloody awful day."

Maggie climbed awkwardly into place and wrapped her arms around Thomas's waist. It was difficult to see with the heavy helmet over her head, and sounds were muted. She felt a bit like an astronaut as they whizzed toward the river.

It wasn't until they crossed into Trastevere that she asked herself where, exactly, her husband had been all day. Burt had taken more than an hour to respond to her texts this afternoon, and then it was just, **In meetings. Talk tonight.** Yet, this man, too busy to call his wife, was out of the office all day, according to his assistant. For all her faults, Burt's Italian assistant was very efficient. Not the sort to mislay her boss.

Thomas accelerated around a corner and veered hard to the left, avoiding two young women smoking outside a bar. Burt had been avoiding her all day. It was completely out of character for him to not return a call. What was Burt keeping secret? Maggie thought of his prickliness over Daniel's infidelity the night before. Maggie didn't worry about Burt. Not really. But he looked different these days. Slimmer. Taking more care with his clothes. And he'd done something with his hair. He looked younger, more handsome.

Thomas crossed through the Piazza Santa Maria, where groups of young people were smoking and drinking beer. There were some families out, children playing a game of tag while their parents talked. An older man sold light sticks and another demonstrated a spinning top.

It was busy for a Wednesday night; then Maggie remembered the next day was Liberation Day. Schools and public offices would be closed. Lots of Italians would take Friday off, as well, to make it a long weekend. No wonder they were out late.

Maggie said a distracted goodbye to Thomas and took the stairs to her apartment as quickly as she could. The French students were having a party. Music and the scent of marijuana had slipped under their door into the hall.

Maggie threw open her door and found Burt on the couch, laptop open on his lap. He took off his reading glasses, and put down the papers he was holding. "Sorry, hon, still finishing up. The Swiss asked about the basis of the projections for the Lagurno project, and I'm still crunching numbers."

His hair was wet. He never showered at night. The knot in her stomach tightened. "Where were you today? I called the office when I couldn't get you, and your assistant said you weren't in." She tried to keep her voice even, but she heard her tone rising. Why were her eyes filling with tears? She ordered herself to keep it together.

Burt rubbed the bridge of his nose. "I wasn't in. We were at the bank. That's what made it so hard. Their firewall was causing all kinds of problems. Had to keep calling the office asking them to look things up. I'm sorry for not calling sooner. You weren't worried, were you?"

His eyes were anxious, concerned.

Relief flooded Maggie's body. "Not at all," she lied. "I just didn't know where you were."

That damn assistant. *Not in.* Any decent assistant would have known what Maggie meant and not been so literal. After all these years, she was flying off the handle. It must be all this time thinking about Daniel and his missteps.

"Let's go for a walk," Maggie said.

They used to walk around their neighborhood at home every night, hand in hand, no particular direction in mind.

Burt looked as if he were going to say no, then he threw his pencil down. "Great idea. I have to go into the office tomorrow anyway—the Swiss don't seem to think Italian holidays apply—so another hour tonight won't make a difference. Gertrude is still out, but she has a key."

Soft music mingled in the narrow streets as they walked into the maze around their apartment, Paul Simon coming from one window, some classical Italian opera out of another. Maggie told Burt about Orsini's suspicions about her and following Daniel and, finally, his death. Burt squeezed her hand, not saying she was overreacting or that she should leave it to the police or that she should have told him sooner.

Maggie snuggled closer to Burt. His coat was soft against her cheek. She sniffed. What was that scent? Perfume? She breathed in again, but she couldn't place it.

Chapter Twenty-Two

Experts say as much as one half of the art on the international market may be fake, and museums bear much of the responsibility. They need sensational pieces to boost ticket sales, and they are sometimes too quick to suppress doubts about the provenance of their finds.
—Masterpiece Tours "Welcome to Rome" pamphlet

Walter Jones called not long after Maggie arrived at the palazzo the next morning. She held the phone to her ear as she struggled out of her wet jacket. The rain had started sometime after midnight. Maggie had still been awake, staring at her ceiling, trying to think of an innocent explanation for perfume to be on Burt's clothing. She'd finally fallen asleep after Gertrude came in and clattered around the kitchen, looking for a snack. Burt was gone when Maggie woke at seven thirty.

The heavy rain meant there were no free taxis, and Maggie's umbrella flipped inside out in a gust of wind as she crossed the river. The buses were running on the weekend schedule due to the Liberation Day holiday, and she had been squished tight against other wet riders when she finally caught one.

"I have some rather interesting news to share about the *White Horse*." Walter's voice was high and excited.

Maggie shifted the phone to her other hand and tried to fluff her wet hair.

"I'd like to come by before Faye's luncheon. Can you arrange for the lawyer fellow representing the estate to be there?"

Maggie promised to try. Rain beat on the windows and her clothes were damp. She should have brought an extra sweater. She pondered what to do about John Aldrich. The first thing would be to check his story about arriving the morning after Lord Philip's death. Maggie searched flights from London to Rome. The first one didn't arrive until 10 a.m. *Got him!* Maggie clicked the browser shut with satisfaction. It must have been eight or nine when Aldrich arrived at the palazzo—a physical impossibility in air travel. Now the question was how to suggest the inspector do the same simple search?

A voice called from the hall. It was Faye's husband, George, who was leading the tour for Masterpiece that day to the Basilica of St. Mary of the Angels and Martyrs. Ilaria had already left to do the shopping, and the guests were in the studio with Thomas. Maggie was glad George would be gone before Walter arrived. He didn't need to know what kind of fortune he'd given away, at least not yet.

"I spoke to a colleague at the university who studies coins. He has some interesting things to say about the ones recovered from the Basilica and is going to meet us." George shook water from his coat and leaned a soggy umbrella against the coat rack. George looked different than when she'd seen him last, relaxed almost. His face was less puffy, the veins on his nose weren't quite so prominent. Lord Philip's death had been good news for him.

What secret had Lord Philip held over him? Stealing another academic's ideas? Cheating at bridge? Having a crazy first wife locked up in an attic?

"I know coins aren't strictly art, but my friend is chock full of facts. Did you know Julius Caesar was the first living individual to appear on a Roman coin? Before that it was just portraits of ancestors. But Cesar turned Roman money into a mini-propaganda machine." He paused, "That is, if you think your guests would be interested."

Maggie hated that these deaths made her think the worst of everyone. It was none of her business. "That sounds perfect. You've really gone above and beyond, George."

She hung his wet coat for him.

He lowered his voice. "I don't suppose you've heard anything from the lawyer?"

Maggie shook her head. Best to say nothing at this point. Could George bring some sort of lawsuit against the estate to get the picture back? Come clean about whatever it was Lord Philip had on him and say he was blackmailed into giving the *White Horse* away?

"I like your scarf." Maggie hung the tartan fabric over the trench coat. It looked just like the one she'd given Burt when they'd first married. Maggie felt a pang, thinking of how innocent she and Burt had been then. Everyone had said marriage was difficult, of course. But she never thought her marriage would have any problems.

She looked closer. George's scarf was missing half its tassels on one end, just like Burt's. "My goodness, don't tell me a vacuum cleaner tried to eat yours, too?"

"Oh, I don't think so…" He glanced down and touched the ends. "Well, look at that. My scarf is green, and brand new. Probably got it mixed up at the party the other night."

Maggie remembered reminding Burt to bring extra layers to Faye's party.

George insisted Maggie take it back to Burt. "I'm sure mine's back at the house somewhere."

She led him down the hall to the studio, where Thomas was leading a session with the guests.

"Mastering the paint-to-water ratio is one of the greatest challenges in water color." Thomas was standing next to a canvas covered with streaks of purple vibrating on yellow. The artists had their own smears of color on their canvasses.

"Don't try to paint a picture of anything right now, just play with the ratios and see what happens. Remember, a syrupy consistency is your workhorse. Go thinner for tints and glazes. Go thicker when you want opacity."

Thomas was dressed simply today, just a dark shirt and dress pants. Maggie wondered if he was too shaken by Daniel's death to choose something more creative. He joined Maggie and George in the back of the room, while the painters made their streaks and dabs. After a few minutes, Thomas introduced George and began moving the group out into the hall.

"I need to stay behind," Maggie murmured to Thomas when George was out of earshot. "Walter's coming back with news on the *White Horse*."

"No trouble, I hope?" Helen was still at her easel, jotting notes. She wore a tunic over wide-legged pants today, and her long grey hair was tied in a loose braid. Maggie could imagine her living in an some artist's colony in New Mexico, the aging earth mother who people came to with their problems. She must have excellent hearing to have caught Maggie's, though.

"Oh no, just some paperwork."

Helen put her pencil down. "I'm feeling a bit tired this morning, and I don't relish the thought of going out into the rain again. I think I'll stay, too, and work on my painting."

Maggie was relieved someone else would be here. Walter Jones was scheduled to arrive at ten, and Maggie had told Aldrich to come at ten fifteen, but people never seemed to arrive when you expected them. And Maggie somehow felt safer knowing this old woman would be in the apartment with her.

Maggie set Helen up with a cup of coffee and retreated to her office to call the hotel. "How are you holding up?" Maggie asked when she was connected with Vicky.

"I'm going a bit mad, to tell you the truth." Vicky sniffed. "I can't face everyone, not yet, but perhaps I could escape to the palazzo this morning, just for a change of scene. You'll be leaving on the tour soon?"

"The group already left, so it's Helen and me here." Maggie thought of Walter and John Aldrich due in an hour. "But the lawyer will be here soon, and the appraiser." The prospect of Aldrich facing his victim's widow made her stomach turn over.

Vicky sighed. "No, I don't think I'm up to see anyone. Maybe tomorrow would be better."

Maggie felt a small flush of relief. She hung up the phone and tried to occupy herself until Walter's arrival. She glanced at the weather forecast. Sunny in Rome tomorrow, thank goodness. The tour was going to Tivoli's Villa d'Este gardens, which would be impractical in the rain. Maggie made her daily check of the international forecasts, as well. She felt more connected, somehow, being able to imagine her children wearing heavy coats when the weather was cold and carrying umbrellas when there was rain.

Then she put a fresh ream of paper in the printer and sharpened her pencils. Maggie was keenly aware of the ticking of her watch. Finally, the hands reached ten and there was a knock at the front door. Walter stood in the doorway, gripping his portfolio. He wore a pink bow tie that perfectly matched his crisp pocket square. His shoes gleamed, despite the rain-soaked streets he must have crossed, and his face was practically glowing. Maggie thought of George. It looked like he had lost a fortune after all.

"Mr. Aldrich hasn't arrived yet." Maggie lead Walter into the dining room.

He followed with his awkward shuffle, dragging his left foot slightly as he walked. He set the folio carefully on the polished table, squaring it in front of him but leaving it zipped.

Aldrich bustled in as Maggie poured Walter a second cup of coffee. He unbuttoned his double-breasted jacket and put his hands into his pants pockets. He looked relaxed and confident. Definitely sinister. "What do you have for me?"

Walter stood and unzipped the portfolio then gently lifted the canvas.

Aldrich leaned in. "Not my style, but people like old stuff, don't they? Well, what's it worth?"

"Not a penny." Walter rubbed his hands together. "I'm sorry to inform you the great Lord Philip was duped at last."

Aldrich slapped his hand on his yellow pad of paper. "Are you having us on? I don't have time for some kind of joke. Not after everything that's happened." He seemed almost genuinely concerned about the picture and the estate.

Walter put on a more serious expression. "No, Mr. Aldrich. I'm afraid not. This picture isn't worth the canvas it's painted on."

Maggie tried to make sense of his words. "But you said it was a masterpiece."

"Not exactly, Mrs. White." Walter's cheeks were pink. "I said Walpole *believed* it was an Abbati. In which case yes, it would have been worth a fortune. This, however, is no Abbati."

It was raining harder now, water splashing against the room's large windows.

"This authentication business is all subjective, isn't it?" One of the dining room's large pendant lights shone right on Aldrich's receding hairline. He looked even more bull-headed than usual. "We'll get a second opinion."

"Certainly, but they'll tell you the same thing." Walter put his hand gently on the picture, short fingers discolored from too many cigarettes. "May I explain?"

Aldrich snorted, but he waved Walter on.

"His lordship told me he acquired a lost painting by Giuseppe Abbati. One of Italy's early impressionists. Said it was picked up at an estate sale in the country. Had probably been in some family's attic for years. Perhaps someone put it up there and forgot about it." He bowed slightly toward Aldrich. "It's not to everyone's taste, as you said."

Maggie wouldn't want the picture in her living room. She preferred images that were more cheerful, that you could match the drapes to.

Walter interlaced his fingers comfortably over his round stomach as he settled into his theme. "And at first glance, the composition is highly suggestive. It certainly harkens to Giuseppe Abbati's *Oxen & Cart* and *Horse In Sunlight*. And there is record of a painting called the *White Horse—Cavallo Bianca*—from an eighteen sixty exhibit, then nothing more. There was a lot of turmoil then uprisings—"

Aldrich rolled his hand in a "hurry it up" gesture.

"And that turmoil is important for the provenance of the picture. For its value. It wouldn't be at all unusual for a picture to go missing during that time. We cannot dismiss Walpole's theory that some family popped it into an attic and forgot about it."

Walter paused to take a sip of coffee. His hand shook slightly as he set the cup down.

"You're telling us why it's worth a fortune," Aldrich said. "Not why it's not."

Aldrich was an impatient man. Someone more careful, more calculating, would have planned Lord Philip's death with more discretion. And Daniel's death, too, showed a certain bull-headedness. Killing a blackmailer rather than giving in to his demands. And that fit with the ruthless young man Thomas had played rugby with.

Walter shook his head. "A moment please, Mr. Aldrich. Abbati's style was all about light effects. He's known for landscapes seen through a dark doorway or window. Or light bouncing off animals in a dark alley. This picture fits. I can understand why Walpole may have thought he had a treasure. At least at first glance." Aldrich sighed, loudly. "There is more to authentication than simple composition. There's technique. And that's where it all goes wrong."

There was a tap at the door and Helen poked her head in. "Am I interrupting something? I heard voices and thought Ilaria might have come. I was looking for a little more cream." The filmy sleeve of her tunic brushed the table as she leaned in closer. "The *White Horse*. Is it worth the fortune Lord Philip hoped?"

Aldrich pursed his lips. "Did you need something else, ma'am?"

Helen shook her head vaguely. "No, no. Well, I won't interrupt you any longer."

Aldrich made a point of looking at his watch when Helen left the room. "Can we get on with it? You were saying?"

Walter's small eyes shone. "This picture isn't very good. The brushstrokes are hurried. There's no sense of movement. It's an amateur effort, at best." He leaned forward. "To be honest, I'm a little surprised Walpole didn't pick up on that himself. But then again, he wasn't a professional, despite his occasional success in the field."

Maggie thought of all the special art exhibits she'd taken her children to over the years. Making sure they had a healthy dose of culture, even if they would all have preferred to stay home and watch television. "Couldn't it have been a sketch or first effort? I've seen those sketches by Picasso. They're worth a fortune and don't even look like anything."

Walter shook his head. "That would have been quite different."

What was it Thomas had said at Bonaventura the day before? That experts couldn't know for sure if the picture in the chapel was a bad Caravaggio or someone just trying to use his style. "Isn't it possible it's just a bad Abbati?"

"The real issue is the paint," Walter said.

Aldrich slammed his hand on the table. "The paint? For bloody sake."

Walter gently pressed a blob of white paint in the corner with a stubby finger. "It's not dry."

Aldrich sank back.

"Someone's artificially aged the paint, a hair dryer is my guess. It's solid enough to pass a quick glance, but oils take years to dry fully. Walpole was, if I may say this without sounding impolite, a bit lazy. He was a dabbler. This acquisition was an error in his lordship's judgment."

Aldrich leaned his chair back, the two front legs lifting off the ground. A lazy smile spread, revealing a small chip on the corner of his front tooth. "Too bad Walpole wasn't alive to hear this report. Might have taken him down a peg or two."

"Mr. Aldrich!" This was the last thing Maggie expected.

Kill the man, maybe, then publicly criticize him? The lawyer was tipping his hand.

"Oh, I'm sorry for Old Neddy and all that," Aldrich rocked his chair back onto all fours. "It would've been nice for him to net a fortune from that painting. But Walpole swindled enough people in his time. Bound to catch up with him eventually."

Lord Philip had boasted about that picture to everyone. Aldrich made it sound as though this wasn't a failure of the eye but an intentional trick someone had played on Lord Philip.

"Well, if there isn't anything else." Walter zipped his folio closed.

Aldrich clapped the appraiser on the shoulder. "I'd appreciate it if you keep this between us. Last thing we need is for the value of his other pictures to come into question before the estate is dissolved. Now I need to get back to work." He opened the door and looked back over his shoulder. "Mrs. White, I'm taking over the office for the present."

Alone with Aldrich. Maggie felt a flash of unease then reminded herself Helen was here too, and Ilaria would be back soon. And then guests. It would be fine.

She would prepare for the visit to Tivoli the next day. Neither she nor Thomas had visited the gardens before. As Maggie walked with Walter to the front door, slowing her pace to match his awkward gait, she had an inspiration. Walter, she remembered from her dinner with him, was a gardener.

"Your schedule must have opened up, with this project completed so quickly."

"Oh, yes, I had the entire week blocked off for it," Walter said. "Not to say it was a fast job. I spoke with a number of experts so I'd be ready even before I picked the picture up."

"I hoped you might help with something else," Maggie said. "A favor, really. We're in a bit of a mess without Lord Philip. We need an expert for the actual tours, someone who can educate the guests. And when you explained about the *White Horse* in such a clever way, I thought perhaps you could assist us. You know the gardens of Tivoli?"

He preened a bit. "Well, certainly I have a working knowledge of the gardens. More than the usual amateur."

She gave him her most persuasive smile, the one with the lots of teeth, eyes crinkled at the corners, and eyebrows raised just so. It worked in every meeting with the CEO. Well, up until the last one, when he told Maggie her department was being given to someone else. "I was thinking a morning with the guests, to share your local knowledge." He hesitated, and she went in for the kill. "The guests are very well off. Perhaps one of them might decide to buy a picture from you as a souvenir."

"When?"

"Tomorrow," Maggie said. "The forecast is perfect."

Walter pursed his lips. "I'm not sure… I'm very busy."

"There must be something." Maggie's voice was light, almost teasing.

"Well, there is one thing. You take my place at Faye's bridge parties."

Maggie had stayed away from the bridge scene at home. Smart women sitting around playing cards instead of doing something valuable with their time. She thought of Burt saying Walter left Faye's early. Did the art dealer get tired of Faye's endless parties, too? "I thought you were friends."

"We are, but I'm partnered with Bernadette. She insists on using the Dutch Doubleton bidding system. I can't take it any longer."

Maggie knew enough about bridge to know complicated bidding conventions were often a cover for poor play. "Why don't you tell her it's outdated and unnecessarily complicated?"

"She's a customer. I can't offend her." He leaned closer and Maggie smelled the tobacco mixed with coffee on his breath. "That's my offer, Mrs. White. Take Bernadette off my hands, and I'll be glad to take the tour off yours."

Maggie heard Helen in the studio down the hall, humming softly as she worked. Maggie sighed. He was right. She needed him more than he needed her. "Fine. But just one party."

"Four." He buttoned his coat. "Take it or leave it."

He had more pluck than she'd given him credit for. But then, the art market was tough. He probably couldn't make a living without being a little cutthroat himself.

"That's outrageous," Maggie whispered. "I'm asking for three hours of your time. I'll go twice."

He shook his head.

"Three times?"

Walter shook her hand. "I'll let Bernadette know to expect you."

Chapter Twenty-Three

*R*ome is a delight in the rain. Outdoor sights are less crowded, cafés are welcoming, and travelers can take comfort in the knowledge that rain typically clears in the afternoon, leaving behind wide skies and glorious sunsets.

—*Masterpiece Tours "Welcome to Rome" pamphlet*

Maggie lingered at the top of the stairs, listening for the street door to close behind Walter. Instead, she heard him offering a greeting and footsteps climbing toward her. Maggie leaned out over the railing and saw Ilaria on the stairs with a bag of produce in each hand. Maggie greeted her on the landing and took the bags while the young woman shook the rain off her coat.

"What was the appraiser so happy about?" Ilaria asked, changing into heels. "He was, what is the word? Whistling?"

Maggie followed Ilaria into the kitchen and told her about Walter's report while helping with lunch preparations.

"We'll have panini and minestrone." Ilaria took fresh bread from one of the bags and onto a wooden cutting board on the counter. She cut two pieces off the end. "Like this, yes?"

Maggie cut while Ilaria set to work with onions and garlic. She added diced tomatoes, and soon the aroma of simmering soup filled the tiny room.

"Is the picture related to the deaths, you think?" Ilaria asked when Maggie finished her story.

"I don't see how. Lord Philip made a mistake."

177

Rain beat against the room's one window. Helen had made a good decision to stay behind today. The guests would have to move quickly from the van to the church and back again to avoid getting soaked. She hoped Thomas was managing them all right.

"That doesn't sound like the man we worked for. Lord Philip didn't make mistakes. Isn't it more likely he had the real picture, and the one you saw today is the fake?"

She added broth and herbs to the soup then began slicing cheese and meat for the toasted sandwiches. "How do you know Walter Jones isn't the one who swapped the picture?"

Maggie felt like she was at the end of the line in a game of crack the whip. She thought she was going one direction then suddenly was jerked in another. She spoke slowly as she tried to follow Ilaria's logic. "You're suggesting Lord Philip acquired a genuine Abbati that was worth a fortune. But when Walter heard Lord Philip died, he decided to tell us it was worthless? So he could, what? Sell the original on the side market and keep the money for himself?"

Ilaria set down her knife. She leaned back against the counter and her eyes were serious. "He could have made a forgery after picking the picture up. An opportunist, unrelated to Lord Philip's death. But no. I was going back further. What if he is the one who killed Lord Philip in the first place?"

Maggie tried to imagine Walter leaving Faye's, sneaking into Lord Philip's with a plan of stealing from his client, then killing him when things went wrong. It wasn't hard to imagine. She thought back to Walter's arrival to pick up the *White Horse*. The way he'd drummed his fingers while she made small talk. How he'd asked if the police had any leads. His eagerness to share the gossip. She had an uneasy feeling he'd been hiding something.

The front door slammed, interrupting her thoughts. Maggie hurried to the hall, but it was empty. She stepped onto the landing and saw Aldrich hurrying down the stairs.

"Is everything all right?"

He just waved an arm at her.

"What was that?" Ilaria asked when Maggie returned to the kitchen.

"John Aldrich." What could have sent the lawyer running? She ignored the knot in her stomach. "Walter wasn't at Bonaventura," Maggie said to herself as much as to Ilaria. "We need to focus on the people who were there when Daniel died."

"You're talking about Eloise?"

The soup and the toasting sandwiches were making the room stuffy. Maggie opened the door to the hall to let in some fresh air. "Of course not. John Aldrich. I checked the flights. There's no way he arrived that morning. I think he was already here when Lord Philip died. He probably slipped into the palazzo during the fireworks for a meeting and shot Lord Philip. If Daniel had seen him, he would have recognized Aldrich when he came back in the morning. Daniel tries to blackmail Aldrich, but instead, Aldrich kills him. He's the obvious suspect."

"With what possible motive?" Ilaria asked.

"I don't know. Maybe they were in business together. Maybe the drug idea was right all along but with Aldrich, not Daniel. He was pleased when Walter said Lord Philip didn't have an Abbati after all, so there must have been some kind of bad blood."

Ilaria shook her head. "Those stories about Lord Philip and drugs were expat fairy tales. I would have heard if he'd been involved."

Maggie gave her a sharp look, but Ilaria's face was impassive. Maggie thought of all those DeMarco vans crisscrossing the city. "You'd hear that in the laundry business?"

"No one in Sicily is in just one business." Ilaria smiled. "We do favors for people. They do favors for us."

Maggie fought to keep her expression neutral. Burt had suggested Ilaria's family might be "connected," but Maggie had said no. Now she wasn't so sure.

"That doesn't clear Aldrich."

"No, but you must keep an open mind."

The artists returned to the palazzo just as Ilaria toasted the last panini. Maggie helped with coats, bags, and umbrellas, soaking her blouse and skirt in the process as she took one dripping item after another.

"But where's Thomas?" Maggie shook out the last umbrella.

"The inspector came by the church," Len said. "He asked Thomas to come to the police station to answer a few more questions."

Maggie ignored Ilaria clicking her tongue. This was promising. And working on Liberation Day, no less. The police must be getting more background on Lord Philip. Talking to his long-time employees was a smart place to begin.

The group settled in to eat soup and sandwiches, Italian style. Maggie bit into her panini—melted mozzarella, roasted red peppers, and an olive tapenade, pure heaven—then she caught sight of herself in the giant mirror and shifted uncomfortably. Her damp blouse and flat hair gave her the appearance of a drowned rat. Did Burt compare her to sparkling Faye? Maggie pushed her plate away. Best not to think about it.

"Tell me about the church this morning," she said with forced enthusiasm. "I haven't visited it yet."

"Those columns." Shelia's tight Western shirt pulled around its pearl snaps as she reached down beside her chair. She put a guidebook on the table and opened to a page. "Red granite straight from ancient Rome."

Maggie had read that Michelangelo had retained some of the original features from the ancient bath when he converted it into a church. She waited to hear more, but Shelia closed the book.

"The popes were quite economical," Helen said after a pause. Her braid had slipped over her shoulder and she shifted it back into place before beginning a lecture. "The Catholic building boom did more to damage the ancient history of this city than anything the barbarians did, stripping the marble veneer off buildings and tearing down others to use their stones. It's a miracle anything's left."

Helen trailed off, as if realizing it wasn't the time for an animated discussion about the Renaissance. They finished their lunch in silence, and the guests elected to return to the hotel to rest. Maggie called a taxi for Charles and the Potter sisters, but Shelia and Len refused the offer of a ride.

"Rain is such a treat after sunbaked Lubbock." Shelia tied a plastic rain cap over her head. "And it's just around the corner."

Maggie walked with them. She would check on Vicky while she was at the hotel.

"I do hope everything's all right with Thomas." Shelia tucked her arm through Len's.

He held a rainbow-striped umbrella big enough to cover a baseball team.

The hotel's maroon awning came into sight. A couple was sheltering near the door, map and guidebook in hand, looking as though they would rather be doing anything than setting off sightseeing in the rain.

"Why shouldn't he be?" Maggie asked. "The police are being thorough. That's a good thing."

She left the couple and checked with the front desk, who reported Vicky wasn't up to visitors. Maggie remembered when her mother died. Sometimes she was frantic for company; other times she wanted to be alone. She'd give Vicky her space.

Maggie passed a group of middle-aged tourists on her walk back to the palazzo.

They wore matching yellow ponchos, the kind that did nothing to keep out the rain. They looked stoic as they marched behind their leader, who was walking backward and talking into a microphone. "Like so many of the city's great landmarks, Piazza Navona sits on the site of an ancient monument, the Stadium of Domitian. Notice the oblong shape of the original racetrack..."

A scooter raced by, splashing Maggie up to the knee. It was time to get inside.

Chapter Twenty-Four

T he Italian judicial system is one of the most dysfunctional in Europe. The system is slow, complicated, and expensive, and the backlog of cases is staggering. Despite improvements, defendants can wait years for a trial, which, in turn, may last several years more.
—Masterpiece Tours "Welcome to Rome" pamphlet

"Where the bloody hell were you?" Thomas was flopped on the big cream couch in the salon when Maggie returned. His face was pale and his hair ruffled. "Ilaria's off someplace with her family, and you were nowhere to be found."

Aldrich was sitting opposite. The two men looked grim. Maggie swallowed. She'd never heard Thomas raise his voice.

"Buck up, Mittens." Aldrich sounded exasperated. "This whole thing will pass. They don't have any evidence."

Maggie looked from one young man to another. A knot of dread formed in her stomach. Was this about Thomas's conversation with Orsini? "What happened?" She hung up her coat and took the upright chair next to Thomas. "Has the inspector made progress?"

"He thinks I'm the one who bumped off Daniel, Mrs. W. And Lord Philip, too." Thomas sat up and played with the gold fringe on one of the couch cushions.

She shook her head. Thomas must have it wrong. But she remembered Shelia's worry for Thomas and knew he had understood Orsini perfectly.

"It was Vicky's idea that Daniel was blackmailing Lord Philip's killer."

Thomas tossed the cushion to the other end of the couch and sat up. "The inspector put two and two together and got twelve. Said I was the most likely suspect."

"I told you to leave it alone, Mrs. White," Aldrich said. "This type of thing was bound to happen."

The panini churned in Maggie's stomach. How could Orsini have gone so far astray? She should have told him her theory about Aldrich yesterday. "But why pick on Thomas?"

"He found out I was fired from my job at the auction house. Said it was proof I was corrupt. That was his word, 'corrupt.' I may as well turn up at the prison this afternoon and meet my new cell mates."

"What he said," Aldrich interrupted, "is that you had the best opportunity of anyone on the tour, and that fact, coupled with your history, made you a suspect. He doesn't have any evidence. You need to keep your chin up, Mittens. This will blow over."

The rain was coming down harder again. It drummed on the metal roof of the studio all the way down the hall.

"I'd like to know how he heard the story about the auction house forgeries in the first place." Thomas narrowed his eyes. "Did you tell him, Mrs. W.? Try to clear your name by dropping me in the soup?"

"Absolutely not!" Maggie's skirt had only half dried, and it clung to her thighs. She remembered Orsini's question about who else had the opportunity to kill Daniel. Why hadn't she realized he would get to Thomas eventually? She could have at least warned Thomas, given him time to prepare.

"I'll call the inspector and tell him he's got it all wrong." Maggie would explain everything and put him on to Aldrich. Then Maggie remembered the *White Horse*. "You didn't tell Orsini about the results of the appraisal, Mr. Aldrich, did you?"

"Why would I do that?" Aldrich asked. "If this Orsini fellow finds out the *White Horse* is a modern picture masquerading as an old one, he'll add that to Thomas's history as a forger and sign Thomas's arrest warrant this afternoon. I hope we can agree to keep that to ourselves."

Maggie nodded. So, this was how people got on the wrong side of the law. If she, Maggie White, could decide to withhold information from the police so easily, what would other people with a less developed sense of justice do?

Aldrich let out his breath. Maggie thought of the lawyer thundering down the stairs. It must have been to go meet Thomas at the station. Aldrich wouldn't have framed his friend on purpose. Maggie watched as the man shifted in his seat, as though trying to get more comfortable. Would he do the right thing and fess up? He had a weak chin. Somehow, she didn't think so.

"I'd like to avoid your getting arrested," Aldrich said. "But it's not the end of the world. You'd never be convicted."

The rain had given the palazzo a musty smell. As though billions of mold spores had blossomed overnight. Wet raincoats and umbrellas by the door were adding to the humidity. Maggie wished Thomas had an alibi for Lord Philip's death. He'd come upstairs to the terrace right after Eloise. Orsini might say Thomas shot Lord Philip then strolled upstairs to the terrace, all calm and collected. But no one who knew Thomas would believe that. He would have muddled it somehow, been out of breath, gotten blood on his sleeve. There was no way he could have pulled it off.

His friend, however, would have been cool under fire. Aldrich began polishing his glasses. "I don't think much of this blackmail idea. I'm sure there's some other explanation for what Vicky heard, or says she heard. We can start there."

"I disagree," Maggie said. "Daniel was downstairs at the right time—that's why we suspected him in the first place."

"And how, exactly, would Daniel have known the killer? He couldn't exactly ask for the chap's name and phone number," Aldrich said.

Maggie picked her words carefully. "I think he saw the killer later and recognized him."

"Leave it alone, Mrs. White. You've done enough damage." Aldrich's voice was cold.

A shiver ran down Maggie's spine.

"The police are fishing, and Thomas will be fine."

The rain continued drumming against the windows, but slower now. Maggie should feel dry and safe, but instead, she felt trapped. Was this a wise idea, calmly discussing the murders with this man? Thomas was hardly protection against a two-time killer.

But still, she went ahead. "Daniel knew *you*, Jonathan."

His expression was blank. "And?"

She swallowed. "He knew you. If he'd seen you kill Lord Philip, he would have known whom to blackmail."

Aldrich's mouth dropped open. If she didn't know better, she might think he was truly surprised. "You're serious? First Daniel, now me? Who else are you going to finger?"

She didn't say anything.

"Mrs. W. explained her idea last night," Thomas said. "I told her it was mad."

"You lied about when you came to Rome," Maggie said. "*And* you told the police not to investigate. It was all very convenient."

"And my motive?" His voice was hard.

This was the tricky bit she hadn't quite worked out. She thought of his pleasure at the idea Lord Philip had acquired a forgery. Was his motive personal, rather than some business venture?

"Thomas said your family has fallen on hard times," she began slowly. "Maybe your siblings got hit harder by the diamond mine scheme than everyone else."

Aldrich laughed. Not bitter or sarcastic, but a genuine belly laugh. "That's your theory? Every family with any kind of land was ruined by death duties, Mrs. White. My home was open to the public long before old Walpole stole his first lollipop, I can assure you."

"But—" She stopped, the first niggle of doubt creeping up. "Well, the family shame of the scandal then?"

The rain had finally stopped and a bit of sun broke through the clouds. The wet rooftops shimmered in the light.

"Walpole tried to swizzle nearly every member of the peerage between eighteen and thirty before he left England," Aldrich said. "Nothing special

185

about my family."

Thomas stretched. "When *did* you get to Rome, old man? Mrs. W. raised an interesting point there."

"I'm dating a girl in the Foreign Office." Aldrich made it sound like it should answer the question. When Maggie and Thomas didn't say anything, he continued, "She picked up a notification about the death of a UK citizen. She told me about it, and I knew Walpole was one of our clients. I thought if I was the first one on the scene, the boys in the office would have to let me handle it, so I caught the last flight out of Heathrow."

"You weren't in cahoots with Lord Philip, then?" Maggie knew it was a lost cause. The man was a hustler, not a murderer.

Aldrich shook his head. "Just his solicitor, nothing more. Would you like to see my boarding pass?" He took out his phone and made a show of tapping on the screen until Thomas waved for him to stop.

"Wasn't that the night of the Hospital Gala?" Thomas looked relaxed now, fingers laced together behind his head, long legs stretched out in front of him.

"Afraid I had to take a miss," Aldrich said.

"The Hospital Gala is the social event of the season," Thomas explained to Maggie. "For Johnnie Boy to miss it is saying something. My parents wanted me to go home for it. Now I wish I had."

Church bells rang outside. Maggie could imagine the crowds of tourists, holed up in churches and cafés for most of the day, streaming outside to take in the city as it was meant to be enjoyed: outdoors.

"Look, Mr. Aldrich," Maggie said in a low voice. "I was wrong. But you had to admit that asking the police to back off the investigation was suspicious."

"Don't make me the bad guy here." Aldrich stood. "If you hadn't stuck your nose in, having the widow tell the police Daniel was blackmailing someone, Thomas wouldn't be in this situation."

Maggie felt like she'd been kicked. It hadn't occurred to her the police would take Vicky's statement as evidence against her friend. "Thomas, you don't blame me?"

Thomas pushed himself to his feet. "Just leave it alone, Mrs. W. You've done enough damage as it is."

Chapter Twenty-Five

A tour of the Capitoline Museum isn't complete without pausing to stare into the eyes of the bronze Capitoline Wolf as she suckles two hungry babies. The wolf portion of the sculpture is believed to be ancient, but the iconic twins are a relatively modern addition dating to the 15th Century.
—Masterpiece Tours "Welcome to Rome" pamphlet

The afternoon passed in a blur. Maggie worked out the transportation requirements for the coming tour of Tivoli.

Aldrich left to prepare for the arrival of the heir. "If you think I can go that far without topping anyone, Mrs. White."

Maggie told Thomas to go home. There was no point in him brooding at the apartment with so few guests to entertain. There would be just Charles, Len, and Shelia for dinner.

After cocktails in the salon, the small group moved to the dining room, which made their party seem even smaller. Six were missing: two dead, two off licking their emotional wounds, and two—the Potter sisters—were off on a pre-arranged dinner with a friend's son.

A gloomy feeling hung over the meal. Maggie halfheartedly twirled a fork in her spaghetti carbonara, then her stomach turned over as the aroma of cream and pepper hit her. She pushed the plate away. Len didn't touch his wine, and Charles sat absently crumbling a piece of bread onto his plate. Shelia talked of her painting, but Maggie could see her heart wasn't in it. They were silent as Ilaria stood to clear the plates.

"Everything's all right with Thomas, isn't it?" Shelia asked when Ilaria returned with the dessert. Chocolate gelato with some sort of cookies.

"Oh yes," Maggie said. "He'll be with us tomorrow."

Ilaria looked pained, but Maggie glanced away, unwilling to meet the woman's eye. Maggie had told herself she'd find the killer and clear her name, and Thomas's. But what had she discovered? She'd learned that Lord Philip was an all-around unlikeable person, one who'd given plenty of people reasons to want him dead. And she'd learned Daniel had been blackmailing someone, probably the person who killed Lord Philip. That was the sum of her progress. *Wonderful work, Watson.*

"Would it be helpful, do you think, if we spoke with the police?" Shelia asked. Her eyes were serious and her voice lacked her usual giggle. "Give him a recommendation or something?"

"He's not applying for a job, Shelia." The creases in his forehead deepened.

"The police were just questioning Thomas," Maggie said. "He's fine."

"Vicky told me Daniel might have been murdered by the same person who killed Lord Philip," Shelia said. "I preferred the suicide theory."

The group lapsed into silence while the guests ate their dessert. Maggie left hers untouched and watched as the ice cream slowly melted.

"I read something interesting this afternoon," Charles said with determined cheerfulness, putting down his spoon. "Did you know that Romulus and Remus weren't raised by a wolf?"

"But that's the symbol of Rome," Shelia said. "We saw the wolf when we went to the Capitoline museum. What day was that, Len? It feels like a lifetime ago."

"Exactly." There was a spot of chocolate on Charles' cuff, and Maggie resisted the urge to wipe it away for him... "It was chosen for effect. Turns out it's a translation issue. 'Lupa,' Latin for she-wolf, was also the ancient term for prostitute. Who do you think was more likely to find two little abandoned babies and raise them up? A friendly wolf or a prostitute with a heart of gold?"

"Well I'll be damned," Len said.

"Weren't Romulus and Remus the sons of some hero?" Shelia said. "Hercules? Or maybe Odysseus?"

"Eloise would know," Ilaria said.

"She must have been a wonderful secretary," Maggie said absently.

Charles gave her a curious look. "Secretary? Whatever gave you that idea? Eloise managed one of her university's art collections."

Maggie blushed. What *had* given her the idea Eloise was a secretary? Just another assumption on her part. If only Eloise had waited to use the restroom until after Thomas had come up to the terrace. He would have an airtight alibi right now. Maggie remembered Ilaria, asking how they knew Eloise was telling the truth about hearing Lord Philip alive. The only artist without an alibi for Daniel's death, or Lord Philip's. Maggie shook herself. She was doing the same thing she'd done with Aldrich, suspecting people without any kind of motive.

"Rome was actually named by the Etruscans. They called it Ruma, which was their name for the Tiber," Charles said. "But it wasn't a good enough story for the Romans, so they came up with a better one."

"Seems like a lot of effort," Shelia said. "Len and I live in Lubbock. But I can't tell you where the name comes from."

"It's named for Thomas Lubbock," Len said. "A big secessionist."

"Well you see?" Shelia's turquoise necklace glittered in the light of the chandelier. "Sometimes you'd rather not know. Though it's all part of our state's history, like it or not."

"You're saying the twins were made up?" Len asked.

"Not sure," Charles said. "Exaggerated, if nothing else. The end gets even more fuzzy. Romulus ruled the city for a long time then eventually disappeared. They said he turned into a wind god, whatever that means."

Burt would enjoy this story. He used to read aloud from a big book of myths when the kids were small. He read the story about Odin and Thor when the children worried about thunder. Athena when they saw a spider. She wondered if he knew this explanation for the origins of Romulus and Remus's "wolf."

Maggie nibbled a cookie. Lemon shortbread that practically dissolved in her mouth. Even if Orsini saw sense and left Thomas alone, the guests would be gone in a few days. Masterpiece would surely close, and she'd be back where she started.

Burt had done such a good job of making a life here. She would make more of an effort. So what if everyone liked to gossip and play bridge? She could do that. She knew her trumps from her tricks. She was already committed to filling in for Walter at three games. That would be a good opportunity to get back into the expat group.

Maggie sighed, thinking about it. This was what defeat felt like. She'd tried her best and failed. Now she'd spend the next two years back as a bored housewife.

"What happened to Remus?" Ilaria's voice lacked its usual musical quality tonight.

"Oh, Romulus killed him," Charles said. "But he wasn't all bad. Old Romulus made all men citizens, even slaves."

"Better than our Lubbock." Shelia took a spoonful of ice cream. "Why'd he do it?"

"There was some disagreement, and Romulus shoved Remus off a wall."

Shelia choked and Charles turned pale.

"Forgive me. Stupid to tell that story."

Maggie looked at her bowl, a muddy puddle now surrounding the soft ice cream.

Shelia forced a bright smile. "Well, we can hope Vicky's up for company tomorrow."

"Sometimes space is just what the doctor ordered," Charles said.

"Poor girl's been through it before," Len said. "Maybe she knows what she needs."

"She has, hasn't she?" Shelia said. "I hope the circumstances of her first husband's death were less, well, sudden."

"She said something about an illness," Charles said. "I didn't like to press."

They finished dinner and returned to the hotel with murmurings about getting a good night's sleep.

Maggie offered to help clean up, but Ilaria pushed her to the door. "Go. I have some thinking to do."

"About Gregorio?" Maggie asked. "I don't want to be one of those nosey old women who think they know everything, but I have been married a long time. Marrying a man because he's comfortable is a mistake, Ilaria. Marriage is hard enough when you marry the *right* man, let alone the wrong one."

Ilaria squeezed Maggie's hand. "I know that, Maggie. But sometimes in life we must think about others, must we not? To think of the greater happiness, not just our own?"

Gertrude would have a snappy response, but Maggie was at a loss. She hugged Ilaria goodnight and walked downstairs.

Taxis were lined up at the stand, but Maggie wasn't ready to go home. Burt wouldn't say this mess was her fault. Burt would never do that. But he'd tell her to do what Thomas asked, to leave it alone.

Maggie walked toward home. As soon as she left the Piazza Navona, she tripped over a bag of garbage some resident had left out for the morning pickup. It seemed like an omen somehow. Maggie turned up her collar and kept walking. She passed a couple in a tight embrace as she crossed the bridge to Trastevere. Maggie looked away and hurried across, not even pausing to glance back at the city lit up beyond the dark river.

Chapter Twenty-Six

*R*omans live their lives outdoors. Piazzas are communal living rooms. The pre-dinner passeggiata—*stroll*—is a daily opportunity to see and be seen. And balconies, no matter how small, are maintained as a reflection of the people within.
   —Masterpiece Tours "Welcome to Rome" pamphlet

High, tinkling laughter greeted Maggie as she unlocked the door to her apartment. Maggie didn't see anyone at first, but there was no mistaking Faye's tones. Then she glimpsed the two figures on the balcony. Burt and Faye sitting with their feet on the railing and a carafe of between them. There was no sign of Gertrude.

Maggie took her time before making her presence known to the couple outside. She picked up the mail, sitting on the coffee table next to a deck of cards and Burt's keys. Just two bills and an advertising circular.

She dropped the mail, thinking about that unfamiliar scent on Burt's coat the night before. The phone call he took in the hall when they were getting ready for bed the other day. And she remembered Faye at the market, knowing the police weren't investigating the drug angle. Had Burt been the one to tell her?

Maggie reflexively clenched her hands into fists. She felt like a fool for thinking she needed to make more of an effort with Faye and her friends, while all the time Burt was here flirting with the queen bee herself. Maggie heard Faye's laughter again and gritted her teeth.

The lock on the front door clicked. "Oh good, you're home." Gertrude stood in the doorway loaded down with shopping bags. "Here, help me with these. Burt took me out to lunch, then I spent the afternoon shopping until I dropped." If Gertrude had dropped, she'd bounced back. Her hair was sleek, her makeup looked fresh, and even the crease on her pants was crisp. Maggie didn't think she'd ever looked that put together at 9 a.m., let alone after being out all day.

Maggie took two of the bags. They felt like they were filled with bricks. How was Gertrude going to pack it all?

"What's happening with your dead men?" Gertrude asked. "Have you made any progress?"

Maggie thought of Thomas telling her to stay out of it and swallowed hard. "It appears Daniel was blackmailing the killer. His wife heard him making threats."

Burt's voice drifted in from the balcony.

"A nightcap outside?" Gertrude said. "What a good idea." Gertrude had the door open before Maggie could answer.

"Didn't hear you come in, Aunt Gertrude." Burt's voice was relaxed, loose, after his wine. "Oh, Maggie, too. Hi dear." He stood for a perfunctory kiss. "Faye dropped off some dinner." He gestured to two dirty plates on the concrete between the chairs.

"I was so sorry you and Burt had to miss the party today." Faye took a sip of wine. She had Burt's blue cardigan around her shoulders, and her slim legs peeked out from her striped shirtdress. "George told me you've been working nonstop, so I thought I'd bring some leftovers and keep Burt company."

Was that this woman's angle? A wave of anger washed over Maggie. Was Faye trying to lure Maggie's husband with home cooking while Maggie worked?

Maggie's stomach knotted. And what was she supposed to do if this flirtation went further? Go back home? It wasn't as though she could drop back into her old life. She didn't have a job to go back to. The house was rented for two years. And for heaven's sake, what would she tell the children? No, she was stuck here.

Burt unfolded two wooden chairs. There were puddles on the balcony floor from the day's rain, but the seats were dry. Gertrude's chair creaked as she settled in. "Is that cake?"

It looked like Faye's famous *Millefoglie*—thousand layer cake—with sweetened mascarpone and almonds layered between puff pastry. Maggie caught a whiff of Faye's familiar perfume as she leaned over to pass a plate to Gertrude. It was the scent from Burt's coat.

Maggie refused the slice Faye held out to her. She would be forced to eat the woman's cucumber sandwiches at her awful bridge parties soon enough. Then she caught herself. Would she really play bridge with the woman who was trying to steal her husband?

"Watching your figure, Maggie?" Faye sounded almost sympathetic. "Rome can so be so hard on us women, can't it?"

Maggie wasn't going to let this woman get under her skin. Burt was flattered by Faye's attention. Fine. But it hadn't gone further than that. And it wouldn't. Maggie would see to that. And if Faye thought Maggie needed to lose a pound or two, Maggie would show her she was happy just the way she was.

"On second thought, Faye dear, that sounds lovely." And it was, Maggie thought grimly, as she swallowed her first bite of flaky sweetness. Just the right balance of pastry and cream.

"George said the police pulled the tour guide in for questioning," Faye said. "Is he a suspect?"

"They're grasping at straws." Maggie certainly wasn't going to tell them about Thomas's prank at the auction house. She was too tired to defend him to this group. Maggie set her plate on the concrete floor. "I found your scarf."

"What's that?" Her husband looked blank.

"The scarf I gave you for our first anniversary." Maggie hated the edge in her voice, but she couldn't do anything about it. "George was wearing it this morning. I brought it home for you."

"Typical George," Faye laughed. She patted Burt's leg. "You must have left it the night of the fireworks." She let her hand linger a moment, and Burt

195

didn't move his leg away.

"It would have been foolish of Daniel to try to blackmail Lord Philip's murderer," Gertrude said. "Blackmailers often meet ugly ends."

Faye blinked. "I don't follow."

"Daniel's widow has some idea her husband saw something he shouldn't have," Burt said. "And that he was threatening to tell the police if he didn't get paid. That could be why he was killed."

"But she doesn't know who it was?" Faye's tone suggested that any wife worth her merit would have gotten this information out of her husband.

Vicky had kept her head in the ground. She didn't want to know. Perhaps that was what all wives did. Hoped their husbands were trustworthy, despite all the evidence to the contrary.

If Faye had any idea her husband had done something so shameful he'd given a masterpiece away rather than let Lord Philip spill the beans, she certainly wasn't letting on. Or a near masterpiece, Maggie corrected herself. They couldn't know for sure whether the *White Horse* was a poor forgery of a masterpiece or a dreary picture recently painted.

Had Burt told Faye about the picture? Maggie didn't think so. "There is the matter of the painting Lord Philip hired Walter to appraise." Maggie ignored Burt, who caught her eye and shook his head. The issue of the original owner didn't have to come up, and Faye was unlikely to connect a hidden masterpiece with a boring old painting she'd hated.

Maggie ignored the voice in her head telling her she was being petty, bringing up a subject that would embarrass Faye if only she knew the full story. Maggie told them about the picture that Lord Philip pressured "an acquaintance" to sell.

"How exactly did he do that?" Faye pulled Burt's sweater tighter around her shoulders.

Maggie shifted in her seat. The wooden slats were digging into her bottom. "He knew something about the owner, and he threatened to tell it."

"He wasn't a good man." It wasn't clear if Burt was talking about Lord Philip or George.

"Lord Philip was sure the picture was worth a fortune, but Walter completed his analysis. It's worthless. More than worthless," Maggie said. "A forgery, perhaps, painted to fool someone into thinking it was an Abbati. And not a very good one at that."

Faye looked at her watch and gave a dramatic yawn. If only she knew whose picture they were discussing.

"Well done, Maggie." Gertrude said. "You're looking for Pierre, I suppose?"

For a wild moment, Maggie thought Gertrude knew Pierre personally. One of her many chums scattered around the globe. Then Maggie remembered she'd told Gertrude about Ilaria's list of suspects and the mysterious Pierre.

"Who's Pierre?" Faye asked. "Is he new in town?"

"He's an art thief who swore revenge on Lord Philip," Gertrude said. "Some kind of master criminal."

Faye raised her eyebrows. It did sound ridiculous when Gertrude put it that way.

"We don't even know if he exists," Maggie said. "Lord Philip double-crossed someone named Pierre, and Thomas told us there are rumors about some kind of brilliant thief who can acquire pictures from private collections without the owner even realizing they're missing."

"How's that?" Faye asked.

"He swaps them with brilliant forgeries." Maggie found herself defending Gertrude's story in the face of Faye's skepticism.

"But didn't you say Walter said it was a poor forgery?"

"Oh, for heaven's sake." Gertrude's neat bob swung as she turned to face Maggie . "One of the suspects is an art thief and known forger, and now we have a picture that turns out to be a forgery. What more do we need?"

Maggie took a sip of wine, most likely from a jug filled at the *vino sfuso* down the street, a bulk wine shop that filled customers' empty bottles from a giant barrel. Faye had tipped Maggie off to it when they moved to the city, telling them it was good quality and cheap. "No reason to pay for a fancy label." And she'd been right.

"It doesn't connect," Burt said. "The only people at Bonaventura when Daniel died were Maggie's group and a bunch of Germans. Are you sure you can trust Walter, Maggie? You only have his word the picture isn't authentic."

"Walter is a darling," Faye finished her wine. "And by all accounts very good at what he does, despite whatever beef Lord Philip had with him. No, my money is on your tour guide. Who else is there? Just some old folks on vacation."

"Maybe that's what they want you to think," Gertrude said. "Maybe one of these 'old folks' is a secret assassin. Young people forget that the elderly weren't always old. It's the perfect cover. But I think this picture is the key to the whole thing. Find Pierre and you'll find the solution."

Maggie's head was spinning as she tried to follow their logic. The others seemed to be having a good time, throwing ideas around, as if unconcerned there were two people dead and Thomas was under suspicion. Not that they knew about Thomas.

"Any chance Thomas is Pierre?" Typical Burt. He'd be happy to have both Gertrude and Faye be right about their favorite suspects.

"Pierre *is* supposed to be English," Maggie said. "But older. He sold something to Thomas's great aunt once."

"More like Gertrude?" Faye's tone was teasing.

Had Burt told her about the couple's joke that Gertrude led a double life?

"Tell us, Gertrude," Burt said in a mock-serious tone. "Did you come to Rome to steal priceless works of art?"

"In my experience, everything has its price," Gertrude said. "But I'm afraid not. I'd hardly have travelled second class on the train if I were your thief."

"Well that's no good, then," Burt said. "Tell us about these geriatric models of decorum, Maggie."

Maggie had told him all about the guests, several times. But he seemed to have adopted the role of master of ceremonies for Faye and Gertrude's benefit.

"Anyone have a dark past working for a secret organization?" Faye asked. "Retired spy come out of retirement for one last job?"

"Charles has been very helpful." Maggie forced herself to match Faye's light tone. "A professor now, mostly retired, who worked in military intelligence. But he was on the terrace when Lord Philip died."

CHAPTER TWENTY-SIX

"Who else is there?" Burt asked, "Geriatric or otherwise."

"There's Helen, a New England spinster. Very skilled artist."

Faye leaned back in her chair. "What's her story?"

"She manages the most marvelous pictures with just a few brush strokes. And a real sense of humor. Crazy for cats."

Gertrude snorted. "Never trust a cat lady. They aren't quite balanced. Dogs are much better." To Maggie's knowledge, Gertrude had never kept a pet. Said they were the moss of a rolling stone, or some such thing.

"Who else?" Faye asked.

"Helen's sister, Eloise. Former curator of some sort. She's the one who established the timeline for Lord Philip's death. She was the last one to hear him alive."

A car splashed through a puddle in the street below. The smell of wet earth from the neighboring balcony's potted plants filled Maggie's nostrils. Normally she loved the city after it rained, but tonight the air felt oppressive.

"Then there are the oil tycoons," Maggie went on. "Len and Shelia are a rags-to-riches couple. I think what you see is what you get with them."

"If they pulled themselves up from their bootstraps, they're more than smart," Faye said. "I once dated a man who started out with nothing and owns half of San Francisco now. He cornered the trout market or something, and that's not as easy as it sounds. He was ruthless."

"They were with me when both men died," Maggie said. "They couldn't possibly be involved."

"What about that lawyer?" Gertrude asked. "You said he was at Bonaventura."

Maggie colored at the memory of her accusation. "He's just what he seems: an aggressive lawyer out to make his name."

"How about the wife?" Faye asked. "Daniel was cheating on her, wasn't he? That's the most powerful motive there is."

Faye was wrong. Maggie would fight for Burt—if it came to that—but never kill him. That would defeat the purpose. And Vicky felt the same way. That was why she had brought Daniel on the trip, to get a little revenge, but to still save her marriage.

"No opportunity," Maggie said. "She wasn't at Bonaventura when Daniel died."

"Could she be in league with someone?" Faye asked. "Maybe she killed Lord Philip for someone, and that person killed Daniel in return? Like that Hitchcock movie. The one on the train."

Gertrude snorted.

"The timeline wouldn't work, even if Vicky were the murdering type. She was back to the terrace before Eloise even went downstairs." A fresh wave of hopelessness rolled over Maggie. She had no leads. No clue what had happened. Sitting here talking about it with Burt and Gertrude and Faye wasn't going to do Thomas any good. It was this type of speculation that had gotten him into trouble in the first place.

After silence, Burt rubbed his eyes. "I need to get to bed. I'm back with the Swiss in the morning. Faye, thank you for a lovely dinner."

Faye snapped the Tupperware lid back on her cake, popping it into her tote bag without asking if Maggie would like to keep the leftovers. "I'll be going, too. Even George wonders where I've gotten off to eventually."

Maggie carried the plates, glasses, and carafe into the kitchen. She stood motionless in front of the sink, trying to summon the energy to tackle the detritus of her husband's dinner with Faye. She swallowed hard as she heard Burt humming in the bedroom.

Maggie squirted soap onto a sponge and began washing. The hot water, at least, was working tonight. The plates were caked with remnants of lasagna Bolognese, one of Burt's favorites. She scrubbed harder, trying not to think.

Gertrude was right. The *White Horse* had to be involved. Was it possible the picture Walter had picked up from the palazzo was a very old, very valuable Abbati, which the art dealer had swapped with a fake? With Lord Philip dead, there'd be no one to challenge him.

But Walter wasn't at Bonaventura. Maggie began drying the dishes. He couldn't have killed Daniel. Not unless he had a partner. Someone who helped with the forgeries. Maggie thought of Thomas. Walter might have known why he was fired from the auction house and recruited him into the plot.

She carefully folded the damp towel over the edge of the sink. She wasn't prepared to make things worse for Thomas, no matter the logical conclusion.

Gertrude came in from the balcony and settled into a kitchen chair. "What will you do now?"

"Thomas told me to leave it alone." Maggie wiped off the kitchen counter. She could feel Gertrude's eyes on her.

"Since when do you shy away from a cause, Maggie White?" Gertrude's tone was sharp.

Maggie didn't know what to say. Thomas was right. She'd made things worse. The woman at the advertising agency had said the same thing when Maggie ordered changes to the ad campaign for a new line of chocolate after some last-minute market research raised questions. It had been a debacle, calling the entire brand strategy into question. When Maggie's retirement was announced, the leadership team had given her a lovely crystal vase as a thank you for her service, but Maggie couldn't help feeling they were pleased her position had been eliminated.

Maggie focused back on Gertrude.

"Fighting the odds," Gertrude was saying. "Doing what's right and damn the consequences. That's you, Maggie."

Wonderful. They could put that on her tombstone. She clicked off the florescent light under the cabinets. She'd go to Masterpiece tomorrow, and every day until the tour was done, then go back to being Mrs. Burt White, bridge player, lifelong student, and lady who lunches. That would have to be enough.

"It doesn't always make you popular, but that was never your thing," Gertrude said.

Maggie focused on Gertrude. The creases around her eyes were deeper than Maggie remembered, the lines around her mouth exaggerated by her serious expression. "What are you talking about?"

"I admire you for it. You don't take the easy way out."

It was the closest Gertrude had ever come to giving Maggie a compliment. "Thomas will thank you for interfering when it's all over. You're a mother. A leader. You know how to do a thankless job. It's called taking the long view."

Maggie shook her head. The only viable suspects were people she wasn't willing to put in front of the police.

"You'll figure it out." Gertrude patted her hand. "You always do."

Chapter Twenty-Seven

V isitors to Rome are often treated as nameless, faceless paying guests, cattle lining up to enter a sight, crowding to follow a guide waiving a garish flag. At Masterpiece Tours, our guests are special friends, visitors with whom it's a pleasure to spend our time.
—Masterpiece Tours "Welcome to Rome" pamphlet

Burt was gone when Maggie woke the next day. More meetings with the Swiss. Gertrude's gentle snores filled the apartment, but she'd left a note.

> Your professor checks out. I called his university, and they said he's on tour in Rome. I think the assistant might have a crush on him. Even described his painting style. That's one off your list.

Maggie put the note to the side. Charles hadn't even been a suspect. She couldn't help feeling let down. Maggie had gone to sleep half hoping she'd wake up with the solution magically laid out in her mind, but this morning she had nothing.

Maggie sliced a piece of bread and put it under the broiler—she had promised she'd cut back on cornetti and there was no time like the present—and tried to think. Gertrude said Pierre was the key to the whole thing. As off-kilter as Gertrude sometimes was, she was sensible.

Maggie needed to understand when the forgery might have happened. By all accounts, no one knew what the original *White Horse* looked like. That meant the forgery would have had to have been made by someone who had seen the painting at George's or Lord Philip's.

Maggie forgot about her bread until she smelled the toasty aroma. She retrieved it from the oven—dark but not burnt—and took a bite. Dry and crunchy and nothing she wanted. Maggie reached for a pad of paper and pencil instead.

She thought about Walter's announcement that Lord Philip had been deceived, acquiring a poor forgery. It was possible, but it wasn't the only explanation for the forgery. She brainstormed a list.

Possibilities
   1) Walter replaced original with forgery during the appraisal
   2) Lord Philip never had original—George commissioned forgery when Lord Philip pressured sale of picture
   3) Lord Philip commission forgery himself—planning some kind of fraud (Insurance? Swindle?)
   4) Original swapped with forgery night of murder—thief shot L.P., then took original (Pierre?)

Maggie stretched and looked at the list, then added another possibility:
   5) Original swapped with forgery night of murder—thief shot L.P., then took original (Pierre?)
   6) Walter is wrong—there is no forgery (Motive for lying? Or is he incompetent???)

Six nice ideas and no way to prove any of them. Gertrude had said they should look at Pierre, but if she was playing the odds, Walter was a better bet. He was at the heart of three of them. And what was it Faye had said last night about the art dealer having a beef with Lord Philip? She should have followed up on that. But none of this helped with the Bonaventura problem. It had only been the Masterpiece group and the Germans.

Maggie dumped her toast into the trash and left the apartment with her list in her pocket. The streets were dry and the sky was a brilliant, cloudless blue, so Maggie opted to walk. Scooters dodged in and out of rows of cars.

Savvy pedestrians crossed in the middle of streets, while tourists clutching guidebooks waited tentatively at the corners for breaks that never came.

Maggie watched a group of Japanese trailing their guide toward Michelangelo's Piazza del Campidoglio, the civic plaza on top of the Capitoline Hill. The buildings were all Renaissance grandeur, turning their backs on the crumbling Forum just behind.

The Renaissance must have been a bit like today. A magical time of science and technology, where everyone thought they'd made the biggest advances the human race would ever see. In Michelangelo's time it was the printing presses and telescopes that were so amazing. Now it was reprogramming stem cells and spacecraft landing on Mars.

Maggie watched the Japanese. It was easy enough to identify their nationality. Just like the well-dressed French and the noisy American groups who crowded the sidewalks each day. Funny how you could never spot a German from a distance, though.

They were inconspicuous. Comfortably dressed like Americans, but in clothes a little less bright. Quiet, but not as reserved as the French. Until they spoke or you saw "Rom" on the cover of their guidebooks, you weren't sure what country they came from.

Maggie headed toward the Piazza Navona then stopped at a light. She looked back, but the tourists had disappeared around a corner. No one really looked at tourists, did they? In a city like Rome, where visitors were everywhere, you took them for granted. Just a faceless group.

What made her so sure the only visitors to Bonaventura on the day Daniel died were the German tour group and Masterpiece Tours? If you're expecting a German and see someone dressed plainly, waiting politely in line, you think he's a German.

Her fingers twitched with excitement. This was it. The solution she'd been looking for. It didn't have to be Thomas at the church. *Anyone* could have snuck in with the Germans and pushed Daniel off the tower. Maggie walked faster, striding downhill beside the Victor Emmanuel Monument, all shiny white marble, looking somehow *nouveau riche* among all the Renaissance buildings.

Maggie cut through the Campo Fiori, zigzagging around market stalls and striding past strolling shoppers. She moved as fast as she could along a winding street and then across the Piazza Navona with its outdoor café tables full of coffee drinkers taking in the sun after yesterday's rain. She almost sprinted up the stairs of the palazzo, using the worn wooden handrail to boost herself up as fast as she could.

Ilaria and Thomas were already in the apartment, setting up the morning coffee. From the dark circles under their eyes, it was clear neither had slept well.

"I've got it!" Maggie puffed slightly.

"Got what?" Ilaria was pouring coffee into an urn.

"I think someone snuck into Bonaventura with the Germans. Daniel's killer wasn't one of us after all. " She paused a moment to catch her breath. "It hit me when I passed a group of tourists. Some you can tell their nationality right away. But Germans? Not a chance." Maggie was grinning from ear to ear. She'd been worried about Thomas, no matter what she'd told the others. But this cleared him.

Ilaria put the pot down and gave Maggie her full attention. "What are you talking about?"

Maggie's stomach dropped when she noticed a diamond ring on Ilaria's left hand. "Did you and Gregorio get engaged last night?"

Ilaria nodded. Maggie had never seen a less enthusiastic bride-to-be.

"I'm about to be arrested and Ilaria decides it's the right time to get married." Thomas's tone was bitter. "You're marrying your childhood sweetheart, even if he bores you to pieces. I don't get it."

"Someone snuck into Bonaventura dressed in regular, nondescript clothes." Maggie said brightly, trying to get the two back on track. "He blended in with the tourists getting off the buses then followed Daniel up to the tower. He pushed him off the top then blended into the crowd again and disappeared. He probably just walked out as the police were arriving. They didn't make any effort to keep us all there."

Thomas looked up from the coffee cups he was supposed to be organizing on the tray. "Can you just sneak into a tour, Mrs. W.?"

"Two tour buses pulling up? They're not counting individuals." Maggie was guessing, but really, there was no way they could keep track of all those people. "And people on those big tours don't know everyone. That's part of why Lord Philip's tours are so special. 'Intimate setting to forge friendships that last a lifetime.' Isn't that what the brochure says? Everyone would just assume the stranger was someone from the other bus."

"It would be a risk," Ilaria said slowly. "But if someone was trying to cover his tracks after killing Lord Philip, it would be a risk worth taking."

A smile broke out over Thomas's face, and he squeezed Maggie in a bear hug. She inhaled the scent of his shampoo, something clean and minty. "It's brilliant, Mrs. W."

If he remembered telling her to leave it alone, he wasn't saying anything. Just as it should be between good friends.

Ilaria's pinched expression relaxed, and she looked almost like herself again. "You did it, Maggie. The police have to look past Thomas now." She shook her head. "I asked my father to call in a favor, to get the police away from Thomas, and he refused. I thought if Gregorio and I were engaged, he'd see things differently, but he still said no."

"You did what?" Thomas's eyes were wide. "You agreed to marry Gregorio for me? You silly old thing!"

He made as if to hug Ilaria, too, but she pushed him away. "Don't give yourself too much credit, Thomas. Me marrying Gregorio would make a lot of people very happy."

Thomas sobered. "But you're won't, not now. Will you?"

Ilaria didn't answer him. "Who do you suspect, Maggie? His heir?" She poured three cups of coffee.

They could go into the salon, but it was cozier here. Maggie's kitchen back home was much bigger, with a brick floor, baskets hanging from the high ceiling, and a built-in banquette with ample room for guests. This room was more utilitarian, but crowded in here with Ilaria and Thomas just felt right.

Maggie thought back to Ilaria's original list of suspects. The heir should always be a prime suspect. "He must need money if his fiancée is terribly poor."

"Poor?" Thomas put down his cup. "Neddy's fiancée? Are you mad?" He looked like any other young man in the city today in his jeans and dress shirt, as if he hadn't had the energy to choose something more original.

"But you said…" Maggie paused. What was it Thomas had said? "You said his fiancée wasn't from your set."

"Exactly. Edward Innes-Fox is marrying the only child of Europe's biscuit king. Actually, he makes the machines that roll the biscuits into their tubes. No history. No land. No title. His fiancée is common, but she's rich common." Thomas laughed. "Old Neddy, hard up. Johnnie Boy will love that." He took a big satisfied sip of his coffee, the picture of relaxation.

"Just because he's marrying someone whose father is well off doesn't mean he doesn't need money." Ilaria tapped a painted fingernail on her cup as she considered. "Maybe he gambles?"

Thomas shook his head. "Never. Not even at college. But even if he were in need of cash, he's a non-starter. Neddy's fiancée is one of the chairs of the Hospital League fundraiser, and he'd never have gotten out of it. Lord Philip's siblings would have been there, too, in case you are thinking of looking deeper into the family tree."

"I think the *White Horse* is tied up in this," Maggie said.

"Pierre," Ilaria said. "Could he and John Aldrich, perhaps, be one and the same?"

"Nice try, Ilaria," Thomas said. "Even if Pierre were real, which I'm not at all sure he is, old Johnnie Boy would be about twenty years too young to be the master thief."

"How can you know that?" Ilaria asked. "I searched for him online. Nothing came up. If there are as many rumors about Pierre as you say, there should be something about him online, even if it's just dealers talking about the rumors. It's as if someone is deleting any digital footprint of Pierre."

Thomas shrugged. "That stuff's all over my head. All I know is family lore has it my godmother's cousin bought a Remington through Pierre about thirty years ago."

Maggie leaned back against the refrigerator, thinking.

CHAPTER TWENTY-SEVEN

"Aldrich may be an agent for Pierre," Ilaria said.

"I've known him for years," Thomas said. "He can't tell a brush from a palette knife."

"My money's on Walter," Maggie said.

Thomas and Ilaria both swiveled to look at her. Maggie thought back to her list this morning. Every explanation of the *White Horse's* forgery could be linked to him. That didn't feel like a coincidence.

Maggie took out her list and smoothed it on the marble counter. "He had the best opportunity of anyone to make a forgery. He's probably an artist himself. Or if he's not, he'd know someone who could forge a picture."

Thomas picked up the list. "Your first possibility was that George Masters swapped the picture out himself. How does that connect to Walter?"

"George wouldn't have been able to paint a forgery," Maggie said. "He'd have asked Walter. They're friends. It would be a natural connection. But that was just an idea. I don't think George was involved. He wouldn't have come here for the picture if he still had the original."

"What is it you think happened?" Ilaria asked.

Maggie took a sip of her coffee. Ilaria had been generous with the milk, and the creaminess softened the bitter punch. It almost made up for her dry toast this morning.

"I think Walter wanted to get his hands on the original Abbati for himself," Maggie said. "He couldn't do that with Lord Philip alive—Lord Philip would have spotted it. I think Walter snuck out of Faye's party and killed his client."

"Hardly sneaking if everyone saw him go," Thomas said.

Maggie ignored him.

"And you think he replaced the picture with the forgery then?" Ilaria asked.

"Walter probably needed the time to get it done," Maggie replied. "No one knew what the *White Horse* looked like, remember? He just picked up the original then made a forgery while he was supposed to be appraising it. And he would have gotten away with everything if Daniel hadn't spotted him."

She looked at the two expectantly. Ilaria was frowning.

Thomas shook his head. "It doesn't hold water. I've been thinking about the day Walpole died. He was in a bad mood all afternoon, do you remember?"

Maggie did. He'd been rude to her, of course, but he'd also been rude to the guests. That was very much out of character.

"I don't know Abbati's work, but I told Walpole I didn't think his new picture was any good."

"How did he take it?" Maggie asked.

"That's the thing. I think I told him something he already suspected," Thomas said. "If there was a swap, it happened before he died, not after."

Maggie picked up a dishtowel and began polishing the already spotless spoons Thomas had abandoned next to the coffee tray. "OK. Then maybe Walter swapped the real picture with the forgery earlier, when Lord Philip was out with the tour. Lord Philip could have shown the original to him a few days earlier, so he'd know what to copy. But then he got cold feet for some reason, and he went back to swap it out with the real picture during the fireworks."

"He snuck in to replace a forgery with an original?" Ilaria didn't bother to hide her disbelief. "Then what happened?"

Maggie gripped the spoon tighter. "Lord Philip caught him in the act, so Walter had no choice but to shoot him. And since a man was already dead, he decided to keep the original picture. He had to declare the new one a fake."

"Sounds awfully complicated, Mrs. W."

"Complicated doesn't mean wrong." She picked up another spoon, avoiding eye contact. Her explanation *did* sound contrived. She needed to learn more about Walter and his disagreement with Lord Philip. That could have been the motive all along, and the *White Horse* was simply an ancillary issue.

"Could he be working for Pierre?" Ilaria asked. "Maybe that was Walter's connection."

"Pierre's forgeries are perfect." Thomas sounded like one of those know-it-all students whose patience was nearing its limit. "That's the whole point. This one doesn't fit the bill."

"Well, the important thing is Walter is a person of interest," Maggie said briskly.

If they found proof of the crime, they could work the motive backward.

"Now, how would he go about selling it?"

Thomas shrugged. "There are special markets for collectors who want something particular and don't care how it's acquired."

"Lord Philip was a blackmailer and a swindler. Shouldn't we be looking at his other victims?" Ilaria had confirmed the investment opportunity Lord Philip had proposed to Len and Shelia was bogus—the land was owned by the city and not for sale.

"If we knew where to look, certainly." But what was Maggie supposed to do? Contact everyone who had ever taken a Masterpiece tour and ask if they had invested with Lord Philip and, if so, did they have an alibi for the night he died? And blackmail victims didn't exactly raise their hands and say Lord Philip was holding some secret over their head. No, Walter was their best lead.

Voices drifted in from the hall. The artists were arriving for their lesson and the excursion to Tivoli with Walter, her prime suspect.

Ilaria seemed to read Maggie's mind. She put a hand on Maggie's. "You're sure it's safe, putting him together with the guests today?"

Maggie shrugged off a tiny twinge of doubt. "It's perfectly safe. He has no idea we're on to him."

Chapter Twenty-Eight

V illa d'Este is justifiably famous for its fountains. More than five hundred dragons, gargoyles, dolphins, and every other sculpture imaginable send jets of water skyward without the use of pumps or gadgets. It's a 16th Century miracle that still dazzles visitors today.
—*Masterpiece Tours "Welcome to Rome" pamphlet*

Walter arrived for the tour promptly at ten. He had dressed for the occasion with a green silk scarf knotted around his neck, a blue yachting blazer, and white pants. "Meet the customer where they are, you know." He winked at Maggie as he handed her a straw hat.

Could she picture this man walking into Lord Philip's office and pulling out a gun? Maggie had certainly imagined shoving Lord Philip in front of a bus, but did Walter have it in him to actually pull a trigger?

Maggie walked him to the studio. Where had his limp come from? A childhood accident? Arthritis? Faye would know. Maggie stood with Thomas as Walter shook hands with the guests. The dealer focused in on Shelia, asking her about her hometown and admiring her work strung up on the clothesline across the room.

Maggie sat next to Walter for the ride to Tivoli. He smelled of tobacco and eggs, and his bulk seemed to inch closer each time they made a turn. Maggie forced platitudes as the van moved onto the highway, while her mind went in circles. She should call Orsini and tell him her suspicions, but she couldn't do that without introducing the *White Horse*, and that would give him more evidence against Thomas. They didn't even know if Walter had an alibi for Daniel's death.

"I'm looking forward to joining the bridge games. Did you play on Wednesday, by any chance?" It was a clumsy way to ask him about his whereabouts on the day Daniel died, but she couldn't think of anything else.

Walter drew his brows and wrinkled his forehead. "Wednesday? Was there a game that day?" His attempt to recall the date seemed almost exaggerated. Was he putting on an act?

"I'm not sure," Maggie said. "What *did* you do on Wednesday?"

Walter answered quickly. "Hard at work evaluating the *White Horse*. I was at the office all day."

He didn't show any obvious signs of lying, but many people didn't. She used to think she could always tell when Burt was hiding something, but now she wasn't so sure. And Walter's answer seemed a little too quick.

"Did you see anyone?" Maggie asked. "Talk to anyone on the phone?"

Walter tapped a finger on his stocky thigh. Maggie wondered idly how long you needed to smoke for your fingers to be permanently stained, like Walters. She was glad she'd never gone down that path. "Just Faye. She called at a critical moment, and I remember it took me some time to get back into it."

Maggie would call Faye as soon as they got back to the palazzo. She needed to eliminate that call as a potential alibi.

"I'm tempted to renegotiate," Walter said. "I'm leaving town on Sunday and would have missed the games anyway."

A jolt zinged through Maggie. Her prime suspect was leaving town? "When are you coming back?"

He pursed his lips. "Not sure. I've decided to visit my mother in Milwaukee for a few weeks. I need a break from the city."

"But." Maggie's mouth felt like sandpaper. She desperately needed a drink of water. "But, can you just leave the business?"

"With this appraisal done, I have some time. Telephones and email will keep me connected." Had he already sold the Abbati? Was that why he had the resources to walk away from his business? Start a new life?

The van moved from the outskirts of Tivoli to the town proper, with its narrow, winding streets and old stucco homes. A knot was forming in Maggie's stomach. Another visit to a garden with a man she suspected of killing Lord Philip.

But her feelings evaporated as they entered the Renaissance estate. The meticulously maintained terraced gardens were packed with Baroque fountains, and the gentle sound of flowing water was soothing. Maggie would figure out what to do with Walter when they returned to the city.

She followed along as Walter took charge, guiding them to his favorite fountains and plantings. He was patient with the group's slow pace up and down the many flights of stone stairs, and he spoke of the garden's history, designed by the archaeologist in charge of excavating Hadrian's Villa nearby, which provided much of the statuary and stonework for the garden.

Finally, it was time for free painting, and Thomas helped the guests arrange their easels. Charles settled in front of a stone mask spitting water in the Alley of One Hundred Fountains while Helen and Eloise began painting the *Rometta* fountain with its woman in battle gear surveying a water-spewing ship. Romulus and Remus suckled the she-wolf nearby. Maggie couldn't look at that wolf the same after Charles's story. Where would Helen add a cat? Next to the twins?

Len took Maggie aside by the Fountain of Dragons, where he and Shelia had their easels. He looked serious. "What do you know about Walter?"

Was Len concerned Shelia would buy an expensive picture from Walter? The dealer and Shelia had been talking about the art market in Rome for both modern and old work. "He's an art dealer and an active member of the community here."

Len hooked his thumbs over his big leather belt. "He was at the piazza, the night of the murder."

"What?"

A couple loaded down with bulky knapsacks glanced over.

Maggie continued more quietly. "What makes you say that?"

"It's his walk. I remember seeing a man when we were watching the police cars drive up after Lord Philip died. It wasn't crowded on the Piazza Navona anymore, and I saw someone with that same step-shuffle. I've been watching

Walter this morning, and I'm sure he's the same man."

Maggie drew in her breath. She was aware of the spray from the fountain landing on her bare arms.

"This is good news for Thomas, isn't it? Shelia and I have been worried. I know you said he's fine, but..."

"It might be." Maggie's heart was pounding.

The two dragons in the fountain appeared to be grinning at her. Lord Philip had talked about how dragons were treated as evil monsters in Western art, but Maggie thought the Chinese had it right. They were benevolent creatures, bringing her good luck.

"I'll take care of it."

The drive back to the city was a quiet one. Charles and Shelia talked in low voices about favorite books while Helen and Eloise slept, probably relaxed from the picnic lunch they'd all eaten before climbing back into the van. Len was silent, not taking his gaze off of Walter.

Maggie slipped into her office as soon as the group returned to the palazzo. She intended to confirm Walter's possible alibi before calling Orsini with what she knew. Maggie held her breath while she waited for Faye to answer.

She suspected the woman of making advances to her husband, advances he seemed to welcome. But Maggie pushed those thoughts aside. She didn't have a choice. Walter was leaving the country in two days. She needed to move now.

They agreed to meet at Café Antica in half an hour, but it was Gertrude who was sitting with a coffee outside the café. She was deep in conversation with Mario.

"You're alive!" Mario looked genuinely happy to see Maggie, even though it had only been three days since Maggie was last in. He gave her a hug, then pulled out a chair for her. "I was telling Gertrude about Carletta."

"Something new?"

He grinned. "She cancelled the camping trip, just like you said. I think, perhaps, she was relieved."

"It's hard for kids to say no. Parents make good bad guys," Maggie said. "But what are you doing here, Gertrude?"

"I couldn't leave Rome without having Mario and Giovanna's wonderful pastries one more time."

Maggie eyed the half-eaten sfogliatella on Gertrude's plate. She could almost smell the ricotta and orange filling and asked Mario to bring her the same. Gertrude's train left that evening, and Maggie couldn't help feeling Burt's aunt was abandoning her, leaving with the case still open. It was unfair to blame the old woman, but she would miss Gertrude.

"You have some very nice flowers waiting for you at home, dear." Gertrude brought Maggie back to the present.

"You brought us flowers?"

Gertrude's hostess gifts were usually more elaborate. Maggie still wore the scarf Gertrude had brought from Morocco six years ago.

"From your husband," Gertrude said.

Maggie didn't say anything. It wasn't her birthday or their anniversary. Was Burt sending them now as an apology for something? Maggie took a sip of her coffee. Bitter, not milky like her usual. Mario had taken her at her word when she said she wanted what Gertrude had.

"Do you think people change, Gertrude?"

Burt's aunt didn't hesitate. "Never. Once a leopard, always a leopard." Gertrude took a sip of her coffee and wiped her lips on a napkin. Maggie wondered how she managed to do all that without smudging her lipstick, then pushed the thought aside as Faye stepped out of a taxi.

She looked impossibly fashionable in her white jumpsuit cinched with a red belt. Maggie sighed and brushed the crumbs off her own skirt. She stood to give Faye an obligatory kiss, and the hairs on her neck stood up as she smelled Faye's perfume.

Faye settled into her chair. "Now, what did you want to know that was too important to discuss over the phone?"

Maggie wanted this conversation over as quickly as possible, so she got right to the point. "What can you tell me about Walter?"

Faye ran a hand through her short hair. "He's a dear friend. Always good for a laugh. A great shopping partner. Makes amazing crab dip. Solid bridge player who doesn't mind taking the dummy."

"Maggie's not vetting him for her next party," Gertrude said. "What have you learned, dear?"

Maggie explained her theory about someone blending into the crowd the day of Daniel's death. Not a German tourist, and not a member of her group. "He led a tour today, and one of the guests recognized his walk. He was outside the palazzo the night Lord Philip died."

"Forging a picturing? Killing Lord Philip?" Faye didn't make an effort to conceal her disbelief. "Walter would never do anything like that."

"You said he had a disagreement with Lord Philip. What was it about?"

"It was Lord Philip who had a disagreement with Walter," Faye said. "I don't know the details, but he'd made some comments about Walter being a lightweight in the art world. Frankly, I was surprised when you said Lord Philip asked Walter to appraise his new picture."

"You didn't tell anyone?"

"Of course not." Faye became serious now. "Walter and I are friends. I wouldn't do anything to hurt his business."

Maggie thought about the *White Horse* at the center of this mess. Walter claimed not to know who the original owner was. Was he keeping a secret from Faye? Or was it possible he'd never seen it in George's study?

"Could Walter be your mysterious Pierre?" Gertrude took a sip of coffee. "Or perhaps his agent?"

"Now you're saying Walter is some kind of genius thief?" Faye asked. "I don't see it. He makes the most foolish mistakes in bridge. Can't keep track of the cards."

"Thomas said Pierre was supposed to be clever," Maggie added. "Just shooting Lord Philip hardly fits the bill." She didn't like being on Faye's side of the argument, but she was sure Gertrude had it wrong.

A young couple took the table next to the them, sitting close together, heads nearly touching over a guidebook.

"Walter said he spoke with you on Wednesday," Maggie said. "Do you remember what time it was, Faye?"

"It was the afternoon," Faye said slowly. "I know that. I wanted his help on a crossword puzzle I was working on over lunch." Faye didn't strike Maggie as a crossword puzzler. She didn't seem, well, smart enough. "Do you want me to look up the time?"

"No need. Daniel was killed in the morning." Gertrude rubbed her hands together. "No alibi, then. This is a good theory, Maggie."

An old man sat on a bench across the piazza and began sprinkling bread crumbs. Pigeons mobbed his corner of the square. Why hadn't Maggie appreciated Gertrude's loyalty before? It felt good to have a cheerleader in her corner. Maybe that was why the children had doted on her. Though the endless supply of sweets she offered when they were young certainly helped.

"You're wrong about Walter," Faye said. "He wouldn't have done this."

"He's leaving town," Maggie said. "Did you know that?"

A flicker of doubt crossed over Faye's face. "When?"

"Sunday." Just two days. Maggie tried to ignore her heart rate picking up speed as she thought about how soon that was.

"What are you two going to do about it?" Gertrude asked.

Maggie should tell Orsini. Now she was sure Walter didn't have an alibi, the inspector couldn't dismiss the theory out of hand. But she would have to tell him about the *White Horse,* and if, somehow, she was wrong, the inspector would twist the information into evidence against Thomas. "I wish we had something concrete we could take to the police. Something linking Walter to the forgery."

"You should search his office," Gertrude said. "Take Faye along."

"Why would I do that?" Faye asked. "Walter's my friend."

"Maggie needs a witness to prove she didn't plant any evidence. Who better than a woman who believes in Walter's innocence."

Faye smiled. "I'm sure we wouldn't find anything. But it might be fun. We'd be like Cagney and Lacy, only with better hair."

Fun. That was Faye in a nutshell. "It would be breaking and entering." Maggie hadn't always been the practical one. But someone had to make sure the children had clean clothes and lunches every day. After twenty years of that, plus scheduling doctors' appointments, tracking soccer games, and organizing costumes for the school plays, not to mention climbing the corporate ladder, Maggie had lost a little of her free spirit. "We might not even find anything."

Faye crossed her legs and leaned back. "One minute you're accusing poor Walter, the next you're saying there's no evidence."

Maggie glanced away.

"I guess some people aren't cut out for adventure."

"I take risks."

"I'm sure you do," Faye said.

The Santa Maria bells began to chime.

"That's my cue to leave. I'll do you the favor of not telling Walter about any of this."

Maggie clenched her fists. "I wish you'd done me the same favor of not telling Lord Philip about me being let go from Bells & Wallace."

Faye appeared astonished. "Tell Lord Philip? I never. I didn't tell anyone, Maggie."

Maggie didn't want to believe her, but she thought of how quickly Orsini had discovered her background. Why hadn't it occurred to her that Lord Philip might have just called Bells & Wallace himself?

Maggie watched as Faye clicked away on the cobblestone street into the maze of Trastevere streets, a bright red scarf floating behind her. Maggie thought of Burt's scarf. Burt and Faye both said it had been lost the night of the fireworks party. But that wasn't right, Maggie realized now. She'd seen it at her apartment when she was tidying up the next day. The only way that scarf had gotten to Faye's was if Burt had gone back to Faye's apartment another time. A visit he hadn't told Maggie anything about.

Maggie gripped her coffee cup as she thought of Burt's evening shower. His whistling. The long hours at the job. And beautiful Faye, making dinner for Maggie's husband. Faye might not have shared Maggie's secret, but her relationship wasn't just a flirtation. Maggie distractedly agreed to walk with Gertrude, who was on her way to tour the Colosseum.

Maggie only half listened to Gertrude as they walked.

"There's something about the two sisters that I don't trust," Gertrude was saying when they reached the famous ruin.

Maggie looked around at the structure of sunbaked stone. Shelia had said just one-third of the original Colosseum remained. Earthquakes had destroyed some of it, but most of the marble and stones were carted off as a pre-cut quarry to supply the construction of other buildings during the Middle Ages and Renaissance. "What's that?"

"They're a little too perfect, don't you think?"

Two men dressed as gladiators were posing for photos with tourists a few feet away. They were dressed in matching gold helmets with plumes of feathers, gold chest plates, and knee-length red skirts. Maggie noticed one was wearing white socks with his leather sandals. An emperor lingered nearby, smiling hopefully at passing tourists.

"The Potters? They're sweet old women. End of story."

Gertrude got into the ticket line. "Keep an open mind, Maggie. You might be surprised."

Chapter Twenty-Nine

S *tanding in line for an attraction can dampen the spirit of even the most dedicated tourist. Guests who wish to visit sights not on the Masterpiece itinerary are encouraged to engage a private guide, who will expedite entry.*

—*Masterpiece Tours "Welcome to Rome" pamphlet*

Maggie watched as Gertrude made her way toward the entrance then started back toward the palazzo. Maggie passed a family, the husband carrying a son on his shoulders, the mother pushing a baby in a stroller, relaxed and happy. How long ago those days felt to Maggie.

Her eyes burned. Her husband had crossed the line with Faye. Her husband who had promised, "Never again." She'd nip it in the bud. Tell him it had to end, plain and simple. They would find a marriage counselor. Come through the affair stronger than before. Maybe it was a wake-up call. She didn't realize her eyes were running until she wiped a tear from her cheek. *Pull it together.* She'd come through this.

Maggie passed tour buses lined up at the group entrance of the Colosseum. She paused to watch one unload. A group of middle-aged Americans or Canadians. She was sure her theory was right. She looked at them. Someone could have snuck into Bonaventura by joining a group.

Maggie felt wired, a mix of anger at Burt and grief for her marriage. A second bus started unloading. She should join that tour group, she thought wildly. Just to show her theory about sneaking in was possible.

A woman in a frilly blouse stood at the bus door, handing passengers down to the pavement. What was the worst that could happen if she got caught? She'd be sent away, embarrassed in front of a group of strangers she'd never see again.

Before she realized she'd made a decision, Maggie found herself at the tail end of the group. She ducked her head and moved with the others. Best not to be at the very end of the line. She pushed her way forward.

"I hope lunch is going to be earlier today," a man in a Boston Celtics T-shirt said. His belly was pronounced, stretching the material. "Can't expect us to be on the same schedule as the locals. Americans eat at seven, noon, and six, that's what I told the girl in charge."

A metal gate was open and the travelers passed through, three or four wide. Maggie held her breath and got on the far side of the Celtics fan.

A shrill woman's voice rang out. "Hey, what do you think you're doing?"

Maggie's face blazed with embarrassment. "I'm, I'm..." she began to stammer, but the woman was scolding a large man in a yellow polo for cutting. The group moved forward again, and Maggie swept past the guards and into the Colosseum. She'd done it.

Maggie quickly distanced herself from the group and made her way to the exit. She paused for a moment in the shade of a tree outside, her heart racing. She'd snuck in with a tour group undetected. She'd proven her theory was possible. She felt like she was on cloud nine.

Maggie power walked back to the palazzo, striding past tourists clutching maps and dodging speeding scooters with confidence. She opted for the stairs up to the apartment. She was still feeling a rush from proving her theory when she found John Aldrich in her office chair.

He closed his laptop when he saw her. "Ah, Mrs. White. Here at last. I'm getting buttoned up for Neddy's arrival and have a few more questions." The light from the window accentuated his thinning hair.

Maggie glanced at the page he handed her, still warm from the printer. More details about office supplies and telephone expenses, probably.

Maggie had had enough. She pulled her shoulders back and stood with her spine straight. "Jonathan, I have humored you. I counted paper clips. I pushed paper. But there's a limit. My time is valuable, as is yours." She was her old self again: Maggie White, a woman who made things happen. He opened his mouth, but she went on. "You want to look good for your client. I want you to look good. But paperwork isn't the answer."

He pursed his lips, giving him a fishlike expression.

"Don't pull that face, Jonathan. I'm telling you the truth and you know it. What you need to do is show initiative."

"That's what I was doing when I told the police not to dig into this business." Aldrich's tone was prim.

"I'm not talking about subverting the police. You need to show Neddy the value of keeping Masterpiece Tours open."

He tapped a pencil on his notepad. "And have Neddy drain his assets? This business is losing money, Mrs. White."

"Today, maybe. But it doesn't have to." She was certain about this. She'd put together a good marketing plan for Lord Philip—the one he'd tossed aside after she skipped her anniversary dinner to prepare it. Guests paid a premium for the tour. Masterpiece just needed more of them to cover the overhead. "The concept is a gold mine," Maggie said. "What we need is marketing. Advertising."

Aldrich took his glasses off and began polishing. "Are you suggesting Edward actually invest in the business? If it had such a bright future, why didn't Lord Philip put money into it?"

Maggie had been thinking about this. A man like Lord Philip wouldn't be interested in anything as pedestrian as a travel business with a decent bottom line. At first, he might have enjoyed the adoration of the guests impressed with his title and knowledge. Just like Michelangelo, Lord Phillip had had a deep need to be admired.

But Maggie suspected it became something more. Everything she'd learned painted a picture of a swindler and a cheat, but he couldn't exactly scam all the members of Rome's expat community. Word would have gotten around.

But what if he imported victims, instead? Wealthy people. Dreamers. Visitors impressed by his title and knowledge. Masterpiece brought potential victims right to his door. What were they called? Marks? Len and Shelia had been his most recent targets, and Len said they wouldn't have invested, but perhaps Lord Philip could have closed the deal if he'd had more time.

"Lord Philip's lack of vision shouldn't be a reason to say no." Maggie made her final push. "I understand Neddy has responsibilities in London, and I'd be delighted to manage all this for him." With Thomas and Ilaria, running Masterpiece would be simple compared to her work in the past. Maggie held her breath, waiting for Aldrich to answer.

Aldrich put his glasses back on and leaned back in his chair. Her chair. "You've been here all of two weeks, Mrs. White. Is that right?"

"I'm a seasoned marketing professional with a new perspective on this business. I'm confident the tours can make money."

Aldrich sniffed. "I'll take it under consideration."

Maggie knew that meant no. She'd done her best and should let it go. But she'd had enough of playing by the rules. What had that gotten her? Her department handed over to someone fifteen years her junior and a husband who cheated the moment her back was turned. "I'd hate for Neddy to find out you came here without your firm's approval. And skipping the Hospital Gala? That's quite important to his fiancée, I believe."

Aldrich's eyebrows shot up. "Are you threatening me, Mrs. White?"

She supposed she was, and it felt good. Was this rush why Lord Philip did what he did? "I'm just asking for you to give it some serious thought."

He coughed. "Get me some numbers. Maybe you're on to something." He picked up his computer and hurried down the hall. Maggie listened with satisfaction as the front door closed behind the young man. Did this make her a terrible person? She'd only use her power for good.

Maggie sat in her seat and closed her eyes, inhaling the scent of garlic and onions wafting down the hall. The guests would be returning for dinner soon.

Burt would say she should call Orsini and tell him her suspicions about Walter and the *White Horse*. But what, exactly, did she expect Orsini to do? He thought he had a suspect, and telling him about the *White Horse* would only add fuel to his suspicions about Thomas.

No. Maggie would do what Gertrude suggested and get proof Walter was the man who committed these murders. If he'd stolen the original *White Horse*, the picture might still be at his office. Or, at least, a sketch, or forger's tools. Maybe, if she was really lucky, the gun he'd used was still there, just waiting to be disposed of.

A tingle of excitement electrified her. She, Maggie White, was going to break and enter. And Faye said she wasn't cut out for adventure. Maggie would show her. She would search Walter's office first thing in the morning. It was the only option.

Maggie sat at her desk, enjoying the warm breeze through her open window, imagining the scene, creeping toward Walter's office, jimmying a lock. Maggie needed a partner, like Gertrude said. Someone to keep watch and vouch for any evidence she found.

She couldn't ask Thomas. He was Orsini's prime suspect. Anything he found would be tainted. She couldn't even ask Ilaria. It had to be someone not involved in the investigation. Maggie stared off across the tile roofs stretching out in front of her. If only Gertrude weren't leaving for Amsterdam. And Burt was out. He would never approve.

Maggie frowned. Would she really have to ask Faye, the woman who was having an affair with her husband? She swiveled back and forth in her chair. Well, why not? It would be letting Faye win somehow if Maggie didn't ask her, even if Faye didn't know it. And besides, it would give Maggie a chance to look Faye in the eye and ask that woman what exactly she thought she was doing with Maggie's husband.

Chapter Thirty

R ome, *like any major city, has its unsavory neighborhoods. Guests of Masterpiece Tours will have no reason to visit them, and your hosts will ensure you remain in the areas of our great city appropriate for foreign visitors.*

—Masterpiece Tours "Welcome to Rome" pamphlet

Faye knocked on Maggie's door before dawn on Saturday morning, the last full day of the tour. She was dressed in a thin trench coat, with white trousers peeping out below. She'd be cold, Maggie thought with satisfaction.

Burt was still asleep. Maggie hadn't told him her plan. He'd eaten by the time she got home and was starting a movie when she walked through the door. He paused it and offered to start it over, but Maggie refused. She couldn't sit with him tonight.

The two women tiptoed down to the street, and Faye led the way to her shiny pink scooter parked with its front wheel on the curb. A metal grille covered a jeweler's display window, and even the block's two cafés were still locked tight. The city felt deserted, and butterflies danced in Maggie's stomach as Faye unlocked the heavy chain from around the bike's front tire.

Faye pulled on a big black helmet that obscured her face. "You coming?"

The idea of touching this woman was almost too much, but Maggie commanded herself to get on with it. Faye followed Via Portuense south along the Tiber then onto Via Ettore Rolli, away from the tourist sites. With each block there were fewer restaurants. More litter. Not dangerous. Not exactly. But not a place Maggie would ever have had a reason to visit.

"This is it." Faye pulled the scooter to a stop.

"This" was an ugly graffiti-covered building. Walter's office was squeezed between a hair salon and a laundromat. How on earth did he attract customers here? If this was the best location he could afford, it was evidence he was in need of a cash infusion. The proceeds from the sale of an original Abbati would pay the rent in a better part of town for years to come.

Gertrude would say it was evidence Walter was Pierre. Customers would come to him through discrete private channels. They would never visit his office or even see him face to face.

"What do we do?" Faye asked. "Park here or something?"

"Around the corner. We don't want anyone to see your scooter."

Maggie tried to appear nonchalant as they walked back around the block, searching for a rear entrance. There was none. They'd have to go in the front door. A young man dressed for heavy labor gave Faye an admiring glance, but he kept going. Too early even for catcalls.

When the man was safely down the street, Maggie pulled a thin screwdriver from her purse and knelt in front of the door.

"We're not really going to break in, are we?"

"What did you think we were going to do?" Maggie fit the screwdriver between the door and the frame and jiggled hard. A neighbor back home had once shown her how to jimmy a lock when she'd locked herself out.

"I don't know. I just thought it was a lark. I didn't think we'd actually, you know, go through with it." Faye looked up and down the street. "What if Walter comes?"

Her talk about fun was just that, talk. "That's why we were up before dawn." The lock didn't give. How did it go? Press down then to the side? Maggie gripped the handle and tried again. The latch popped.

"There. Let's get to it." Maggie led the way inside and paused, taking it all in.

The space was more of an office than a gallery. A big wooden desk occupied one corner, covered with a jumble of reference books and leaflets. Two guest chairs sat in front of it. A bookcase was packed with thick, leather-bound tomes, magazines at odd angles, and piles of paper everywhere. There was a wide table on the other side, empty, but with an angled light and a collection of tools on a cart next to it. Five or six canvases were stacked against the wall. The old heating system was humming and whistling at intervals. A partition closed off the area in the back, probably a bathroom or kitchen. The scent of stale cigarette smoke gave the space a faintly down-at-the-heels impression.

"What exactly are you looking for?" Faye whispered, keeping her hand on the doorknob as though she might bolt at any moment.

Maggie realized Faye didn't even know which picture they were looking for. If they found the *White Horse*, Faye would certainly recognize it, and George would have to fess up. Maggie sent a mental apology to Faye's husband.

"A painting of a horse, or a sketch." Maggie tried to be vague. "Anything tying Walter to the forgery. Or the murders."

Faye sniffed. It was clear she didn't expect to find anything. Maggie glanced through the stacked canvases. Old-looking pictures, but nothing like the *White Horse*. The original wouldn't be sitting in plain sight. Perhaps he had a safe?

Maggie was about to look in the back when she saw something moving from the corner of her eye. Her heart leapt into her throat and she froze. How foolish she was to come to the lair of a suspected killer. Because it was a lair, wasn't it? His home turf.

Maggie scanned the room but couldn't see anything moving now. It was silent, except for Faye's shuffling of papers and the wheezing of the heating system. Then she saw the movement again and let out a sigh of relief. A black cat was slinking across the room, nearly camouflaged against the dim light.

"For heaven's sake." Maggie caught her breath. Her hands were still shaking.

"What did you find? Smoking gun?"

"Just a cat. I'm checking the back. If there's anything here, it won't be on display." Maggie pulled the curtain aside and yelped again.

Walter Jones was lying motionless on a couch. Then his barrel chest jerked and he let out a very nasal, very load snore. He was the sound she'd thought was the heating system.

"Oh, God." Faye came up behind her. "Walter, what's going on?"

Walter had a makeshift bed-sit here, with a camp cot, a microwave, and clothes hanging from a rod.

"Shh," Maggie hissed.

But it was too late. Walter woke with a snort, and squinted as he looked around. "Faye? Maggie? What are you doing here?"

"The question is, what are you doing here?" Faye said. "I thought you patched things up with Morgan."

Walter rubbed his eyes and shook himself, as if trying to get fully alert. "I thought so, too. Until I found my bags lined up in the hall when I got home last week. Took up with another man. True love, apparently."

Faye's eyes softened. "I'm sorry, Walter. I had no idea. You should have told me."

He adjusted his pajama shirt, a red and white striped button-down. "But what are you doing here? How did you get in?"

"Maggie broke in," Faye said. "I came along to protect your honor."

Walter looked confused. "What do you mean you broke in? What are you talking about?" Then his face turned red and he clenched and unclenched his hands as the reality of the two women in his office seemed to sink in.

Gertrude was wrong about Walter being Pierre. A master criminal wouldn't be sleeping on a cot and cooking in a microwave. Walter was clearly down on his luck. And maybe his breakup wasn't a coincidence. It could have pushed him over the edge.

Maggie took a breath. "I know you were at the palazzo the night Lord Philip died."

His face turned a deeper crimson. "Out. Now." He took a step toward Maggie, and his hot breath brushed her cheek.

She stepped back.

"Maggie's right?" Faye's voice went up an octave. "You killed Lord Philip over a picture?"

"What? *Killed?* No! Is that what you think?" He looked at Maggie and his body sagged.

She felt the first inkling of doubt.

Walter sank onto his camp bed. "I was at the palazzo, but I didn't kill anyone."

"You said you were leaving the party to work," Faye said.

"I was. When I got outside, I picked up a voice mail from Walpole that I'd missed during the party. He said he didn't want the *White Horse* appraised after all. I'd just spent the whole night boasting about the commission, so I went to the palazzo to try to get him to change his mind. But I didn't kill him."

The cat darted under the curtain then raced around the make-shift bedroom for a purpose known only to himself.

"I'll play you the message." Walter reached for his phone and tapped the screen a few times.

A chill ran down Maggie's spine as she heard Lord Philip's icy tone. "Walter, Walpole here. I've had second thoughts about that commission. I'm sending it to someone with more expertise in this area. Someone whose judgment is more widely known."

Maggie thought about Thomas's idea that Lord Philip knew there was something wrong with the *White Horse*. That his mood had been black that afternoon, even before Thomas pointed out the issues. It fit that Lord Philip would call off the appraisal rather than risk humiliation.

"What happened when you got to the palazzo?" Maggie asked.

"Nothing. Police cars pulled up before I could get to the door. I didn't know what was going on, but it sobered me up enough to realize what a bad idea it was. I decided I'd just come back the next morning as if nothing had happened. Say the message must have been deleted or something. I was as surprised as anyone when you told me he was dead."

"Walter's telling the truth," Faye said. "I've played bridge against him long enough to know when he's bluffing. He's not."

Maggie felt sorry for the man, who looked so deflated sitting in his shabby office in his pajamas. "And you didn't have anything to do with forging the *White Horse*, either? You're not working for Pierre?"

He laughed. "Pierre? You really are reaching, Maggie. I'd hardly be here if that were the case."

Maggie looked him straight in the eyes, and he held her gaze. He looked tired. Relieved even. But not shifty. She looked away. It wouldn't take much for someone with the right skills to forge the picture. Some brushes, some oil paints—and the canvas itself was small. It would have been easy for someone to transport it in a backpack or tote bag. But she believed him.

Maggie heard the sounds of the city, fully awake outside now. A truck was honking out front. Two men shouted angrily back and forth in Italian. Maggie had been so sure the *White Horse* was at the heart of everything. Maybe it still was.

"Who knew Lord Philip had acquired an Abbati?" Maggie asked.

"That picture was hardly an Abbati, Maggie. I can assure you."

She sighed. "Who knew Lord Philip *thought* he had an Abbati?"

"I'm not sure." Walter's fingers shook a bit as he lit a cigarette. "Lord Philip had told everyone high and low he'd acquired a hidden gem. And I was doing my due diligence. Someone could have pieced it together, I suppose."

"What did you do?"

The cat wandered back, winding itself around Maggie's ankles. Walter waved the women to the guest chairs in the main room and took the seat behind the desk, incongruous behind the oaken expanse with his pajamas and mussed hair.

"I got up to speed." Walter looked more relaxed as he pulled on his cigarette. "I called some collectors of Abbatis. I read articles. I looked at auction records."

"What is it you suspect, Maggie?" Faye said.

"I think Pierre heard about the picture and arranged for it to be replaced with a forgery." As far as she knew, no one had ever seen the original *White Horse*. Walter had said it was described in a catalog, but it was too early for photographs. The only people who'd seen it were Lord Philip and the guests. And George and Faye, even if they hadn't known what it was.

"How long would it have taken to make the copy, do you think?" Maggie asked.

"A few days, maybe, depending on how quickly the artist worked." Walter leaned back in his chair, reminding Maggie of some long-dead railroad baron. Whether it was his stout build or conceited smile, Maggie couldn't say. She wished she weren't so sure he was innocent. "Are you suggesting Walpole had Abbati's original *White Horse* and it was stolen right out from under his nose? By someone who—what?—caught a glimpse of it, then painted a substitute and swapped it in?"

Pierre probably heard about Lord Philip's picture when Walter was doing his advance work for the appraisal, calling experts in the field about the picture he was about to receive. Word would have made its way to a man like Pierre.

"Why go to all that bother?" Faye brushed her bangs back. "Why not just steal the picture if it's so valuable?"

"That's not Pierre's approach," Walter said. "He swaps them so it takes ages before anyone realizes a picture is gone. They just see the same picture hanging on the wall they always have."

"And Lord Philip couldn't exactly go to the police claiming theft of a picture when he still had a perfectly decent painting. It hadn't been appraised yet, so there was no evidence he ever even had an original Abbati."

Maggie remembered Thomas's story about Pierre's revenge on the dealer who tried to back out. A man like Pierre wouldn't have wanted Lord Philip dead. He'd want him alive and squirming, knowing his picture had been stolen and humiliated after talking up his big find.

"Have you ever seen him?" Maggie asked. "Pierre?"

"Gracious, no," said Walter.

"Do you think Lord Philip had? Would he know Pierre if he met him?"

"I have no idea." Walter ground out his cigarette.

An idea nagged at Maggie, that she was missing something.

Faye scraped her chair back. "This has all been fascinating, but I have commitments to get on to. Will you be joining us this weekend, Walter? A last game before you fly home?"

Walter shook his head. "Didn't Maggie tell you? She's kindly offered to fill in for me. Funny, I never connected you with Burt, Maggie," Walter said.

"His game's really coming along."

Maggie's confusion must have shown on her face.

"His bridge. His bidding is spot on."

Maggie noticed Faye waving her hand at Walter, trying to shush him.

"Burt doesn't play bridge," Maggie said.

"Of course he does. We played Tuesday night. Give him my best."

Maggie said goodbye in a daze. Burt's missing scarf. The cards on the coffee table. Her husband wanting to tell her something that night she came home so excited about overhearing Daniel's conversation in the studio.

"Why didn't you tell me you were playing bridge with my husband?" she asked Faye when they returned to the scooter.

Faye looked away, not meeting Maggie's gaze.

"That's what you and Burt have been doing, isn't it?"

"It was a surprise for you. He thought if he learned, you could join us for the couples parties. Walter is right—Burt's a natural."

Maggie looked at Faye. When had she decided this woman was so bad? So what if Faye didn't want to join Maggie's volunteer crusades. So what if she was happy playing cards and flirting with painting instructors. The two women might, just might, be friends.

Chapter Thirty-One

G uests will be delighted to work in a studio stocked with everything a serious artist will need to complete a masterpiece.
—*Masterpiece Tours "Welcome to Rome" pamphlet*

Maggie found a well-dressed young man waiting in the salon when she returned to the palazzo. He was about Thomas's age and something about his jawline suggested he was English before he opened his mouth.

He stood and extended his hand. "I'm Edward Innes-Fox. John Aldrich told me what's happened. Bloody awful."

So this was Neddy, heir to Lord Philip's estate. The man she needed to impress if she had any hope of Masterpiece staying open. He had a slight build—smaller than Thomas and John Aldrich—and an open, easy smile. "Maggie White. Please accept my condolences."

"It's all a bit of a surprise." Neddy sat back down on the plush couch. "Johnnie Boy has brought me up to speed on the whole tour business. Says the top line doesn't come close to covering my uncle's lifestyle."

The palazzo was quiet. The guests had already left for their painting session on Janiculum Hill, Rome's second highest point with tremendous views over the city's domes and piazzas. Maggie sat down across from the heir. "I've been looking into that and—"

He shook his head. "I'd rather not know, if you don't mind. You've heard Walpole was strictly persona non grata at home? I don't want to find out anything that's going to put me in an uncomfortable position about accepting this inheritance." He looked so relaxed in this grand room. Maggie could imagine him ordering household staff around in whatever bygone era the decor was meant to capture.

"I don't want to be indiscreet, but Mr. Aldrich suggested you have, well, pots of money."

Neddy laughed. "I will. And that rather leads to what I wanted to discuss with you."

She folded her hands in her lap and waited, not sure what to expect.

"Look here. I'm jolly impressed that you and Thomas and that woman—Hilary?—that you kept it all going. The place could be a sound investment, and I want you to keep doing it. What do you say?" He held his fingers in front of him in a bridge. His signet ring shone on his right hand.

Maggie sank back on the soft cushions. The best she'd hoped for was Neddy being willing to look at a business plan, to consider some preliminary financial estimates. But this? She beamed. "I can't tell you how happy I am to hear that. With some advertising and a more regular schedule of tours, I'm confident we'll build something very big here."

Maggie had thought it all through. A few advertisements in carefully selected publications would increase the tour's visibility. Two tours a month should pay for themselves, and a few months of that schedule would allow Maggie to hire guides and run tours at the same time. Maybe even branch out to other cities. She imagined herself dashing off texts to old colleagues. *Just got back from the new office in Florence. Plans for Venice to open soon.* She'd go to the office dressed in new suits, Italian ones, not the boring old Talbots ones she wore back home.

Edward twisted the heavy signet ring on his right hand. "That's all fine, Mrs. W. Is it all right if I call you Mrs. W.? I don't mind if the business grows a little. But I do need it to keep losing money."

Maggie came crashing back to Earth. "I don't think I understand."

"It's called a tax shelter, Mrs. White." Edward flicked a piece of invisible lint off his pants. "I need a place to park my earnings. Write them off. That kind of thing."

She saw her stylish wardrobe vanish, along with the bevy of underlings awaiting instruction. She was a fool to think Neddy was asking her to really take charge.

She spoke slowly, coolly. "That sounds very interesting, Edward, I'm sure. But a tax shelter isn't what I'm looking for right now." Maggie said the words "tax shelter" as though they were pornographic. "I joined Masterpiece Tours to be part of something real. If you're looking for someone to corral the guests, I'm your woman. You want someone to beat the bushes for new clients, that's me. But if you want someone to run this place poorly, you'll need to look elsewhere."

"I'm offering you the chance to run *something*." Neddy's voice was exasperated. "What more do you want?"

"I want to be taken seriously. And if you won't, I'll find someone who will."

Maggie went into the studio and began wiping tables. She needed to put the conversation with Neddy out of her mind. She'd done the right thing, she knew she had, but she didn't want to replay it over and over again.

They would be using the studio for the farewell party that evening. It was to be a gallery-style exhibition, with the artists' favorite works on display, fancy appetizers, and lots of prosecco. She would make sure there was a festive feel to it, even with the small group.

Maggie had wiped off the third table when her phone rang.

It was Burt. "Faye said you know everything."

Maggie ran her fingers through her hair. "My husband playing bridge doesn't exactly have to be a secret."

"You've seemed a little down about life here. Not seeing much of Faye and the rest of the set. I thought if I learned to play, we could be more a part of the group. Go to the bridge parties together so you wouldn't have to be alone. It was supposed to be a surprise..."

Maggie thought about the party Burt threw for her fortieth birthday. He'd sworn everyone to secrecy, so not a single friend called to wish her a happy birthday. Burt had refused to explain why he wouldn't take Maggie to her favorite restaurant for dinner, and Maggie hadn't understood why he insisted she go run a very tedious errand to get her out of the house. The party was lovely, of course, but she wished she hadn't had to feel so hurt and neglected first.

"Walter says you're pretty good," Maggie said now. "Are you looking for a partner?"

"Any time." She imagined her husband in their living room, feet up on the couch, cradling the phone against his cheek.

How could she have doubted him? "I'm promised to Bernadette for three weeks, then I'm free. Maybe you can give me a refresher."

"I have a great app." Burt's voice became excited and the couch springs squeaked beneath him. "I'm only at level three, but you can use it. You'll be ready to play in no time. How's it going there? No one else dead?"

"All alive and accounted for. Why don't you come to the farewell party tonight?" It would be nice to have Burt there, to meet everyone.

"Nothing would give me greater pleasure." Burt was still Burt. The husband who loved her. Rome hadn't changed him. Not really.

A bell was chiming the hour outside. Eleven. Maggie could see Janiculum Hill from the studio window, and she imagined the artists all hard at work. It was the last day of painting. She'd tell Len that Walter was just what he seemed. Maybe even encourage him to buy a picture to make up for this morning's invasion.

Pots and pans clanged in the kitchen. Ilaria must be setting up. Maggie took one last look around the studio. She'd just said no to the opportunity of a lifetime. This would all be closing in a day or two.

Maggie rinsed out a painter's water cup by the sink and grabbed a handful of Thomas's demonstration brushes to put away. He kept them in a neat cabinet in the middle of the room. She thought of that afternoon, when she'd come in looking for Daniel, only to find Eloise at the sink.

Maggie's heart thumped as she remembered the scene. The sink. She'd been a fool.

Maggie called to the kitchen. "Ilaria!"

The cook came down the hall, wiping her hands on an apron.

"How do you wash out a watercolor stain?"

But Maggie knew the answer to her question before Ilaria answered.

"Watercolor? Water. Why?"

Maggie fought to keep the excitement from her voice. "Not turpentine?"

"Certainly not. That is for oils." Ilaria tried to ask another question, but Maggie waved her away.

Eloise had been using turpentine to remove paint from her knitting bag. A solvent that has no use in cleaning up water color messes, but is used for removing oil paint.

Maggie took a deep breath and told herself to slow down and think it through. She'd rushed down enough dead ends today.

She forced an image of Walter in his pajamas from her head and considered Eloise and Helen. She'd taken everything they said at face value, no matter how improbable. Eloise's knitting that didn't go anywhere. Helen's stories about innumerable cats. The lost reservation. And, finally, the statement Lord Philip was still alive when Eloise went downstairs.

She swallowed. Those two had been playing parts the entire time. What better cover could there be than two doddering old women? Daniel might still be alive if she hadn't been so gullible.

Maggie began pacing and her eyes wandered over one of Shelia's pictures proudly displayed on an easel. It was the sculpture of Romulus and Remus suckling the she-wolf. The great lie, if Charles was to be believed. A story everyone accepted, despite its improbability. And poor Remus, just a footnote in history now.

Though, really, he'd been a bit of a bully, hadn't he? Goading his brother until Romulus snapped. And that was what had happened to Lord Philip. Just like Remus, he'd underestimated the wrong person, an underdog who finally bit back.

Maggie smiled. There was so much talk about history being shaped by the powerful. The kings and the emperors. But really, wasn't it the underdogs, the counselors, the wives, who were pulling the strings? She had been bending over backward trying to fit square pegs into round holes, but no more. It was time to act.

Chapter Thirty-Two

B etween nuns and widows, the streets of Rome are filled with elderly females dressed in black. Don't pity these women. The unmarried geriatrics tend to be happier than their married peers.
—Masterpiece Tours "Welcome to Rome" pamphlet

Maggie forced herself to tidy the studio while she waited for the guests to return. She'd scrubbed all the tables and half the stools before she heard the front door open. She found Thomas in the hall with Len, Shelia, and Charles.

"Where are the Potters?" There was no sound of the elevator creaking upward.

"They're walking back," Thomas said. "They wanted to spoil their lunches with gelato."

"Do you know where?"

Thomas gave her a quizzical look. "I suggested Lupo."

Maggie knew it. Twenty-four flavors of gelato, churned on site, and displayed in a giant case. It was near Rome's parliament building, and she could be there in ten minutes.

"What's wrong?" Len asked. "Does this have something to do with Walter?"

"Walter Jones? What does he have to do with anything?" Charles leaned on his cane and looked concerned.

"Not a thing." Maggie steered the group toward the terrace stairs. "In fact, I think it would be a good idea for you to give him a call, Len. He has some art you and Shelia might be interested in. Now, upstairs, everyone. Lunch is ready."

Thomas hung back. "What's all this about Helen and Eloise?"

"We've been looking at things all wrong," Maggie said. "Listening to the wrong people. Eloise lied. I'm sure of it. I've got to find them."

Ilaria came down the stairs and seemed to read Maggie's expression. "You have solved it? You know the answer?"

Maggie nodded. "Eloise lied about hearing Lord Philip alive."

Thomas stared at her. "You're not saying the old dear is involved?"

"Helen painted the forgery and Eloise made the swap."

"Oh, come on, Mrs. W." Thomas frowned. "What proof do you have?"

"Turpentine," Maggie said. "You take care of the guests. I'll explain everything when I get back."

Ilaria put a hand on Maggie's elbow. "Is it wise to go alone? I can have men here in a matter of moments to accompany you."

Thomas shook his head. "No more favors from your father. I'll go with Maggie."

"My father's not going to be doing me any favors for a long time." Ilaria bit her lip. "I ended it with Gregorio once and for all."

"You what?" Thomas stared at her, as if not sure he'd understood.

"It's over." The young woman smiled. Maggie should have realized there was something different about her this morning. Ilaria had even been whistling in the kitchen.

Thomas stared at her, as if still processing the news, then pulled her into him for a kiss.

Ilaria pushed him away. "Don't get any ideas, Thomas. I should have done it a long time ago." But her grin was as wide as his.

Maggie couldn't wait any longer. "I'm leaving now. If you're coming, Thomas, get a move on."

Thomas gave Ilaria another kiss and jogged after Maggie, his face as pink as if he'd spent the day at the beach. They took the stairs as fast as they could then headed away from the Piazza Navona along a cobblestone street too narrow for sidewalks. A car came toward them, and Thomas maneuvered Maggie to the side.

"What does turpentine have to do with anything?" he asked.

"Eloise was using it to clean her knitting bag, but she's painting with watercolors. Turpentine wouldn't help." Maggie trotted next to Thomas, hurrying to keep up with his long stride. "They're agents for Pierre, Thomas."

They crossed a tiny street, and a car honked loudly.

"This picture doesn't fit his style, remember?"

"This was a different assignment. Pierre wanted to embarrass Lord Philip. It was revenge, plain and simple." It felt good to say it out loud.

Thomas didn't say anything.

"The picture you saw in Lord Philip's office was terrible. You said so yourself. Imagine if word had gotten out he thought such a poor picture was genuine?" Maggie was surprised at how confident she was. But she knew she was right.

They turned the corner to the piazza in front of the parliament building. Lupo Gelato's purple sign was across the square. A yellow wolf with a sundae.

"How do the Potters fit in?" Thomas asked.

"Pierre hired them to forge the *White Horse* and swap it for the original."

"Why the sisters?"

"Why *not* the sisters? Helen has the talent. Eloise carries that silly bag everywhere. We all just saw a pair of old women who like cats and knitting, but Helen can't keep track of how many pets she owns, and Eloise never manages to actually knit anything." Maggie had been as taken in by their acts as everyone else, believing them to be a pair of harmless old women.

"Maybe." Thomas slowed his pace.

"I think Helen painted the replacement *White Horse* when she was pretending to have a migraine at the start of the tour. Remember? Lord Philip showed everyone his picture the first night, then Helen got sick the next day. I'm sure she was in her room painting the entire time. Then Eloise hid it in her knitting bag, probably making the swap the morning Lord Philip died."

The timeline fit. Helen could have painted the picture in a day then used a hair dryer to accelerate the drying time. And it would have been easy enough for Eloise to pop into Lord Philip's study during breakfast before the group left for the Natale di Roma celebrations.

They paused by the giant obelisk in the center of the square. Yet another ancient artifact in this modern city. There were so many, she'd stopped really looking at them. Just like she'd overlooked Helen and Eloise.

"And then later Eloise killed Lord Philip?" Thomas shook his head at vendor walking past offering leather bags for sale.

"Oh, no. They didn't want Lord Philip dead. They wanted him embarrassed. Remember how pleased Walter and Aldrich were that the *White Horse* was worthless? Now imagine if the whole expat community had heard that. 'Old Walpole losing his touch.' He would have hated it. *That* was Pierre's revenge."

"Presumably Pierre has an original Abbati now, as well," Thomas said. "Unless the sisters still have it?"

Maggie thought of the dinner the Potters missed. Chances were, it was a cover story to sneak out and get the picture to Pierre. "I don't think so."

Maggie and Thomas spotted the sisters at the same time, sitting on a concrete wall ringing the piazza. Eloise was laughing at something Helen said. They looked relaxed and happy.

"Well, what now?" Thomas asked.

"We get them to tell us the truth."

Maggie led the way to the sisters, who were eating their ice cream in the shade. Eloise calmly licked her cone. It was stracciatella, vanilla with shards of chocolate mixed in. Her blue eyes moved, looking between Maggie and Thomas. Maggie felt a charge of excitement. She was looking forward to this, she realized.

"Here for dessert?" Eloise asked. "Thomas was right. This gelato is heavenly."

"We know everything," Maggie said.

Helen wiped her mouth with a napkin. "I don't know what you're talking about." Her tone was cold, her vague fluffiness gone.

"The paint Eloise was cleaning in the studio," Maggie said. "It was oil. Why would she be using oil paint in a watercolor class?" Her voice was calm.

She was the old Maggie. The one who stood up for herself, the one who delivered results.

Eloise sighed. "I hoped you wouldn't catch that."

Helen ran her spoon around the small paper cup for the last bit of gelato. Strawberry, judging from the smudges left inside. "What are you here for?"

"Your help." Maggie sat down next to the women.

Helen set the cup and spoon on the ground next to her straw hat, the one with the cats on it. "What is it you think you know?"

"I know Eloise replaced the original *White Horse* with a forgery then gave the original to Pierre when you said you were meeting your nephew for dinner."

"Goddaughter's son, I think it was." Eloise was wearing her usual sturdy walking shoes. Maggie wondered what she wore when she wasn't in character. Something impractical, maybe. Sandals? Heels?

"If what you've said is true," Helen said, "the picture is gone. What is it you want?"

"To clear things up." Maggie looked at the cobblestones. She'd read they'd been thrown at police during the riots twenty years ago. Easy to collect, easy to throw. "You lied about hearing Lord Philip on the phone the night he died, Eloise."

Two men with briefcases walked by, deep in conversation.

"She didn't kill him," Helen's eyes were clear as she looked straight at Maggie.

"I know. Pierre wanted Lord Philip alive to suffer his humiliation."

Eloise let out her breath. "Smart girl. Lord Philip was already dead."

It was just as Maggie had thought. After all of her false steps, she finally had it right.

"This is all hypothetical," Helen said. "You can't prove a thing. Lord Philip had a painting of a white horse when we arrived, and he had a painting of a white horse when he died. There's no one who can prove anything different."

"I'm not going to the police," Maggie said.

Helen was right. Even if Orsini believed her, there'd be no way to prove

Lord Philip had a different picture than the one Walter had appraised. Maggie told herself it didn't matter, that knowing the truth was the important thing. Bringing them to justice wasn't her responsibility.

"But why did you go in that night?" Thomas asked. "You'd already made the switch, hadn't you?"

"I swapped it just after breakfast." Eloise finished her cone and brushed a few crumbs off her skirt. She shooed away some pigeons who waddled hopefully toward her.

"I went in during the fireworks to see if Lord Philip had noticed the difference," Eloise explained. "We were supposed to make the handoff to Pierre the next day, and I wanted to report that Lord Philip knew something was wrong. I was going to ask to see the *White Horse* and hesitate when I saw it, saying it didn't look very skillful, just in case he hadn't picked up on the problems on his own."

Thomas smiled. "Walpole knew."

"Pierre will be pleased," Eloise said. "He hated thinking all this was for nothing."

"Speaking hypothetically." Even Helen seemed more relaxed now.

Out of their characters, the sisters appeared younger. Helen was focused, not at all flighty. Eloise's posture was better.

"Working for Pierre must pay fantastically well." Thomas looked like his old self, boyish and animated. Maggie didn't like the light in his eyes.

"Eloise and Helen are thieves, Thomas. It's immoral and unethical, not to mention illegal."

"Pierre does pay his agents well," Helen said. "But that's hardly the point. He hires the best and trusts them to do their jobs. That's a rewarding feeling."

"At one place I pretended to be the granddaughter of a former cook looking to recapture my family's roots," Eloise said. "Another time we said we got left behind on a coach tour through gardens of Cumbria. Whenever there's trouble, we just mention cats. People lose interest, and you're immediately labeled a little batty."

"Hypothetically," Helen said.

"Hypothetically," Eloise amended.

Two young women in tight jeans strolled by, wrists loaded down with bright plastic bracelets, teetering on their heels. They looked like sisters, so similar in build and features. Maggie looked again at Eloise and Helen, so different physically. One tall, one small. Nothing physical in common, yet everyone accepted them as siblings.

"What have you forged?" Thomas asked.

Eloise waved her hand. "Oh Helen's done everything. Manet. Monet. Picasso. Old masters. Modern. You name it. Helen's versatile."

How could Eloise be so proud of larceny? She made it sound like it was all fun and games, something to be celebrated. Eloise must have noticed Maggie's disapproval. "The original artist isn't getting hurt. He got paid, or didn't get paid, years ago. Now it's just wealthy folks dealing pictures back and forth."

"They're just possessions to the owners." Helen smoothed her hair, tucking a stray piece back into her bun. "Many of the ones we work with were purchased generations ago. At best, the owners like them as pretty pictures and never even notice the swap. The *White Horse* was an exception, remember."

"And the original pictures go to people who truly love them." Eloise was earnest. "That's how Pierre works. A collector contacts him about a special piece, and he obtains it. They're not just investments to the new owners. They're prized for what they are."

The two women sounded like they truly believed what they were saying, but Maggie suspected it was the pulling of the wool over everyone's eyes they loved. She remembered the charge she'd gotten from pressuring Aldrich, the sense of power. She shifted uncomfortably on the hard concrete.

"What about Charles?" Thomas asked. "Was he part of the plan?"

Helen and Eloise exchanged a glance.

"I'm afraid so," Eloise said. "We've found chasing eligible men is one of the best ways to neutralize a potential threat. Put him on the defensive. That way he spends his time trying to get away from us, not asking any difficult questions."

The women made it sound like a game. "Daniel might still be alive if you hadn't lied," Maggie said. She ignored the voice telling her he might have been alive if she hadn't been so eager to believe them.

"I had no way of knowing that would happen." Eloise's tone was defensive. "I just didn't want the police investigating me because I found a dead body. They would have dug into our pasts, noticed some—" she paused, "irregularities."

Helen frowned at Maggie. "What are you going to do about all this?"

Maggie had the information she needed. She was going to call Orsini as soon as she got back to the palazzo and he would arrest the murderer. She and Thomas would be in the clear. Simple as that.

But she wasn't going to tell the inspector about the *White Horse*. Helen was right. There was no proof Lord Philip's original picture was missing. And George Masters wouldn't thank Maggie for bringing his name into it if there wasn't a way to recover the original.

Whatever secret Lord Philip was holding over George would stay hidden, and that was all right, wasn't it? He had paid enough with the loss of his picture, even if he didn't have any idea of its value until it was gone.

"I'm sure Pierre would come to some sort of arrangement," Eloise said. "One that would be mutually beneficial if we keep this to ourselves."

How much money would be mutually beneficial? Enough to buy Masterpiece Tours from Edward Innes-Fox? Then she caught herself. It was one thing to keep silent because there was no benefit to speaking. It was quite another to take money in return.

"I won't say any more than I have to," she said. Despite herself, she liked the women. She was glad that she didn't have any evidence to take to the police.

Eloise patted her hand. "Lord Philip and Daniel weren't good men. Remember that."

But Eloise was wrong. Daniel wasn't a bad man, not really. He wasn't working for a drug cartel, and he wasn't a blackmailer. He was a man who worked too much and cheated on his wife. If he hadn't died, who knows? Maybe he would have redeemed himself.

Chapter Thirty-Three

I t is said Rome has just two problems: traffic and tourists.
  —*Masterpiece Tours "Welcome to Rome" pamphlet*

Maggie and Thomas lingered on the sidewalk after walking the Potter sisters back to the hotel.

"You think Lord Philip was killed by someone from the outside, after all?" Thomas ran his fingers through his hair. "If it was one of Lord Philip's victims, we'll never find him. I may as well turn myself in at the station now."

Maggie inhaled. The aroma of coffee mixed with baked goods from the café around the corner lingered in the air. She didn't have any doubts now. The meeting with Eloise and Helen had confirmed her suspicions. "It was Vicky."

Thomas stared. "Vicky? Have you forgotten she has a very tidy alibi for both deaths?"

"She doesn't. Eloise's lie about hearing Lord Philip just made us think she did." Would things have been different if Eloise had told the truth? Maybe not, Maggie thought. There was no reason to suspect one of the guests. "Vicky went downstairs during the fireworks before Eloise, remember? She had the perfect opportunity."

Thomas looked skeptical. "And Daniel?"

"She pretended to be sick so Daniel would have to go to Bonaventura in her place. She probably slipped out of the hotel, using the fire escape, and then snuck into the gardens with the Germans."

A family walked past into the hotel, two parents with scowling teenagers. "You think she was blackmailing her own husband?"

"Vicky made up the blackmail story to throw us off." Maggie was cold, the letdown after the rush of the interview, probably. She moved into the sun. "We were all so focused on Lord Philip, we looked at everything through the lens of his murder. It seemed logical that Daniel's death was somehow caused by Lord Philip's. But I think it was the other way around. Lord Philip died because Daniel was going to die."

Maggie remembered how eager Vicky had been to keep Bonaventura on the tour schedule, asking Maggie to confirm the date of the trip, and even who else would be touring the garden the same day. Vicky had planned to kill her husband there from the start. She rubbed her arms, still trying to get warm.

"Remember the Bonaventura manager saying how dangerous the tower was if you got too close to the edge? If Lord Philip hadn't died a few days earlier, everyone would have treated Daniel's death like an accident."

"Vicky read that article the manager mentioned and brought her husband here to kill him?"

Maggie nodded.

"And she killed Lord Philip, why? You're not thinking of that Agatha Christie with the train schedules are you? The one where there are lots of murders to hide the one with the motive?"

"Lord Philip's death wasn't part of her plan," Maggie said. "Not originally. Vicky booked the trip to kill her cheating husband, and Lord Philip got in the way."

Maggie thought of the bracelet Vicky said was stolen but had hidden in her suitcase. She should have realized its importance then, right after Daniel died. "Lord Philip was blackmailing Vicky over something. She pretended her jewelry was stolen so she could give it to him to keep quiet. But she shot him instead, kept the jewelry, and proceeded with her plan to kill her husband." What had Gertrude said? Never blackmail a murderer. Or a murderess.

Thomas still didn't look convinced.

"Do you know what happened to Remus? He was the powerful one, always criticizing his brother. Then one day Romulus had had enough. He pushed his brother right off the city wall. Maybe Vicky got tired of being pushed around, too." Maggie remembered thinking she and Vicky were alike, both underdogs, underestimated by the men in their lives. She shivered.

"Even if your theory is right, Lord Philip couldn't know what she had planned for Daniel. What could he have had on Vicky?" Thomas stepped aside to make room for two guests exiting the hotel, an elderly couple walking hand in hand.

"It could have been anything, but I do have a guess."

Thomas waved away the bellhop approaching from the hotel, probably wanting to know why these two nonresidents were blocking the front door. "Well, what is it?"

Maggie thought of Thomas and Aldrich telling the story about their friend, Tancred's uncle, who'd died sightseeing in Madrid. "I think Vicky is your friend Tancred's aunt."

"You've lost me, Mrs. W. Tancred doesn't have an aunt."

"Yes, he does," Maggie said. "The uncle who died on his honeymoon—I think Vicky was his wife."

"The old geezer who fell from a tower..." Understanding dawned on Thomas's face.

"Exactly. Tancred's aunt was called Tory, wasn't she? That's a nickname for Victoria, just like Vicky. And Aldrich keeps saying Vicky looks familiar. He probably met her at some event with Tancred's family."

"But her first husband was young, wasn't he? Died of some terrible disease or something?"

That was what Vicky had told everyone the first night. Maggie remembered Vicky's sad blue eyes and perfect white teeth biting her lower lip when she told them all. "She lied, Thomas. She told the same story she'd told Daniel. If Lord Philip made the connection and told Daniel his wife had been lying to him about her past, he'd have left her. He may have even gone back to the secretary he was cheating with."

Thomas opened and closed his mouth several times. "Terrible Tory is

249

Vicious Victoria?"

"We all go by different names, don't we?" She was Margaret on legal documents, Peggy to her parents, Meg to college friends, and Maggie to all who knew her now. Except for Thomas, and she rather liked Mrs. W.

"A name is hardly proof. But it *could* be something." He spoke faster. "If she got away with it in Spain, maybe she thought she'd found a foolproof method of disposing of rich husbands."

"We need to call the inspector. He can make sure she doesn't make her flight tomorrow while he's digging into her past."

"You think he'll believe you?"

"He won't have a choice." She'd convince him. Maggie had always been a great closer when she truly believed in her project.

Thomas put his hands in his pockets, as though unconcerned. "You'll tell him about the *White Horse*?"

"Only what I have to: that Eloise was confused and that Vicky was downstairs during the critical time." There was no point in complicating the story with the stolen picture. Orsini wouldn't be able to prove anything. Maggie dialed the inspector and was put through almost immediately.

"You and Thomas Evans are close friends, are you not?" Orsini asked when she finished her story. "Are you telling me this theory, I wonder, because you're trying to take my attention from the two of you? It is perhaps understandable, Signora White, but misguided. I am working today—a Saturday, yes?—because I have learned Mr. Evans has been asking about buyers for a valuable painting. An Abbati, I think it was."

Maggie's stomach turned over. She'd forgotten she'd asked Thomas to look into people Walter might have approached with the *White Horse*. Yet another mistake. She gripped the phone. "Inspector, Vicky killed two men, and she's booked on a flight out of the country tomorrow. We can't stand by."

She heard papers rustling on the other end of the line. She wished she were there in person, to read his body language. It had been easy enough to understand when she and Vicky had gone to the station together, but, over the phone, it was impossible to know if she was making headway.

He sighed. "I cannot go after everyone you suspect of committing a crime, Signora White. Do you have any proof?"

Maggie remembered her first meeting with Orsini at the station, how hot she'd been waiting in the long line. She'd forced Vicky to join her that afternoon. The young woman been so reluctant to file the police report over the jewelry. It had been the one thing Orsini had been helpful with.

Then it clicked. The police report. "Yes. Yes, I do, Inspector." Maggie was finally warm again, she realized. Whatever regret she'd felt was gone. "Vicky filed a false police report when she said she had jewelry stolen, but it wasn't. I saw the jewelry in her things." Maggie held her breath, waiting for him to answer.

He grunted. "I will come to the apartment. We will sort this out there."

The palazzo was silent when Maggie and Thomas opened the front door. Maggie hoped Len and Shelia had called Walter to look at some artwork. Charles was probably painting on this final day, and Ilaria was off somewhere. Telling her father about the breakup?

Maggie walked over to the big living room windows. The view really was magnificent. Red tiles and green roof gardens, small piazzas and big fountains. She would miss this apartment. She'd done the right thing, saying no to Neddy, though. She didn't need to trade a domineering boss for one who was banking on her failure.

Maggie was still looking out over the city when a floorboard squeaked. She looked at Thomas, who was flopped on the salon's deep couch. He sat up. The sound had come from the hall. There was another squeak, then the sound of drawers being opened.

Thomas put a finger to his lips and moved toward the hall. Maggie's heart thudded as she followed him. The door to Lord Philip's study was open. Maggie knew they should back up, go outside the apartment, but she couldn't stop herself.

She moved forward and saw a woman rifling through a drawer in Lord Philip's desk. Her head was down, long blond hair hiding her face. It was Vicky.

The young woman rummaged for another moment, then pulled out a magazine. That was when she noticed the pair in the doorway. Slowly, with almost deliberate casualness, she put the magazine down.

"I thought everyone was out for the afternoon." Vicky's voice was neutral, as though she hadn't decided how to play it yet.

"We're meeting the police." Maggie kept her voice light. Not accusing. Not knowing. Maybe even a little dumb. "Taking care of some paperwork."

Vicky cocked her head at Maggie, as if weighing the words. Maggie made an effort to relax her shoulders. Orsini would be here soon, and Thomas could overpower Vicky if it came to that. Maggie forced a sympathetic expression. "I'm happy to see you out of the hotel."

Thomas coughed. "I say, yes, it is good to see you, Vicky. Is that a copy of *Tattler*?" He reached for the magazine. A brunette wearing a colorful polka-dot dress was on the cover. "It's five years old. Gossip's going to be a bit out of date."

He laughed awkwardly and started leafing through it. A page was marked with a sticky note, and Thomas read the caption. "Albert Puffington-Scott marries Victoria Kathleen Thomas."

He coughed again, and his voice was strained. "Fancy old Walpole flagging a picture of Tancred's uncle." He held the magazine up to Maggie.

She saw a photo of an ancient man in a morning suit standing with a mousy girl in a glittering white dress. There was no question Vicky was the woman in the photograph.

"I'll take that." Vicky reached for the magazine with her left hand, holding a shiny pistol in her right.

Chapter Thirty-Four

*I*talians do everything slowly, except speak and drive. Nothing will ever be done "today" or "this week," no matter how simple or how urgent the request. The wise traveler will embrace this as one of the country's charms.
—*Masterpiece Tours "Welcome to Rome" pamphlet*

"Oh, I say... You really are Terrible Tori?"

Vicky took the magazine from Thomas and tucked it into her purse, keeping the gun trained on him. "Step away from the desk, please."

Orsini would be here any minute. They needed to keep Vicky talking, just like in the movies.

"There is one thing I don't understand," Maggie said.

"Just one? Oh, I doubt that." Vicky wore the same superior smile Lucy's childhood friend Tanya adopted whenever she was up to something.

Maggie had been glad when Tanya's family moved to Pittsburgh.

"What's so important about the magazine?" Maggie worked to keep her voice steady. "Your first marriage isn't proof of anything."

Vicky spoke slowly, as if addressing a particularly slow child. "You're right, there's no crime in being a widow. But this magazine shows Lord Philip knew about my marriage. Something Daniel did not. If the police knew that, it would be a problem, don't you agree?"

"Cutting it a bit close, aren't you?" Thomas said.

Maggie shot him a look. They shouldn't be antagonizing this woman.

"Just taking care of loose ends," Vicky said. "By the time I realized it was important, it wasn't easy to slip in."

Maggie remembered seeing Vicky in the hallway outside the study, pretending to have lost something. Then always hanging back when the group was heading down to the van. And after Daniel died—or, more accurately, after Vicky killed him—the woman couldn't exactly trail along on the tour. This afternoon might have been her best opportunity.

"And you'll just take it and be off?" Thomas asked. His reminded Maggie of a child who's asked for a second helping of dessert. He knows what the answer is going to be, but still holds onto a glimmer of hope.

Vicky gave a tight smile. She looked very young. Impetuous. "I wish you hadn't dug your nose into this, Mrs. White." Vicky shook her head, her hoop earrings bouncing against her cheeks. "Not that I don't appreciate your help. Confusing everything with theories about drugs and art thieves."

The room was hot from being closed off. Maggie edged back toward the door, a trickle of sweat running down her back. Where was that inspector? Maggie listened hard, hoping to hear the sound of the elevator creaking or the front door opening, but there was only silence.

"I wasn't overly concerned with alibis," Vicky went on, almost preening. "The police were bound to focus on finding an intruder from outside. But it was a nice surprise when Eloise said she heard Lord Philip alive. And then the lawyer told the police not to investigate. All in all, I've been rather lucky."

Vicky was wrong. If the police had made a reasonable attempt to find the killer, Maggie would have left it in their hands and Orsini would never have dug into the case. It would have been dropped, just as Aldrich had arranged. At least until Daniel died.

"Bit of bad luck old Walpole recognizing you." Thomas had his hands in pockets. He could have been casually chatting with a friend about relationship troubles.

Vicky shrugged. "He dug out that magazine the first night I was here. Said he never forgot a face." Her voice had lost its BBC polish and was rougher now. "He thought I was a gold digger hiding a little secret from my husband about marrying an old man. He had no idea I'd pushed my beloved husband."

"Tancred's family couldn't figure out why you'd done it." Thomas managed to sound genuinely curious, as if untroubled by Vicky's admission of guilt. "He'd have died soon enough, and you didn't inherit anything."

Vicky winced, her pretty face momentarily transforming into that of bitter old woman . "My late husband lied to me. He said we'd be out in society when we married. Then, on our, honeymoon he told me he sold the London flat so we could spend all our time in the country. I was furious. I didn't realize until too late he'd also lied about fixing his will."

"Was the fake jewelry theft Lord Philip's idea?" Maggie asked.

Vicky's lip curled. "Lord Philip thought I would pay him off like all the other saps he twisted his knife into. When I came into the study that night, he thought it was to give him the bracelet."

"It was clever to use Lord Philip's gun." Maggie wanted to keep this girl feeling secure.

Vicky nodded. "I picked it up during dinner. He didn't give me any choice. You must understand that, don't you? When Daniel died, Lord Philip would have made the connection to Madrid. And then, who knows what he would have asked for? Daniel's life insurance policy? My house? Nothing would ever have been enough."

A sensible woman would have cancelled her plans to kill Daniel. Or at least delay them until she got back home, away from Lord Philip. But Vicky hadn't been able to change course or adjust her plans when Lord Philip threw a curve ball at her.

For the first time, it occurred to Maggie that Vicky might actually shoot them. She was crazy enough to think she could just remove the obstacles in her way, that two more bodies wouldn't hurt her.

Maggie felt her blood pounding in her ears. Orsini wasn't going to get here in time to save them. She had to do something herself.

"Lord Philip underestimated you." Maggie tried to sound understanding, sympathetic. "And you couldn't put off your plans for Daniel. You'd gone to a lot of trouble."

"It'd be months before I could convince Daniel to go on another trip. It was now or never."

"Why not do it at home? There have to be loads of opportunities there."

Thomas's words were strained. The reality of the situation must be hitting him, too.

"Police would investigate, wouldn't they?" Vicky said. "Ask about the state of our marriage. The will. Sticky things like that. But on a trip, it's different. We're just tourists to them. The police in Madrid didn't even bat an eye."

Vicky gestured for Maggie to sit in the wooden visitor's chair in front of Lord Philip's desk. "Maggie, you go here. Thomas, on the floor by the door."

Maggie ignored her sweaty shirt clinging to her back. She focused only on appearing in total control, the way she had when the Bells & Wallace CEO told Maggie her services were no longer needed. She'd survived that meeting. Just the way she'd survive this.

Her mind raced. What was it Vicky wanted? Recognition that she'd outsmarted them?

"The police can't prove anything," Maggie said. "You were too clever."

"Committed the perfect crimes," Thomas chimed in from the floor. He looked like an obedient preschooler sitting with his legs crossed, elbows on his knees.

Vicky looked smug.

"How did you think of it?" Maggie's chair was hard, all the better for keeping her posture. She couldn't let Vicky see she was afraid.

"I read an article in a magazine about the restoration," Vicky said. "I'd just found out about Daniel's affair, and it seemed like the perfect solution. Take him there and push him off when no one was looking. It was easy enough with my first husband."

Vicky let the gun dip a few inches as she spoke. She couldn't keep it trained on both of them at the same time. No matter how many hours Vicky spent in Pilates studios, her arm would get tired from holding the gun on them.

"It must have been hard getting inside the grounds," Maggie said.

"It couldn't have been easier. I put on my most drab clothes, carried a backpack, and wore a sun hat. I climbed down the fire escape at the hotel and took a taxi to Bonaventura. I waited at a café across the street for the tour buses to arrive then just joined the group as they were getting off the bus. No one gave me a second look."

"You got lucky with Daniel being in the tower at the right time," Thomas said.

Maggie eyed Lord Philip's heavy paperweight in the shape of an Eskimo. She wondered if she could scoot her chair a few inches closer. If she got close enough, she could reach the paperweight, but then what?

"I didn't leave that to chance, Thomas. I told him he needed to be there at just the right time for the sun angles to be perfect for the pictures. And I said he should be alone, so he wouldn't have anyone talking in his ear. He hated crowds, so that was easy enough."

"And you were waiting for him?" Thomas said.

Maggie scooted the chair an inch closer to the desk while Vicky was looking at Thomas.

"I was in the church, and I climbed up after a wave of Germans came down. He was so surprised to see me it was almost too easy."

Maggie scooted another inch closer. Her chair scraped loudly.

"Stop that, Mrs. White." Vicky swung the gun in her direction. "Move your chair back, please. This isn't going to end with you grabbing a pair of scissors from the desk and stabbing me or something."

Maggie scooted the chair back an inch.

"Farther." Vicky kept the gun trained on Maggie while she opened the drawer and put a roll of packing tape on the desk. "Now, Thomas, I need you to tie Mrs. White up."

"Tie her up?" Thomas's voice squeaked.

She waved her gun at him. "What, you think I'm going to kill her and let you tackle me while I'm distracted?"

"Kill her?" Thomas coughed. "And me? That hardly seems wise, Vicky. The police won't stop, not with four deaths."

"People die in struggles all the time," Vicky said. "It'll look like Maggie managed to get a shot against you before you killed her, and then you both took your last breaths. I watch a lot of television. This is textbook."

The air in the room still smelled of Lord Philip's blood. Maggie suddenly felt like she'd suffocate if she stayed here longer. "You're the hero of your own story," Gertrude had told Lucy one year, when she was hoping a boy she liked would ask her to the homecoming dance. "Take charge."

Gertrude was right. Vicky might have killed a philandering husband and a blackmailing lord, but Maggie wasn't going to be a sitting duck like those men. Vicky's gun arm was shaking. It was time.

"It's all right, Thomas," Maggie said. "Remember the Scout Motto."

He looked at her, his gaze meeting hers in an unspoken question. She nodded.

"What's that?" Vicky said. "Some special knot they teach you? Hard with tape, I think."

"No." Maggie kept her gaze on Vicky. "It's to be prepared."

She reached forward from her chair and grabbed the big glass paper weight off the corner of the desk. She stood and slammed it into Vicky's gun hand. The gun landed on the ornate rug with a dull thud, and Maggie kicked it away with her foot while Thomas sprang from the floor and tackled Vicky. She yelped as she lay spread eagle on her stomach with Thomas's knee against her back.

Maggie picked up the gun and held it trained on Vicky. Her arms were weak, as though she'd swam a hundred laps. She took several deep breaths. "Nice work," Maggie said, when she could finally speak.

Thomas winked. "I told you I was a good rugger player."

Chapter Thirty-Five

W   hen you bid arrivederci *at the end of the tour, you're not saying*
         goodbye, but, quite literally, "until we meet again."
                    —Masterpiece Tours "Welcome to Rome" pamphlet

John Aldrich and Neddy Innes-Fox arrived as Orsini walked Vicky out in handcuffs.

"What's going on?" Aldrich asked. "What are they doing with the widow?"

Maggie's heart rate had finally returned to normal during the police questioning. "Vicky Barlow killed Daniel. And Lord Philip."

"She tried to kill us, too, but we showed her," Thomas broke in. "It was rather a good show."

The two were still in the salon, where they'd given their statements to Orsini. Aldrich and Neddy joined them and made a satisfying audience, gasping and "jolly good old man"ing in all the right moments.

"She was some kind of black widow?" Neddy asked when they finished.

"I don't think she married intending to kill her husbands," Maggie said. "I think they let her down, and she couldn't forgive them for it."

"Once the trust is broken, you can't go back." Neddy exuded all the piety of a man about to take the vows of matrimony. Maggie thought of Burt. You couldn't go back, but you could go forward. "Well done, Mrs. W." Neddy reached to shake her hand. "Solving the case when the police were stumped."

Maggie smiled at him. She had made missteps, but Neddy was right. She *had* solved it.

Shelia's breathless voice broke in from the hall. "Is everything all right?"

She came into the salon, her face red, as if she'd run all the way up. "I saw police cars downstairs. What's going on?"

Ilaria, Len, and Charles followed a moment later, dressed and ready for the party an hour early.

Thomas answered, "They've arrested Vicky for both murders. Maggie figured it out, and Vicky tried to kill us both and frame me. You explain, Maggie. I'm exhausted."

Maggie told the story from the beginning.

Ilaria squeezed Thomas's hand. "You should have let me send my men. They are trained for this type of thing."

He puffed out his chest. "I'll admit it was tight there for a minute, but I did just fine."

"I understood it was Maggie who saved you?" Ilaria's eyes twinkled.

"More like a team effort," Thomas said.

"And Daniel wasn't doing anything illegal?" Charles asked.

"He was a cheating workaholic," Maggie said. "That was enough for Vicky."

"Such a shame." The crimson ruffles around the deep v-neckline of Shelia's party dress rippled as she spoke. "He'd just gotten a big promotion, too."

"What promotion?" Len asked.

"Daniel told me about it during dinner the night before he died. He'd gotten a call from New York with the news. He was really excited."

Maggie caught Thomas and Charles's eyes. Was that phone call from New York the one she'd heard in the studio? The one that had led her down such a rabbit hole?

"He was certainly a hard worker." Shelia tugged her dress lower over her knees, unaware of the silent exchange. "That's what he was doing the day he lied about going to the museum, working on some big deal that was about to close. He said the timing of the trip was terrible—right during his busy period—but Vicky wouldn't put it off."

Maggie realized she'd never confided her suspicions about Daniel to Shelia. If she had, maybe Shelia would have told her all this and Maggie wouldn't have suspected him.

"Vicky's problem was a lack of imagination." Ilaria stood near the fireplace, one hand on the mantle. She was a woman at home in this grand room. "She had a good idea with her first husband, but she should have gotten rid of Lord Philip another way. More discrete. Then this would never have come to light."

Maggie was glad she and Ilaria had become friends. This wasn't a woman to cross. She hoped Thomas knew how to watch his step.

Shelia tapped the toe of her shoes embellished with red sequins. "Did she intend to frame Thomas all along?"

Maggie considered, thinking back to her visit to Vicky's room after Daniel's death. "Maybe not at first. But when it was clear the police weren't going to rule Daniel's death an accident, she had to come up with another suspect."

Vicky hadn't known the police already suspected Maggie.

"She made up the story about hearing Daniel blackmailing someone then told the police about Thomas's trick at the auction house to give him some semblance of a motive."

"What about the *White Horse*?" Charles asked. "Was it involved?"

"Just a misunderstanding. Nothing to do with Lord Philip's death." Then Maggie excused herself to call Burt.

"The police just arrested Vicky Barlow. She came on the trip to kill her husband. Lord Philip was collateral damage."

"The wronged wife?"

Maggie heard music in the background—a medley of earnest Italian crooners mixed with American pop. Burt must have the window open. Maggie gave him an abridged version of the events.

"I'm proud of you, honey," he said.

Maggie leaned back, smiling. "What are you doing now?"

"Just killing time until the party. I've been reading *Bid Better, Play Better*. It says the way to improve your bridge is to cut down on your mistakes. It makes sense, doesn't it?"

Maggie waved at Thomas and Ilaria, who passed back and forth on their way to the studio, carrying tablecloths, silver trays, and all the other bits and pieces that went into preparing a party.

"You're already dressed?"

Burt never got ready early, not unless he was really looking forward to something.

"And shaved."

"Come now," Maggie said. "I'm ready to pop the prosecco."

She returned to the salon, where she found Eloise and Helen with the group. Shelia was telling them the story of Vicky's capture. "But, Maggie, how did you know Eloise was confused about hearing Lord Philip alive?"

Maggie had glossed over this point when she first told the story. Maggie avoided Eloise's gaze. "We all get confused sometimes, don't we? I just thought, maybe, that was what had happened here."

Eloise hunched slightly and said in a weak voice, "It's not easy getting old. The mind isn't what it once was…"

Maggie thought the woman might be overacting, but Shelia patted Eloise's hand.

"Regular Sherlock Holmes." Aldrich pushed himself to his feet. "The Puffington-Scotts should know about this. They may need local representation to keep them apprised of everything. Our firm has some excellent relationships in Madrid that I could enlist. I'm going to call Tancred."

"Are you sure he wasn't involved?" Shelia said when he left the room. "The lawyer always seemed a bit cold blooded to me."

Neddy stretched. "Old Johnnie Boy isn't so bad. Just a hair overenthusiastic."

Ilaria and Thomas had transformed the studio into a high-end gallery. Twinkling fairy lights were strung across the ceiling, white tablecloths covered the work tables, and there were a full bar and silver trays loaded with more food than the assembled group could eat in a week. On the easels and hanging on the walls were selections of the artists' favorite work.

Maggie tucked her arm into Burt's and walked him through the exhibition. She took a bruschetta from the buffet and chewed thoughtfully. Artichoke pureed with, what? White beans? She'd have to ask Ilaria.

Helen asked for a moment alone with Maggie. "I have a message from Pierre."

Maggie's stomach tightened. She had watched *The Godfather* with Burt at least five times, and rule number one was not to get involved with criminals. She followed Helen into the hall.

The tall woman's demeanor changed. She'd lost her ethereal quality and was all business. "Pierre said to tell you he owes you."

"Owes me what?" Maggie's mouth was dry. Retribution?

"He's at your service if you ever need assistance." Helen pressed a card into Maggie's hand. "Keep it. You never know."

Helen wandered back into the studio, her carriage changing as she slipped back into character, and Maggie was left looking at the card, crisp and white with a foreign number on it. The phone number for a criminal. What would Aunt Gertrude say?

She was still looking at it when Neddy Innes-Fox approached. "May I have a moment, Mrs. White?"

I am not going to run a tax dodge for him. No matter how nicely he asks. I won't do it. It's not who I am. She followed him into the salon and sat on the edge of the couch, shoulders back, readying herself. She'd find something else to do in Rome. She would play bridge. She would try harder with the expat set. She'd be fine.

"Well, what do you think?" He looked at her expectantly.

She'd missed what he said. "Could you explain it again?"

He ran his fingers through his hair. "I've muddled this all up. Look here, Mrs. W. I want you to make a success of Masterpiece Tours. I'll invest whatever you need. What do you say?"

Maggie heard laughter from the studio. It sounded like Len was making a toast. He and Shelia had bought two pictures with Walter's assistance that afternoon. Souvenirs, he'd called them, but, judging from Walter's grateful phone call, they sounded like sizable investments with commissions large enough to get Walter's office back into the city center.

"But what's changed your mind?" she asked.

"It was what you said, actually. That you wanted to be part of something real. To make a difference." Neddy swallowed. "I'm about to marry a very wealthy woman. If I can't help something like this grow, what good am I?"

"I'm not a cause, Edward."

"No, no. I didn't mean that. I'm making an investment in you. I expect it to pay off. I've got to show my father-in-law-to-be that he's not the only one with a head for business."

"It'll take money for marketing and advertising." She looked him in the eye. "We need more staff, too. And I'd want to get started right away so we don't miss the summer."

He nodded. "Anything you recommend."

There was just one more thing. "There's the matter of the *White Horse.*"

"My uncle's picture? Johnnie Boy said it's worthless."

"It is, and the owner would very much like it back."

Neddy gave a dismissive wave. "That's fine."

Maggie would call George that evening and tell him he could have his picture. He didn't need to know the original was gone. He hadn't known what he had in the first place. And maybe, just maybe, he'd realize how close he'd come to having his secret exposed. Sometimes a close call was all it took to make you appreciate what you've got.

She held out her hand. "You won't regret it."

"Aldrich will be in touch about the details." Neddy got to his feet. "I've got to dash. Fiancée arranged a cake tasting at the Savoy in the morning and I'm booked on the evening flight."

Maggie sank back on the couch and looked at the lights of Rome, twinkling in front of her. Music drifted up from the restaurants on the piazza, and she imagined she could smell the aroma of fresh pasta. She was home at last.

Acknowledgements

So many people have generously shared their time and wisdom as I worked to bring this story to life. Special thanks go to my parents Holly and David Collins and my sister Holly Storck for their support and wisdom throughout this journey, my agent Dawn Dowdle, my editor Shawn Reilly Simmons, my writing group, Jaclyn Hamer, Dorothy Lam, Roberta Levin, Raegan O'Lone, and Lisa Rothstein, my fellow students at Story Studio Chicago and especially my instructor, Abby Geni, my beta readers Jeannie Taylor and Mindy Dickler, my Mystery Writers of America Midwest Chapter Critique Readers Jessie Chandler and Andrew Shaffer, my fellow newbie Jen Sinclair Johnson, and everyone who has been a booster along the way, most especially Pete, Harry, and Gus Moore, whose love and support has made it all possible.

About the Author

Jen Collins Moore is an established marketer and entrepreneur living in Chicago. A transplanted New Englander and avid traveler, she lives with her husband and two boys. *Murder in the Piazza* is her first novel.

Author Photo Credit: Ian McLaren Photography

9 781947 915534